DREAMS: An A-Z of Dream InterpretationsThe interpretations in this book are by ALFRED CESARE

What's In A Dream - A to C

AAbandonTo dream that you are abandoned, denotes that you will have difficulty in framing yourplans for future success.To abandon others, you will see unhappy conditions piled thick around you, leaving littlehope of surmounting them.If it is your house that you abandon, you will soon come to grief in experimenting withfortune.If you abandon your sweetheart, you will fail to recover lost valuables, and friends willturn aside from your favors.If you abandon a mistress, you will unexpectedly come into a goodly inheritance.If it is religion you abandon, you will come to grief by your attacks on prominent people.To abandon children, denotes that you will lose your fortune by lack of calmness andjudgment.To abandon your business, indicates distressing circumstances in which there will bequarrels and suspicion. (This dream may have a literal fulfilment if it is impressed onyour waking mind, whether you abandon a person, or that person abandons you, or, asindicated, it denotes other worries.)To see yourself or friend abandon a ship, suggests your possible entanglement in somebusiness failure, but if you escape to shore your interests will remain secure.AbbeyTo see an abbey in ruins, foretells that your hopes and schemes will fall into ignobleincompletion.

To dream that a priest bars your entrance into an abbey, denotes that you will be savedfrom a ruinous state by enemies mistaking your embarrassment for progress.For a young woman to get into an abbey, foretells her violent illness. If she converseswith a priest in an abbey, she will incur the censure of true friends for indiscretion.AbbessFor a young woman to dream that she sees an abbess, denotes that she will be compelledto perform distasteful tasks, and will submit to authority only after unsuccessfulrebellion.To dream of an abbess smiling and benignant, denotes you will be surrounded by truefriends and pleasing prospects.AbbotTo dream that you are an abbot, warns you that treacherous plots are being laid for yourdownfall.If you see this pious man in devotional exercises, it forewarns you of smooth flattery anddeceit pulling you a willing victim into the meshes of artful bewilderment.For a young woman to talk with an abbot, portends that she will yield to insinuatingflatteries, and in yielding she will besmirch her reputation. If she marries one, she willuphold her name and honor despite poverty and temptation.See similar words in connection with churches, priests, etc.AbdomenTo see your abdomen in a dream, foretells that you will have great expectations, but youmust curb hardheadedness and redouble your energies on your labor, as pleasure isapproaching to your hurt.To see your abdomen shriveled, foretells that you will be persecuted and defied by falsefriends.To see it swollen, you will have tribulations, but you will overcome them and enjoy thefruits of your labor.To see blood oozing from the abdomen, foretells an accident or tragedy in your family.The abdomen of children in an unhealthy state, portends that contagion will pursue you.See Belly.

dreamer who falls overboard while sailing upon stormy waters.BobbinTo dream of bobbins, denotes that important work will devolve on you, and yourinterests will be adversely affected if you are negligent in dispatching the same work.BogBogs, denotes burdens under whose weight you feel that endeavors to rise are useless.Illness and other worries may oppress you.See Swamp.BoilerTo dream of seeing a boiler out of repair, signifies you will suffer from bad managementor disappointment.For a woman to dream that she goes into a cellar to see about a boiler foretells thatsickness and losses will surround her.BoilsTo dream of a boil running pus and blood, you will have unpleasant things to meet inyour immediate future. May be that the insincerity of friends will cause you greatinconvenience.To dream of boils on your forehead, is significant of the sickness of some one near you.BoltsTo dream of bolts, signifies that formidable obstacles will oppose your progress. If thebolts are old or broken, your expectations will be eclipsed by failures.Bomb ShellTo dream of bomb shells, foretells anger and disputes, ending in law suits. Manydispleasing incident[s] follow this dream.BonesTo see your bones protruding from the flesh, denotes that treachery is working to ensnareyou.

To see a pile of bones, famine and contaminating influences surround you.BonnetBonnet, denotes much gossiping and slanderous insinuations, from which a womanshould carefully defend herself.For a man to see a woman tying her bonnet, denotes unforeseen good luck near by. Hisfriends will be faithful and true.A young woman is likely to engage in pleasant and harmless flirtations if her bonnet isnew and of any color except black.Black bonnets, denote false friends of the opposite sex.BooksPleasant pursuits, honor and riches to dream of studying them. For an author to dream ofhis works going to press, is a dream of caution; he will have much trouble in placingthem before the public.To dream of spending great study and time in solving some intricate subjects, and thehidden meaning of learned authors, is significant of honors well earned.To see children at their books, denotes harmony and good conduct of the young.To dream of old books, is a warning to shun evil in any form.BookcaseTo see a bookcase in your dreams, signifies that you will associate knowledge with yourwork and pleasure. Empty bookcases, imply that you will be put out because of lack ofmeans or facility for work.Book StoreTo visit a book store in your dream, foretells you will be filled with literary aspirations,which will interfere with your other works and labors.BootsTo see your boots on another, your place will be

usurped in the affections of yoursweetheart.To wear new boots, you will
be lucky in your dealings. Bread winners will commandhigher wages.

Old and torn boots, indicate sickness and snares before
you.BorrowingBorrowing is a sign of loss and meagre support. For a banker
to dream of borrowing fromanother bank, a run on his own will leave him
in a state of collapse, unless he accepts thiswarning. If another borrows
from you, help in time of need will be extended or offeredyou. True
friends will attend you.BosomFor a young woman to dream that her bosom is
wounded, foretells that some affliction isthreatening her.To see it
soiled or shrunken, she will have a great disappointment in love and many
rivalswill vex her. If it is white and full she is soon to be possessed
of fortune. If her lover isslyly observing it through her sheer corsage,
she is about to come under the softpersuasive influence of a too ardent
wooer.BottlesBottles are good to dream of if well filled with transparent
liquid. You will overcome allobstacles in affairs of the heart,
prosperous engagements will ensue. If empty, comingtrouble will envelop
you in meshes of sinister design, from which you will be forced touse
strategy to disengage yourself.BouquetTo dream of a bouquet beautifully
and richly colored, denotes a legacy from somewealthy and unknown
relative; also, pleasant, joyous gatherings among young folks.To see a
withered bouquet, signifies sickness and death.Bow and ArrowBow and arrow
in a dream, denotes great gain reaped from the inability of others to
carryout plans.To make a bad shot means disappointed hopes in carrying
forward successfully businessaffairs.BoxOpening a goods box in your
dream, signifies untold wealth and that delightful journeysto distant
places may be made with happy results. If the box is empty disappointment
inworks of all kinds will follow.

To see full money boxes, augurs cessation from business cares and a
pleasant retirement.BraceletTo see in your dreams a bracelet encircling
your arm, the gift of lover or friend, isassurance of an early marriage
and a happy union.If a young woman lose her bracelet she will meet with
sundry losses and vexations.To find one, good property will come into her
possession.BrainTo see your own brain in a dream, denotes uncongenial
surroundings will irritate anddwarf you into an unpleasant companion. To
see the brains of animals, foretells that youwill suffer mental
trouble.If you eat them, you will gain knowledge, and profit
unexpectedly.BramblesTo dream of brambles entangling you, is a messenger
of evil. Law suits will go againstyou, and malignant sickness attack you,
or some of your family.BrandyTo dream of brandy, foretells that while you
may reach heights of distinction and wealth,you will lack that innate
refinement which wins true friendship from people whom youmost wish to
please.BranchIt betokens, if full of fruit and green leaves, wealth, many

delightful hours with friends. Ifthey are dried, sorrowful news of the absent.BrassTo dream of brass, denotes that you will rise rapidly in your profession, but while ofapparently solid elevation you will secretly fear a downfall of fortune.BrayHearing an ass bray, is significant of unwelcome tidings or intrusions.

BreadFor a woman to dream of eating bread, denotes that she will be afflicted with children ofstubborn will, for whom she will spend many days of useless labor and worry.To dream of breaking bread with others, indicates an assured competence through life.To see a lot of impure bread, want and misery will burden the dreamer. If the bread isgood and you have access to it, it is a favorable dream.See Baking and Crust.BreakBreakage is a bad dream. To dream of breaking any of your limbs, denotes badmanagement and probable failures. To break furniture, denotes domestic quarrels and anunquiet state of the mind.To break a window, signifies bereavement. To see a broken ring order will be displacedby furious and dangerous uprisings, such as jealous contentions often cause.BreakfastIs favorable to persons engaged in mental work. To see a breakfast of fresh milk and eggsand a well filled dish of ripe fruit, indicates hasty, but favorable changes.See Meals.BreathTo come close to a person in your dreaming with a pure and sweet breath, commendablewill be your conduct, and a profitable consummation of business deals will follow.Breath if fetid, indicates sickness and snares.Losing one's breath, denotes signal failure where success seemed assured.BrewingTo dream of being in a vast brewing establishment, means unjust persecution by publicofficials, but you will eventually prove your innocence and will rise far above yourpersecutors.

Brewing in any way in your dreams, denotes anxiety at the outset, but usually ends inprofit and satisfaction.BriarsTo see yourself caught among briars, black enemies are weaving cords of calumny andperjury intricately around you and will cause you great distress, but if you succeed indisengaging yourself from the briars, loyal friends will come to your assistance in everyemergency.BrickBrick in a dream, indicates unsettled business and disagreements in love affairs. To makethem you will doubtless fail in your efforts to amass great wealth.BrideFor a young woman to dream that she is a bride, foretells that she will shortly come intoan inheritance which will please her exceedingly, if she is pleased in making her bridaltoilet. If displeasure is felt she will suffer disappointments in her anticipations.To dream that you kiss a bride, denotes a happy reconciliation between friends. For abride to kiss others, foretells for you many friends and pleasures; to kiss you, denotes youwill enjoy health and find that your sweetheart will inherit unexpected fortune.To kiss a bride and find that she looks careworn and ill, denotes you will be displeasedwith your success and the action of your friends.If a bride dreams that she is indifferent to her husband, it foretells that many unhappycircumstances will pollute her pleasures.See Wedding.BridgeTo see a long bridge dilapidated, and mysteriously winding into darkness, profoundmelancholy over the loss of dearest possessions and dismal situations will fall upon you.To the young and those in love, disappointment in the heart's fondest hopes, as the lovedone will fall below your ideal.To cross a bridge safely, a final surmounting of difficulties, though the means seemhardly safe to use. Any obstacle or delay denotes disaster.To see a bridge give way before you, beware of treachery and false admirers. Affluencecomes with clear waters. Sorrowful returns of best efforts are experienced after lookingupon or coming in contact with muddy or turbid water in dreams.

BridleTo dream of a bridle, denotes you will engage in some enterprise which will afford muchworry, but will eventually terminate in pleasure and gain. If it is old or broken you willhave difficulties to encounter, and the probabilities are that you will go down beforethem.A blind bridle signifies you will be deceived by some wily enemy, or some woman willentangle you in an intrigue.Bridle BitsTo see bridle bits in your dreams, foretells you will subdue and overcome any obstacleopposing your advancement or happiness. If they break or are broken you will besurprised into making concessions to enemies,BrimstoneTo dream of brimstone, foretells that discreditable dealings will lose you many friends. ifyou fail to rectify the mistakes you are making.To see fires of brimstone, denotes you will be threatened with loss by contagion in yourvicinity.BronchitisTo dream that you are affected with bronchitis, foretells you will be detained frompursuing your views and plans by unfortunate complications of sickness in your home.To suffer with bronchitis in a dream, denotes that discouraging prospects of winningdesired objects will soon loom up before you.BronzeFor a woman to dream of a bronze statue, signifies that she will fail in her efforts to winthe person she has determined on for a husband.If the statue simulates life, or moves, she will be involved in a love affair, but nomarriage will occur. Disappointment to some person may follow the dream.To dream of bronze serpents or insects, foretells you will be pursued by envy and ruin.To see bronze metals, denotes your fortune will be uncertain and unsatisfactory.

BroodTo see a fowl with her brood, denotes that, if you are a woman, your cares will be variedand irksome. Many children will be in your care, and some of them will prove waywardand unruly.Brood, to others, denotes accumulation of wealth.BroomTo dream of brooms, denotes thrift and rapid improvement in your fortune, if the brooms are new. If they are seen in use, you will lose in speculation. For a woman to lose a broom, foretells that she will prove a disagreeable and slovenly wife and housekeeper.Broth Broth denotes the sincerity of friends. They will uphold you in all instances. If you need pecuniary aid it will be forthcoming. To lovers, it promises a strong and lasting attachment.To make broth, you will rule your own and others' fate.Brothel To dream of being in a brothel, denotes you will encounter disgrace through your material indulgence.Brothers To see your brothers, while dreaming, full of energy, you will have cause to rejoice at your own, or their good fortune; but if they are poor and in distress, or begging for assistance, you will be called to a deathbed soon, or some dire loss will overwhelm you or them.Brush To dream of using a hair-brush, denotes you will suffer misfortune from your mismanagement. To see old hair brushes, denotes sickness and ill health. To see clothes brushes, indicates a heavy task is pending over you.If you are busy brushing your clothes, you will soon receive reimbursement for laborious work. To see miscellaneous brushes, foretells a varied line of work, yet withal, rather pleasing and remunerative.

Buckle To dream of buckles, foretells that you will be beset with invitations to places of pleasure, and your affairs will be in danger of chaotic confusion.Buffalo If a woman dreams that she kills a lot of buffaloes, she will undertake a stupendous enterprise, but by enforcing will power and leaving off material pleasures, she will win commendation from men, and may receive long wished for favors. Buffalo, seen in a dream, augurs obstinate and powerful but stupid enemies. They will boldly declare against you but by diplomacy you will escape much misfortune.Bugle To hear joyous blasts from a bugle, prepare for some unusual happiness, as a harmony of good things for you is being formed by unseen powers.Blowing a bugle, denotes fortunate dealings.Bugs To dream of bugs denotes that some disgustingly revolting complications will rise in your daily life. Families will suffer from the carelessness of servants, and sickness may follow.Buildings To see large and magnificent buildings, with green lawns stretching out before them, is significant of a long life of plenty, and travels and explorations into distant countries.Small and newly built houses, denote happy homes and profitable undertakings; but, if old and filthy buildings, ill health and decay of love and business will follow.Bull To see one pursuing you, business trouble, through envious and jealous competitors, will harass you.If a young woman meets a bull, she will have an offer of marriage, but, by declining this offer, she will better her fortune.To see a bull goring a person, misfortune from unwisely using another's possessions will overtake you.

To dream of a white bull, denotes that you will lift yourself up to a higher plane of life than those who persist in making material things their God. It usually denotes gain. Bulldog To dream of entering strange premises and have a bulldog attack you, you will be in danger of transgressing the laws of your country by using perjury to obtain your desires. If one meets you in a friendly way, you will rise in life, regardless of adverse criticisms and seditious interference of enemies. See Dog. Bullock Denotes that kind friends will surround you, if you are in danger from enemies. Good health is promised you. See Bull. Burden To dream that you carry a heavy burden, signifies that you will be tied down by oppressive weights of care and injustice, caused from favoritism shown your enemies by those in power. But to struggle free from it, you will climb to the topmost heights of success. Burr To dream of burrs, denotes that you will struggle to free self from some unpleasant burden, and will seek a change of surroundings. Burglars To dream that they are searching your person, you will have dangerous enemies to contend with, who will destroy you if extreme carefulness is not practised in your dealings with strangers. If you dream of your home, or place of business, being burglarized, your good standing in business or society will be assailed, but courage in meeting these difficulties will defend you. Accidents may happen to the careless after this dream. Burial To attend the burial of a relative, if the sun is shining on the procession, is a sign of the good health of relations, and perhaps the happy marriage of some one of them is about to

occur. But if rain and dismal weather prevails, sickness and bad news of the absent will soon come, and depressions in business circles will be felt A burial where there are sad rites performed, or sorrowing faces, is indicative of adverse surroundings or their speedy approach. See Funeral. Buried Alive To dream that you are buried alive. denotes that you are about to make a great mistake, which your opponents will quickly turn to your injury. If you are rescued from the grave, your struggle will eventually correct your misadventure. Burns Burns stand for tidings of good. To burn your hand in a clear and flowing fire, denotes purity of purpose and the approbation of friends. To burn your feet in walking through coals, or beds of fire, denotes your ability to accomplish any endeavor, however impossible it may be to others. Your usual good health will remain with you, but, if you are overcome in the fire, it represents that your interests will suffer through treachery of supposed friends. Butcher To see them slaughtering cattle and much blood, you may expect long and fatal sickness in your family. To see a butcher cutting meat, your character will be dissected by society to your detriment. Beware of writing letters or documents. Butter To dream of eating fresh, golden butter, is a sign of good health and plans well carried out; it will bring unto you possessions, wealth and knowledge. To eat rancid butter, denotes a competency acquired through struggles of manual labor. To sell butter, denotes small gain. Butterfly To see a butterfly among flowers and green grasses, indicates prosperity and fairattainments.To see them flying about, denotes news from absent friends by letter, or from some onewho has seen them. To a young woman, a happy love, culminating in a life union.

ButtonsTo dream of sewing bright shining buttons on a uniform, betokens to a young woman thewarm affection of a fine looking and wealthy partner in marriage. To a youth, it signifiesadmittance to military honors and a bright career.Dull, or cloth buttons, denotes disappointments and systematic losses and ill health.The loss of a button, and the consequent anxiety as to losing a garment, denotesprospective losses in trade.ButtermilkDrinking buttermilk, denotes sorrow will follow some worldly pleasure, and someimprudence will impair the general health of the dreamer.To give it away, or feed it to pigs, is bad still.To dream that you are drinking buttermilk made into oyster soup, denotes that you willbe called on to do some very repulsive thing, and ill luck will confront you. There arequarrels brewing and friendships threatened. If you awaken while you are drinking it, bydiscreet maneuvering you may effect a pleasant understanding of disagreements.BuzzardTo dream that you hear a buzzard talking, foretells that some old scandal will arise andwork you injury by your connection with it.To see one sitting on a railroad, denotes some accident or loss is about to descend uponyou. To see them fly away as you approach, foretells that you will be able to smooth oversome scandalous disagreement among your friends, or even appertaining to yourself.To see buzzards in a dream, portends generally salacious gossip or that unusual scandalwill disturb you.CCabTo ride in a cab in dreams, is significant of pleasant avocations, and average prosperityyou will enjoy.

To ride in a cab at night, with others, indicates that you will have a secret that you willendeavor to keep from your friends.To ride in a cab with a woman, scandal will couple your name with others of bad repute.To dream of driving a public cab, denotes manual labor, with little chance ofadvancement.CabbageIt is bad to dream of cabbage. Disorders may run riot in all forms. To dream of seeingcabbage green, means unfaithfulness in love and infidelity in wedlock.To cut heads of cabbage, denotes that you are tightening the cords of calamity aroundyou by lavish expenditure.CableTo dream of a cable, foretells the undertaking of a decidedly hazardous work, which, ifsuccessfully carried to completion, will abound in riches and honor to you.To dream of receiving cablegrams, denotes that a message of importance will reach yousoon, and will cause disagreeable comments.CabinThe cabin of a ship is rather unfortunate to be in in a dream. Some mischief is brewingfor you. You will most likely be engaged in a law suit, in which you will lose from theunstability of your witness.For log cabin, see House.CackleTo hear the cackling of hens denotes a sudden shock produced by the news of anunexpected death in your neighborhood, Sickness will cause poverty.CageIn your dreaming if you see a cageful of birds, you will be the happy possessor ofimmense wealth and many beautiful and charming children. To see only one bird, youwill contract a desirable and wealthy marriage. No bird indicates a member of the familylost, either by elopement or death.To see wild animals caged, denotes that you will triumph over your enemies andmisfortunes. If you are in the cage with them, it denotes harrowing scenes from accidents

while traveling.CakesBatter or pancakes, denote that the affections of the dreamer are well placed, and a homewill be bequeathed to him or her.To dream of sweet cakes, is gain for the laboring and a favorable opportunity for theenterprising. Those in love will prosper.Pound cake is significant of much pleasure either from society or business. For a youngwoman to dream of her wedding cake is the only bad luck cake in the category. Bakingthem is not so good an omen as seeing them or eating them.CalomelTo dream of calomel shows some person is seeking to deceive and injure you through theunconscious abetting of friends. For a young woman to dream of taking it, foretells thatshe will be victimized through the artful designing of persons whom she trusts. If it isapplied externally, she will close her eyes to deceit in order to enjoy a short season ofpleasure.CalvesTo dream of calves peacefully grazing on a velvety lawn, foretells to the young, happy,festive gatherings and enjoyment. Those engaged in seeking wealth will see it rapidlyincreasing.See Cattle.CalledTo hear your name called in a dream by strange voices, denotes that your business willfall into a precarious state, and that strangers may lend you assistance, or you may fail tomeet your obligations.To hear the voice of a friend or relative, denotes the desperate illness of some one ofthem, and may be death; in the latter case you may be called upon to stand as guardianover some one, in governing whom you should use much discretion.Lovers hearing the voice of their affianced should heed the warning. If they have beennegligent in attention they should make amends. Otherwise they may suffer separationfrom misunderstanding.To hear the voice of the dead may be a warning of your own serious illness or somebusiness worry from bad judgment may ensue. The voice is an echo thrown back fromthe future on the subjective mind, taking the sound of your ancestor's voice from coming

in contact with that part of your ancestor which remains with you. A certain portion ofmind matter remains the same in lines of family descent.CalendarTo dream of keeping a calendar, indicates that you will be very orderly and systematic inhabits throughout the year.To see a calendar, denotes disappointment in your calculations.CalmTo see calm seas, denotes successful ending of doubtful undertaking.To feel calm and happy, is a sign of a long and well-spent life and a vigorous old age.CalumnyTo dream that you are the subject of calumny, denotes that your interests will suffer atthe hands of evil-minded gossips. For a young woman, it warns her to be careful of herconduct, as her movements are being critically observed by persons who claim to be herfriends.CameraTo dream of a camera, signifies that changes will bring undeserved environments. For ayoung woman to dream that she is taking pictures with a camera, foretells that herimmediate future will have much that is displeasing and that a friend will subject her toacute disappointment.Cameo BroochTo dream of a cameo brooch, denotes some sad occurrence will soon claim yourattention.CamelsTo see this beast of burden, signifies that you will entertain great patience and fortitude intime of almost unbearable anguish and failures that will seemingly sweep every vestigeof hope from you.To own a camel, is a sign that you will possess rich mining property.To see a herd of camels on the desert, denotes assistance when all human aid seems at alow ebb, and of sickness from which you will arise, contrary to all expectations.

CampTo dream of camping in the open air, you may expect a change in your affairs, alsoprepare to make a long and wearisome journey.To see a camping settlement, many of your companions will remove to new estates andyour own prospects will appear gloomy.For a young woman to dream that she is in a camp, denotes that her lover will havetrouble in getting her to name a day for their wedding, and that he will prove a kindhusband. If in a military camp she will marry the first time she has a chance.A married woman after dreaming of being in a soldier's camp is in danger of having herhusband's name sullied, and divorce courts may be her destination.CampaignTo dream of making a political one, signifies your opposition to approved ways ofconducting business, and you will set up original plans for yourself regardless ofenemies' working against you. Those in power will lose.If it is a religious people conducting a campaign against sin, it denotes that you will becalled upon to contribute from your private means to sustain charitable institutions.For a woman to dream that she is interested in a campaign against fallen women, denotesthat she will surmount obstacles and prove courageous in time of need.CaneTo see cane growing in your dream, foretells favorable advancement will be made towardfortune. To see it cut, denotes absolute failure in all undertakings.CancerTo have one successfully treated in a dream, denotes a sudden rise from obscure povertyto wealthy surroundings.To dream of a cancer, denotes illness of some one near you, and quarrels with those youlove. Depressions may follow to the man of affairs after this dream.To dream of a cancer, foretells sorrow in its ugliest phase. Love will resolve itself intocold formality, and business will be worrying and profitless.CanalTo see the water of a canal muddy and stagnant-looking, portends sickness and disorders of the stomach and dark designs of enemies. But if its waters are clear a placid life andthe devotion of friends is before you.For a young woman to glide in a canoe across a canal, denotes a chaste life and anadoring husband. If she crossed the canal on a bridge over clear water and gathers fernsand other greens on the banks, she will enjoy a life of ceaseless rounds of pleasure andattain to high social distinction. But if the water be turbid she will often find herselftangled in meshes of perplexity and will be the victim of nervous troubles.Canary BirdsTo dream of this sweet songster, denotes unexpected pleasures. For the young to dreamof possessing a beautiful canary, denotes high class honors and a successful passagethrough the literary world, or a happy termination of love's young dream.To dream one is given you, indicates a welcome legacy. To give away a canary, denotesthat you will suffer disappointment in your dearest wishes.To dream that one dies, denotes the unfaithfulness of dear friends.Advancing, fluttering, and singing canaries, in luxurious apartments, denotes feasting anda life of exquisite refinement, wealth, and satisfying friendships. If the light is weird orunnaturally bright, it augurs that you are entertaining illusive hopes. Yourover-confidence is your worst enemy. A young woman after this dream should beware,lest flattering promises react upon her in disappointment. Fairy-like scenes in a dreamare peculiarly misleading and treacherous to women.CandlesTo see them burning with a clear and steady flame, denotes the constancy of those aboutyou and a well-grounded fortune.For a maiden to dream that she is molding candles, denotes that she will have anunexpected offer of marriage and a pleasant visit to distant relatives. If she is lighting acandle, she will meet her lover clandestinely because of parental objections.To see a candle wasting in a draught, enemies are circulating detrimental reports aboutyou.To snuff a candle, portends sorrowful news. Friends are dead or in distressful straits.CandlestickTo see a candlestick bearing a whole candle, denotes that a bright future lies before youfilled with health, happiness and loving companions. If empty, the reverse.

CankerTo dream of seeing canker on anything, is an omen of evil. It foretells death andtreacherous companions for the young. Sorrow and loneliness to the aged.Cankerous growths in the flesh, denote future distinctions either as head of State or stagelife.The last definition is not consistent with other parts of this book, but I let it stand, as Ifind it among my automatic writings.CannonThis dream denotes that one's home and country are in danger of foreign intrusion, fromwhich our youth will suffer from the perils of war.For a young woman to hear or see cannons, denotes she will be a soldier's wife and willhave to bid him godspeed as he marches in defense of her and honor.The reader will have to interpret dreams of this character by the influences surroundinghim, and by the experiences stored away in his subjective mind. If you have thoughtabout cannons a great deal and you dream of them when there is no war, they are mostlikely to warn you against struggle and probable defeat. Or if business is manipulated byyourself successful engagements after much worry and ill luck may ensue.Cannon-BallThis means that secret enemies are uniting against you. For a maid to see a cannon-ball,denotes that she will have a soldier sweetheart. For a youth to see a cannon-ball, denotesthat he will be called upon to defend his country.CanoeTo paddle a canoe on a calm stream, denotes your perfect confidence in your own abilityto conduct your business in a profitable way.To row with a sweetheart, means an early marriage and fidelity. To row on rough watersyou will have to tame a shrew before you attain connubial bliss. Affairs in the businessworld will prove disappointing after you dream of rowing in muddy waters. If the watersare shallow and swift, a hasty courtship or stolen pleasures, from which there can be nolasting good, are indicated.Shallow, clear and calm waters in rowing, signifies happiness of a pleasing character, butof short duration.Water is typical of futurity in the dream realms. If a pleasant immediate future awaits thedreamer he will come in close proximity with clear water. Or if he emerges from

disturbed watery elements into waking life the near future is filled with crosses for him.CandyTo dream of making candy, denotes profit accruing from industry.To dream of eating crisp, new candy, implies social pleasures and much love-makingamong the young and old. Sour candy is a sign of illness or that disgusting annoyanceswill grow out of confidences too long kept.To receive a box of bonbons, signifies to a young person that he or she will be therecipient of much adulation. It generally means prosperity. If you send a box you willmake a proposition, but will meet with disappointment.CanopyTo dream of a canopy or of being beneath one, denotes that false friends are influencingyou to undesirable ways of securing gain. You will do well to protect those in your care.CapFor a woman to dream of seeing a cap, she will be invited to take part in some festivity.For a girl to dream that she sees her sweetheart with a cap on, denotes that she will bebashful and shy in his presence.To see a prisoner's cap, denotes that your courage is failing you in time of danger.To see a miner's cap, you will inherit a substantial competency.CaptainTo dream of seeing a captain of any company, denotes your noblest aspirations will berealized. If a woman dreams that her lover is a captain, she will be much harassed inmind from jealousy and rivalry.CaptiveTo dream that you are a captive, denotes that you may have treachery to deal with, and ifyou cannot escape, that injury and misfortune will befall you.To dream of taking any one captive, you will join yourself to pursuits and persons oflowest status.For a young woman to dream that she is a captive, denotes that she will have a husbandwho will be jealous of her confidence in others; or she may be censured for her indiscretion.CardinalIt is unlucky to dream you see a cardinal in his robes. You will meet such misfortunes aswill necessitate your removal to distant or foreign lands to begin anew your ruinedfortune. For a woman to dream this is a sign of her downfall through false promises. Ifpriest or preacher is a spiritual adviser and his services are supposed to be needed,especially in the hour of temptation, then we find ourselves dreaming of him as a warningagainst approaching evil.CardsIf playing them in your dreams with others for social pastime, you will meet with fairrealization of hopes that have long buoyed you up. Small ills will vanish. But playing forstakes will involve you in difficulties of a serious nature.If you lose at cards you will encounter enemies. If you win you will justify yourself in theeyes of the law, but will have trouble in so doing.If a young woman dreams that her sweetheart is playing at cards, she will have cause toquestion his good intentions.In social games, seeing diamonds indicate wealth; clubs, that your partner in life will beexacting, and that you may have trouble in explaining your absence at times; heartsdenote fidelity and cosy surroundings; spades signify that you will be a widow andencumbered with a large estate.CarnivalTo dream that you are participating in a carnival, portends that you are soon to enjoysome unusual pleasure or recreation. A carnival when masks are used, or whenincongruous or clownish figures are seen, implies discord in the home; business will beunsatisfactory and love unrequited.CarpenterTo see carpenters at their labor, foretells you will engage in honest endeavors to raiseyour fortune, to the exclusion of selfish pastime or so-called recreation.CarpetTo see a carpet in a dream, denotes profit, and wealthy friends to aid you in need.To walk on a carpet, you will be prosperous and happy.

To dream that you buy carpets, denotes great gain. If selling them, you will have cause togo on a pleasant journey, as well as a profitable one.For a young woman to dream of carpets, shows she will own a beautiful home andservants will wait upon her.CarriageTo see a carriage, implies that you will be gratified, and that you will make visits.To ride in one, you will have a sickness that will soon pass, and you will enjoy health andadvantageous positions.To dream that you are looking for a carriage, you will have to labor hard, but willeventually be possessed with a fair competency.CarrotTo dream of carrots, portends prosperity and health For a young woman to eat them,denotes that she will contract an early marriage and be the mother of several hardychildren.CarsTo dream of seeing cars, denotes journeying and changing in quick succession. To get onone shows that travel which you held in contemplation will be made under differentauspices than had been calculated upon.To miss one, foretells that you will be foiled in an attempt to forward your prospects.To get off of one, denotes that you will succeed with some interesting schemes whichwill fill you with self congratulations.To dream of sleeping-cars, indicates that your struggles to amass wealth is animated bythe desire of gratifying selfish and lewd principles which should be mastered andcontrolled.To see street-cars in your dreams, denotes that some person is actively interested incausing you malicious trouble and disquiet.To ride on a car, foretells that rivalry and jealousy will enthrall your happiness.To stand on the platform of a street-car while it is running, denotes you will attempt tocarry on an affair which will be extremely dangerous, but if you ride without accidentyou will be successful.If the platform is up high, your danger will be more apparent, but if low, you will barely

accomplish your purpose.CartTo dream of riding in a cart, ill luck and constant work will employ your time if youwould keep supplies for your family.To see a cart, denotes bad news from kindred or friends.To dream of driving a cart, you will meet with merited success in business and otheraspirations.For lovers to ride together in a cart, they will be true in spite of the machinations ofrivals.CartridgeTo dream of cartridges, foretells unhappy quarrels and dissensions.Some untoward fate threatens you or some one closely allied to you.If they are empty, there will be foolish variances in your associations.CarvingTo dream of carving a fowl, indicates you will be poorly off in a worldly way.Companions will cause you vexation from continued ill temper.Carving meat, denotes bad investments, but, if a change is made, prospects will bebrighter.CashTo dream that you have plenty of cash, but that it has been borrowed, portends that youwill be looked upon as a worthy man, but that those who come in close contact with youwill find that you are mercenary and unfeeling.For a young woman to dream that she is spending borrowed money, foretells that she willbe found out in her practice of deceit, and through this lose a prized friend.See Money.Cash boxTo dream of a full cash box, denotes that favorable prospects will open around you. Ifempty, you will experience meager reimbursements.

CashierTo see a cashier in your dream, denotes that others will claim your possessions. If youowe any one, you will practice deceit in your designs upon some wealthy person.CaskTo see one filled, denotes prosperous times and feastings. If empty, your life will be voidof any joy or consolation from outward influences.CastleTo dream of being in a castle, you will be possessed of sufficient wealth to make life asyou wish. You have prospects of being a great traveler, enjoying contact with people ofmany nations.To see an old and vine-covered castle, you are likely to become romantic in your tastes,and care should be taken that you do not contract an undesirable marriage or engagement.Business is depressed after this dream.To dream that you are leaving a castle, you will be robbed of your possessions, or loseyour lover or some dear one by death.Castor oilTo dream of castor oil, denotes that you will seek to overthrow a friend who is secretlyabetting your advancement.CastoriaTo dream of castoria, denotes that you will fail to discharge some important duty, andyour fortune will seemingly decline to low stages.CatechismTo dream of the catechism, foretells that you will be offered a lucrative position, but thestrictures will be such that you will be worried as to accepting it.CaterpillarTo see a caterpillar in a dream, denotes that low and hypocritical people are in yourimmediate future, and you will do well to keep clear of deceitful appearances. You maysuffer a loss in love or business.To dream of a caterpillar, foretells you will be placed in embarrassing situations, and

there will be small honor or gain to be expected.CattleTo dream of seeing good-looking and fat cattle contentedly grazing in green pastures,denotes prosperity and happiness through a congenial and pleasant companion.To see cattle lean and shaggy, and poorly fed, you will be likely to toil all your lifebecause of misspent energy and dislike of details of work. Correct your habits after thisdream.To see cattle stampeding, means that you will have to exert all the powers of commandyou have to keep your career in a profitable channel.To see a herd of cows at milking time, you will be the successful owner of wealth thatmany have worked to obtain. To a young woman this means that her affections will notsuffer from the one of her choice.To dream of milking cows with udders well filled, great good fortune is in store for you.If the calf has stolen the milk, it signifies that you are about to lose your lover byslowness to show your reciprocity, or your property from neglect of business.To see young calves in your dream, you will become a great favorite in society and winthe heart of a loyal person. For business, this dream indicates profit from sales. For alover, the entering into bonds that will be respected. If the calves are poor, look for aboutthe same, except that the object sought will be much harder to obtain.Long-horned and dark, vicious cattle, denote enemies.See Calves.CathedralTo dream of a wast cathedral with its domes rising into space, denotes that you will bepossessed with an envious nature and unhappy longings for the unattainable, both mentaland physical; but if you enter you will be elevated in life, having for your companions thelearned and wise.CatsTo dream of a cat, denotes ill luck, if you do not succeed in killing it or driving it fromyour sight. If the cat attacks you, you will have enemies who will go to any extreme toblacken your reputation and to cause you loss of property. But if you succeed inbanishing it, you will overcome great obstacles and rise in fortune and fame.If you meet a thin, mean and dirty-looking cat, you will have bad news from the absent.Some friend lies at death's door; but if you chase it out of sight, your friend will recover

after a long and lingering sickness.To hear the scream or the mewing of a cat, some false friend is using all the words andwork at his command to do you harm.To dream that a cat scratches you, an enemy will succeed in wrenching from you theprofits of a deal that you have spent many days making.If a young woman dreams that she is holding a cat, or kitten, she will be influenced intosome impropriety through the treachery of others.To dream of a clean white cat, denotes entanglements which, while seemingly harmless,will prove a source of sorrow and loss of wealth.When a merchant dreams of a cat, he should put his best energies to work, as hiscompetitors are about to succeed in demolishing his standard of dealing, and he will beforced to other measures if he undersells others and still succeeds.To dream of seeing a cat and snake on friendly terms signifies the beginning of an angrystruggle. It denotes that an enemy is being entertained by you with the intention of usinghim to find out some secret which you believe concerns yourself; uneasy of hisconfidences given, you will endeavor to disclaim all knowledge of his actions, as you arefearful that things divulged, concerning your private life, may become public.CauliflowerTo dream of eating it, you will be taken to task for neglect of duty. To see it growing,your prospects will brighten after a period of loss.For a young woman to see this vegetable in a garden, denotes that she will marry topleaose her parents and not herself.CavalryTo dream that you see a division of cavalry, denotes personal advancement anddistinction. Some little sensation may accompany your elevation.Cavern or CaveTo dream of seeing a cavern yawning in the weird moonlight before you, manyperplexities will assail you, and doubtful advancement because of adversaries. Work andhealth is threatened.To be in a cave foreshadows change. You will probably be estranged from those who arevery dear to you.For a young woman to walk in a cave with her lover or friend, denotes she will fall in

love with a villain and will suffer the loss of true friends.CedarsTo dream of seeing them green and shapely, denotes pleasing success in an undertaking.To see them dead or blighted, signifies despair. No object will be attained from seeingthem thus.CeleryTo dream of seeing fresh, crisp stalks of celery, you will be prosperous and influentialbeyond your highest hopes.To see it decaying, a death in your family will soon occur.To eat it, boundless love and affection will be heaped upon you.For a young woman to eat it with her lover, denotes she will come into rich possessions.Celestial SignsTo dream of celestial signs, foretells unhappy occurrences will cause you to makeunseasonable journeys. Love or business may go awry, quarrels in the house are alsopredicted if you are not discreet with your engagements.See Illumination.CellarTo dream of being in a cold, damp cellar, you will be oppressed by doubts. You will loseconfidence in all things and suffer gloomy forebodings from which you will fail to escapeunless you control your will. It also indicates loss of property.To see a cellar stored with wines and table stores, you will be offered a share in profitscoming from a doubtful source. If a young woman dreams of this she will have an offerof marriage from a speculator or gambler.CemeteryTo dream of being in a beautiful and well-kept cemetery, you will have unexpected newsof the recovery of one whom you had mourned as dead, and you will have your title goodto lands occupied by usurpers.To see an old bramble grown and forgotten cemetery, you will live to see all your lovedones leave you, and you will be left to a stranger's care.

For young people to dream of wandering through the silent avenues of the deadforeshows they will meet with tender and loving responses from friends, but will have tomeet sorrows that friends are powerless to avert.Brides dreaming of passing a cemetery on their way to the wedding ceremony, will bebereft of their husbands by fatal accidents occurring on journeys.For a mother to carry fresh flowers to a cemetery, indicates she may expect the continuedgood health of her family.For a young widow to visit a cemetery means she will soon throw aside her weeds forrobes of matrimony. If she feels sad and depressed she will have new cares and regrets.Old people dreaming of a cemetery, shows they will soon make other journeys wherethey will find perfect rest.To see little children gathering flowers and chasing butterflies among the graves, denotesprosperous changes and no graves of any of your friends to weep over. Good health willhold high carnival.ChaffTo see chaff, denotes an empty and fruitless undertaking and ill health causing muchanxiety.Women dreaming of piles of chaff, portends many hours spent in useless and degradinggossip, bringing them into notoriety and causing them to lose husbands who would havemaintained them without work on their part.ChainsTo dream of being bound in chains, denotes that unjust burdens are about to be thrownupon your shoulders; but if you succeed in breaking them you will free yourself fromsome unpleasant business or social engagement.To see chains, brings calumny and treacherous designs of the envious.Seeing others in chains, denotes bad fortunes for them.ChairTo see a chair in your dream, denotes failure to meet some obligation. If you are notcareful you will also vacate your most profitable places.To see a friend sitting on a chair and remaining motionless, signifies news of his death orillness.

Chair MakerTo dream of seeing a chair maker, denotes that worry from apparently pleasant labor willconfront you.ChairmanTo dream that you see the chairman of any public body, foretells you will seek elevationand be recompensed by receiving a high position of trust. To see one looking out ofhumor you are threatened with unsatisfactory states.If you are a chairman, you will be distinguished for your justice and kindness to others.ChalkFor a woman to dream of chalking her face, denotes that she will scheme to obtainadmirers.To dream of using chalk on a board, you will attain public honors, unless it is theblackboard; then it indicates ill luck.To hold hands full of chalk, disappointment is foretold.ChaliceTo dream of a chalice, denotes pleasure will be gained by you to the sorrow of others. Tobreak one foretells your failure to obtain power over some friend.ChallengeIf you are challenged to fight a duel, you will become involved in a social difficultywherein you will be compelled to make apologies or else lose friendships.To accept a challenge of any character, denotes that you will bear many ills yourself inyour endeavor to shield others from dishonor.ChamberTo find yourself in a beautiful and richly furnished chamber implies sudden fortune,either through legacies from unknown relatives or through speculation. For a youngwoman, it denotes that a wealthy stranger will offer her marriage and a fineestablishment. If the chamber is plainly furnished, it denotes that a small competency andfrugality will be her portion.

ChambermaidTo see a chambermaid, denotes bad fortune and decided changes will be made.For a man to dream of making love to a chambermaid, shows he is likely to find himselfan object of derision on account of indiscreet conduct and want of tact.ChameleonTo dream of seeing your sweetheart wearing a chameleon chained to her, shows she willprove faithless to you if by changing she can better her fortune. Ordinarily chameleonssignify deceit and self advancement, even though others suffer.ChampionTo dream of a champion, denotes you will win the warmest friendship of some person byyour dignity and moral conduct.ChandelierTo dream of a chandelier, portends that unhoped-for success will make it possible foryou to enjoy pleasure and luxury at your caprice.To see a broken or ill-kept one, denotes that unfortunate speculation will depress yourseemingly substantial fortune. To see the light in one go out, foretells that sickness anddistress will cloud a promising future.ChapelTo dream of a chapel, denotes dissension in social circles and unsettled business.To be in a chapel, denotes disappointment and change of business.For young people to dream of entering a chapel, implies false loves and enemies.Unlucky unions may entangle them.CharcoalTo dream of charcoal unlighted, denotes miserable situations and bleak unhappiness. If itis burning with glowing coals, there is prospects of great enhancement of fortune, andpossession of unalloyed joys.ChariotTo dream of riding in a chariot, foretells that favorable opportunities will present

themselves resulting in your good if rightly used by you.To fall or see others fall from one, denotes displacement from high positions.CharityTo dream of giving charity, denotes that you will be harassed with supplications for helpfrom the poor and your business will be at standstill.To dream of giving to charitable institutions, your right of possession to paving propertywill be disputed. Worries and ill health will threaten you.For young persons to dream of giving charity, foreshows they will be annoyed bydeceitful rivals. To dream that you are an object of charity, omens that you will succeedin life after hard times with misfortunes.ChastiseTo dream of being chastised, denotes that you have not been prudent in conducting youraffairs.To dream that you administer chastisement to another, signifies that you will have anill-tempered partner either in business or marriage.For parents to dream of chastising their children, indicates they will be loose in theirmanner of correcting them, but they will succeed in bringing them up honorably.CheatedTo dream of being cheated in business, you will meet designing people who will seek toclose your avenues to fortune.For young persons to dream that they are being cheated in games, portend they will losetheir sweethearts through quarrels and misunderstandings.ChecksTo dream of palming off false checks on your friends, denotes that you will resort tosubterfuge in order to carry forward your plans.To receive checks you will be able to meet your payments and will inherit money.To dream that you pay out checks, denotes depression and loss in business.

CheckersTo dream of playing checkers, you will be involved in difficulties of a serious character,and strange people will come into your life, working you harm.To dream that you win the game, you will succeed in some doubtful enterprise.CheeseTo dream of eating cheese, denotes great disappointments and sorrow. No good of anynature can be hoped for. Cheese is generally a bad dream.ChemiseFor a woman to dream of a chemise, denotes she will hear unfavorable gossip aboutherself.CherriesTo dream of cherries, denotes you will gain popularity by your amiability andunselfishness. To eat them, portends possession of some much desired object. To seegreen ones, indicates approaching good fortune.CherubsTo dream you see cherubs, foretells you will have some distinct joy, which will leave animpression of lasting good upon your life.To see them looking sorrowful or reproachful, foretells that distress will comeunexpectedly upon you.ChessTo dream of playing chess, denotes stagnation of business, dull companions, and poorhealth.To dream that you lose at chess, worries from mean sources will ensue; but if you win,disagreeable influences may be surmounted.ChestnutsTo dream of handling chestnuts, foretells losses in a business way, but indicates anagreeable companion through life.Eating them, denotes sorrow for a time, but final happiness.

For a young woman to dream of eating or trying her fortune with them, she will have awell-to-do lover and comparative plenty.ChickensTo dream of seeing a brood of chickens, denotes worry from many cares, some of whichof which will prove to your profit.Young or half grown chickens, signify fortunate enterprises, but to make them so youwill have to exert your physical strength.To see chickens going to roost, enemies are planning to work you evil.To eat them, denotes that selfishness will detract from your otherwise good name.Business and love will remain in precarious states.ChiffonierTo see or search through a chiffonier, denotes you will have disappointing anticipations.To see one in order, indicates pleasant friends and entertainments.ChilblainsTo dream of suffering with chilblains, denotes that you will be driven into some baddealing through over anxiety of a friend or partner. This dream also portends your ownillness or an accident.ChildbedTo dream of giving child birth, denotes fortunate circumstances and safe delivery of ahandsome child.For an unmarried woman to dream of being in childbed, denotes unhappy changes fromhonor to evil and low estates.Children"Dream of children sweet and fair,To you will come suave debonair,Fortune robed in shining dress,Bearing wealth and happiness."To dream of seeing many beautiful children is portentous of great prosperity andblessings.For a mother to dream of seeing her child sick from slight cause, she may see it enjoying

robust health, but trifles of another nature may harass her.To see children working or studying, denotes peaceful times and general prosperity.To dream of seeing your child desperately ill or dead, you have much to fear, for itswelfare is sadly threatened.To dream of your dead child, denotes worry and disappointment in the near future.To dream of seeing disappointed children, denotes trouble from enemies, and anxiousforebodings from underhanded work of seemingly friendly people.To romp and play with children, denotes that all your speculating and love enterpriseswill prevail.ChimesTo dream of Christmas chimes, denotes fair prospects for business men and farmers.For the young, happy anticipations fulfilled. Ordinary chimes, denotes some smallanxiety will soon be displaced by news of distant friends.ChimneyTo dream of seeing chimneys, denotes a very displeasing incident will occur in your life.Hasty intelligence of sickness will be borne you. A tumble down chimney, denotessorrow and likely death in your family. To see one overgrown with ivy or other vines,foretells that happiness will result from sorrow or loss of relatives.To see a fire burning in a chimney, denotes much good is approaching you. To hide in achimney corner, denotes distress and doubt will assail you. Business will appear gloomy.For a young woman to dream that she is going down a chimney, foretells she will beguilty of some impropriety which will cause consternation among her associates. Toascend a chimney, shows that she will escape trouble which will be planned for her.ChinaFor a woman to dream of painting or arranging her china, foretells she will have apleasant home and be a thrifty and economical matron.China StoreFor a china merchant to dream that his store looks empty, foretells he will have reversesin his business, and withal a gloomy period will follow.See Crockery.

ChocolateTo dream of chocolate, denotes you will provide abundantly for those who are dependenton you. To see chocolate candy, indicates agreeable companions and employments. Ifsour, illness or other disappointments will follow. To drink chocolate, foretells you willprosper after a short period of unfavorable reverses.ChoirTo dream of a choir, foretells you may expect cheerful surroundings to replace gloomand discontent. For a young woman to sing in a choir, denotes she will be miserable overthe attention paid others by her lover.CholeraTo dream of this dread disease devastating the country, portends sickness of virulent typewill rage and many disappointments will follow.To dream that you are attacked by it, denotes your own sickness.ChristTo dream of beholding Christ, the young child, worshiped by the wise men, denotesmany peaceful days, full of wealth and knowledge, abundant with joy, and content.If in the garden of the Gethsemane, sorrowing adversity will fill your soul, great longingsfor change and absent objects of love will be felt.To see him in the temple scourging the traders, denotes that evil enemies will be defeatedand honest endeavors will prevail.Christmas TreeTo dream of a Christmas tree, denotes joyful occasions and auspicious fortune. To seeone dismantled, foretells some painful incident will follow occasions of festivity.ChrysanthemumTo dream that you gather white chrysanthemums, signifies loss and much perplexity;colored ones, betokens pleasant engagements.To see them in bouquets, denotes that love will be offered you, but a foolish ambitionwill cause you to put it aside. To pass down an avenue of white chrysanthemums, withhere and there a yellow one showing among the white, foretells a strange sense of lossand sadness, from which the sensibilities will expand and take on new powers. Whilelooking on these white flowers as you pass, and you suddenly feel your spirit leave your

body and a voice shouts aloud "Glory to God, my Creator," foretells that a crisis ispending in your near future. If some of your friends pass out, and others take up trueideas in connection with spiritual and earthly needs, you will enjoy life in its deepestmeaning. Often death is near you in these dreams.ChurchTo dream of seeing a church in the distance, denotes disappointment in pleasures longanticipated.To enter one wrapt in gloom, you will participate in a funeral. Dull prospects of bettertimes are portended.ChurchyardTo dream of walking in a churchyard, if in winter, denotes that you are to have a long andbitter struggle with poverty, and you will reside far from the home of your childhood, andfriends will be separated from you; but if you see the signs of springtime, you will walkup in into pleasant places and enjoy the society of friends.For lovers to dream of being in a churchyard means they will never marry each other, butwill see others fill their places.ChurningTo dream of churning, you will have difficult tasks set you, but by diligence and industryyou will accomplish them and be very prosperous. To the farmer, it denotes profit from aplenteous harvest; to a young woman, it denotes a thrifty and energetic husband.CiderTo dream of cider, denotes fortune may be won by you if your time is not squanderedupon material pleasure. To see people drinking it, you will be under the influence ofunfaithful friends.CipherTo dream of reading cipher, indicates that you are interested in literary researches, and byconstant study you will become well acquainted with the habits and lives of the ancients.CircleTo dream of a circle, denotes that your affairs will deceive you in their proportions ofgain. For a young woman to dream of a circle, warns her of indiscreet involvement to theexclusion of marriage.

CisternTo dream of a cistern, denotes you are in danger of trespassing upon the pleasures andrights of your friends. To draw from one, foretells that you will enlarge in your pastimeand enjoyment in a manner which may be questioned by propriety.To see an empty one, foretells despairing change from happiness to sorrow.CityTo dream that you are in a strange city, denotes you will have sorrowful occasion tochange your abode or mode of living.City CouncilTo dream of a city council, foretells that your interests will clash with public institutionsand there will be discouraging outlooks for you.City HallTo dream of a city hall, denotes contentions and threatened law suits.To a young woman this dream is a foreboding of unhappy estrangement from her loverby her failure to keep virtue inviolate.ClamsTo dream of clams, denotes you will have dealings with an obstinate but honest person.To eat them, foretells you will enjoy another's prosperity.For a young woman to dream of eating baked clams with her sweetheart, foretells thatshe will enjoy his money as well as his confidence.ClayTo dream of clay, denotes isolation of interest and probable insolvency. To dig in a claybank, foretells you will submit to extraordinary demands of enemies. If you dig in an ashbank and find clay, unfortunate surprises will combat progressive enterprises or newwork. Your efforts are likely to be misdirected after this dream.Women will find this dream unfavorable in love, social and business states, andmisrepresentations will overwhelm them.

ClaretTo dream of drinking claret, denotes you will come under the influence of ennoblingassociation. To dream of seeing broken bottles of claret, portends you will be induced tocommit immoralities by the false persuasions of deceitful persons.Claret Cup and PunchTo dream of claret cup or punch, foretells that you will be much pleased with theattention shown you by new acquaintances.ClarionetTo dream of a claironet, foretells that you will indulge in frivolity beneath your usualdignity. If it is broken, you will incur the displeasure of a close friend.ClairvoyanceTo dream of being a clairvoyant and seeing yourself in the future, denotes signal changesin your present occupation, followed by a series of unhappy conflicts with designingpeople.To dream of visiting a clairvoyant, foretells unprosperous commercial states and unhappyunions.ClergymanTo dream that you send for a clergyman to preach a funeral sermon, denotes that you willvainly strive against sickness and to ward off evil influences, but they will prevail in spiteof your earnest endeavors.If a young woman marries a clergyman in her dream, she will be the object of muchmental distress, and the wayward hand of fortune will lead her into the morass ofadversity.See Minister.ClimbingTo dream of climbing up a hill or mountain and reaching the top, you will overcome themost formidable obstacles between you and a prosperous future; but if you should fail toreach the top, your dearest plans will suffer being wrecked.To climb a ladder to the last rung, you will succeed in business; but if the ladder breaks,you will be plunged into unexpected straits, and accidents may happen to you.

To see yourself climbing the side of a house in some mysterious way in a dream, and tohave a window suddenly open to let you in, foretells that you will make or have madeextraordinary ventures against the approbation of friends, but success will eventuallycrown your efforts, though there will be times when despair will almost enshroud you.See Ascend,Hill, and Mountain.ClockTo dream that you see a clock, denotes danger from a foe. To hear one strike, you willreceive unpleasant news. The death of some friend is implied.CloisterTo dream of a cloister, omens dissatisfaction with present surroundings, and you willsoon seek new environments. For a young woman to dream of a cloister, foretells that herlife will be made unselfish by the chastening of sorrow.ClothesTo dream of seeing clothes soiled and torn, denotes that deceit will be practised to yourharm. Beware of friendly dealings with strangers.For a woman to dream that her clothing is soiled or torn, her virtue will be dragged in themire if she is not careful of her associates. Clean new clothes, denotes prosperity.To dream that you have plenty, or an assortment of clothes, is a doubtful omen; you maywant the necessaries of life. To a young person, this dream denotes unsatisfied hopes anddisappointments.See Apparel.CloudsTo dream of seeing dark heavy clouds, portends misfortune and bad management. If rainis falling, it denotes troubles and sickness.To see bright transparent clouds with the sun shining through them, you will besuccessful after trouble has been your companion.To see them with the stars shining, denotes fleeting joys and small advancements.CloverWalking through fields of fragrant clover is a propitious dream. It brings all objectsdesired into the reach of the dreamer. Fine crops is portended for the farmer and wealth

for the young. Blasted fields of clover brings harrowing and regretful sighs.To dream of clover, foretells prosperity will soon enfold you. For a young woman todream of seeing a snake crawling through blossoming clover, foretells she will be earlydisappointed in love, and her surroundings will be gloomy and discouraging, though toher friends she seems peculiarly fortunate.Cloven FootTo dream of a cloven foot, portends some unusual ill luck is threatening you, and youwill do well to avoid the friendship of strange persons.ClubTo dream of being approached by a person bearing a club, denotes that you will beassailed by your adversaries, but you will overcome them and be unusually happy andprosperous; but if you club any one, you will undergo a rough and profitless journey.CoachTo dream of riding in a coach, denotes continued losses and depressions in business.Driving one implies removal or business changes.CoalsTo see bright coals of fire, denotes pleasure and many pleasant changes. To dream youhandle them yourself, denotes unmitigated joy. To see dead coals implies trouble anddisappointments.Coal-hodTo dream of a coal-hod, denotes that grief will be likely to fill a vacancy made byreckless extravagance. To see your neighbor carrying in hods, foretells your surroundingswill be decidedly distasteful and inharmonious.CoatTo dream of wearing another's coat, signifies that you will ask some friend to go securityfor you. To see your coat torn, denotes the loss of a close friend and dreary business.To see a new coat, portends for you some literary honor.To lose your coat, you will have to rebuild your fortune lost through beingover-confident in speculations.See Apparel and Clothes.

Coat-of-ArmsTo dream of seeing your coat-of-arms, is a dream of ill luck. You will never possess atitle.CocoaTo dream of cocoa, denotes you will cultivate distasteful friends for your ownadvancement and pleasure.CocoanutCocoanuts in dreams, warns you of fatalities in your expectations, as sly enemies areencroaching upon your rights in the guise of ardent friends. Dead cocoanut trees are asign of loss and sorrow. The death of some one near you may follow.Cock-CrowingTo dream of hearing a cock crowing in the morning, is significant of good. If you besingle, it denotes an early marriage and a luxurious home.To hear one at night is despair, and cause for tears you will have.To dream of seeing cocks fight, you will leave your family because of quarrels andinfidelity. This dream usually announces some unexpected and sorrowful events. Thecock warned the Apostle Peter when he was about to perjure himself. It may also warnyou in a dream when the meshes of the world are swaying you from "the straight line'' ofspiritual wisdom.CockadeThis dream denotes that foes will bring disastrous suits against you. Beware of titles.CocktailTo drink a cocktail while dreaming, denotes that you will deceive your friends as to yourinclinations and enjoy the companionship of fast men and women while posing as aserious student and staid home lover. For a woman, this dream portends fast living and anignoring of moral and set rules.Coca-ColaFor a woman to dream that she is drinking coca-cola signifies that she will lose healthand a chance for marrying a wealthy man by her abandonment to material delights.

CoffinThis dream is unlucky. You will, if you are a farmer, see your crops blasted and yourcattle lean and unhealthy. To business men it means debts whose accumulation they arepowerless to avoid. To the young it denotes unhappy unions and death of loved ones.To see your own coffin in a dream, business defeat and domestic sorrow may beexpected.To dream of a coffin moving of itself, denotes sickness and marriage in closeconjunction. Sorrow and pleasure intermingled. Death may follow this dream, but therewill also be good.To see your corpse in a coffin, signifies brave efforts will be crushed in defeat andignominy,To dream that you find yourself sitting on a coffin in a moving hearse, denotes desperateif not fatal illness for you or some person closely allied to you.Quarrels with the opposite sex is also indicated. You will remorsefully consider yourconduct toward a friend.CoffeeTo dream of drinking coffee, denotes the disapproval of friends toward your marriageintentions. If married, disagreements and frequent quarrels are implied.To dream of dealing in coffee, portends business failures. If selling, sure loss. Buying it,you may with ease retain your credit.For a young woman to see or handle coffee she will be made a by-word if she is notdiscreet in her actions.To dream of roasting coffee, for a young woman it denotes escape from evil by luckilymarrying a stranger.To see ground coffee, foretells successful struggles with adversity. Parched coffee, warnsyou of the evil attentions of strangers.Green coffee, denotes you have bold enemies who will show you no quarter, but willfight for your overthrow.Coffee MillTo see a coffee mill in your dreams, denotes you are approaching a critical danger, andall your energy and alertness will have to stand up with obduracy to avert its disastrousconsequences. To hear it grinding, signifies you will hardly overthrow some evil pitted

against your interest.Coffee HouseTo see or visit a coffee house in your dreams, foretells that you will unwisely entertainfriendly relations with persons known to be your enemies. Designing women mayintrigue against your morality and possessions.CoinsTo dream of gold, denotes great prosperity and much pleasure derived from sight-seeingand ocean voyages.Silver coin is unlucky to dream about. Dissensions will arise in the most orderly families.For a maiden to dream that her lover gives her a silver coin, signifies she will be jilted byhim.Copper coins, denotes despair and physical burdens. Nickel coins, imply that work of thelowest nature will devolve upon you.If silver coins are your ideal of money, and they are bright and clean, or seen distinctly inyour possession, the dream will be a propitious one.CokeTo dream of coke, denotes affliction and discord will enter your near future.Coke OvenTo see coke ovens burning, foretells some unexpected good fortune will result fromfailure in some enterprise.ColdTo dream of suffering from cold, you are warned to look well to your affairs. There areenemies at work to destroy you. Your health is also menaced.ColonelTo dream of seeing or being commanded by a colonel, denotes you will fail to reach anyprominence in social or business circles.If you are a colonel, it denotes you will contrive to hold position above those of friends oracquaintances.

Collar To dream of wearing a collar, you will have high honors thrust upon you that you willhardly be worthy of. For a woman to dream of collars, she will have many admirers, butno sincere ones, She will be likely to remain single for a long while.**College** To dream of a college, denotes you are soon to advance to a position long sought after.To dream that you are back in college, foretells you will receive distinction through somewell favored work.**Colliery or Coal-Mine** To dream of being in a coal-mine or colliery and seeing miners, denotes that some evilwill assert its power for your downfall; but if you dream of holding a share in acoal-mine, it denotes your safe investment in some deal.For a young woman to dream of mining coal, foreshows she will become the wife of areal-estate dealer or dentist.**Collision** To dream of a collision, you will meet with an accident of a serious type anddisappointments in business.For a young woman to see a collision, denotes she will be unable to decide betweenlovers, and will be the cause of wrangles.**Combat** To dream of engaging in combat, you will find yourself seeking to ingratiate youraffections into the life and love of some one whom you know to be another's, and youwill run great risks of losing your good reputation in business. It denotes struggles tokeep on firm ground.For a young woman to dream of seeing combatants, signifies that she will have choicebetween lovers, both of whom love her and would face death for her.**Combing** To dream of combing one's hair, denotes the illness or death of a friend or relative. Decayof friendship and loss of property is also indicated by this dream.See Hair.

Comedy To dream of being at a light play, denotes that foolish and short-lived pleasures will beindulged in by the dreamer.To dream of seeing a comedy, is significant of light pleasures and pleasant tasks.**Comet** To dream of this heavenly awe-inspiring object sailing through the skies, you will havetrials of an unexpected nature to beset you, but by bravely combating these foes you willrise above the mediocre in life to heights of fame.For a young person, this dream portends bereavement and sorrow.**Comic Songs** To hear comic songs in dreams, foretells you will disregard opportunity to advance youraffairs and enjoy the companionship of the pleasure loving. To sing one, proves you willenjoy much pleasure for a time, but difficulties will overtake you.**Command** To dream of being commanded, denotes that you will be humbled in some way by yourassociates for scorn shown your superiors.To dream of giving a command, you will have some honor conferred upon you. If this isdone in a tyrannical or boastful way disappointments will follow.**Commandment** To dream of receiving commands, foretells you will be unwisely influenced by personsof stronger will than your own. To read or hear the Ten Commandments read, denotesyou will fall into errors from which you will hardly escape, even with the counsels offriends of wise and unerring judgment.**Commerce** To dream that you are engaged in commerce, denotes you will handle your opportunitieswisely and advantageously. To dream of failures and gloomy outlooks in commercialcircles, denotes trouble and ominous threatening of failure in real business life.CommitteeTo dream of a committee, foretells that you will be surprised into doing some distasteful

work. For one to wait on you, foretells some unfruitful labor will be assigned you.CompanionTo dream of seeing a wife or husband, signifies small anxieties and probable sickness.To dream of social companions, denotes light and frivolous pastimes will engage yourattention hindering you from performing your duties.CompassTo dream of a compass, denotes you will be forced to struggle in narrow limits, thusmaking elevation more toilsome but fuller of honor.To dream of the compass or mariner's needle, foretells you will be surrounded byprosperous circumstances and honest people will favor you.To see one pointing awry, foretells threatened loss and deception.CompletionTo dream of completing a task or piece of work, denotes that you will have acquired acompetency early in life, and that you can spend your days as you like and wherever youplease.For a young woman to dream that she has completed a garment, denotes that she willsoon decide on a husband.To dream of completing a journey, you will have the means to make one whenever youlike.ComplexionTo dream that you have a beautiful complexion is lucky. You will pass through pleasingincidents.To dream that you have bad and dark complexion, denotes disappointment and sickness.ComposingTo see in your dreams a composing stick, foretells that difficult problems will disclosethemselves, and you will be at great trouble to meet them.

ConcertTo dream of a concert of a high musical order, denotes delightful seasons of pleasure,and literary work to the author. To the business man it portends successful trade, and tothe young it signifies unalloyed bliss and faithful loves.Ordinary concerts such as engage ballet singers, denote that disagreeable companions andungrateful friends will be met with. Business will show a falling off.ConcubineFor a man to dream that he is in company with a concubine, forecasts he is in danger ofpublic disgrace, striving to keep from the world his true character and state of business.For a woman to dream that she is a concubine, indicates that she will degrade herself byher own improprieties.For a man to dream that his mistress is untrue, denotes that he has old enemies toencounter. Expected reverses will arise.ConfectionaryTo dream of impure confectionary, denotes that an enemy in the guise of a friend willenter your privacy and discover secrets of moment to your opponents.ConfettiTo dream of confetti obstructing your view in a crowd of merry-makers, denotes thatyou will lose much by first seeking enjoyment, and later fulfil tasks set by duty.ConjurerTo dream of a conjuror, denotes unpleasant experience will beset you in your search forwealth and happiness.ConjuringTo dream that you are in a hypnotic state or under the power of others, portendsdisastrous results, for your enemies will enthrall you; but if you hold others under a spellyou will assert decided will power in governing your surroundings.For a young woman to dream that she is under strange influences, denotes her immediateexposure to danger, and she should beware.To dream of seeing hypnotic and slight-of-hand performances, signifies worries andperplexities in business and domestic circles, and unhealthy conditions of state.

ConflagrationTo dream of a conflagration, denotes, if no lives are lost, changes in the future which willbe beneficial to your interests and happiness.See Fire.ConspiracyTo dream that you are the object of a conspiracy, foretells you will make a wrong movein the directing of your affairs.ConscienceTo dream that your conscience censures you for deceiving some one, denotes that youwill be tempted to commit wrong and should be constantly on your guard.To dream of having a quiet conscience, denotes that you will stand in high repute.ConsumptionTo dream that you have consumption, denotes that you are exposing yourself to danger.Remain with your friends.ContemptTo dream of being in contempt of court, denotes that you have committed business orsocial indiscretion and that it is unmerited.To dream that you are held in contempt by others, you will succeed in winning theirhighest regard, and will find yourself prosperous and happy. But if the contempt ismerited, your exile from business or social circles is intimated.ConventTo dream of seeking refuge in a convent, denotes that your future will be signally freefrom care and enemies, unless on entering the building you encounter a priest. If so, youwill seek often and in vain for relief from worldly cares and mind worry.For a young girl to dream of seeing a convent, her virtue and honestly will be questioned.ConvictsTo dream of seeing convicts, denotes disasters and sad news. To dream that you are aconvict, indicates that you will worry over some affair; but you will clear up all mistakes.

For a young woman to dream of seeing her lover in the garb of a convict, indicates shewill have cause to question the character of his love.ConvictedSee Accuse.ConventionTo dream of a convention, denotes unusual activity in business affairs and finalengagement in love. An inharmonious or displeasing convention brings youdisappointment.CookingTo cook a meal, denotes some pleasant duty will devolve on you. Many friends will visityou in the near future. If there is discord or a lack of cheerfulness you may expectharassing and disappointing events to happen.Cooking StoveTo see a cooking stove in a dream, denotes that much unpleasantness will be modified byyour timely interference. For a young woman to dream of using a cooking stove, foretellsshe will be too hasty in showing her appreciation of the attention of some person andthereby lose a closer friendship.Cooling BoardFor a young woman to see a cooling board in her dreams, foretells sickness and quarrelswith her lover. To dream of some living person as dead and rising up from a coolingboard, denotes she will be indirectly connected with that person in some trouble, but willfind out that things will work out satisfactorily.To see her brother, who has long since been dead, rising from a cooling board, warns herof complications which may be averted if she puts forth the proper will and energy instruggling against them.CopperTo dream of copper, denotes oppression from those above you in station.CopperasTo dream of copperas, foretells unintentional wrong will be done you which will bedistressing and will cause you loss.

Copper PlateCopper plate seen in a dream, is a warning of discordant views causing unhappinessbetween members of the same household.CoppersmithTo dream of a coppersmith, denotes small returns for labor, but withal contentment.CopyingTo dream of copying, denotes unfavorable workings of well tried plans.For a young woman to dream that she is copying a letter, denotes she will be prejudicedinto error by her love for a certain class of people.CoralTo dream of coral, is momentous of enduring friend ship which will know no wearinessin alleviating your trouble. Colored coral is meant in this dream.White coral, foretells unfaithfulness and warning of love.CornetA cornet seen or heard in a dream, denotes kindly attentions from strangers.CoronationTo dream of a coronation, foretells you will enjoy acquaintances and friendships withprominent people. For a young woman to be participating in a coronation, foretells thatshe will come into some surprising favor with distinguished personages. But if thecoronation presents disagreeable incoherence in her dreams, then she may expectunsatisfactory states growing out of anticipated pleasure.CordsSee Rope.CorkTo dream of drawing corks at a banquet, signifies that you will soon enter a state ofprosperity, in which you will revel in happiness of the most select kind.To dream of medicine corks, denotes sickness and wasted energies.

To dream of seeing a fishing cork resting on clear water, denotes success. If water isdisturbed you will be annoyed by unprincipled persons.To dream that you are corking bottles, denotes a well organized business and system inyour living.For a young woman to dream of drawing champagne corks, indicates she will have a gayand handsome lover who will lavish much attention and money on her. She should lookwell to her reputation and listen to the warning of parents after this dream.CornTo dream of husking pied ears of corn, denotes you will enjoy varied success andpleasure. To see others gathering corn, foretells you will rejoice in the prosperity offriends or relatives.Corn and Corn-FieldTo dream of passing through a green and luxurious corn-field, and seeing full earshanging heavily, denotes great wealth for the farmer. It denotes fine crops and richharvest and harmony in the home. To the young it promises much happiness and truefriends, but to see the ears blasted, denotes disappointments and bereavements.To see young corn newly ploughed, denotes favor with the powerful and coming success.To see it ripe, denotes fame and wealth. To see it cribbed, signifies that your highestdesires will be realized.To see shelled corn, denotes wealthy combines and unstinted favors.To dream of eating green corn, denotes harmony among friends and happy unions for theyoung.CornsTo dream that your corns hurt your feet, denotes that some enemies are undermining you,and you will have much distress; but if you succeed in clearing your feet of corns, youwill inherit a large estate from some unknown source.For a young woman to dream of having corns on her feet, indicates she will have to bearmany crosses and be coldly treated by her sex.CorkscrewTo dream of seeing a corkscrew, indicates an unsatisfied mind, and the dreamer shouldheed this as a warning to curb his desires, for it is likely they are on dangerous grounds.

To dream of breaking a corkscrew while using it, indicates to the dreamer periloussurroundings, and he should use force of will to abandon unhealthful inclinations.CorpseTo dream of a corpse is fatal to happiness, as this dream indicates sorrowful tidings of theabsent, and gloomy business prospects. The young will suffer many disappointments andpleasure will vanish.To see a corpse placed in its casket, denotes immediate troubles to the dreamer.To see a corpse in black, denotes the violent death of a friend or some desperate businessentanglement.To see a battle-field strewn with corpses, indicates war and general dissatisfactionbetween countries and political factions.To see the corpse of an animal, denotes unhealthy situation, both as to business andhealth.To see the corpse of any one of your immediate family, indicates death to that person, orto some member of the family, or a serious rupture of domestic relations, also unusualbusiness depression. For lovers it is a sure sign of failure to keep promises of a sacrednature.To put money on the eyes of a corpse in your dreams, denotes that you will seeunscrupulous enemies robbing you while you are powerless to resent injury. If you onlyput it on one eye you will be able to recover lost property after an almost hopelessstruggle. For a young woman this dream denotes distress and loss by unfortunatelygiving her confidence to designing persons.For a young woman to dream that the proprietor of the store in which she works is acorpse, and she sees while sitting up with him that his face is clean shaven, foretells thatshe will fall below the standard of perfection in which she was held by her lover. If shesees the head of the corpse falling from the body, she is warned of secret enemies who, inharming her, will also detract from the interest of her employer. Seeing the corpse in thestore, foretells that loss and unpleasantness will offset all concerned. There are those whoare not conscientiously doing the right thing. There will be a gloomy outlook for peaceand prosperous work.CornmealTo see cornmeal, foretells the consummation of ardent wishes. To eat it made into bread,denotes that you will unwittingly throw obstructions in the way of your ownadvancement.

CornerThis is an unfavorable dream if the dreamer is frightened and secretes himself in a cornerfor safety.To see persons talking in a corner, enemies are seeking to destroy you. The chances arethat some one whom you consider a friend will prove a traitor to your interest.CorpulenceFor a person to dream of being corpulent, indicates to the dreamer bountiful increase ofwealth and pleasant abiding places.To see others corpulent, denotes unusual activity and prosperous times.If a man or woman sees himself or herself looking grossly corpulent, he or she shouldlook well to their moral nature and impulses. Beware of either concave or convextelescopically or microscopically drawn pictures of yourself or others, as they forbodeevil.CorsetTo dream of a corset, denotes that you will be perplexed as to the meaning of attentionswon by you. If a young woman is vexed over undoing or fastening her corset, she will bestrongly inclined to quarrel with her friends under slight provocations.CossackTo dream of a Cossack, denotes humiliation of a personal character, brought about bydissipation and wanton extravagance.CotTo dream of a cot, foretells some affliction, either through sickness or accident. Cots inrows signify you will not be alone in trouble, as friends will be afflicted also.CottonTo dream of young growing cotton-fields, denotes great business and prosperous times.To see cotton ready for gathering, denotes wealth and abundance for farmers.For manufacturers to dream of cotton, means that they will be benefited by theadvancement of this article. For merchants, it denotes a change for the better in their lineof business.To see cotton in bales, is a favorable indication for better times.

To dream that cotton is advancing, denotes an immediate change from low to high prices,and all will be in better circumstances.Cotton CapIt is a good dream, denoting many sincere friends.Cotton ClothTo see cotton cloth in a dream, denotes easy circumstances. No great changes follow thisdream.For a young woman to dream of weaving cotton cloth, denotes that she will have a thriftyand enterprising husband. To the married it denotes a pleasant yet a humble abode.Cotton GinTo dream of a cotton gin, foretells you will make some advancement toward fortunewhich will be very pleasing and satisfactory. To see a broken or dilapidated gin, signifiesmisfortune and trouble will overthrow success.CouchTo dream of reclining on a couch, indicates that false hopes will be entertained. Youshould be alert to every change of your affairs, for only in this way will your hopes berealized.CoughTo dream that you are aggravated by a constant cough indicates a state of low health; butone from which you will recuperate if care is observed in your habits.To dream of hearing others cough, indicates unpleasant surroundings from which youwill ultimately emerge.CounterTo dream of counters, foretells that active interest will debar idleness from infecting yourlife with unhealthful desires. To dream of empty and soiled counters, foretells unfortunate engagements which will bring great uneasiness of mind lest your interest will be wholly swept away. Counterfeit Money To dream of counterfeit money, denotes you will have trouble with some unruly and

worthless person. This dream always omens evil, whether you receive it or pass it. Counselor To dream of a counselor, you are likely to be possessed of some ability yourself, and you will usually prefer your own judgment to that of others. Be guarded in executing your ideas of right. Countenance To dream of a beautiful and ingenuous countenance, you may safely look for some pleasure to fall to your lot in the near future; but to behold an ugly and scowling visage, portends unfavorable transactions. Counterpane A counterpane is very good to dream of, if clean and white, denoting pleasant occupations for women; but if it be soiled you may expect harassing situations. Sickness usually follows this dream. Counting To dream of counting your children, and they are merry and sweet-looking, denotes that you will have no trouble in controlling them, and they will attain honorable places. To dream of counting money, you will be lucky and always able to pay your debts; but to count out money to another person, you will meet with loss of some kind. Such will be the case, also, in counting other things. If for yourself, good; if for others, usually bad luck will attend you. Country To dream of being in a beautiful and fertile country, where abound rich fields of grain and running streams of pure water, denotes the very acme of good times is at hand. Wealth will pile in upon you, and you will be able to reign in state in any country. If the country be dry and bare, you will see and hear of troublous times. Famine and sickness will be in the land. Courtship Bad, bad, will be the fate of the woman who dreams of being courted. She will often think that now he will propose, but often she will be disappointed. Disappointments will follow illusory hopes and fleeting pleasures. For a man to dream of courting, implies that he is not worthy of a companion.

Cousin Dreaming of one's cousin, denotes disappointments and afflictions. Saddened lives are predicted by this dream. To dream of an affectionate correspondence with one's cousin, denotes a fatal rupture between families. Cows To dream of seeing cows waiting for the milking hour, promises abundant fulfilment of hopes and desires. See Cattle. Cowslip To dream of gathering cowslips, portends unhappy ending of seemingly close and warm friendships; but seeing them growing, denotes a limited competency for lovers. This is a sinister dream. To see them in full bloom, denotes a crisis in your affairs. The breaking up of happy homes may follow this dream. Coxcomb To dream of a coxcomb, denotes a low state of mind. The dreamer should endeavor to elevate his mind to nobler thoughts. Cradle To dream of a cradle, with a beautiful infant occupying it, portends prosperity and theaffections of beautiful children.To rock your own baby in a cradle, denotes the serious illness of one of the family.For a young woman to dream of rocking a cradle is portentous of her downfall. Sheshould beware of gossiping.CrabsTo dream of crabs, indicates that you will have many complicated affairs, for the solvingof which you will be forced to exert the soundest judgment. This dream portends tolovers a long and difficult courtship.

CraneTo dream of seeing a flight of cranes tending northward, indicates gloomy prospects forbusiness. To a woman, it is significant of disappointment; but to see them flyingsouthward, prognosticates a joyful meeting of absent friends, and that lovers will remainfaithful.To see them fly to the ground, events of unusual moment are at hand.CrapeTo dream of seeing crape hanging from a door, denotes that you will hear of the suddendeath of some relative or friend.To see a person dressed in crape, indicates that sorrow, other than death, will possessyou. It is bad for business and trade. To the young, it implies lovers' disputes andseparations.CrawfishDeceit is sure to assail you in your affairs of the heart, if you are young, after dreaming ofthis backward-going thing.CrawlTo dream that you are crawling on the ground, and hurt your hand, you may expecthumiliating tasks to be placed on you.To crawl over rough places and stones, indicates that you have not taken properadvantage of your opportunities. A young woman, after dreaming of crawling, if not verycareful of her conduct, will lose the respect of her lover.To crawl in mire with others, denotes depression in business and loss of credit. Yourfriends will have cause to censure you.CreamTo dream of seeing cream served, denotes that you will be associated with wealth if youare engaged in business other than farming.To the farmer, it indicates fine crops and pleasant family relations.To drink cream yourself, denotes immediate good fortune.To lovers, this is a happy omen, as they will soon be united.

CreditTo dream of asking for credit, denotes that you will have cause to worry, although youmay be inclined sometimes to think things look bright.To credit another, warns you to be careful of your affairs, as you are likely to trust thosewho will eventually work you harm.CreekTo dream of a creek, denotes new experiences and short journeys. If it is overflowing,you will have sharp trouble, but of brief period.If it is dry, disappointment will be felt by you, and you will see another obtain the thingsyou intrigued to secure.CremateTo dream of seeing bodies cremated, denotes enemies will reduce your influence inbusiness circles. To think you are being cremated, portends distinct failure in enterprises,if you mind any but your own judgment in conducting them.CrewTo dream of seeing a crew getting ready to leave port, some unforeseen circumstancewill cause you to give up a journey from which you would have gained much.To see a crew working to save a ship in a storm, denotes disaster on land and sea. To theyoung, this dream bodes evil.CricketTo hear a cricket in one's dream, indicates melancholy news, and perhaps the death ofsome distant friend.To see them, indicates hard struggles with poverty.CriesTo hear cries of distress, denotes that you will be engulfed in serious troubles, but bybeing alert you will finally emerge from these distressing straits and gain by thistemporary gloom.To hear a cry of surprise, you will receive aid from unexpected sources.To hear the cries of wild beasts, denotes an accident of a serious nature.

To hear a cry for help from relatives, or friends, denotes that they are sick or in distress.CriminalTo dream of associating with a person who has committed a crime, denotes that you willbe harassed with unscrupulous persons, who will try to use your friendship for their ownadvancement.To see a criminal fleeing from justice, denotes that you will come into the possession ofthe secrets of others, and will therefore be in danger, for they will fear that you willbetray them, and consequently will seek your removal.CrippledTo dream of the maimed and crippled, denotes famine and distress among the poor, andyou should be willing to contribute to their store. It also indicates a temporary dulness intrade.Crochet WorkTo dream of doing crochet work, foretells your entanglement in some silly affair growingout of a too great curiosity about other people's business. Beware of talking too franklywith over-confidential women.CrockeryTo dream of having an abundance of nice, clean crockery, denotes that you will be a tidyand economical housekeeper. To be in a crockery store, indicates, if you are a merchantor business man, that you will look well to the details of your business and therebyexperience profit. To a young woman, this dream denotes that she will marry a sturdyand upright man. An untidy store, with empty shelves, implies loss.CrocodileAs sure as you dream of this creature, you will be deceived by your warmest friends.Enemies will assail you at every turn.To dream of stepping on a crocodile's back, you may expect to fall into trouble, fromwhich you will have to struggle mightily to extricate yourself. Heed this warning whendreams of this nature visit you. Avoid giving your confidence even to friends.CrossTo dream of seeing a cross, indicates trouble ahead for you. Shape your affairsaccordingly. To dream of seeing a person bearing a cross, you will be called on bymissionaries to aid in charities.

Cross-BonesTo dream of cross-bones, foretells you will be troubled by the evil influence of others,and prosperity will assume other than promising aspects.To see cross-bones as a monogram on an invitation to a funeral, which was sent out by asecret order, denotes that unnecessary fears will be entertained for some person, andevents will transpire seemingly harsh, but of good import to the dreamer.Cross RoadsTo dream of cross roads, denotes you will be unable to hold some former favorableopportunity for reaching your desires. If you are undecided which one to take, you arelikely to let unimportant matters irritate you in a distressing manner. You will be betterfavored by fortune if you decide on your route. It may be after this dream you will havesome important matter of business or love to decide.CroupTo dream that your child has the croup, denotes slight illness, but useless fear for itssafety. This is generally a good omen of health and domestic harmony.CrowTo dream of seeing a crow, betokens misfortune and grief. To hear crows cawing, youwill be influenced by others to make a bad disposal of property. To a young man, it isindicative of his succumbing to the wiles of designing women.See Raven.CrowdTo dream of a large, handsomely dressed crowd of people at some entertainment, denotespleasant association with friends; but anything occurring to mar the pleasure of theguests, denotes distress and loss of friendship, and unhappiness will be found whereprofit and congenial intercourse was expected. It also denotes dissatisfaction ingovernment and family dissensions.To see a crowd in a church, denotes that a death will be likely to affect you, or someslight unpleasantness may develop.To see a crowd in the street, indicates unusual briskness in trade and a general air ofprosperity will surround you.To try to be heard in a crowd, foretells that you will push your interests ahead of allothers.

To see a crowd is usually good, if too many are not wearing black or dull costumes.To dream of seeing a hypnotist trying to hypnotize others, and then turn his attention onyou, and fail to do so, indicates that a trouble is hanging above you which friends will notsucceed in warding off. Yourself alone can avert the impending danger.CrownTo dream of a crown, prognosticates change of mode in the habit of one's life. Thedreamer will travel a long distance from home and form new relations. Fatal illness mayalso be the sad omen of this dream.To dream that you wear a crown, signifies loss of personal property.To dream of crowning a person, denotes your own worthiness.To dream of talking with the President of the United States, denotes that you areinterested in affairs of state, and sometimes show a great longing to be a politician.CrucifixionIf you chance to dream of the crucifixion, you will see your opportunities slip away,tearing your hopes from your grasp, and leaving you wailing over the frustration ofdesires.CrucifixTo see a crucifix in a dream, is a warning of distress approaching, which will involveothers beside yourself. To kiss one, foretells that trouble will be accepted by you withresignation.For a young woman to possess one, foretells she will observe modesty and kindness inher deportment, and thus win the love of others and better her fortune.CrueltyTo dream of cruelty being shown you, foretells you will have trouble and disappointmentin some dealings. If it is shown to others, there will be a disagreeable task set for othersby you, which will contribute to you own loss.CrustTo dream of a crust of bread, denotes incompetency, and threatened misery throughcarelessness in appointed duties.

Crutches To dream that you go on crutches, denotes that you will depend largely on others for your support and advancement. To see others on crutches, denotes unsatisfactory results from labors. **Crying** To dream of crying, is a forerunner of illusory pleasures, which will subside into gloom, and distressing influences affecting for evil business engagements and domestic affairs. To see others crying, forbodes unexpected calls for aid from you. **Crystal** To dream of crystal in any form, is a fatal sign of coming depression either in social relations or business transactions. Electrical storms often attend this dream, doing damage to town and country. For a woman to dream of seeing a dining-room furnished in crystal, even to the chairs, she will have cause to believe that those whom she holds in high regard no longer deserve this distinction, but she will find out that there were others in the crystal-furnished room, who were implicated also in this sinister dream. **Cuckoo** To dream of a cuckoo, prognosticates a sudden ending of a happy life caused by the downfall of a dear friend. To dream that you hear a cuckoo, denotes the painful illness of the death of some absent loved one, or accident to some one in your family. **Cucumber** This is a dream of plenty, denoting health and prosperity. For the sick to dream of serving cucumbers, denotes their speedy recovery. For the married, a pleasant change. **Cunning** To dream of being cunning, denotes you will assume happy cheerfulness to retain the friendship of prosperous and gay people. If you are associating with cunning people, it warns you that deceit is being practised upon you in order to use your means for their own advancement.

Cupboard To see a cupboard in your dream, is significant of pleasure and comfort, or penury and distress, according as the cupboard is clean and full of shining ware, or empty and dirty. See Safe. **Curbstone** To dream of stepping on a curbstone, denotes your rapid rise in business circles, and that you will be held in high esteem by your friends and the public. For lovers to dream of stepping together on a curb, denotes an early marriage and consequent fidelity; but if in your dream you step or fall from a curbstone your fortunes will be reversed. **Currycomb** To dream of a currycomb foretells that great labors must be endured in order to obtain wealth and comfort. **Currying a Horse** To dream of currying a horse, signifies that you will have a great many hard licks to make both with brain and hand before you attain to the heights of your ambition; but if you successfully curry him you will attain that height, whatever it may be. **Curtains** To dream of curtains, foretells that unwelcome visitors will cause you worry and unhappiness. Soiled or torn curtains seen in a dream means disgraceful quarrels and reproaches. **Cushion** To dream of reclining on silken cushions, foretells that your ease will be procured at the expense of others; but to see the cushions, denotes that you will prosper in business andlove-making.For a young woman to dream of making silken cushions, implies that she will be a bridebefore many months.CuspidorTo see a cuspidor in a dream, signifies that an unworthy attachment will be formed by

you, and that your work will be neglected.To spit in one, foretells that reflections will be cast upon your conduct.CustardFor a married woman to dream of making or eating custard, indicates she will be calledupon to entertain an unexpected guest. A young woman will meet a stranger who will intime become a warm friend. If the custard has a sickening sweet taste, or is insipid,nothing but sorrow will intervene where you had expected a pleasant experience.See Baking.Custom HouseTo dream of a custom-house, denotes you will have rivalries and competition in yourlabors.To enter a custom-house, foretells that you will strive for, or have offered you, a positionwhich you have long desired.To leave one, signifies loss of position, trade or failure of securing some desired object.CutTo dream of a cut, denotes sickness or the treachery of a friend will frustrate yourcheerfulness.CymbalHearing a cymbal in your dreams, foretells the death of a very aged person of youracquaintance. The sun will shine, but you will see it darkly because of gloom.

What's In A Dream - D to H

DDaggerIf seen in a dream, denotes threatening enemies. If you wrench the dagger from the handof another, it denotes that you will be able to counteract the influence of your enemiesand overcome misfortune.DahliaTo see dahlias in a dream, if they are fresh and bright, signifies good fortune to thedreamer.See Bouquet.DairyDairy is a good dream both to the married and unmarried.See Churning Butter.DaisyTo dream of a bunch of daisys, implies sadness, but if you dream of being in a fieldwhere these lovely flowers are in bloom, with the sun shining and birds singing,happiness, health and prosperity will vie each with the other to lead you through thepleasantest avenues of life.To dream of seeing them out of season, you will be assailed by evil in some guise.Damask RoseTo dream of seeing a damask rosebush in full foliage and bloom, denotes that a weddingwill soon take place in your family, and great hopes will be fulfilled.

For a lover to place this rose in your hair, foretells that you will be deceived. If a woman receives a bouquet of damask roses in springtime, she will have a faithful lover; but if she received them in winter, she will cherish blasted hopes. Damson This is a peculiarly good dream if one is so fortunate. as to see these trees lifting their branches loaded with rich purple fruit and dainty foliage; one may expect riches compared with his present estate. To dream of eating them at any time, forebodes grief. Dance To dream of seeing a crowd of merry children dancing, signifies to the married, loving, obedient and intelligent children and a cheerful and comfortable home. To young people, it denotes easy tasks and many pleasures. To see older people dancing, denotes a brighter outlook for business. To dream of dancing yourself, some unexpected good fortune will come to you. See Ball. Dancing Master To dream of a dancing master, foretells you will neglect important affairs to pursue frivolities. For a young woman to dream that her lover is a dancing master, portends that she will have a friend in accordance with her views of pleasure and life. Dandelion Dandelions blossoming in green foliage, foretells happy unions and prosperous surroundings. Danger To dream of being in a perilous situation, and death seems imminent, denotes that you will emerge from obscurity into places of distinction and honor; but if you should not escape the impending danger, and suffer death or a wound, you will lose in business and be annoyed in your home, and by others. If you are in love, your prospects will grow discouraging.

Dark To dream of darkness overtaking you on a journey, augurs ill for any work you may attempt, unless the sun breaks through before the journey ends, then faults will be overcome. To lose your friend, or child, in the darkness, portends many provocations to wrath. Try to remain under control after dreaming of darkness, for trials in business and love will beset you. Dates To dream of seeing them on their parent trees, signifies prosperity and happy union; but to eat them as prepared for commerce, they are omens of want and distress. Daughter To dream of your daughter, signifies that many displeasing incidents will give way to pleasure and harmony. If in the dream, she fails to meet your wishes, through any cause, you will suffer vexation and discontent. Daughter-In-Law To dream of your daughter-in-law, indicates some unusual occurrence will add to happiness, or disquiet, according as she is pleasant or unreasonable. David To dream of David, of Bible fame, denotes divisions in domestic circles, and unsettled affairs, will tax heavily your nerve force. Day To dream of the day, denotes improvement in your situation, and pleasant associations. A gloomy or cloudy day, foretells loss and ill success in new enterprises. Daybreak To watch the day break in a dream, omens successful undertakings, unless the scene is indistinct and weird; then it may imply disappointment when success in business or love seems assured.

DeadTo dream of the dead, is usually a dream of warning. If you see and talk with your father,some unlucky transaction is about to be made by you. Be careful how you enter intocontracts, enemies are around you. Men and women are warned to look to theirreputations after this dream.To see your mother, warns you to control your inclination to cultivate morbidness and illwill towards your fellow creatures. A brother, or other relatives or friends, denotes thatyou may be called on for charity or aid within a short time.To dream of seeing the dead, living and happy, signifies you are letting wrong influencesinto your life, which will bring material loss if not corrected by the assumption of yourown will force.To dream that you are conversing with a dead relative, and that relative endeavors toextract a promise from you, warns you of coming distress, unless you follow the advicegiven you. Disastrous consequences could often be averted if minds could grasp the innerworkings and sight of the higher or spiritual self. The voice of relatives is only thathigher self taking form to approach more distinctly the mind that lives near the materialplane. There is so little congeniality between common or material natures that personsshould depend upon their own subjectivity for true contentment and pleasure.Paracelsus says on this subject:It may happen that the soul of persons who have died perhaps fifty yearsago may appear to us in a dream, and if it speaks to us we should payspecial attention to what it says, for such a vision is not an illusion ordelusion, and it is possible that a man is as much able to use his reasonduring the sleep of his body as when the latter is awake; and if in such acase such a soul appears to him and he asks questions, he will then hearthat which is true. Through these solicitous souls we may obtain a greatdeal of knowledge to good or to evil things if we ask them to reveal themto us. Many persons have had such prayers granted to them. Some peoplethat were sick have been informed during their sleep what remedies theyshould use, and after using the remedies, they became cured, and suchthings have happened not only to Christians, but also to Jews, Persians,and heathens, to good and to bad persons.The writer does not hold that such knowledge is obtained from external or excarnatespirits, but rather through the personal Spirit Glimpses that is in man.AUTHOR.Death.To dream of seeing any of your people dead, warns you of coming dissolution or sorrow.Disappointments always follow dreams of this nature.

To hear of any friend or relative being dead, you will soon have bad news from some ofthem.Dreams relating to death or dying, unless they are due to spiritual causes, are misleadingand very confusing to the novice in dream lore when he attempts to interpret them. Aman who thinks intensely fills his aura with thought or subjective images active with thepassions that gave them birth; by thinking and acting on other lines, he may supplantthese images with others possessed of a different form and nature. In his dreams he maysee these images dying, dead or their burial, and mistake them for friends or enemies. Inthis way he may, while asleep, see himself or a relative die, when in reality he has beenwarned that some good thought or deed is to be supplanted by an evil one. To illustrate:If it is a dear friend or relative whom he sees in the agony of death, he is warned againstimmoral or other improper thought and action, but if it is an enemy or some repulsiveobject dismantled in death, he may overcome his evil ways and thus give himself orfriends cause for joy. Often the end or beginning of suspense or trials are foretold bydreams of this nature. They also frequently occur when the dreamer is controlled byimaginary states of evil or good. A man in that state is not himself, but is what thedominating influences make him. He may be warned of approaching conditions or hisextrication from the same. In our dreams we are closer to our real self than in waking life.The hideous or pleasing incidents seen and heard about us in our dreams are all of ourown making, they reflect the true state of our soul and body, and we cannot flee fromthem unless we drive them out of our being by the use of good thoughts and deeds, by thepower of the spirit within us.See Corpse.DebtDebt is rather a bad dream, foretelling worries in business and love, and struggles for acompetency; but if you have plenty to meet all your obligations, your affairs will assumea favorable turn.DecemberTo dream of December, foretells accumulation of wealth, but loss of friendship.Strangers will occupy the position in the affections of some friend which was formerlyheld by you.DeckTo dream of being on a ship and that a storm is raging, great disasters and unfortunatealliances will overtake you; but if the sea is calm and the light distinct, your way is clearto success. For lovers, this dream augurs happiness.See Boat.

DecorateTo dream of decorating a place with bright-hued flowers for some festive occasion, issignificant of favorable turns in business, and, to the young, of continued rounds of socialpleasures and fruitful study.To see the graves or caskets of the dead decorated with white flowers, is unfavorable topleasure and worldly pursuits.To be decorating, or see others decorate for some heroic action, foretells that you will beworthy, but that few will recognize your ability.DeedTo dream of seeing or signing deeds, portends a law suit, to gain which you should becareful in selecting your counsel, as you are likely to be the loser. To dream of signingany kind of a paper, is a bad omen for the dreamer.See Mortgage.DeerThis is a favorable dream, denoting pure and deep friendships for the young and a quietand even life for the married.To kill a deer, denotes that you will be hounded by enemies. For farmers, or businesspeople, to dream of hunting deer, denotes failure in their respective pursuits.DelayTo be delayed in a dream, warns you of the scheming of enemies to prevent yourprogress.DelightTo dream of experiencing delight over any event, signifies a favorable turn in affairs. Forlovers to be delighted with the conduct of their sweethearts, denotes pleasant greetings.To feel delight when looking on beautiful landscapes, prognosticates to the dreamer verygreat success and congenial associations.DemandTo dream that a demand for charity comes in upon you, denotes that you will be placed inembarrassing situations, but by your persistency you will fully restore your goodstanding. If the demand is unjust, you will become a leader in your profession. For a

lover to command you adversely, implies his, or her, leniency.DentistTo dream of a dentist working on your teeth, denotes that you will have occasion todoubt the sincerity and honor of some person with whom you have dealings.To see him at work on a young woman's teeth, denotes that you will soon be shocked bya scandal in circles near you.DerrickDerricks seen in a dream, indicate strife and obstruction in your way to success.DesertTo dream of wandering through a gloomy and barren desert, denotes famine and uprisalof races and great loss of life and property.For a young woman to find herself alone in a desert, her health and reputation is beingjeopardized by her indiscretion. She should be more cautious.DeskTo be using a desk in a dream, denotes unforeseen ill luck will rise before you. To seemoney on your desk, brings you unexpected extrication from private difficulties.DespairTo be in despair in dreams, denotes that you will have many and cruel vexations in theworking world.To see others in despair, foretells the distress and unhappy position of some relative orfriend.DetectiveTo dream of a detective keeping in your wake when you are innocent of chargespreferred, denotes that fortune and honor are drawing nearer to you each day; but if youfeel yourself guilty, you are likely to find your reputation at stake, and friends will turnfrom you. For a young woman, this is not a fortunate dream.DevotionFor a farmer to dream of showing his devotion to God, or to his family, denotes

plenteous crops and peaceful neighbors. To business people, this is a warning thatnothing is to be gained by deceit.For a young woman to dream of being devout, implies her chastity and an adoringhusband.DevilFor farmers to dream of the devil, denotes blasted crops and death among stock, alsofamily sickness. Sporting people should heed this dream as a warning to be careful oftheir affairs, as they are likely to venture beyond the laws of their State. For a preacher,this dream is undeniable proof that he is over-zealous, and should forebear worshipingGod by tongue-lashing his neighbor.To dream of the devil as being a large, imposingly dressed person, wearing manysparkling jewels on his body and hands, trying to persuade you to enter his abode, warnsyou that unscrupulous persons are seeking your ruin by the most ingenious flattery.Young and innocent women, should seek the stronghold of friends after this dream, andavoid strange attentions, especially from married men. Women of low character, arelikely to be robbed of jewels and money by seeming strangers.Beware of associating with the devil, even in dreams. He is always the forerunner ofdespair. If you dream of being pursued by his majesty, you will fall into snares set foryou by enemies in the guise of friends. To a lover, this denotes that he will be won awayfrom his allegiance by a wanton.DewTo feel the dew falling on you in your dreams, portends that you will be attacked by feveror some malignant disease; but to see the dew sparkling through the grass in the sunlight,great honors and wealth are about to be heaped upon you. If you are single, a wealthymarriage will soon be your portion.DiademTo dream of a diadem, denotes that some honor will be tendered you for acceptance.DiamondsTo dream of owning diamonds is a very propitious dream, signifying great honor andrecognition from high places.For a young woman to dream of her lover presenting her with diamonds, foreshows thatshe will make a great and honorable marriage, which will fill her people with honestpride; but to lose diamonds, and not find them again, is the most unlucky of dreams,foretelling disgrace, want and death.

For a sporting woman to dream of diamonds, foretells for her many prosperous days andmagnificent presents. For a speculator, it denotes prosperous transactions. To dream ofowning diamonds, portends the same for sporting men or women.Diamonds are omens of good luck, unless stolen from the bodies of dead persons, whenthey foretell that your own unfaithfulness will be discovered by your friends.DiceTo dream of dice, is indicative of unfortunate speculations, and consequent misery anddespair. It also foretells contagious sickness.For a girl to dream that she sees her lover throwing dice, indicates his unworthiness.DictionaryTo dream that you are referring to a dictionary, signifies you will depend too much uponthe opinion and suggestions of others for the clear management of your own affairs,which could be done with proper dispatch if your own will was given play.DifficultyThis dream signifies temporary embarrassment for business men of all classes, includingsoldiers and writers. But to extricate yourself from difficulties, foretells your prosperity.For a woman to dream of being in difficulties, denotes that she is threatened with illhealth or enemies. For lovers, this is a dream of contrariety, denoting pleasant courtship.DiggingTo dream of digging, denotes that you will never be in want, but life will be an uphillaffair.To dig a hole and find any glittering substance, denotes a favorable turn in fortune; but todig and open up a vast area of hollow mist, you will be harrassed with real misfortunesand be filled with gloomy forebodings. Water filling the hole that you dig, denotes that inspite of your most strenuous efforts things will not bend to your will.DinnerTo dream that you eat your dinner alone, denotes that you will often have cause to thinkseriously of the necessaries of life.For a young woman to dream of taking dinner with her lover, is indicative of a lovers'quarrel or a rupture, unless the affair is one of harmonious pleasure, when the reversemay be expected.

To be one of many invited guests at a dinner, denotes that you will enjoy the hospitalitiesof those who are able to extend to you many pleasant courtesies.DirtTo dream of seeing freshly stirred dirt around flowers or trees, denotes thrift andhealthful conditions abound for the dreamer.To see your clothes soiled with unclean dirt, you will be forced to save yourself fromcontagious diseases by leaving your home or submitting to the strictures of the law.To dream that some one throws dirt upon you, denotes that enemies will try to injureyour character.DisasterTo dream of being in any disaster from public conveyance, you are in danger of losingproperty or of being maimed from some malarious disease.For a young woman to dream of a disaster in which she is a participant, foretells that shewill mourn the loss of her lover by death or desertion.To dream of a disaster at sea, denotes unhappiness to sailors and loss of their gains. Toothers, it signifies loss by death; but if you dream that you are rescued, you will be placedin trying situations, but will come out unscathed.To dream of a railway wreck in which you are not a participant, you will eventually beinterested in some accident because of some relative or friend being hurt, or you willhave trouble of a business character.DiseaseTo dream that you are diseased, denotes a slight attack of illness, or of unpleasantdealings with a relative.For a young woman to dream that she is incurably diseased, denotes that she will belikely to lead a life of single blessedness.DisgraceTo be worried in your dream over the disgraceful conduct of children or friends, willbring you unsatisfying hopes, and worries will harass you. To be in disgrace yourself,denotes that you will hold morality at a low rate, and you are in danger of lowering yourreputation for uprightness. Enemies are also shadowing you.

DishTo dream of handling dishes, denotes good fortune; but if from any cause they should bebroken, this signifies that fortune will be short-lived for you.To see shelves of polished dishes, denotes success in marriage.To dream of dishes, is prognostic of coming success and gain, and you will be able tofully appreciate your good luck. Soiled dishes, represent dissatisfaction and anunpromising future.See Crockery.DisinheritedTo dream that you are disinherited, warns you to look well to your business and socialstanding.For a young man to dream of losing his inheritance by disobedience, warns him that hewill find favor in the eyes of his parents by contracting a suitable marriage. For a woman,this dream is a warning to be careful of her conduct, lest she meet with unfavorablefortune.DisputeTo dream of holding disputes over trifles, indicates bad health and unfairness in judgingothers.To dream of disputing with learned people, shows that you have some latent ability, butare a little sluggish in developing it.DistaffTo dream of a distaff, denotes frugality, with pleasant surroundings. It also signifies thata devotional spirit will be cultivated by you.DistanceTo dream of being a long way from your residence, denotes that you will make a journeysoon in which you may meet many strangers who will be instrumental in changing lifefrom good to bad.To dream of friends at a distance, denotes slight disappointments.To dream of distance, signifies travel and a long journey. To see men plowing with oxenat a distance, across broad fields, denotes advancing prosperity and honor. For a man to

see strange women in the twilight, at a distance, and throwing kisses to him, foretells thathe will enter into an engagement with a new acquaintance, which will result in unhappyexposures.DitchTo dream of falling in a ditch, denotes degradation and personal loss; but if you jumpover it, you will live down any suspicion of wrong-doing.DivingTo dream of diving in clear water, denotes a favorable termination of someembarrassment. If the water is muddy, you will suffer anxiety at the turn your affairsseem to be taking.To see others diving, indicates pleasant companions. For lovers to dream of diving,denotes the consummation of happy dreams and passionate love.DividendTo dream of dividends, augments successful speculations or prosperous harvests. To failin securing hoped-for dividends, proclaims failure in management or love affairs.Divining RodsTo see a divining rod in your dreams, foretells ill luck will dissatisfy you with presentsurroundings.DivorceTo dream of being divorced, denotes that you are not satisfied with your companion, andshould cultivate a more congenial atmosphere in the home life. It is a dream of warning.For women to dream of divorce, denotes that a single life may be theirs through theinfidelity of lovers.DocksTo dream of being on docks, denotes that you are about to make an unpropitious journey.Accidents will threaten you. If you are there, wandering alone, and darkness overtakesyou, you will meet with deadly enemies, but if the sun be shining, you will escapethreatening dangers.

DoctorThis is a most auspicious dream, denoting good health and general prosperity, if youmeet him socially, for you will not then spend your money for his services. If you beyoung and engaged to marry him, then this dream warns you of deceit.To dream of a doctor professionally, signifies discouraging illness and disagreeabledifferences between members of a family.To dream that a doctor makes an incision in your flesh, trying to discover blood, butfailing in his efforts, denotes that you will be tormented and injured by some evil person,who may try to make you pay out money for his debts. If he finds blood, you will be theloser in some transaction.DogsTo dream of a vicious dog, denotes enemies and unalterable misfortune. To dream that adog fondles you, indicates great gain and constant friends.To dream of owning a dog with fine qualities, denotes that you will be possessed of solidwealth.To dream that a blood-hound is tracking you, you are likely to fall into some temptation,in which there is much danger of your downfall.To dream of small dogs, indicates that your thoughts and chief pleasures are of afrivolous order.To dream of dogs biting you, foretells for you a quarrelsome companion either inmarriage or business.Lean, filthy dogs, indicate failure in business, also sickness among children.To dream of a dog-show, is indicative of many and varied favors from fortune.To hear the barking of dogs, foretells news of a depressing nature. Difficulties are morethan likely to follow. To see dogs on the chase of foxes, and other large game, denotes anunusual briskness in all affairs.To see fancy pet dogs, signifies a love of show, and that the owner is selfish and narrow.For a young woman, this dream foretells a fop for a sweetheart.To feel much fright upon seeing a large mastiff, denotes that you will experienceinconvenience because of efforts to rise above mediocrity. If a woman dreams this, shewill marry a wise and humane man.To hear the growling and snarling of dogs, indicates that you are at the mercy ofdesigning people, and you will be afflicted with unpleasant home surroundings.

To hear the lonely baying of a dog, foretells a death or a long separation from friends.To hear dogs growling and fighting, portends that you will be overcome by your enemies,and your life will be filled with depression.To see dogs and cats seemingly on friendly terms, and suddenly turning on each other,showing their teeth and a general fight ensuing, you will meet with disaster in love andworldly pursuits, unless you succeed in quelling the row.If you dream of a friendly white dog approaching you, it portends for you a victoriousengagement whether in business or love. For a woman, this is an omen of an earlymarriage.To dream of a many-headed dog, you are trying to maintain too many branches ofbusiness at one time. Success always comes with concentration of energies. A man whowishes to succeed in anything should be warned by this dream.To dream of a mad dog, your most strenuous efforts will not bring desired results, andfatal disease may be clutching at your vitals. If a mad dog succeeds in biting you, it is asign that you or some loved one is on the verge of insanity, and a deplorable tragedy mayoccur.To dream of traveling alone, with a dog following you, foretells stanch friends andsuccessful undertakings.To dream of dogs swimming, indicates for you an easy stretch to happiness and fortune.To dream that a dog kills a cat in your presence, is significant of profitable dealings andsome unexpected pleasure.For a dog to kill a snake in your presence, is an omen of good luckDolphinTo dream of a dolphin, indicates your liability to come under a new government. It is nota very good dream.DomeTo dream that you are in the dome of a building, viewing a strange landscape, signifies afavorable change in your life. You will occupy honorable places among strangers.To behold a dome from a distance, portends that you will never reach the height of yourambition, and if you are in love, the object of your desires will scorn your attention.

DominoesTo dream of playing at dominoes, and lose, you will be affronted by a friend, and muchuneasiness for your safety will be entertained by your people, as you will not be discreetin your affairs with women or other matters that engage your attention.If you are the winner of the game, it foretells that you will be much courted and admiredby certain dissolute characters, bringing you selfish pleasures, but much distress to yourrelatives.DonkeyTo dream of a donkey braying in your face, denotes that you are about to be publiclyinsulted by a lewd and unscrupulous person.To hear the distant braying filling space with melancholy, you will receive wealth andrelease from unpleasant bonds by the death of some person close to you.If you see yourself riding on a donkey, you will visit foreign lands and make manyexplorations into places difficult of passage.To see others riding donkeys, denotes a meagre inheritance for them and a toiling life.To dream of seeing many of the old patriarchs traveling on donkeys, shows that theinfluence of Christians will be thrown against you in your selfish wantonness, causingyou to ponder over the rights and duties of man to man.To drive a donkey, signifies that all your energies and pluck will be brought into playagainst a desperate effort on the part of enemies to overthrow you. If you are in love, evilwomen will cause you trouble.If you are kicked by this little animal, it shows that you are carrying on illicitconnections, from which you will suffer much anxiety from fear of betrayal.If you lead one by a halter, you will be master of every situation, and lead women intoyour way of seeing things by flattery.To see children riding and driving donkeys, signifies health and obedience for them.To fall or be thrown from one, denotes ill luck and disappointment in secular affairs.Lovers will quarrel and separate.To see one dead, denotes satiated appetites, resulting from licentious excesses.To dream of drinking the milk of a donkey, denotes that whimsical desires will begratified, even to the displacement of important duties.

If you see in your dreams a strange donkey among your stock, or on your premises, youwill inherit some valuable effects.To dream of coming into the possession of a donkey by present, or buying, you willattain to enviable heights in the business or social world, and if single, will contract acongenial marriage.To dream of a white donkey, denotes an assured and lasting fortune, which will enableyou to pursue the pleasures or studies that lie nearest your heart. For a woman, it signalsentrance into that society for which she has long entertained the most ardent desire.Woman has in her composition those qualities, docility and stubbornness, which tallieswith the same qualities in the donkey; both being supplied from the same storehouse,mother Nature; and consequently, they would naturally maintain an affinity, and theugliest phase of the donkey in her dreams are nothing but woman's nature being soundedfor her warning, or vice versa when pleasure is just before her.DoomsdayTo dream that you are living on, and looking forward to seeing doomsday, is a warningfor you to give substantial and material affairs close attention, or you will find that theartful and scheming friends you are entertaining will have possession of what they desirefrom you, which is your wealth, and not your sentimentality.To a young woman, this dream encourages her to throw aside the attention of men aboveher in station and accept the love of an honest and deserving man near her.DoorTo dream of entering a door, denotes slander, and enemies from whom you are trying invain to escape. This is the same of any door, except the door of your childhood home. Ifit is this door you dream of entering, your days will be filled with plenty andcongeniality.To dream of entering a door at night through the rain, denotes, to women, unpardonableescapades; to a man, it is significant of a drawing on his resources by unwarranted vice,and also foretells assignations.To see others go through a doorway, denotes unsuccessful attempts to get your affairsinto a paying condition. It also means changes to farmers and the political world. To anauthor, it foretells that the reading public will reprove his way of stating facts by refusingto read his later works.To dream that you attempt to close a door, and it falls from its hinges, injuring some one,denotes that malignant evil threatens your friend through your unintentionally wrongadvice. If you see another attempt to lock a door, and it falls from its hinges, you willhave knowledge of some friend's misfortune and be powerless to aid him.

Door BellTo dream you hear or ring a door bell, foretells unexpected tidings, or a hasty summonsto business, or the bedtide of a sick relative.DovesDreaming of doves mating and building their nests, indicates peacefulness of the worldand joyous homes where children render obedience, and mercy is extended to all.To hear the lonely, mournful voice of a dove, portends sorrow and disappointmentthrough the death of one to whom you looked for aid. Often it portends the death of afather.To see a dead dove, is ominous of a separation of husband and wife, either through deathor infidelity.To see white doves, denotes bountiful harvests and the utmost confidence in the loyaltyof friends.To dream of seeing a flock of white doves, denotes peaceful, innocent pleasures, andfortunate developments in the future.If one brings you a letter, tidings of a pleasant nature from absent friends is intimated,also a lovers' reconciliation is denoted.If the dove seems exhausted, a note of sadness will pervade the reconciliation, or a sadtouch may be given the pleasant tidings by mention of an invalid friend; if of business, aslight drop may follow. If the letter bears the message that you are doomed, it foretellsthat a desperate illness, either your own or of a relative, may cause you financialmisfortune.DowryTo dream that you fail to receive a dowry, signifies penury and a cold world to depend onfor a living. If you receive it, your expectations for the day will be fulfilled. The oppositemay be expected if the dream is superinduced by the previous action of the waking mind.DragonTo dream of a dragon, denotes that you allow yourself to be governed by your passions,and that you are likely to place yourself in the power of your enemies through thoseoutbursts of sardonic tendencies. You should be warned by this dream to cultivateself-control.See Devil.

DramaTo see a drama, signifies pleasant reunions with distant friends.To be bored with the performance of a drama, you will be forced to accept anuncongenial companion at some entertainment or secret affair.To write one, portends that you will be plunged into distress and debt, to be extricated asif by a miracle.Dram-DrinkingTo be given to dram-drinking in your dreams, omens ill-natured rivalry and contentionfor small possession. To think you have quit dram-drinking, or find that others havedone so, shows that you will rise above present estate and rejoice in prosperity.Draw-KnifeTo see or use a draw-knife, portends unfulfiled hopes or desires.Some fair prospect will loom before you, only to go down in mistake anddisappointment.DressingTo think you are having trouble in dressing, while dreaming, means some evil personswill worry and detain you from places of amusement.If you can't get dressed in time for a train, you will have many annoyances through thecarelessness of others. You should depend on your own efforts as far as possible, afterthese dreams, if you would secure contentment and full success.DrinkingFor a woman to dream of hilarious drinking, denotes that she is engaging in affairs whichmay work to her discredit, though she may now find much pleasure in the same. If shedreams that she fails to drink clear water, though she uses her best efforts to do so, shewill fail to enjoy some pleasure that is insinuatingly offered her.See Water.DrivingTo dream of driving a carriage, signifies unjust criticism of your seeming extravagance.You will be compelled to do things which appear undignified.

To dream of driving a public cab, denotes menial labor, with little chance foradvancement. If it is a wagon, you will remain in poverty and unfortunate circumstancesfor some time. If you are driven in these conveyances by others, you will profit bysuperior knowledge of the world, and will always find some path through difficulties. Ifyou are a man, you will, in affairs with women, drive your wishes to a speedyconsummation. If a woman, you will hold men's hearts at low value after succeeding ingetting a hold on them.See Cab or Carriage.DromedaryTo dream of a dromedary, denotes that you will be the recipient of unexpectedbeneficence, and will wear your new honors with dignity; you will dispense charity witha gracious hands. To lovers, this dream foretells congenial dispositions.DropsyTo dream of being afflicted with the dropsy, denotes illness for a time, but from whichyou will recover with renewed vigor. To see others thus afflicted, denotes that you willhear from the absent shortly, and have tidings of their good health.DrouthThis is-an evil dream, denoting warring disputes between nations, and much bloodshedtherefrom. Shipwrecks and land disasters will occur, and families will quarrel andseparate; sickness will work damage also. Your affairs will go awry, as well.DrowningTo dream of drowning, denotes loss of property and life; but if you are rescued, you willrise from your present position to one of wealth and honor.To see others drowning, and you go to their relief, signifies that you will aid your friendto high places, and will bring deserved happiness to yourself.For a young woman to see her sweetheart drowned, denotes her bereavement by death.DrumTo hear the muffled beating of a drum, denotes that some absent friend is in distress andcalls on you for aid.To see a drum, foretells amiability of character and a great aversion to quarrels anddissensions. It is an omen of prosperity to the sailor, the farmer and the tradesman alike.

DrunkThis is an unfavorable dream if you are drunk on heavy liquors, indicating profligacy andloss of employment. You will be disgraced by stooping to forgery or theft.If drunk on wine, you will be fortunate in trade and love-making, and will scale exaltedheights in literary pursuits. This dream is always the bearer of aesthetic experiences.To see others in a drunken condition, foretells for you, and probably others, unhappystates.Drunkenness in all forms is unreliable as a good dream. All classes are warned by thisdream to shift their thoughts into more healthful channels.DucksTo dream of seeing wild ducks on a clear stream of water, signifies fortunate journeys,perhaps across the sea. White ducks around a farm, indicate thrift and a fine harvest.To hunt ducks, denotes displacement in employment in the carrying out of plans.To see them shot, signifies that enemies are meddling with your private affairs.To see them flying, foretells a brighter future for you. It also denotes marriage, andchildren in the new home.DuetTo dream of hearing a duet played, denotes a peaceful and even existence for lovers. Noquarrels, as is customary in this sort of thing. Business people carry on a mild rivalry. Tomusical people, this denotes competition and wrangling for superiority.To hear a duet sung, is unpleasant tidings from the absent; but this will not last, as somenew pleasure will displace the unpleasantness.DulcimerTo dream of a dulcimer, denotes that the highest wishes in life will be attained by exaltedqualities of mind. To women, this is significant of a life free from those petty jealousieswhich usually make women unhappy.DumbTo dream of being dumb, indicates your inability to persuade others into your mode ofthinking, and using them for your profit by your glibness of tongue. To the dumb, itdenotes false friends.

DunTo dream that you receive a dun, warns you to look after your affairs and correct alltendency towards neglect of business and love.DungeonTo dream of being in a dungeon, foretells for you struggles with the vital affairs of lifebut by wise dealing you will disenthrall yourself of obstacles and the designs of enemies.For a woman this is a dark foreboding; by her wilful indiscretion she will lose herposition among honorable people.To see a dungeon lighted up, portends that you are threatened with entanglements ofwhich your better judgment warns you.DunghillTo dream of a dunghill, you will see profits coming in through the most unexpectedsources. To the farmer this is a lucky dream, indicating fine seasons and abundantproducts from soil and stock. For a young woman, it denotes that she will unknowinglymarry a man of great wealth.DuskThis is a dream of sadness; it portends an early decline and unrequited hopes. Darkoutlook for trade and pursuits of any nature is prolonged by this dream.DustTo dream of dust covering you, denotes that you will be slightly injured in business bythe failure of others. For a young woman, this denotes that she will be set aside by herlover for a newer flame. If you free yourself of the dust by using judicious measures, youwill clear up the loss.DwarfThis is a very favorable dream. If the dwarf is well formed and pleasing in appearance, itomens you will never be dwarfed in mind or stature. Health and good constitution willadmit of your engaging in many profitable pursuits both of mind and body.To see your friends dwarfed, denotes their health, and you will have many pleasuresthrough them.Ugly and hideous dwarfs, always forebodes distressing states.

DyeTo see the dyeing of cloth or garments in process, your bad or good luck depends on thecolor. Blues, reds and gold, indicate prosperity; black and white, indicate sorrow in allforms.DyingTo dream of dying, foretells that you are threatened with evil from a source that hascontributed to your former advancement and enjoyment.To see others dying, forebodes general ill luck to you and to your friends.To dream that you are going to die, denotes that unfortunate inattention to your affairswill depreciate their value. Illness threatens to damage you also.To see animals in the throes of death, denotes escape from evil influences if the animalbe wild or savage.It is an unlucky dream to see domestic animals dying or in agony.[As these events of good or ill approach you they naturally assume these forms ofagonizing death, to impress you more fully with the joyfulness or the gravity of thesituation you are about to enter on awakening to material responsibilities, to aid you inthe mastery of self which is essential to meeting all conditions with calmness anddetermination.]See Death.DynamiteTo see dynamite in a dream, is a sign of approaching change and the expanding of one'saffairs. To be frightened by it, indicates that a secret enemy is at work against you, and ifyou are not careful of your conduct he will disclose himself at an unexpected andhelpless moment.DynamoTo dream of a dynamo, omens successful enterprises if attention is shown to details ofbusiness. One out of repair, shows you are nearing enemies who will involve you introuble.E

EaglesTo see one soaring above you, denotes lofty ambitions which you will struggle fiercely torealize, nevertheless you will gain your desires.To see one perched on distant heights, denotes that you will possess fame, wealth and thehighest position attainable in your country.To see young eagles in their eyrie, signifies your association with people of highstanding, and that you will profit from wise counsel from them. You will in time comeinto a rich legacy.To dream that you kill an eagle, portends that no obstacles whatever would be allowed tostand before you and the utmost heights of your ambition. You will overcome yourenemies and be possessed of untold wealth.Eating the flesh of one, denotes the possession of a powerful will that would not turnaside in ambitious struggles even for death. You will come immediately into richpossessions.To see a dead eagle killed by others than yourself, signifies high rank and fortune will bewrested from you ruthlessly.To ride on an eagle's back, denotes that you will make a long voyage into almostunexplored countries in your search for knowledge and wealth which you will eventuallygain.EarsTo dream of seeing ears, an evil and designing person is keeping watch over yourconversation to work you harm.EarringsTo see earrings in dreams, omens good news and interesting work is before you. To seethem broken, indicates that gossip of a low order will be directed against you.EarthquakeTo see or feel the earthquake in your dream, denotes business failure and much distresscaused from turmoils and wars between nations.

EarwigTo dream that you see an earwig or have one in your ear, denotes that you will haveunpleasant news affecting your business or family relations.EatingTo dream of eating alone, signifies loss and melancholy spirits. To eat with others,denotes personal gain, cheerful environments and prosperous undertakings.If your daughter carries away the platter of meat before you are done eating, it foretellsthat you will have trouble and vexation from those beneath you or dependent upon you.The same would apply to a waiter or waitress.See other subjects similar.EbonyIf you dream of ebony furniture or other articles of ebony, you will have many distressingdisputes and quarrels in your home.EchoTo dream of an echo, portends that distressful times are upon you. Your sickness maylose you your employment, and friends will desert you in time of need.EclipseTo dream of the eclipse of the sun, denotes temporary failure in business and othersecular affairs, also disturbances in families.The eclipse of the moon, portends contagious disease or death.EcstasyTo dream of feeling ecstasy, denotes you will enjoy a visit from a long-absent friend. Ifyou experience ecstasy in disturbing dreams you will be subjected to sorrow anddisappointment.EducationTo dream that you are anxious to obtain an education, shows that whatever yourcircumstances in life may be there will be a keen desire for knowledge on your part,which will place you on a higher plane than your associates. Fortune will also be morelenient to you.

To dream that you are in places of learning, foretells for you many influential friends.EelTo dream of an eel is good if you can maintain your grip on him. Otherwise fortune willbe fleeting.To see an eel in clear water, denotes, for a woman, new but evanescent pleasures.To see a dead eel, signifies that you will overcome your most maliciously inclinedenemies. To lovers, the dream denotes an end to long and hazardous courtship bymarriage.EggsTo dream of finding a nest of eggs, denotes wealth of a substantial character, happinessamong the married and many children. This dream signifies many and varied love affairsto women.To eat eggs, denotes that unusual disturbances threaten you in your home.To see broken eggs and they are fresh, fortune is ready to shower upon you her richestgifts. A lofty spirit and high regard for justice will make you beloved by the world.To dream of rotten eggs, denotes loss of property and degradation.To see a crate of eggs, denotes that you will engage in profitable speculations.To dream of being spattered with eggs, denotes that you will sport riches of doubtfulorigin.To see bird eggs, signifies legacies from distant relations, or gain from an unexpected risein staple products.ElbowsTo see elbows in a dream, signifies that arduous labors will devolve upon you, and forwhich you will receive small reimbursements.For a young woman, this is a prognostic of favorable opportunities to make a reasonablywealthy marriage. If the elbows are soiled, she will lose a good chance of securing ahome by marriage.ElderberriesTo dream of seeing elderberries on bushes with their foliage, denotes domestic bliss andan agreeable county home with resources for travel and other pleasures.

Elderberries is generally a good dream.ElectionTo dream that you are at an election, foretells you will engage in some controversy whichwill prove detrimental to your social or financial standing.ElectricityTo dream of electricity, denotes there will be sudden changes about you, which will notafford you either advancement or pleasure. If you are shocked by it you will face adeplorable danger.To see live electrical wire, foretells that enemies will disturb your plans, which havegiven you much anxiety in forming. To dream that you can send a package or yourselfout over a wire with the same rapidity that a message can be sent, denotes you will finallyovercome obstacles and be able to use your enemies' plans to advance yourself.ElephantTo dream of riding an elephant, denotes that you will possess wealth of the most solidcharacter, and honors which you will wear with dignity. You will rule absolutely in alllines of your business affairs and your word will be law in the home.To see many elephants, denotes tremendous prosperity. One lone elephant, signifies youwill live in a small but solid way.To dream of feeding one, denotes that you will elevate yourself in your community byyour kindness to those occupying places below you.ElevatorTo dream of ascending in an elevator, denotes you will swiftly rise to position andwealth, but if you descend in one your misfortunes will crush and discourage you. If yousee one go down and think you are left, you will narrowly escape disappointment in someundertaking. To see one standing, foretells threatened danger.Elixir of LifeTo dream of the elixir of life, denotes that there will come into your environments newpleasures and new possibilities.ElopementTo dream of eloping is unfavorable. To the married, it denotes that you hold places whichyou are unworthy to fill, and if your ways are not rectified your reputation will be at

stake. To the unmarried, it foretells disappointments in love and the unfaithfulness ofmen.To dream that your lover has eloped with some one else, denotes his or herunfaithfulness.To dream of your friend eloping with one whom you do not approve, denotes that youwill soon hear of them contracting a disagreeable marriage.EloquentIf you think you are eloquent of speech in your dreams, there will be pleasant news foryou concerning one in whose interest you are working.To fail in impressing others with your eloquence, there will be much disorder in youraffairs.EmbalmingTo see embalming in process, foretells altered positions in social life and threatenedpoverty. To dream that you are looking at yourself embalmed, omens unfortunatefriendships for you, which will force you into lower classes than you are accustomed tomove in.EmbankmentTo dream that you drive along an embankment, foretells you will be threatened withtrouble and unhappiness. If you continue your drive without unpleasant incidents arising,you will succeed in turning these forebodings to useful account in your advancement. Toride on horseback along one, denotes you will fearlessly meet and overcome all obstaclesin your way to wealth and happiness. To walk along one, you will have a weary strugglefor elevation, but will finally reap a successful reward.EmbarrassmentSee Difficulty.EmbraceTo dream of embracing your husband or wife, as the case may be, in a sorrowing orindifferent way, denotes that you will have dissensions and accusations in your family,also that sickness is threatened.To embrace relatives, signifies their sickness and unhappiness.For lovers to dream of embracing, foretells quarrels and disagreements arising from

infidelity. If these dreams take place under auspicious conditions, the reverse may beexpected.If you embrace a stranger, it signifies that you will have an unwelcome guest.EmbroideryIf a woman dreams of embroidering, she will be admired for her tact and ability to makethe best of everything that comes her way. For a married man to see embroidery, signifiesa new member in his household, For a lover, this denotes a wise and economical wife.EmeraldTo dream of an emerald, you will inherit property concerning which there will be sometrouble with others.For a lover to see an emerald or emeralds on the person of his affianced, warns him thathe is about to be discarded for some wealthier suitor.To dream that you buy an emerald, signifies unfortunate dealings.EmperorTo dream of going abroad and meeting the emperor of a nation in your travels, denotesthat you will make a long journey, which will bring neither pleasure nor muchknowledge.EmployeeTo see one of your employees denotes crosses and disturbances if he assumes adisagreeable or offensive attitude. If he is pleasant and has communications of interest,you will find no cause for evil or embarrassing conditions upon waking.EmploymentThis is not an auspicious dream. It implies depression in business circles and loss ofemployment to wage earners. It also denotes bodily illness.To dream of being out of work, denotes that you will have no fear, as you are alwayssought out for your conscientious fulfilment of contracts, which make you a desired help.Giving employment to others, indicates loss for yourself. All dreams of this nature maybe interpreted as the above.

EmpressTo dream of an empress, denotes that you will be exalted to high honors, but you will letpride make you very unpopular.To dream of an empress and an emperor is not particularly bad, but brings one nosubstantial good.EnchantmentTo dream of being under the spell of enchantment, denotes that if you are not careful youwill be exposed to some evil in the form of pleasure. The young should heed thebenevolent advice of their elders.To resist enchantment, foretells that you will be much sought after for your wise counselsand your liberality.To dream of trying to enchant others, portends that you will fall into evil.EncyclopediaTo dream of seeing or searching through encyclopedias, portends that you will secureliterary ability to the losing of prosperity and comfort.EnemyTo dream that you overcome enemies, denotes that you will surmount all difficulties inbusiness, and enjoy the greatest prosperity.If you are defamed by your enemies, it denotes that you will be threatened with failuresin your work. You will be wise to use the utmost caution in proceeding in affairs of anymoment.To overcome your enemies in any form, signifies your gain. For them to get the better ofyou is ominous of adverse fortunes. This dream may be literal.EngagementTo dream of a business engagement, denotes dulness and worries in trade.For young people to dream that they are engaged, denotes that they will not be muchadmired.To dream of breaking an engagement, denotes a hasty, and an unwise action in someimportant matter or disappointments may follow.

EngineTo dream of an engine, denotes you will encounter grave difficulties and journeys, butyou will have substantial friends to uphold you.Disabled engines stand for misfortune and loss of relatives.EngineerTo see an engineer, forebodes weary journeys but joyful reunions.EnglishTo dream, if you are a foreigner, of meeting English people, denotes that you will have tosuffer through the selfish designs of others.EntertainmentTo dream of an entertainment where there is music and dancing, you will have pleasanttidings of the absent, and enjoy health and prosperity. To the young, this is a dream ofmany and varied pleasures and the high regard of friends.EntrailsTo dream of the human entrails, denotes horrible misery and despair, shutting out allhope of happiness.To dream of the entrails of a wild beast, signifies the overthrow of your mortal enemy.To tear the entrails of another, signifies cruel persecutions to further your own interests.To dream of your own entrails, the deepest despair will overwhelm you.To dream of the entrails of your own child, denotes that the child's, or your own,dissolution is at hand.See Intestines.EnvelopeEnvelopes seen in a dream, omens news of a sorrowful cast.EnvyTo dream that you entertain envy for others, denotes that you will make warm friends by

your unselfish deference to the wishes of others.If you dream of being envied by others, it denotes that you will suffer someinconvenience from friends overanxious to please you.EpauletFor a man to dream of wearing epaulets, if he is a soldier, denotes his disfavor for a time,but he will finally wear honors.For a woman to dream that she is introduced to a person wearing epaulets, denotes thatshe will form unwise attachments, very likely to result in scandal.EpicureTo dream of sitting at the table with an epicure, denotes that you will enjoy some finedistinction, but you will be surrounded by people of selfish principles.To dream that you an epicure yourself, you will cultivate your mind, body and taste to thehighest polish.For a woman to dream of trying to satisfy an epicure, signifies that she will have adistinguished husband, but to her he will be a tyrant.EpidemicTo dream of an epidemic, signifies prostration of mental faculties and worry fromdistasteful tasks. Contagion among relatives or friends is foretold by dreams of thisnature.ErmineTo dream that you wear this beautiful and costly raiment, denotes exaltation, loftycharacter and wealth forming a barrier to want and misery.To see others thus clothed, you will be associated with wealthy people, polished inliterature and art.For a lover to see his sweetheart clothed in ermine, is an omen of purity and faithfulness.If the ermine is soiled, the reverse is indicated.ErrandsTo go on errands in your dreams, means congenial associations and mutual agreement inthe home circle. For a young woman to send some person on an errand, denotes she willlose her lover by her indifference to meet his wishes.

EscapeTo dream of escape from injury or accidents, is usually favorable.If you escape from some place of confinement, it signifies your rise in the world fromclose application to business.To escape from any contagion, denotes your good health and prosperity. If you try toescape and fail, you will suffer from the design of enemies, who will slander and defraudyou.EstateTo dream that you come into the ownership of a vast estate, denotes that you will receivea legacy at some distant day, but quite different to your expectations. For a youngwoman, this dream portends that her inheritance will be of a disappointing nature. Shewill have to live quite frugally, as her inheritance will be a poor man and a house full ofchildren.EuropeTo dream of traveling in Europe, foretells that you will soon go on a long journey, whichwill avail you in the knowledge you gain of the manners and customs of foreign people.You will also be enabled to forward your financial standing. For a young woman to feelthat she is disappointed with the sights of Europe, omens her inability to appreciatechances for her elevation. She will be likely to disappoint her friends or lover.EveTo dream of this ancient character, denotes your hesitancy to accept this ancient story asauthentic, and you may encounter opposition in business and social circles because ofthis doubt.For a young woman to dream that she impersonates Eve, warns her to be careful. Shemay be wiser than her ancient relative, but the Evil One still has powerful agents in thedisguise of a handsome man. Keep your eye on innocent Eve, young man. That apple treestill bears fruit, and you may be persuaded, unwittingly, to share the wealth of itsproducts.EveningTo dream that evening is about you, denotes unrealized hopes, and you will makeunfortunate ventures.To see stars shining out clear, denotes present distress, but brighter fortune is behind yourtrouble.

For lovers to walk in the evening, denotes separation by the death of one.EvergreenThis dream denotes boundless resources of wealth, happiness and learning. It is a freepresentiment of prosperity to all classes.ExchangeExchange, denotes profitable dealings in all classes of business. For a young woman todream that she is exchanging sweethearts with her friend, indicates that she will do wellto heed this as advice, as she would be happier with another.ExecutionTo dream of seeing an execution, signifies that you will suffer some misfortune from thecarelessness of others.To dream that you are about to be executed, and some miraculous intervention occurs,denotes that you will overthrow enemies and succeed in gaining wealth.ExileFor a woman to dream that she is exiled, denotes that she will have to make a journeywhich will interfere with some engagement or pleasure.See Banishment.ExplosionTo dream of explosions, portends that disapproving actions of those connected with youwill cause you transient displeasure and loss, and that business will also displease you.To think your face, or the face of others, is blackened or mutilated, signifies you will beaccused of indiscretion which will be unjust, though circumstances may convict you.To see the air filled with smoke and de'bris, denotes unusual dissatisfaction in businesscircles and much social antagonism.To think you are enveloped in the flames, or are up in the air where you have been blownby an explosion, foretells that unworthy friends will infringe on your rights and willabuse your confidence. Young women should be careful of associates of the opposite sexafter a dream of this character.

EyeTo dream of seeing an eye, warns you that watchful enemies are seeking the slightestchance to work injury to your business. This dream indicates to a lover, that a rival willusurp him if he is not careful.To dream of brown eyes, denotes deceit and perfidy. To see blue eyes, denotes weaknessin carrying out any intention. To see gray eyes, denotes a love of flattery for the owner.To dream of losing an eye, or that the eyes are sore, denotes trouble.To see a one-eyed man, denotes that you will be threatened with loss and trouble, besidewhich all others will appear insignificant.EyebrowsEyebrows, denotes that you will encounter sinister obstacles in your immediate future.EyeglassTo dream of seeing or wearing an eyeglass, denotes you will be afflicted withdisagreeable friendships, from which you will strive vainly to disengage yourself. For ayoung woman to see her lover with an eyeglass on, omens disruption of love affairs.FFablesTo dream of reading or telling fables, denotes pleasant tasks and a literary turn of mind.To the young, it signifies romantic attachments.To hear, or tell, religious fables, denotes that the dreamer will become very devotional.FaceThis dream is favorable if you see happy and bright faces, but significant of trouble ifthey are disfigured, ugly, or frowning on you.To a young person, an ugly face foretells lovers' quarrels; or for a lover to see the face ofhis sweetheart looking old, denotes separation and the breaking up of happy associations.

To see a strange and weird-looking face, denotes that enemies and misfortunes surroundyou.To dream of seeing your own face, denotes unhappiness; and to the married, threats ofdivorce will be made.To see your face in a mirror, denotes displeasure with yourself for not being able to carryout plans for self-advancement. You will also lose the esteem of friends.FagotIf you dream of seeing a dense smoke ascending from a pile of fagots, it denotes thatenemies are bearing down upon you, but if the fagots are burning brightly, you willescape from all unpleasant complications and enjoy great prosperity.If you walk on burning fagots, you will be injured by the unwise actions of friends. If yousucceed in walking on them without being burned, you will have a miraculous rise inprospects.To dream of seeing fagots piled up to burn you at the stake, signifies that you arethreatened with loss, but if you escape, you will enjoy a long and prosperous life.FailureFor a lover, this is sometimes of contrary significance. To dream that he fails in his suit,signifies that he only needs more masterfulness and energy in his daring, as he hasalready the love and esteem of his sweetheart.(Contrary dreams are those in which the dreamer suffers fear, and not injury.)For a young woman to dream that her life is going to be a failure, denotes that she is notapplying her opportunities to good advantage.For a business man to dream that he has made a failure, forebodes loss and badmanagement, which should be corrected, or failure threatens to materialize in earnest.FaintingTo dream of fainting, signifies illness in your family and unpleasant news of the absent.If a young woman dreams of fainting, it denotes that she will fall into ill health andexperience disappointment from her careless way of living.FairTo dream of being at a fair, denotes that you will have a pleasant and profitable businessand a congenial companion.

For a young woman, this dream signifies a jovial and even-tempered man for a lifepartner.FairyTo dream of a fairy, is a favorable omen to all classes, as it is always a scene with abeautiful face portrayed as a happy child, or woman.FaithlessTo dream that your friends are faithless, denotes that they will hold you in worthyesteem. For a lover to dream that his sweetheart is faithless, signifies a happy marriage.FakirTo dream of an Indian fakir, denotes uncommon activity and phenomenal changes inyour life. Such dreams may sometimes be of gloomy import.FalconTo dream of a falcon, denotes that your prosperity will make you an object of envy andmalice. For a young woman, this dream denotes that she will be calumniated by a rival.FallTo dream that you sustain a fall, and are much frightened, denotes that you will undergosome great struggle, but will eventually rise to honor and wealth; but if you are injured inthe fall, you will encounter hardships and loss of friends.FameTo dream of being famous, denotes disappointed aspirations. To dream of famous people,portends your rise from obscurity to places of honor.FamineTo dream of a famine, foretells that your business will be unremunerative and sicknesswill prove a scourge. This dream is generally bad.If you see your enemies perishing by famine, you will be successful in competition. Ifdreams of famine should break in wild confusion over slumbers, tearing up all heads inanguish, filling every soul with care, hauling down Hope's banners, somber with omensof misfortune and despair, your waking grief more poignant still must grow ere youquench ambition and envy overthrow.

FamishTo dream that you are famishing, foretells that you are meeting disheartening failure insome enterprise which you considered a promising success. To see others famishing,brings sorrow to others as well as to yourself.FamilyTo dream of one's family as harmonious and happy, is significant of health and easycircumstances; but if there is sickness or contentions, it forebodes gloom anddisappointment.FanTo see a fan in your dreams, denotes pleasant news and surprises are awaiting you in thenear future. For a young woman to dream of fanning herself, or that some one is fanningher, gives promise of a new and pleasing acquaintances; if she loses an old fan, she willfind that a warm friend is becoming interested in other women.FarewellTo dream of bidding farewell, is not very favorable, as you are likely to hear unpleasantnews of absent friends.For a young woman to bid her lover farewell, portends his indifference to her. If she feelsno sadness in this farewell, she will soon find oFamishTo†dream†that†you†are†famishing, †foretells†that†you†are†meeting†di sheartening†failure†in some†enterprise†which†you†considered†at†promising†su ccess.†To†see†others†famishing, brings†sorrow†to†others†as†well†as†to†your self.FamilyTo†dream†of†one's†family†as†harmonious†and†happy, †is†significa nt†of†health†and†easy†circumstances;†but†if†there†is†sickne†hers to comfort her.FarmTo dream that you are living on a farm, denotes that you will be fortunate in allundertakings.To dream that you are buying a farm, denotes abundant crops to the farmer, a profitabledeal of some kind to the business man, and a safe voyage to travelers and sailors.If you are visiting a farm, it signifies pleasant associations.See Estate.FatTo dream that you are getting fat, denotes that you are about to make a fortunate changein your life.To see others fat, signifies prosperity.

See Corpulent.FatesTo dream of the fates, unnecessary disagreements and unhappiness is foretold. For ayoung woman to dream of juggling with fate, denotes she will daringly interpose herselfbetween devoted friends or lovers.FatherTo dream of your father, signifies that you are about to be involved in a difficulty, andyou will need wise counsel if you extricate yourself therefrom.If he is dead, it denotes that your business is pulling heavily, and you will have to usecaution in conducting it.For a young woman to dream of her dead father, portends that her lover will, or is,playing her false.Father-in-LawTo dream of your father-in-law, denotes contentions with friends or relatives. To seehim well and cheerful, foretells pleasant family relations.FatigueTo feel fatigued in a dream, foretells ill health or oppression in business. For a youngwoman to see others fatigued, indicates discouraging progress in health.FavorTo dream that you ask favors of anyone, denotes that you will enjoy abundance, and thatyou will not especially need anything.To grant favors, means a loss.FawnTo dream of seeing a fawn, denotes that you will have true and upright friends.To the young, it indicates faithfulness in love.To dream that a person fawns on you, or cajoles you, is a warning that enemies are aboutyou in the guise of interested friends.See Deer.

FearsTo dream that you feel fear from any cause, denotes that your future engagements willnot prove so successful as was expected.For a young woman, this dream forebodes disappointment and unfortunate love.FeastTo dream of a feast, foretells that pleasant surprises are being planned for you. To seedisorder or misconduct at a feast, foretells quarrels or unhappiness through thenegligence or sickness of some person.To arrive late at a feast, denotes that vexing affairs will occupy you.FeatherTo dream of seeing feathers falling around you, denotes that your burdens in

life will belight and easily borne.To see eagle feathers, denotes that
your aspirations will be realized.To see chicken feathers, denotes small
annoyances. To dream of buying or selling geeseor duck feathers, denotes
thrift and fortune.To dream of black feathers, denotes disappointments
and unhappy amours.For a woman to dream of seeing ostrich and other
ornamental feathers, denotes that shewill advance in society, but her
ways of gaining favor will not bear imitating.FebruaryTo dream of
February, denotes continued ill health and gloom, generally. If you
happento see a bright sunshiny day in this month, you will be
unexpectedly and happilysurprised with some good fortune.FeebleTo dream
of being feeble, denotes unhealthy occupation and mental worry. Seek to
makea change for yourself after this dream.FeetTo dream of seeing your
own feet, is ominous of despair. You will be overcome by thewill and
temper of another. To see others' feet, denotes that you will maintain
your rightsin a pleasant, but determined way, and win for yourself a
place above the common walks

of life.To dream that you wash your feet, denotes that you will let
others take advantage of you.To dream that your feet are hurting you,
portends troubles of a humiliating character, asthey usually are family
quarrels.To see your feet swollen and red, you will make a sudden change
in your business byseparating from your family. This is an evil dream, as
it usually foretells scandal andsensation.FenceTo dream of climbing to
the top of a fence, denotes that success will crown your efforts.To fall
from a fence, signifies that you will undertake a project for which you
areincapable, and you will see your efforts come to naught.To be seated
on a fence with others, and have it fall under you, denotes an accident
inwhich some person will be badly injured.To dream that you climb through
a fence, signifies that you will use means not altogetherlegitimate to
reach your desires.To throw the fence down and walk into the other side,
indicates that you will, byenterprise and energy, overcome the
stubbornest barriers between you and success.To see stock jumping a
fence, if into your enclosure, you will receive aid fromunexpected
sources; if out of your lot, loss in trade and other affairs may
follow.To dream of building a fence, denotes that you are, by economy and
industry, laying afoundation for future wealth. For a young woman, this
dream denotes success in loveaffairs; or the reverse, if she dreams of
the fence falling, or that she falls from it.FernsTo see ferns in dreams,
foretells that pleasant hours will break up gloomy forebodings.To see
them withered, indicates that much and varied illness in your family
connectionswill cause you grave unrest.FerryTo wait at a ferry for a boat
and see the waters swift and muddy, you will be baffled inyour highest
wishes and designs by unforeseen circumstances.To cross a ferry while the
water is calm and clear, you will be very lucky in carrying outyour
plans, and fortune will crown you.

Festival To dream of being at a festival, denotes indifference to the cold realities of life, and a love for those pleasures that make one old before his time. You will never want, but will be largely dependent on others. **Fever** To dream that you are stricken with this malady, signifies that you are worrying over trifling affairs while the best of life is slipping past you, and you should pull yourself into shape and engage in profitable work. To dream of seeing some of your family sick with fever, denotes temporary illness for some of them. See Illness. **Fiddle** To dream of a fiddle, foretells harmony in the home and many joyful occasions abroad. See Violin. **Field** To dream of dead corn or stubble fields, indicates to the dreamer dreary prospects for the future. To see green fields, or ripe with corn or grain, denotes great abundance and happiness to all classes. To see newly plowed fields, denotes early rise in wealth and fortunate advancement to places of honor. To see fields freshly harrowed and ready for planting, denotes that you are soon to benefit by your endeavor and long struggles for success. See Cornfields and Wheat. **Fiend** To dream that you encounter a fiend, forbodes reckless living and loose morals. For a woman, this dream signifies a blackened reputation. To dream of a fiend, warns you of attacks to be made on you by false friends. If you overcome one, you will be able to intercept the evil designs of enemies.

Fife To dream of hearing a fife, denotes that there will be an unexpected call on you to defend your honor, or that of some person near to you. To dream that you play one yourself, indicates that whatever else may be said of you, your reputation will remain intact. If a woman has this dream, she will have a soldier husband. **Fight** To dream that you engage in a fight, denotes that you will have unpleasant encounters with your business opponents, and law suits threaten you. To see fighting, denotes that you are squandering your time and money. For women, this dream is a warning against slander and gossip. For a young woman to see her lover fighting, is a sign of his unworthiness. To dream that you are defeated in a fight, signifies that you will lose your right to property. To whip your assailant, denotes that you will, by courage and perseverance, win honor and wealth in spite of opposition. To dream that you see two men fighting with pistols, denotes many worries and perplexities, while no real loss is involved in the dream, yet but small profit is predicted and some unpleasantness is denoted. To dream that you are on your way home and negroes attack you with razors, you will be disappointed in your business, you will be much vexed with servants, and home associations will be unpleasant. To dream that you are fighting negroes, you will be annoyed by them or by some one of low character. **Figs** Figs, signifies a malarious condition of the system, if you are eating them, but usually favorable to health and profit if you see them growing. For a young woman to see figs growing, signifies that she will soon wed a wealthy and prominent man.

FigureTo dream of figures, indicates great mental distress and wrong. You will be the loser in abig deal if not careful of your actions and conversation.FilbertThis is a favorable dream, denoting a peaceful and harmonious domestic life andprofitable business ventures.To dream of eating them, signifies to the young, delightful associations and many truefriends.FileTo dream that you see a file, signifies that you will transact some business which willprove unsatisfactory in the extreme.To see files, to store away bills and other important papers, foretells animated discussionsover subjects which bear relation to significant affairs, and which will cause you muchunrest and disquiet. Unfavorable predictions for the future are also implied in this dream.FingersTo dream of seeing your fingers soiled or scratched, with the blood exuding, denotesmuch trouble and suffering. You will despair of making your way through life.To see beautiful hands, with white fingers, denotes that your love will be requited andthat you will become renowned for your benevolence.To dream that your fingers are cut clean off, you will lose wealth and a legacy by theintervention of enemies.FingernailsTo dream of soiled finger-nails, forbodes disgrace in your family by the wild escapadesof the young.To see well-kept nails, indicates scholarly tastes and some literary attainments; also,thrift.FireFire is favorable to the dreamer if he does not get burned. It brings continued prosperityto seamen and voyagers, as well as to those on land.

To dream of seeing your home burning, denotes a loving companion, obedient children,and careful servants.For a business man to dream that his store is burning, and he is looking on, foretells agreat rush in business and profitable results.To dream that he is fighting fire and does not get burned, denotes that he will be muchworked and worried as to the conduct of his business. To see the ruins of his store after afire, forebodes ill luck. He will be almost ready to give up the effort of amassing ahandsome fortune and a brilliant business record as useless, but some unforeseen goodfortune will bear him up again.If you dream of kindling a fire, you may expect many pleasant surprises. You will havedistant friends to visit.To see a large conflagration, denotes to sailors a profitable and safe voyage. To men ofliterary affairs, advancement and honors; to business people, unlimited success.FirebrandTo dream of a firebrand, denotes favorable fortune, if you are not burned or distressed byit.Fire BudgetTo dream of a fire budget, denotes disagreement over small matters.Fire EngineTo see a fire-engine, denotes worry under extraordinary circumstances, but which willresult in good fortune. To see one broken down, foretells accident or serious loss For ayoung woman to ride on one, denotes she will engage in some unladylike and obnoxiousaffair.FiremanTo see a fireman in your dreams, signifies the constancy of your friends. For a youngwoman to see a fireman crippled, or meet with an accident otherwise, implies gravedanger is threatening a close friend.FireworksTo see fireworks, indicates enjoyment and good health. For a young woman, this dreamsignifies entertainments and pleasant visiting to distant places.

FirmamentTo dream of the firmament filled with stars, denotes many crosses and almostsuperhuman efforts ere you reach the pinnacle of your ambition. Beware of the snare ofenemies in your work.To see the firmament illuminated and filled with the heavenly hosts, denotes greatspiritual research, but a final pulling back on Nature for sustenance and consolation. Youwill often be disappointed in fortune also.To see people you know in the firmament, signifies that they are about to commit someunwise act through you, and others must be the innocent sufferers. Great disasters usuallyfollow this dream.See Illumination.FishTo dream that you see fish in clear-water streams, denotes that you will be favored bythe rich and powerful.Dead fish, signifies the loss of wealth and power through some dire calamity. For ayoung woman to dream of seeing fish, portends that she will have a handsome andtalented lover.To dream of catching a catfish, denotes that you will be embarrassed by evil designs ofenemies, but your luck and presence of mind will tide you safely over the trouble.To wade in water, catching fish, denotes that you will possess wealth acquired by yourown ability and enterprise.To dream of fishing, denotes energy and economy; but if you do not succeed in catchingany, your efforts to obtain honors and wealth will be futile.Eating fish, denotes warm and lasting attachments.FishermanTo dream of a fisherman, denotes you are nearing times of greater prosperity than youhave yet known.FishhooksTo dream of fishhooks, denotes that you have opportunities to make for yourself afortune and an honorable name if you rightly apply them.

Fish MarketTo visit a fish market in your dream, brings competence and pleasure.To see decayed fish, foretells distress will come in the guise of happiness.FishnetTo dream of a fish-net, portends numerous small pleasures and gains. A torn one,represents vexatious disappointments.FishpondTo dream of a fish-pond, denotes illness through dissipation, if muddy. To see one clearand well stocked with fish, portends profitable enterprises and extensive pleasures. Tosee one empty, proclaims the near approach of deadly enemies.For a young woman to fall into a clear pond, omens decided good fortune and reciprocallove. If muddy, the opposite is foretold.FitsTo dream of having fits, denotes that you will fall a prey to ill health and will loseemployment.To see others in this plight, denotes that you will have much unpleasantness in yourcircle, caused by quarrels from those under you.FlagTo dream of your national flag, portends victory if at war, and if at peace, prosperity.For a woman to dream of a flag, denotes that she will be ensnared by a soldier.To dream of foreign flags, denotes ruptures and breach of confidence between nationsand friends.To dream of being signaled by a flag, denotes that you should be careful of your healthand name, as both are threatened.FlameTo dream of fighting flames, foretells that you will have to put forth your best efforts andenergy if you are successful in amassing wealth.See Fire.

FlaxTo see flax in a dream, prosperous enterprises are denoted.Flax SpinningFlax spinning, foretells you will be given to industrious and thrifty habits.FleasTo dream of fleas, indicates that you will be provoked to anger and retaliation by the evilmachinations of those close to you.For a woman to dream that fleas bite her, foretells that she will be slandered by pretendedfriends. To see fleas on her lover, denotes inconstancy.FleetTo see a large fleet moving rapidly in your dreams, denotes a hasty change in thebusiness world. Where dulness oppressed, brisk workings of commercial wheels will goforward and some rumors of foreign wars will be heard.FliesTo dream of flies, denotes sickness and contagious maladies. Also that enemies surroundyou. To a young woman this dream is significant of unhappiness. If she kills orexterminates flies, she will reinstate herself in the love of her intended by her ingenuity.FlightTo dream of flight, signifies disgrace and unpleasant news of the absent.For a young woman to dream of flight, indicates that she has not kept her character abovereproach, and her lover will throw her aside.To see anything fleeing from you, denotes that you will be victorious in any contention.FloatingTo dream of floating, denotes that you will victoriously overcome obstacles which areseemingly overwhelming you. If the water is muddy your victories will not be gratifying.

FloodsTo dream of floods destroying vast areas of country and bearing you on with its muddyde'bris, denotes sickness, loss in business, and the most unhappy and unsettled situationin the marriage state.See Water.FlourTo dream of flour, denotes a frugal but happy life. For a young woman to dream that shesees flour on herself, denotes that she will be ruled by her husband, and that her life willbe full of pleasant cares.To dream of dealing in flour, denotes hazardous speculations.FlowerTo dream of seeing flowers blooming in gardens, signifies pleasure and gain, ifbright-hued and fresh; white denotes sadness. Withered and dead flowers, signifydisappointments and gloomy situations.For a young woman to receive a bouquet of mixed flowers, foretells that she will havemany admirers.To see flowers blooming in barren soil without vestage of foliage, foretells you will havesome grievous experience, but your energy and cheerfulness will enable you to climbthrough these to prominence and happiness.Held in slumber's soft embrace, She enters realms of flowery grace,Where tender love and fond caress, Bids her awake to happiness.See Bouquet.FluteTo dream of hearing notes from a flute, signifies a pleasant meeting with friends from adistance, and profitable engagements.For a young woman to dream of playing a flute, denotes that she will fall in love becauseof her lover's engaging manners.FluxTo dream of having flux, or thinking that you are thus afflicted, denotes desperate or fatalillness will overtake you or some member of your family. To see others thus afflicted,

implies disappointment in carrying out some enterprise through the neglect of others.Inharmonious states will vex you.FlyingTo dream of flying high through a space, denotes marital calamities.To fly low, almost to the ground, indicates sickness and uneasy states from which thedreamer will recover.To fly over muddy water, warns you to keep close with your private affairs, as enemiesare watching to enthrall you.To fly over broken places, signifies ill luck and gloomy surroundings. If you notice greentrees and vegetation below you in flying, you will suffer temporary embarrassment, butwill have a flood of prosperity upon you.To dream of seeing the sun while flying, signifies useless worries, as your affairs willsucceed despite your fears of evil.To dream of flying through the firmament passing the moon and other planets; foretellsfamine, wars, and troubles of all kinds.To dream that you fly with black wings, portends bitter disappointments. To fall whileflying, signifies your downfall. If you wake while falling, you will succeed in reinstatingyourself.For a young man to dream that he is flying with white wings above green foliage,foretells advancement in business, and he will also be successful in love. If he dreamsthis often it is a sign of increasing prosperity and the fulfilment of desires. If the treesappear barren or dead, there will be obstacles to combat in obtaining desires. He will getalong, but his work will bring small results.For a woman to dream of flying from one city to another, and alighting on church spires,foretells she will have much to contend against in the way of false persuasions anddeclarations of love. She will be threatened with a disastrous season of ill health, and thedeath of some one near to her may follow.For a young woman to dream that she is shot at while flying, denotes enemies willendeavor to restrain her advancement into higher spheres of usefulness and prosperity.Flying MachineTo dream of seeing a flying machine, foretells that you will make satisfactory progress inyour future speculations. To see one failing to work, foretells gloomy returns for muchdisturbing and worrisome planning.

FlypaperTo dream of fly-paper, signifies ill health and disrupted friendships.FlytrapTo see a fly-trap in a dream, is signal of malicious designing against you. To see one fullof flies, denotes that small embarrassments will ward off greater ones.FoalTo dream of a foal,

indicates new undertakings in which you will be rather fortunate.FogTo
dream of traveling through a dense fog, denotes much trouble and business
worries.To emerge from it, foretells a weary journey, but profitable.For
a young woman to dream of being in a fog, denotes that she will be mixed
up in asalacious scandal, but if she gets out of the fog she will prove
her innocence and regainher social standing.Foot LogTo dream of crossing
a clear stream of water on a foot-log, denotes pleasant employmentand
profit. If the water is thick and muddy, it indicates loss and temporary
disturbance.For a woman this dream indicates either a quarrelsome
husband, or one of mild temperand regular habits, as the water is muddy
or clear.To fall from a foot-log into clear water, signifies short
widowhood terminating in anagreeable marriage. If the water is not clear,
gloomy prospects.See Bridge.ForestTo dream that you find yourself in a
dense forest, denotes loss in trade, unhappy homeinfluences and quarrels
among families. If you are cold and feel hungry, you will beforced to
make a long journey to settle some unpleasant affair.To see a forest of
stately trees in foliage, denotes prosperity and pleasures. To
literarypeople, this dream foretells fame and much appreciation from the
public. A young ladyrelates the following dream and its fulfilment:I was
in a strange forest of what appeared to be cocoanut trees, with redand
yellow berries growing on them. The ground was covered with

blasted leaves, and I could hear them crackle under my feet as Iwandered
about lost. The next afternoon I received a telegramannouncing the death
of a dear cousin.ForeheadTo dream of a fine and smooth forehead, denotes
that you will be thought well of foryour judgment and fair dealings.An
ugly forehead, denotes displeasure in your private affairs.To pass your
hand over the forehead of your child, indicates sincere praises from
friends,because of some talent and goodness displayed by your
children.For a young woman to dream of kissing the forehead of her lover,
signifies that he will bedispleased with her for gaining notice by
indiscreet conduct.ForkTo dream of a fork, denotes that enemies are
working for your displacement. For awoman, this dream denotes unhappy
domestic relations, and separation for lovers.FormTo see anything ill
formed, denotes disappointment. To have a beautiful form,
denotesfavorable conditions to health and business.ForsakingFor a young
woman to dream of forsaking her home or friend, denotes that she will
havetroubles in love, as her estimate of her lover will decrease with
acquaintance andassociation.See Abandoned and Lover.FortTo dream of
defending a fort, signifies your honor and possessions will be attacked,
andyou will have great worry over the matter.To dream that you attack a
fort and take it, denotes victory over your worst enemy, andfortunate
engagements.

FortressTo dream that you are confined in a fortress, denotes that enemies will succeed in placingyou in an undesirable situation.To put others in a fortress, denotes your ability to rule in business or over women.Fortune TellingTo dream of telling, or having your fortune told, it dicates that you are deliberating oversome vexed affair, and you should use much caution in giving consent to itsconsummation. For a young woman, this portends a choice between two rivals. She willbe worried to find out the standing of one in business and social circles. To dream thatshe is engaged to a fortune-teller, denotes that she has gone through the forest andpicked the proverbial stick. She should be self-reliant, or poverty will attend hermarriage.FountainTo dream that you see a clear fountain sparkling in the sunlight, denotes vast possessions,ecstatic delights and many pleasant journeys.A clouded fountain, denotes the insincerity of associates and unhappy engagements andlove affairs.A dry and broken fountain, indicates death and cessation of pleasures.For a young woman to see a sparkling fountain in the moonlight, signifies ill-advisedpleasure which may result in a desertion.FowlTo dream of seeing fowls, denotes temporary worry or illness. For a woman to dream offowls, indicates a short illness or disagreement with her friends.See Chickens.FoxTo dream of chasing a fox, denotes that you are en gaging in doubtful speculations andrisky love affairs.If you see a fox slyly coming into your yard, beware of envious friendships; yourreputation is being slyly assailed.To kill a fox, denotes that you will win in every engagement.

FraudTo dream that you are defrauding a person, denotes that you will deceive your employerfor gain, indulge in degrading pleasures, and fall into disrepute.If you are defrauded, it signifies the useless attempt of enemies to defame you and causeyou loss.To accuse some one of defrauding you, you will be offered a place of high honor.FrecklesFor a woman to dream that her face is freckled, denotes that many displeasing incidentswill insinuate themselves into her happiness. If she sees them in a mirror, she will be indanger of losing her lover to a rival.FriendTo dream of friends being well and happy, denotes pleasant tidings of them, or you willsoon see them or some of their relatives.To see your friend troubled and haggard, sickness or distress is upon them.To see your friends dark-colored, denotes unusual sickness or trouble to you or to them.To see them take the form of animals, signifies that enemies will separate you from yourclosest relations.To see your friend who dresses in somber colors in flaming red, foretells that unpleasantthings will transpire, causing you anxiety if not loss, and that friends will be implicated.To dream you see a friend standing like a statue on a hill, denotes you will advancebeyond present pursuits, but will retain former impressions of justice and knowledge,seeking these through every change. If the figure below be low, you will ignore yourfriends of former days in your future advancement. If it is on a plane or level with you,you will fail in your ambition to reach other spheres. If you seem to be going from it, youwill force yourself to seek a change in spite of friendly ties or self-admonition.To dream you see a friend with a white cloth tied over his face, denotes that you will beinjured by some person who will endeavor to keep up friendly relations with you.To dream that you are shaking hands with a person who has wronged you, and he istaking his departure and looks sad, foretells you will have differences with a close friendand alienation will perhaps follow. You are most assuredly nearing loss of somecharacter.

FrightenedTo dream that you are frightened at anything, denotes temporary and fleeting worries.See Affrighted.FrogsTo dream of catching frogs, denotes carelessness in watching after your health, whichmay cause no little distress among those of your family.To see frogs in the grass, denotes that you will have a pleasant and even-tempered friendas your confidant and counselor.To see a bullfrog, denotes, for a woman, marriage with a wealthy widower, but there willbe children with him to be cared for.To see frogs in low marshy places, foretells trouble, but you will overcome it by thekindness of others.To dream of eating frogs, signifies fleeting joys and very little gain from associating withsome people.To hear frogs, portends that you will go on a visit to friends, but it will in the end provefruitless of good.FrostTo dream of seeing frost on a dark gloomy morning, signifies exile to a strange country,but your wanderings will end in peace.To see frost on a small sunlit landscape, signifies gilded pleasures from which you willbe glad to turn later in life, and by your exemplary conduct will succeed in making yourcircle forget past escapades.To dream that you see a friend in a frost, denotes a love affair in which your rival will beworsted. For a young woman, this dream signifies the absence of her lover and danger ofhis affections waning. This dream is bad for all classes in business and love.FruitTo dream of seeing fruit ripening among its foliage, usually foretells to the dreamer aprosperous future. Green fruit signifies disappointed efforts or hasty action.For a young woman to dream of eating green fruit, indicates her degradation and loss ofinheritance. Eating fruit is unfavorable usually.

To buy or sell fruit, denotes much business, but not very remunerative.To see or eat ripe fruit, signifies uncertain fortune and pleasure.Fruit SellerTo dream of a fruit seller, denotes you will endeavor to recover your loss too rapidly andwill engage in unfortunate speculations.FuneralTo see a funeral, denotes an unhappy marriage and sickly offspring.To dream of the funeral of a stranger, denotes unexpected worries. To see the funeral ofyour child, may denote the health of your family, but very grave disappointments mayfollow from a friendly source.To attend a funeral in black, foretells an early widowhood. To dream of the funeral ofany relative, denotes nervous troubles and family worries.FurnaceTo dream of a furnace, foretells good luck if it is running. If out of repair, you will havetrouble with children or hired help. To fall into one, portends some enemy willoverpower you in a business struggle.FursTo dream of dealing in furs, denotes prosperity and an interest in many concerns.To be dressed in fur, signifies your safety from want and poverty.To see fine fur, denotes honor and riches. For a young woman to dream that she iswearing costly furs, denotes that she will marry a wise man.FutureTo dream of the future, is a prognostic of careful reckoning and avoiding of detrimentalextravagance.G

GaiterTo dream of gaiters, foretells pleasant amusements and rivalries.GaleTo dream of being caught in a gale, signifies business losses and troubles for workingpeople.GallowsTo dream of seeing a friend on the gallows of execution, foretells that desperateemergencies must be met with decision, or a great calamity will befall you.To dream that you are on a gallows, denotes that you will suffer from the maliciousnessof false friends.For a young woman to dream that she sees her lover executed by this means, denotes thatshe will marry an unscrupulous and designing man.If you rescue any one from the gallows, it portends desirable acquisitions.To dream that you hang an enemy, denotes victory in all spheres.Gambling HouseTo dream that you are gambling and win, signifies low associations and pleasure at theexpense of others. If you lose, it foretells that your disgraceful conduct will be theundoing of one near to you.GameTo dream of game, either shooting or killing or by other means, denotes fortunateundertakings; but selfish motions; if you fail to take game on a hunt, it denotes badmanagement and loss.GangreneTo dream that you see any one afflicted with gangrene, foretells the death of a parent ornear relative.

GaolIf you dream of being confined in a gaol, you will be prevented from carrying forwardsome profitable work by the intervention of envious people; but if you escape from thegaol, you will enjoy a season of favorable business.See Jail.GarbageTo see heaps of garbage in your dreams, indicates thoughts of social scandal andunfavorable business of every character. For females this dream is ominous ofdisparagement and desertion by lovers.GardenTo see a garden in your dreams, filled with evergreen and flowers, denotes great peace ofmind and comfort.To see vegetables, denotes misery or loss of fortune and calumny. To females, this dreamforetells that they will be famous, or exceedingly happy in domestic circles.To dream of walking with one's lover through a garden where flowering shrubs andplants abound, indicates unalloyed happiness and independent means.GarlicTo dream of passing through a garlic patch, denotes a rise from penury to prominenceand wealth. To a young woman, this denotes that she will marry from a sense of business,and love will not be considered.To eat garlic in your dreams, denotes that you will take a sensible view of life and leaveits ideals to take care of themselves.GarretTo dream of climbing to a garret, denotes your inclination to run after theories whileleaving the cold realities of life to others less able to bear them than yourself. To thepoor, this dream is an omen of easier circumstances. To a woman, it denotes that hervanity and selfishness should be curbed.GarterFor a lover to find his lady's garter, foretells that he will lose caste with her. He will findrivals.

For a woman to dream that she loses her garter, signifies that her lover will be jealousand suspicious of a handsomer person.For a married man to dream of a garter, foretells that his wife will hear of his clandestineattachments, and he will have a stormy scene.For a woman to dream that she is admiring beautiful jeweled garters on her limbs,denotes that she will be betrayed in her private movements, and her reputation will hangin the balance of public opinion. If she dreams that her lover fastens them on her, she willhold his affections and faith through all adverse criticisms.GasTo dream of gas, denotes you will entertain harmful opinions of others, which will causeyou to deal with them unjustly, and you will suffer consequent remorse. To think you areasphyxiated, denotes you will have trouble which you will needlessly incur through yourown wastefulness and negligence.To try to blow gas out, signifies you will entertain enemies unconsciously, who willdestroy you if you are not wary.To extinguish gas, denotes you will ruthlessly destroy your own happiness. To light it,you will easily find a way out of oppressive ill fortune.Gas LampsTo see a gas lamp, denotes progress and pleasant surroundings. To see one explode, orout of order other wise, foretells you are threatened with unseasonable distress.GasolineTo dream of gasoline, denotes you have a competency coming to you through astruggling source.GateTo dream of seeing or passing through a gate, foretells that alarming tidings will reachyou soon of the absent. Business affairs will not be encouraging.To see a closed gate, inability to overcome present difficulties is predicted. To lock one,denotes successful enterprises and well chosen friends. A broken one, signifies failureand discordant surroundings. To be troubled to get through one, or open it, denotes yourmost engrossing labors will fail to be remunerative or satisfactory. To swing on one,foretells you will engage in idle and dissolute pleasures.

GauzeTo dream of being dressed in gauze, denotes uncertain fortune. For a lover to see hissweetheart clothed in filmy material, suggests his ability to influence her for good.GavelTo dream of a gavel, denotes you will be burdened with some unprofitable yet notunpleasant pursuit. To use one, denotes that officiousness will be shown by you towardyour friends.GeeseTo dream that you are annoyed by the quacking of geese, denotes a death in your family.To see them swimming, denotes that your fortune is gradually increasing.To see them in grassy places, denotes assured success. If you see them dead, you willsuffer loss and displeasure.For a lover, geese denotes the worthiness of his affianced. If you are picking them, youwill come into an estate.To eat them, denotes that your possessions are disputed.GemsTo dream of gems, foretells a happy fate both in love and business affairs.See Jewelry.Genealogical TreeTo dream of your genealogical tree, denotes you will be much burdened with familycares, or will find pleasure in other domains than your own. To see others studying it,foretells that you will be forced to yield your rights to others. If any of the branches aremissing, you will ignore some of your friends because of their straightenedcircumstances.GeographyTo dream of studying geography, denotes that you will travel much and visit places ofrenown.See Atlas.

GhostTo dream of the ghost of either one of your parents, denotes that you are exposed todanger, and you should be careful in forming partnerships with strangers.To see the ghost of a dead friend, foretells that you will make a long journey with anunpleasant companion, and suffer disappointments.For a ghost to speak to you, you will be decoyed into the hands of enemies. For a woman,this is a prognostication of widowhood and deception.To see an angel or a ghost appear in the sky, denotes the loss of kindred and misfortunes.To see a female ghost on your right in the sky and a male on your left, both of pleasingcountenance, signifies a quick rise from obscurity to fame, but the honor and positionwill be filled only for a short space, as death will be a visitor and will bear you off.To see a female ghost in long, clinging robes floating calmly through the sky, indicatesthat you will make progression in scientific studies and acquire wealth almostmiraculously, but there will be an under note of sadness in your life.To dream that you see the ghost of a living relative or friend, denotes that you are indanger of some friend's malice, and you are warned to carefully keep your affairs underpersonal supervision. If the ghost appears to be haggard, it may be the intimation of theearly death of that friend.See Death and Dead.GiantTo dream of a giant appearing suddenly before you, denotes that there will be a greatstruggle between you and your opponents. If the giant succeeds in stopping your journey,you will be overcome by your enemy. If he runs from you, prosperity and good healthwill be yours.GiftTo dream that you receive gifts from any one, denotes that you will not be behind in yourpayments, and be unusually fortunate in speculations or love matters.To send a gift, signifies displeasure will be shown you, and ill luck will surround yourefforts.For a young woman to dream that her lover sends her rich and beautiful gifts, denotesthat she will make a wealthy and congenial marriage.

GigTo run a gig in your dream, you will have to forego a pleasant journey to entertainunwelcome visitors. Sickness also threatens you.See Cart.**Girdle**To dream of wearing a girdle, and it presses you, denotes that you will be influenced bydesigning people.To see others wearing velvet, or jeweled girdles, foretells that you will strive for wealthmore than honor.For a woman to receive one, signifies that honors will be conferred upon her.**Girls**To dream of seeing a well, bright-looking girl, foretells pleasing prospects and domesticjoys. If she is thin and pale, it denotes that you will have an invalid in your family, andmuch unpleasantness.For a man to dream that he is a girl, he will be weak-minded, or become an actor andplay female parts.**Glass**To dream that you are looking through glass, denotes that bitter disappointments willcloud your brightest hopes.To see your image in a mirror, foretells unfaithfulness and neglect in marriage, andfruitless speculations.To see another face with your own in a mirror indicates that you are leading a double life.You will deceive your friends.To break a mirror, portends an early and accidental death.To break glass dishes, or windows, foretells the unfavorable termination to enterprises.To receive cut glass, denotes that you will be admired for your brilliancy and talent.To make presents of cut glass ornaments, signifies that you will fail in your undertakings.For a woman to see her lover in a mirror, denotes that she will have cause to institute abreach of promise suit.

For a married woman to see her husband in a mirror, is a warning that she will havecause to feel anxiety for her happiness and honor.To look clearly through a glass window, you will have employment, but will have towork subordinately. If the glass is clouded, you will be unfortunately situated.If a woman sees men, other than husband or lover, in a looking glass, she will bediscovered in some indiscreet affair which will be humiliating to her and a source ofworry to her relations.For a man to dream of seeing strange women in a mirror, he will ruin his health andbusiness by foolish attachments.**Glass Blower**To dream that you see glass-blowers at their work, denotes you will contemplate changein your business, which will appear for the better, but you will make it at a loss toyourself.**Glass House**To see a glass house, foretells you are likely to be injured by listening to flattery.For a young woman to dream that she is living in a glass house, her coming trouble andthreatened loss of reputation is emphasized.**Gleaning**To see gleaners at work at harvest time, denotes prosperous business, and, to the farmer,a bountiful yield of crops.If you are working with the gleaners, you will come into an estate, after some trouble inestablishing rights. For a woman, this dream foretells marriage with a stranger.**Gloomy**To be surrounded by many gloomy situations in your dream, warns you of rapidlyapproaching unpleasantness and loss.See Despair.**Gloves**To dream of wearing new gloves, denotes that you will be cautious and economical inyour dealings with others, but not mercenary. You will have law suits, or businesstroubles, but will settle them satisfactorily to yourself.

If you wear old or ragged gloves, you will be betrayed and suffer loss.If you dream that you lose your gloves, you will be deserted and earn your own means oflivelihood.To find a pair of gloves, denotes a marriage or new love affair.For a man to fasten a lady's glove, he has, or will have, a woman on his hands whothreatens him with exposure.If you pull your glove off, you will meet with poor success in business or love.GoatTo dream of goats wandering around a farm, is significant of seasonable weather and afine yield of crops To see them otherwise, denotes cautious dealings and a steadyincrease of wealth.If a billy goat butts you, beware that enemies do not get possession of your secrets orbusiness plans.For a woman to dream of riding a billy goat, denotes that she will be held in disreputebecause of her coarse and ill-bred conduct.If a woman dreams that she drinks goat's milk, she will marry for money and will not bedisappointed.GobletIf you dream that you drink water from a silver goblet, you will meet unfavorablebusiness results in the near future.To see goblets of ancient design, you will receive favors and benefits from strangers.For a woman to give a man a glass goblet full of water, denotes illicit pleasures.GodIf you dream of seeing God, you will be domineered over by a tyrannical womanmasquerading under the cloak of Christianity. No good accrues from this dream.If God speaks to you, beware that you do not fall into condemnation. Business of all sortswill take an unfavorable turn. It is the forerunner of the weakening of health and maymean early dissolution.If you dream of worshiping God, you will have cause to repent of an error of your ownmaking. Look well to observing the ten commandments after this dream.

To dream that God confers distinct favors upon you, you will become the favorite of acautious and prominent person who will use his position to advance yours.To dream that God sends his spirit upon you, great changes in your beliefs will takeplace. Views concerning dogmatic Christianity should broaden after this dream, or youmay be severely chastised for some indiscreet action which has brought shame upon you.God speaks oftener to those who transgress than those who do not. It is the genius ofspiritual law or economy to reinstate the prodigal child by signs and visions. Elijah,Jonah, David, and Paul were brought to the altar of repentence through the vigilantenergy of the hidden forces within.GogglesTo dream of goggles, is a warning of disreputable companions who will wheedle you intolending your money foolishly.For a young woman to dream of goggles, means that she will listen to persuasion whichwill mar her fortune.GoldIf you handle gold in your dream, you will be unusually successful in all enterprises.For a womanto dream that she receives presents of gold, either money or ornaments, shewill marry a wealthy but mercenary man.To find gold, indicates that your superior abilities will place you easily ahead in the racefor honors and wealth.If you lose gold, you will miss the grandest opportunity of your life through negligence.To dream of finding a gold vein, denotes that some uneasy honor will be thrust upon you.If you dream that you contemplate working a gold mine, you will endeavor to usurp therights of others, and should beware of domestic scandals.GoldfishTo dream of goldfish, is a prognostic of many successful and pleasant adventures. For ayoung woman, this dream is indicative of a wealthy union with a pleasing man. If the fishare sick or dead, heavy disappointments will fall upon her.Gold LeavesTo dream of gold leaves, signifies a flattering future is before you.

GolfTo be playing golf or watching the game, denotes that pleasant and successive wishingwill be indulged in by you.To see any unpleasantness connected with golf, you will be humiliated by somethoughtless person.GongTo hear the sound of a gong while dreaming, denotes false alarm of illness, or loss willvex you excessively.GooseberriesTo dream of gathering gooseberries, is a sign of happiness after trouble, and a favorableindication of brighter prospects in one's business affairs.If you are eating green gooseberries, you will make a mistake in your course to pleasure,and be precipitated into the vertex of sensationalism. Bad results are sure to follow thetasting of green gooseberries.To see gooseberries in a dream, foretells you will escape some dreaded work. For ayoung woman to eat them, foretells she will be slightly disappointed in her expectations.GossipTo dream of being interested in common gossip, you will undergo some humiliatingtrouble caused by overconfidence in transient friendships.If you are the object of gossip, you may expect some pleasurable surprise.GoutIf you dream of having the gout, you will be sure to be exasperated beyond endurance bythe silly conduct of some relative, and suffer small financial loss through the sameperson.GownIf you dream that you are in your nightgown, you will be afflicted with a slight illness. Ifyou see others thus clad, you will have unpleasant news of absent friends. Business willreceive a back set.If a lover sees his sweetheart in her night gown, he will be superseded.

See Clothes.GrainGrain is a most fortunate dream, betokening wealth and happiness. For a young woman,it is a dream of fortune. She will meet wealthy and adoring companions.GrammarTo dream that you are studying grammar, denotes you are soon to make a wise choice inmomentous opportunities.GramophoneTo dream of hearing the gramophone, foretells the advent of some new and pleasingcomrade who will lend himself willingly to advance your enjoyment. If it is broken,some fateful occurrence will thwart and defeat delights that you hold in anticipation.GrandparentsTo dreaam of meeting your grandparents and conversing with them, you will meet withdifficulties that will be hard to surmount, but by following good advice you willovercome many barriers.GrapesTo eat grapes in your dream, you will be hardened with many cares; but if you only seethem hanging in profuseness among the leaves, you will soon attain to eminent positionsand will be able to impart happiness to others. For a young woman, this dream is one ofbright promise. She will have her most ardent wish gratified.To dream of riding on horseback and passing musca-dine bushes and gathering andeating some of its fruit, denotes profitable employment and the realization of greatdesires. If there arises in your mind a question of the poisonous quality of the fruit youare eating, there will come doubts and fears of success, but they will gradually cease toworry you.GrassThis is a very propitious dream indeed. It gives promise of a happy and well advancedlife to the tradesman, rapid accumulation of wealth, fame to literary and artistic people,and a safe voyage through the turbulent sea of love is promised to all lovers.To see a rugged mountain beyond the green expanse of grass, is momentous of remotetrouble.

If in passing through green grass, you pass withered places, it denotes your sickness orembarrassments in business.To be a perfect dream, the grass must be clear of obstruction or blemishes. If you dreamof withered grass, the reverse is predicted.GrasshopperTo dream of seeing grasshoppers on green vegetables, denotes that enemies threaten yourbest interests. If on withered grasses, ill health. Disappointing business will beexperienced.If you see grasshoppers between you and the sun, it denotes that you will have avexatious problem in your immediate business life to settle, but using caution it willadjust itself in your favor.To call peoples' attention to the grasshoppers, shows that you are not discreet indispatching your private business.GraveTo dream that you see a newly made grave, you will have to suffer for the wrongdoingsof others.If you visit a newly made grave, dangers of a serious nature is hanging over you. Grave isan unfortunate dream. Ill luck in business transactions will follow, also sickness isthreatened.To dream of walking on graves, predicts an early death or an unfortunate marriage.If you look into an empty grave, it denotes disappointment and loss of friends.If you see a person in a grave with the earth covering him, except the head, somedistressing situation will take hold of that person and loss of property is indicated to thedreamer.To see your own grave, foretells that enemies are warily seeking to engulf you indisaster, and if you fail to be watchful they will succeed.To dream of digging a grave, denotes some uneasiness over some undertaking, asenemies will seek to thwart you, but if you finish the grave you will overcomeopposition. If the sun is shining, good will come out of seeming embarrassments.If you return for a corpse, to bury it, and it has disappeared, trouble will come to youfrom obscure quarters.For a woman to dream that night overtakes her in a graveyard, and she can find no placeto sleep but in an open grave, foreshows she will have much sorrow and disappointment through death or false friends. She may lose in love, and many things seek to work herharm.To see a graveyard barren, except on top of the graves, signifies much sorrow anddespondency for a time, but greater benefits and pleasure await you if you properlyshoulder your burden.To see your own corpse in a grave, foreshadows hopeless and despairing oppression.GravelTo dream of gravel, denotes unfruitful schemes and enterprises.If you see gravel mixed with dirt, it foretells you will unfortunately speculate and losegood property.GravyTo dream of eating gravy, portends failing health and disappointing business.GreaseTo dream you are in grease, is significant of travels being enjoyed with disagreeable butpolished strangers.GreekTo dream of reading Greek, denotes that your ideas will be discussed and finallyaccepted and put in practical use. To fail to read it, denotes that technical difficulties arein your way.GreyhoundA greyhound is a fortunate object to see in your dream. If it is following a young girl, youwill be surprised with a legacy from unknown people. If a greyhound is owned by you, itssignifies friends where enemies were expected.GrindstoneFor a person to dream of turning a grindstone, his dream is prophetic of a life of energyand well directed efforts bringing handsome competency.If you are sharpening tools, you will be blessed with a worthy helpmate.To deal in grindstones, is significant of small but honest gain.

GroansIf you hear groans in your dream, decide quickly on your course, for enemies areundermining your business.If you are groaning with fear, you will be pleasantly surprised at the turn for better inyour affairs, and you may look for pleasant visiting among friends.GroceriesTo dream of general groceries, if they are fresh and clean, is a sign of ease and comfort.GrottoTo see a grotto in your dreams, is a sign of incomplete and inconstant friendships.Change from comfortable and simple plenty will make showy poverty unbearable.GuardianTo dream of a guardian, denotes you will be treated with consideration by your friends.For a young woman to dream that she is being unkindly dealt with by her guardian,foretells that she will have loss and trouble in the future.GuitarTo dream that you have a guitar, or is playing one in a dream, signifies a merry gatheringand serious love making. For a young woman to think it is unstrung or broken, foretellsthat disappointments in love are sure to overtake her. Upon hearing the weird music of aguitar, the dreamer should fortify herself against flattery and soft persuasion, for she is indanger of being tempted by a fascinating evil. If the dreamer be a man, he will becourted, and will be likely to lose his judgment under the wiles of seductive women.If you play on a guitar, your family affairs will be harmonious.GullsTo dream of gulls, is a prophecy of peaceful dealings with ungenerous persons.Seeing dead gulls, means wide separation for friends.GunThis is a dream of distress. Hearing the sound of a gun, denotes loss of employment, andbad management to proprietors of establishments.

If you shoot a person with a gun, you will fall into dishonor.If you are shot, you will be annoyed by evil persons, and perhaps suffer an acute illness.For a woman to dream of shooting, forecasts for her a quarreling and disagreeablereputation connected with sensations. For a married woman, unhappiness through otherwomen.GutterTo dream of a gutter, is a sign of degradation. You will be the cause of unhappiness toothers.To find articles of value in a gutter, your right to certain property will be questioned.GymnastTo dream of a gymnast, denotes you will have misfortune in speculation or trade.GypsyIf you dream of visiting a gypsy camp, you will have an offer of importance and willinvestigate the standing of the parties to your disadvantage.For a woman to have a gypsy tell her fortune, is an omen of a speedy and unwisemarriage. If she is already married, she will be unduly jealous of her husband.For a man to hold any conversation with a gypsy, he will be likely to lose valuableproperty.To dream of trading with a gypsy, you will lose money in speculation. This dreamdenotes that material pleasures are the biggest items in your life.HHaggardTo see a haggard face in your dreams, denotes misfortune and defeat in love matters.To see your own face haggard and distressed, denotes trouble over female affairs, whichmay render you unable to meet business engagements in a healthy manner.

HailIf you dream of being in a hail storm, you will meet poor success in any undertaking.If you watch hail-stones fall through sunshine and rain, you will be harassed by cares fora time, but fortune will soon smile upon you. For a young woman, this dream indicateslove after many slights.To hear hail beating the house, indicates distressing situations.HairIf a woman dreams that she has beautiful hair and combs it, she will be careless in herpersonal affairs, and will lose advancement by neglecting mental application.For a man to dream that he is thinning his hair, foreshadows that he will become poor byhis generosity, and suffer illness through mental worry.To see your hair turning gray, foretells death and contagion in the family of some relativeor some friend.To see yourself covered with hair, omens indulgence in vices to such an extent as willdebar you from the society of refined people. If a woman, she will resolve herself into aworld of her own, claiming the right to act for her own pleasure regardless of moralcodes.If a man dreams that he has black, curling hair, he will deceive people through hispleasing address. He will very likely deceive the women who trust him. If a woman's hairseems black and curly, she will be threatened with seduction.If you dream of seeing a woman with golden hair, you will prove a fearless lover and bewoman's true friend.To dream that your sweetheart has red hair, you will be denounced by the woman youlove for unfaithfulness. Red hair usually suggests changes.If you see brown hair, you will be unfortunate in choosing a career.If you see well kept and neatly combed hair, your fortune will improve.To dream you cut your hair close to the scalp, denotes that you will be generous tolavishness towards a friend. Frugality will be the fruits growing out therefrom.To see the hair growing out soft and luxuriant, signifies happiness and luxury.For a woman to compare a white hair with a black one, which she takes from her head,foretells that she will be likely to hesitate between two offers of seeming fortune, andunless she uses great care, will choose the one that will afford her loss or distress instead

of pleasant fortune.To see tangled and unkempt hair, life will be a veritable burden, business will fall off,and the marriage yoke will be troublesome to carry.If a woman is unsuccessful in combing her hair, she will lose a worthy man's name byneedless show of temper and disdain.For a young woman to dream of women with gray hair, denotes that they will come intoher life as rivals in the affection of a male relative, or displace the love of her affianced.To dream of having your hair cut, denotes serious disappointments.For a woman to dream that her hair is falling out, and baldness is apparent, she will haveto earn her own livelihood, as fortune has passed her by.For man or woman to dream that they have hair of snowy whiteness, denotes that theywill enjoy a pleasing and fortunate journey through life.For a man to caress the hair of a woman, shows he will enjoy the love and confidence ofsome worthy woman who will trust him despite the world's condemnation.To see flowers in your hair, foretells troubles approaching which, when they come, willgive you less fear than when viewed from a distance.For a woman to dream that her hair turns to white flowers, augurs that troubles of avarious nature will confront her, and she does well if she strengthens her soul withpatience, and endeavors to bear her trials with fortitude.To dream that a lock of your hair turns gray and falls out, is a sign of trouble anddisappointment in your affairs. Sickness will cast gloom over bright expectations.To see one's hair turn perfectly white in one night, and the face seemingly young,foretells sudden calamity and deep grief. For a young woman to have this dream,signifies that she will lose her lover by a sudden sickness or accident. She will likelycome to grief from some indiscretion on her part. She should be careful of her associates.Hair-dresserShould you visit a hair-dresser in your dreams, you will be connected with a sensationcaused by the indiscretion of a good looking woman. To a woman, this dream means afamily disturbance and well merited censures.For a woman to dream of having her hair colored, she will narrowly escape the scorn ofsociety, as enemies will seek to blight her reputation. To have her hair dressed, denotesthat she will run after frivolous things, and use any means to bend people to her wishes.

Hairy HandsTo dream that your hands are covered with hair like that of a beast, signifies you willintrigue against innocent people, and will find that you have alert enemies who areworking to forestall your designs.HalterTo dream that you put a halter on a young horse, shows that you will manage a veryprosperous and clean business. Love matters will shape themselves to suit you.To see other things haltered, denotes that fortune will be withheld from you for a while.You will win it, but with much toil.HamTo dream of seeing hams, signifies you are in danger of being treacherously used. To cutlarge slices of ham, denotes that all opposition will be successfully met by you. To dressa ham, signifies you will be leniently treated by others.To dream of dealing in hams, prosperity will come to you. Also good health is foreboded.To eat ham, you will lose something of great value. To smell ham cooking, you will bebenefited by the enterprises of others.HammerTo dream of seeing a hammer, denotes you will have some discouraging obstacles toovercome in order to establish firmly your fortune.HandIf you see beautiful hands in your dream, you will enjoy great distinction, and rise rapidlyin your calling; but ugly and malformed hands point to disappointments and poverty. Tosee blood on them, denotes estrangement and unjust censure from members of yourfamily.If you have an injured hand, some person will succeed to what you are striving most toobtain.To see a detached hand, indicates a solitary life, that is, people will fail to understandyour views and feelings. To burn your hands, you will overreach the bounds of reason inyour struggles for wealth and fame, and lose thereby.To see your hands covered with hair, denotes that you will not become a solid andleading factor in your circle.

To see your hands enlarged, denotes a quick advancement in your affairs. To see themsmaller, the reverse is predicted.To see your hands soiled, denotes that you will be envious and unjust to others.To wash your hands, you will participate in some joyous festivity.For a woman to admire her own hands, is proof that she will win and hold the sincereregard of the man she prizes above all others.To admire the hands of others, she will be subjected to the whims of a jealous man. Tohave a man hold her hands, she will be enticed into illicit engagements. If she lets otherskiss her hands, she will have gossips busy with her reputation. To handle fire withoutburning her hands, she will rise to high rank and commanding positions.To dream that your hands are tied, denotes that you will be involved in difficulties. Inloosening them, you will force others to submit to your dictations.See Fingers.HandbillsTo dream of distributing handbills over the country, is a sign of contentions and possiblelawsuits.If you dream of printing handbills, you will hear unfavorable news.HandcuffsTo find yourself handcuffed, you will be annoyed and vexed by enemies. To see othersthus, you will subdue those oppressing you and rise above your associates.To see handcuffs, you will be menaced with sickness and danger.To dream of handcuffs, denotes formidable enemies are surrounding you withobjectionable conditions. To break them, is a sign that you will escape toils planned byenemies.HandkerchiefsTo dream of handkerchiefs, denotes flirtations and contingent affairs.To lose one, omens a broken engagement through no fault of yours.To see torn ones, foretells that lovers' quarrels will reach such straits that reconciliationwill be improbable if not impossible.

To see them soiled, foretells that you will be corrupted by indiscriminate associations.To see pure white ones in large lots, foretells that you will resist the insistent flattery ofunscrupulous and evil-minded persons, and thus gain entrance into high relations withlove and matrimony.To see them colored, denotes that while your engagements may not be strictly moral, youwill manage them with such ingenuity that they will elude opprobrium.If you see silk handkerchiefs, it denotes that your pleasing and magnetic personality willshed its radiating cheerfulness upon others, making for yourself a fortunate existence.For a young woman to wave adieu or a recognition with her handkerchief, or see othersdoing this, denotes that she will soon make a questionable pleasure trip, or she mayknowingly run the gauntlet of disgrace to secure some fancied pleasure.HandsomeTo see yourself handsome-looking in your dreams, you will prove yourself an ingeniousflatterer.To see others appearing handsome, denotes that you will enjoy the confidence of fastpeople.HandwritingTo dream that you see and recognize your own handwriting, foretells that maliciousenemies will use your expressed opinion to foil you in advancing to some competedposition.HangingTo see a large concourse of people gathering at a hanging, denotes that many enemieswill club together to try to demolish your position in their midst.See Execution.HareIf you see a hare escaping from you in a dream, you will lose something valuable in amysterious way. If you capture one, you will be the victor in a contest.If you make pets of them, you will have an orderly but unintelligent companion.A dead hare, betokens death to some friend. Existence will be a prosy affair.

To see hares chased by dogs, denotes trouble and contentions among your friends, andyou will concern yourself to bring about friendly relations.If you dream that you shoot a hare, you will be forced to use violent measures to maintainyour rightful possessions.See Rabbit.HaremTo dream that you maintain a harem, denotes that you are wasting your best energies onlow pleasures. Life holds fair promises, if your desires are rightly directed.If a woman dreams that she is an inmate of a harem, she will seek pleasure wherepleasure is unlawful, as her desires will be toward married men as a rule. If she dreamsthat she is a favorite of a harem, she will be preferred before others in material pleasures,but the distinction will be fleeting.HarlequinTo dream of a harlequin cheating you, you will find uphill work to identify certain claimsthat promise profit to you. If you dream of a harlequin, trouble will beset you.To be dressed as a harlequin, denotes passionate error and unwise attacks on strength andpurse. Designing women will lure you to paths of sin.HarlotTo dream of being in the company of a harlot, denotes ill-chosen pleasures and troublein your social circles, and business will suffer depression. If you marry one, life will bethreatened by an enemy.HarnessTo dream of possessing bright new harness, you will soon prepare for a pleasant journey.HarpTo hear the sad sweet strains of a harp, denotes the sad ending to what seems a pleasingand profitable enterprise.To see a broken harp, betokens illness, or broken troth between lovers.To play a harp yourself, signifies that your nature is too trusting, and you should be morecareful in placing your confidence as well as love matters.

HarvestTo dream of harvest time, is a forerunner of prosperity and pleasure. If the harvest yieldsare abundant, the indications are good for country and state, as political machinery willgrind to advance all conditions.A poor harvest is a sign of small profits.HashTo dream you are eating hash, many sorrows and vexations are foretold.You will probably be troubled with various little jealousies and contentions over meretrifles, and your health will be menaced through worry.For a woman to dream that she cooks hash, denotes that she will be jealous of herhusband, and children will be a stumbling block to her wantonness.HassockTo dream of a hassock, forebodes the yielding of your power and fortune to another. If awoman dreams of a hassock, she should cultivate spirit and independence.HatTo dream of losing your hat, you may expect unsatisfactory business and failure ofpersons to keep important engagements.For a man to dream that he wears a new hat, predicts change of place and business, whichwill be very much to his advantage. For a woman to dream that she wears a fine new hat,denotes the attainment of wealth, and she will be the object of much admiration.For the wind to blow your hat off, denotes sudden changes in affairs, and somewhat forthe worse.HatchetA hatchet seen in a dream, denotes that wanton wastefulness will expose you to the evildesigns of envious persons. If it is rusty or broken, you will have grief over waywardpeople.HateTo dream that you hate a person, denotes that if you are not careful you will do the partyan inadvertent injury or a spiteful action will bring business loss and worry.

If you are hated for unjust causes, you will find sincere and obliging friends, and yourassociations will be most pleasant. Otherwise, the dream forebodes ill.HawkTo dream of a hawk, foretells you will be cheated in some way by intriguing persons. Toshoot one, foretells you will surmount obstacles after many struggles. For a youngwoman to frighten hawks away from her chickens, signifies she will obtain her mostextravagant desires through diligent attention to her affairs.It also denotes that enemies are near you, and they are ready to take advantage of yourslightest mistakes. If you succeed in scaring it away before your fowls are injured, youwill be lucky in your business.To see a dead hawk, signifies that your enemies will be vanquished.To dream of shooting at a hawk, you will have a contest with enemies, and will probablywin.HayIf you dream of mowing hay, you will find much good in life, and if a farmer your cropswill yield abundantly.To see fields of newly cut hay, is a sign of unusual prosperity.If you are hauling and putting hay into barns, your fortune is assured, and you will realizegreat profit from some enterprise.To see loads of hay passing through the street, you will meet influential strangers whowill add much to your pleasure.To feed hay to stock, indicates that you will offer aid to some one who will return thefavor with love and advancement to higher states.HeadTo see a person's head in your dream, and it is well-shaped and prominent, you will meetpersons of power and vast influence who will lend you aid in enterprises of importance.If you dream of your own head, you are threatened with nervous or brain trouble.To see a head severed from its trunk, and bloody, you will meet sickeningdisappointments, and the overthrow of your dearest hopes and anticipations.To see yourself with two or more heads, foretells phenomenal and rapid rise in life, butthe probabilities are that the rise will not be stable.

To dream that your head aches, denotes that you will be oppressed with worry.To dream of a swollen head, you will have more good than bad in your life.To dream of a child's head, there will be much pleasure ill store for you and signalfinancial success.To dream of the head of a beast, denotes that the nature of your desires will run on a lowplane, and only material pleasures will concern you.To wash your head, you will be sought after by prominent people for your judgment andgood counsel.HeadgearTo dream of seeing rich headgear, you will become famous and successful. To see oldand worn headgear, you will have to yield up your possessions to others.HearseTo dream of a hearse, denotes uncongenial relations in the home, and failure to carry onbusiness in a satisfactory manner. It also betokens the death of one near to you, orsickness and sorrow.If a hearse crosses your path, you will have a bitter enemy to overcome.HeartTo dream of your heart paining and suffocating you, there will be trouble in yourbusiness. Some mistake of your own will bring loss if not corrected.Seeing your heart, foretells sickness and failure of energy.To see the heart of an animal, you will overcome enemies and merit the respect of all.To eat the heart of a chicken, denotes strange desires will cause you to carry out verydifficult projects for your advancement.HeatTo dream that you are oppressed by heat, denotes failure to carry out designs on accountof some friend betraying you. Heat is not a very favorable dream.Heather BellsTo dream of heather bells, foretells that joyous occasions will pass you in happy succession.HeavenIf you ascend to heaven in a dream, you will fail to enjoy the distinction you have laboredto gain,, and joy will end in sadness.If young persons dream of climbing to heaven on a ladder, they will rise from a lowestate to one of unusual prominence, but will fail to find contentment or much pleasure.To dream of being in heaven and meeting Christ and friends, you will meet with manylosses, but will reconcile yourself to them through your true understanding of humannature.To dream of the Heavenly City, denotes a contented and spiritual nature, and trouble willdo you small harm.HedgesTo dream of hedges of evergreens, denotes joy and profit.Bare hedges, foretells distress and unwise dealings.If a young woman dreams of walking beside a green hedge with her lover, it foretells thather marriage will soon be consummated.If you dream of being entangled in a thorny hedge, you will be hampered in yourbusiness by unruly partners or persons working under you. To lovers, this dream issignificant of quarrels and jealousies.HeirTo dream that you fall heir to property or valuables, denotes that you are in danger oflosing what you already possess. and warns you of coming responsibilities. Pleasantsurprises may also follow this dream.HellIf you dream of being in hell, you will fall into temptations, which will almost wreck youfinancially and morally.To see your friends in hell, denotes distress and burdensome cares. You will hear of themisfortune of some friend.To dream of crying in hell, denotes the powerlessness of friends to extricate you from thesnares of enemies.

HelmetTo dream of seeing a helmet, denotes threatened misery and loss will be avoided by wiseaction.HempTo dream of hemp, denotes you will be successful in all undertakings, especially largeengagements. For a young woman to dream that some accident befalls her throughcultivating hemp, foretells the fatal quarrel and separation from her friend.Hemp SeedTo see hemp seed in dreams, denotes the near approach of a deep and continuedfriendship. To the business man, is shown favorable opportunity for money-making.HenTo dream of hens, denotes pleasant family reunions with added members.See Chickens.HerbsTo dream of herbs, denotes that you will have vexatious cares, though some pleasureswill ensue.To dream of poisonous herbs, warns you of enemies.Balm and other useful herbs, denotes satisfaction in business and warm friendships.HermitTo dream of a hermit, denotes sadness and loneliness caused by the unfaithfulness offriends.If you are a hermit yourself, you will pursue researches into intricate subjects, and willtake great interest in the discussions of the hour.To find yourself in the abode of a hermit, denotes unselfishness toward enemies andfriends alike.HerringTo dream of seeing herring, indicates a tight squeeze to escape financial embarrassment, but you will have success later.HideTo dream of the hide of an animal, denotes profit and permanent employment.HiddenTo dream that you have hidden away any object, denotes embarrassment in yourcircumstances.To find hidden things, you will enjoy unexpected pleasures.For a young woman to dream of hiding objects, she will be the object of much adversegossip, but will finally prove her conduct orderly.HieroglyphsHieroglyphs seen in a dream, foretells that wavering judgment in some vital matter maycause you great distress and money loss. To be able to read them, your success inovercoming some evil is foretold.High SchoolTo dream of a high school, foretells ascension to more elevated positions in love, as wellas social and business affairs. For a young woman to be suspended from a high school,foretells she will have troubles in social circles.High TideTo dream of high tide is indicative of favorable progression in your affairs.HillsTo dream of climbing hills is good if the top is reached, but if you fall back, you willhave much envy and contrariness to fight against.See Ascend.HipsTo dream that you admire well-formed hips, denotes that you will be upbraided by yourwife.For a woman to admire her hips, shows she will be disappointed in love matters.

To notice fat hips on animals, foretells ease and pleasure.For a woman to dream that her hips are too narrow, omens sickness and disappointments.If too fat, she is in danger of losing her reputation.HissingTo dream of hissing persons, is an omen that you will be displeased beyond endurance atthe discourteous treatment shown you while among newly made acquaintances. If theyhiss you, you will be threatened with the loss of a friend.HistoryTo dream that you are reading history, indicates a long and pleasant recreation.HivesTo dream that your child is affected with hives, denotes that it will enjoy good health andbe docile.To see strange children thus affected, you will be unduly frightened over the condition ofsome favorite.HoeTo dream of seeing a hoe, denotes that you will have no time for idle pleasures, as therewill be others depending upon your work for subsistence.To dream of using a hoe, you will enjoy freedom from poverty by directing your energyinto safe channels.For a woman to dream of hoeing, she will be independent of others, as she will beself-supporting. For lovers, this dream is a sign of faithfulness.To dream of a foe striking at you with a hoe, your interests will be threatened byenemies, but with caution you will keep aloof from real danger.HogsTo dream of seeing fat, strong-looking hogs, foretells brisk changes in business and safedealings. Lean hogs predict vexatious affairs and trouble with servants and children.To see a sow and litter of pigs, denotes abundant crops to the farmer, and advance in theaffairs of others.To hear hogs squealing, denotes unpleasant news from absent friends, and foretells disappointment by death, or failure to realize the amounts you expected in deals ofimportance.To dream of feeding your own hogs, denotes an increase in your personal belongings.To dream that you are dealing in hogs, you will accumulate considerable property, butyou will have much rough work to perform.HolidayTo dream of a holiday, foretells interesting strangers will soon partake of yourhospitality. For a young woman to dream that she is displeased with a holiday, denotesshe will be fearful of her own attractions in winning a friend back from a rival.Holy CommunionTo dream that you are taking part in the Holy Communion, warns you that you willresign your independent opinions to gain some frivolous desire.If you dream that there is neither bread nor wine for the supper, you will find that youhave suffered your ideas to be proselytized in vain, as you are no nearer your goal.If you are refused the right of communion and feel worthy, there is hope for yourobtaining some prominent position which has appeared extremely doubtful, as youropponents are popular and powerful. If you feel unworthy, you will meet with muchdiscomfort.To dream that you are in a body of Baptists who are taking communion, denotes that youwill find that your friends are growing uncongenial, and you will look to strangers forharmony.HomeTo dream of visiting your old home, you will have good news to rejoice over.To see your old home in a dilapidated state, warns you of the sickness or death of arelative. For a young woman this is a dream of sorrow. She will lose a dear friend.To go home and find everything cheery and comfortable, denotes harmony in the presenthome life and satisfactory results in business.See Abode.HominyTo dream of hominy, denotes pleasant love-making will furnish you interestingrecreation from absorbing study and planning for future progression.

HomesickTo dream of being homesick, foretells you will lose fortunate opportunities to enjoytravels of interest and pleasant visits.HomicideTo dream that you commit homicide, foretells that you will suffer great anguish andhumiliation through the indifference of others, and your gloomy surroundings will causeperplexing worry to those close to you.To dream that a friend commits suicide, you will have trouble in deciding a veryimportant question.See Kill.HoneyTo dream that you see honey, you will be possessed of considerable wealth.To see strained honey, denotes wealth and ease, but there will be an undercurrent in yourlife of unlawful gratification of material desires.To dream of eating honey, foretells that you will attain wealth and love. To lovers, thisindicates a swift rush into marital joys.HoneysuckleTo see or gather, honeysuckles, denotes that you will be contentedly prosperous and yourmarriage will be a singularly happy one.HoodFor a young woman to dream that she is wearing a hood, is a sign she will attempt toallure some man from rectitude and bounden duty.HookTo dream of a hook, foretells unhappy obligations will be assumed by you.HoopTo dream of a hoop, foretells you will form influential friendships. Many will seekcounsel of you. To jump through, or see others jumping through hoops, denotes you willhave discouraging outlooks, but you will overcome them with decisive victory.

HopsTo dream of hops, denotes thrift, energy and the power to grasp and master almost anybusiness proposition. Hops is a favorable dream to all classes, lovers and tradesmen.HornTo dream that you hear the sound of a horn, foretells hasty news of a joyful character.To see a broken horn, denotes death or accident.To see children playing with horns, denotes congeniality in the home.For a woman to dream of blowing a horn, foretells that she is more anxious for marriagethan her lover.HornetTo dream of a hornet, signals disruption to lifelong friendship, and loss of money.For a young woman to dream that one stings her, or she is in a nest of them, foretells thatmany envious women will seek to disparage her before her admirers.HoroscopeTo dream of having your horoscope drawn by an astrologist, foretells unexpectedchanges in affairs and a long journey; associations with a stranger will probably happen.If the dreamer has the stars pointed out to him, as his fate is being read, he will finddisappointments where fortune and pleasure seem to await him.HorseIf you dream of seeing or riding a white horse, the indications are favorable for prosperityand pleasurable commingling with congenial friends and fair women. If the white horseis soiled and lean, your confidence will be betrayed by a jealous friend or a woman. If thehorse is black, you will be successful in your fortune, but you will practice deception, andwill be guilty of assignations. To a woman, this dream denotes that her husband isunfaithful.To dream of dark horses, signifies prosperous conditions, but a large amount ofdiscontent. Fleeting pleasures usually follow this dream.To see yourself riding a fine bay horse, denotes a rise in fortune and gratification ofpassion. For a woman, it foretells a yielding to importunate advances. She will enjoymaterial things.

To ride or see passing horses, denotes ease and comfort.To ride a runaway horse, your interests will be injured by the folly of a friend oremployer.To see a horse running away with others, denotes that you will hear of the illness offriends.To see fine stallions, is a sign of success and high living, and undue passion will masteryou.To see brood mares, denotes congeniality and absence of jealousy between the marriedsweethearts.To ride a horse to ford a stream, you will soon experience some good fortune and willenjoy rich pleasures. If the stream is unsettled or murky, anticipated joys will besomewhat disappointing.To swim on a horse's back through a clear and beautiful stream of water, your conceptionof passionate bliss will be swiftly realized. To a business man, this dream portends greatgain.To see a wounded horse, foretells the trouble of friends.To dream of a dead horse, signifies disappointments of various kinds.To dream of riding a horse that bucks, denotes that your desires will be difficult ofconsummation. To dream that he throws you, you will have a strong rival, and yourbusiness will suffer slightly through competition.To dream that a horse kicks you, you will be repulsed by one you love. Your fortune willbe embarrassed by ill health.To dream of catching a horse to bridle and saddle, or harness it, you will see a greatimprovement in business of all kinds, and people of all callings will prosper. If you fail tocatch it, fortune will play you false.To see spotted horses, foretells that various enterprises will bring you profit.To dream of having a horse shod, your success is assured. For a woman, this dreamomens a good and faithful husband.To dream that you shoe a horse, denotes that you will endeavor to and perhaps makedoubtful property your own.To dream of race horses, denotes that you will be surfeited with fast living, but to thefarmer this dream denotes prosperity.To dream that you ride a horse in a race, you will be prosperous and enjoy life.

To dream of killing a horse, you will injure your friends through selfishness.To mount a horse bareback, you will gain wealth and ease by hard struggles.To ride bareback in company with men, you will have honest people to aid you, and yoursuccess will be merited. If in company with women, your desires will be loose, and yourprosperity will not be so abundant as might be if women did not fill your heart.To curry a horse, your business interests will not be neglected for frivolous pleasures.To dream of trimming a horse's mane, or tail, denotes that you will be a good financier orfarmer. Literary people will be painstaking in their work and others will look after theirinterest with solicitude.To dream of horses, you will amass wealth and enjoy life to its fullest extent.To see horses pulling vehicles, denotes wealth with some incumbrance, and love will findobstacles.If you are riding up a hill and the horse falls but you gain the top, you will win fortune,though you will have to struggle against enemies and jealousy. If both the horse and youget to the top, your rise will be phenomenal, but substantial.For a young girl to dream that she rides a black horse, denotes that she should be dealtwith by wise authority. Some wishes will be gratified at an unexpected time. Black inhorses, signifies postponements in anticipations.To see a horse with a tender foot, denotes that some unexpected unpleasantness willinsinuate itself into your otherwise propitious state.If you attempt to fit a broken shoe which is too small for the horse's foot, you will becharged with making fraudulent deals with unsuspecting parties.To ride a horse down hill, your affairs will undoubtedly disappoint you. For a youngwoman to dream that a friend rides her on a horse, denotes that she will beforemost in the favors of many prominent and successful men. If she was frightened, sheis likely to stir up jealous sensations. If after she alights from the horse it turns into a pig,she will carelessly pass by honorable offers of marriage, preferring freedom until herchances of a desirable marriage are lost. If afterward she sees the pig sliding gracefullyalong the telegraph wire, she will by intriguing advance her position,For a young woman to dream that she is riding a white horse up and down hill, oftenlooking back and seeing some one on a black horse, pursuing her, denotes she will have amixed season of success and sorrow, but through it all a relentless enemy is working toovershadow her with gloom and disappointment.To see a horse in human flesh, descending on a hammock through the air, and as it nearsyour house is metamorphosed into a man, and he approaches your door and throwssomething at you which seems to be rubber but turns into great bees, denotes miscarriage

of hopes and useless endeavors to regain lost valuables. To see animals in human flesh,signifies great advancement to the dreamer, and new friends will be made by modestwearing of well-earned honors. If the human flesh appears diseased or freckled, themiscarriage of well-laid plans is denoted.HorseshoeTo dream of a horseshoe, indicates advance in business and lucky engagements forwomen.To see them broken, ill fortune and sickness is portrayed.To find a horseshoe hanging on the fence, denotes that your interests will advancebeyond your most sanguine expectations.To pick one up in the road, you will receive profit from a source you know not of.HorseradishTo dream of horseradish, foretells pleasant associations with intellectual and congenialpeople. Fortune is also expressed in this dream. For a woman, it indicates a rise above herpresent station.To eat horseradish, you will be the object of pleasant raillery.Horse-traderTo dream of a horse-trader, signifies great profit from perilous ventures.To dream that you are trading horses, and the trader cheats you, you will lose in trade orlove. If you get a better horse than the one you traded, you will better yourself in fortune.HospitalIf you dream that you are a patient in a hospital. you will have a contagious disease inyour community, and will narrowly escape affliction. If you visit patients there, you willhear distressing news of the absent.HotelTo dream of living in a hotel, denotes ease and profit.To visit women in a hotel, your life will be rather on a dissolute order.To dream of seeing a fine hotel, indicates wealth and travel.

If you dream that you are the proprietor of a hotel, you will earn all the fortune you willever possess.To work in a hotel, you could find a more remunerative employment than what you have.To dream of hunting a hotel, you will be baffled in your search for wealth and happiness.HoundsTo dream of hounds on a hunt, denotes coming delights and pleasant changes. For awoman to dream of hounds, she will love a man below her in station. To dream thathounds are following her, she will have many admirers, but there will be no real love feltfor her.See Dogs.HouseTo dream of building a house, you will make wise changes in your present affairs.To dream that you own an elegant house, denotes that you will soon leave your home fora better, and fortune will be kind to you.Old and dilapidated houses, denote failure in business or any effort, and declining health.See Building.HousekeeperTo dream that you are a housekeeper, denotes you will have labors which will occupyyour time, and make pleasure an ennobling thing. To employ one, signifies comparativecomfort will be possible for your obtaining.HuggingIf you dream of hugging, you will be disappointed in love affairs and in business.For a woman to dream of hugging a man, she will accept advances of a doubtfulcharacter from men.For a married woman to hug others than her husband, she will endanger her honor inaccepting attentions from others in her husband's absence.HumidityTo dream that you are overcome with humidity, foretells that you will combat enemies

fiercely, but their superior force will submerge you in overwhelming defeat.See Air.HunchbackTo dream of a hunchback, denotes unexpected reverses in your prospects.HungerTo dream that you are hungry, is an unfortunate omen. You will not find comfort andsatisfaction in your home, and to lovers it means an unhappy marriage.HuntingIf you dream of hunting, you will struggle for the unattainable.If you dream that you hunt game and find it, you will overcome obstacles and gain yourdesires.HurtIf you hurt a person in your dreams, you will do ugly work, revenging and injuring.If you are hurt, you will have enemies who will overcome you.HurricaneTo hear the roar and see a hurricane heading towards you with its frightful force, you willundergo torture and suspense, striving to avert failure and ruin in your affairs.If you are in a house which is being blown to pieces by a hurricane, and you struggle inthe awful gloom to extricate some one from the falling timbers, your life will suffer achange. You will move and remove to distant places, and still find no improvement indomestic or business affairs.If you dream of looking on de'bris and havoc wrought by a hurricane, you will comeclose to trouble, which will be averted by the turn in the affairs of others.To see dead and wounded caused by a hurricane, you will be much distressed over thetroubles of others.HusbandTo dream that your husband is leaving you, and you do not understand why, there will bebitterness between you, but an unexpected reconciliation will ensue. If he mistreats and

upbraids you for unfaithfulness, you will hold his regard and confidence, but otherworries will ensue and you are warned to be more discreet in receiving attention frommen.If you see him dead, disappointment and sorrow will envelop you.To see him pale and careworn, sickness will tax you heavily, as some of the family willlinger in bed for a time.To see him gay and handsome, your home will be filled with happiness and brightprospects will be yours. If he is sick, you will be mistreated by him and he will beunfaithful.To dream that he is in love with another woman, he will soon tire of his presentsurroundings and seek pleasure elsewhere.To be in love with another woman's husband in your dreams, denotes that you are nothappily married, or that you are not happy

unmarried, but the chances for happiness aredoubtful.For an unmarried
woman to dream that she has a husband, denotes that she is wanting inthe
graces which men most admire.To see your husband depart from you, and as
he recedes from you he grows larger,inharmonious surroundings will
prevent immediate congeniality. If disagreeableconclusions are avoided,
harmony will be reinstated.For a woman to dream she sees her husband in a
compromising position with anunsuspected party, denotes she will have
trouble through the indiscretion of friends. Ifshe dreams that he is
killed while with another woman, and a scandal ensues, she will bein
danger of separating from her husband or losing property. Unfavorable
conditionsfollow this dream, though the evil is often exaggerated.HutTo
dream of a hut, denotes indifferent success.To dream that you are
sleeping in a hut, denotes ill health and dissatisfaction.To see a hut in
a green pasture, denotes prosperity, but fluctuating happiness.HyacinthTo
dream that you see, or gather, hyacinths, you are about to undergo a
painful separationfrom a friend, which will ultimately result in good for
you.

HydrophobiaTo dream that you are afflicted with hydrophobia, denotes
enemies and change ofbusiness.To see others thus afflicted, your work
will be interrupted by death or ungratefuldependence.To dream that an
animal with the rabies bites you, you will be betrayed by your
dearestfriend, and much scandal will be brought to light.HyenaIf you see
a hyena in your dreams, you will meet much disappointment and much ill
luckin your undertakings, and your companions will be very uncongenial.
If lovers have thisdream, they will often be involved in quarrels.If one
attacks you, your reputation will be set upon by busybodies.HymnsTo dream
of hearing hymns sung, denotes contentment in the home and
averageprospects in business affairs.See Singing.HypocriteTo dream that
anyone has acted the hypocrite with you, you will be turned over to
yourenemies by false friends.To dream that you are a hypocrite, denotes
that you will prove yourself a deceiver and befalse to friends.HyssopTo
dream of hyssop, denotes you will have grave charges preferred against
you; and, if awoman, your reputation will be endangered.

IIceTo dream of ice, betokens much distress, and evil-minded persons will
seek to injure youin your best work.To see ice floating in a stream of

clear water, denotes that your happiness will beinterrupted by
ill-tempered and jealous friends.To dream that you walk on ice, you risk
much solid comfort and respect for evanescentjoys.For a young woman to
walk on ice, is a warning that only a thin veil hides her fromshame.To
see icicles on the eaves of houses, denotes misery and want of comfort.
Ill health isforeboded.To see icicles on the fence, denotes suffering
bodily and mentally.To see them on trees, despondent hopes will grow
gloomier.To see them on evergreens, a bright future will be overcast with
the shadow of doubtfulhonors.To dream that you make ice, you will make a
failure of your life through egotism andselfishness.Eating ice, foretells
sickness. If you drink ice-water, you will bring ill health
fromdissipation.Bathing in ice-water, anticipated pleasures will be
interrupted with an unforeseen event.

Ice CreamTo dream that you are eating ice cream, foretells you will have
happy success in affairsalready undertaken. To see children eating it,
denotes prosperity and happiness willattend you most favorably.For a
young woman to upset her ice cream in the presence of her lover or
friend, denotesshe will be flirted with because of her unkindness to
others.To see sour ice cream, denotes some unexpected trouble will
interfere with yourpleasures. If it is melted, your anticipated pleasure
will reach stagnation before it isrealized.IciclesTo see icicles falling
from trees, denotes that some distinctive misfortune, or trouble,
willsoon vanish.See Ice.IdealFor a young woman to dream of meeting her
ideal, foretells a season of uninterruptedpleasure and contentment.For a
bachelor to dream of meeting his ideal, denotes he will soon experience a
favorablechange in his affairs.IdiotIdiots in a dream, foretells
disagreements and losses.To dream that you are an idiot, you will feel
humiliated and downcast over themiscarriage of plans.To see idiotic
children, denotes affliction and unhappy changes in life.IdleIf you dream
of being idle, you will fail to accomplish your designs.To see your
friends in idleness, you will hear of some trouble affecting them.For a
young woman to dream that she is leading an idle existence, she will fall
into badhabits, and is likely to marry a shiftless man.

IdolsShould you dream of worshiping idols, you will make slow progress to
wealth or fame,as you will let petty things tyrannize over you.To break
idols, signifies a strong mastery over self, and no work will deter you
in yourupward rise to positions of honor.To see others worshiping idols,
great differences will rise up between you and warmfriends.To dream that
you are denouncing idolatry, great distinction is in store for you
throughyour understanding of the natural inclinations of the human
mind.IllnessFor a woman to dream of her own illness, foretells that some
unforeseen event will throwher into a frenzy of despair by causing her to

miss some anticipated visit orentertainment.See Sickness.IlluminationIf you see strange and weird illuminations in your dreams, you will meet withdisappointments and failures on every hand.Illuminated faces, indicate unsettled business, both private and official.To see the heavens illuminated, with the moon in all her weirdness, unnatural stars and ared sun, or a golden one, you may look for distress in its worst form. Death, familytroubles, and national upheavals will occur.To see children in the lighted heavens, warns you to control your feelings, as irrevocablewrong may be done in a frenzy of feeling arising over seeming neglect by your dear ones.To see illuminated human figures or animals in the heavens, denotes failure and trouble;dark clouds overshadow fortune. To see them fall to the earth and men shoot them withguns, many troubles and obstacles will go to nought before your energy anddetermination to rise.To see illuminated snakes, or any other creeping thing, enemies will surround you, anduse hellish means to overthrow you.

ImageIf you dream that you see images, you will have poor success in business or love.To set up an image in your home, portends that you will be weak minded and easily ledastray. Women should be careful of their reputation after a dream of this kind. If theimages are ugly, you will have trouble in your home.ImitationTo dream of imitations, means that persons are working to deceive you.For a young woman to dream some one is imitating her lover or herself, foretells she willbe imposed upon, and will suffer for the faults of others.ImplementsTo dream of implements, denotes unsatisfactory means of accomplishing some work. Ifthe implements are broken, you will be threatened with death or serious illness ofrelatives or friends, or failure n business.ImpsTo see imps in your dream, signifies trouble from what seems a passing pleasure.To dream that you are an imp, denotes that folly and vice will bring you to poverty.InaugurationTo dream of inauguration, denotes you will rise to higher position than you have yetenjoyed.For a young woman to be disappointed in attending an inauguration, predicts she will failto obtain her wishes.IncantationTo dream you are using incantations, signifies unpleasantness between husband and wife,or sweethearts. To hear others repeating them, implies dissembling among your friends.IncestTo dream of incestuous practices, denotes you will fall from honorable places, and willalso suffer loss in business.

IncoherentTo dream of incoherency, usually denotes extreme nervousness and excitement throughthe oppression of changing events.IncomeTo dream of coming into the possession of your income, denotes that you may deceivesome one and cause trouble to your family and friends.To dream that some of your family inherits an income, predicts success for you.For a woman to dream of losing her income, signifies disappointments in life.To dream that your income is insufficient to support you, denotes trouble to relatives orfriends.To dream of a portion of your income remaining, signifies that you will be verysuccessful for a short time, but you may expect more than you receive.IncreaseTo dream of an increase in your family, may denote failure in some of your plans, andsuccess to another.To dream of an increase in your business, signifies that you will overcome existingtroubles.IndependentTo dream that you are very independent, denotes that you have a rival who may do youan injustice.To dream that you gain an independence of wealth, you may not be so successful at thattime as you expect, but good results are promised.India RubberTo dream of India rubber, denotes unfavorable changes in your affairs. If you stretch it,you will try to establish a greater business than you can support.IndifferenceTo dream of indifference, signifies pleasant companions for a very short time.

For a young woman to dream that her sweetheart is indifferent to her, signifies that hemay not prove his affections in the most appropriate way. To dream that she is indifferentto him, means that she will prove untrue to him.IndigoTo see indigo in a dream, denotes you will deceive friendly persons in order to cheatthem out of their be longings.To see indigo water, foretells you will be involved in an ugly love affair.IndigestionTo dream of indigestion, indicates unhealthy and gloomy surroundings.IndestinctIf in your dreams you see objects indistinctly, it portends unfaithfulness in friendships,and uncertain dealings.IndulgenceFor a woman to dream of indulgence, denotes that she will not escape unfavorablecomment on her conduct.IndustryTo dream that you are industrious, denotes that you will be unusually active in planningand working out ideas to further your interests, and that you will be successful in yourundertakings.For a lover to dream of being industriously at work, shows he will succeed in business,and that his companion will advance his position.To see others busy, is favorable to the dreamer.InfantsTo dream of seeing a newly born infant, denotes pleasant surprises are nearing you.For a young woman to dream she has an infant, foretells she will be accused ofindulgence in immoral pastime.To see an infant swimming, portends a fortunate escape from some entanglement.

InfirmaryTo dream that you leave an infirmary, denotes your escape from wily enemies who willcause you much worry.See Hospital.InfirmitiesTo dream of infirmities, denotes misfortune in love and business; enemies are not to bemisunderstood, and sickness may follow.To dream that you see others infirm, denotes that you may have various troubles anddisappointments in business.InfluenceIf you dream of seeking rank or advancement through the influence of others, yourdesires will fail to materialize; but if you are in an influential position, your prospectswill assume a bright form.To see friends in high positions, your companions will be congenial, and you will be freefrom vexations.InheritanceTo dream that you receive an inheritance, foretells that you will be successful in easilyobtaining your desires.See Estate.InjuryTo dream of an injury being done to you, signifies that an unfortunate occurrence willsoon grieve and vex you.See Hurt.InkTo see ink spilled over one's clothing, many small and spiteful meannesses will bewrought you through envy.If a young woman sees ink, she will be slandered by a rival.

To dream that you have ink on your fingers, you will be jealous and seek to injure someone unless you exercise your better nature. If it is red ink, you will be involved in aserious trouble.To dream that you make ink, you will engage in a low and debasing business, and youwill fall into disreputable associations.To see bottles of ink in your dreams, indicates enemies and unsuccessful interests.Ink StandEmpty ink stands denote that you will narrowly escape public denunciation for somesupposed injustice.To see them filled with ink, if you are not cautious, enemies will succeed incalumniation.InnTo dream of an inn, denotes prosperity and pleasures, if the inn is commodious and wellfurnished.To be at a dilapidated and ill kept inn, denotes poor success, or mournful tasks, orunhappy journeys.InquestTo dream of an inquest, foretells you will be unfortunate in your friendships.InquisitionTo dream of an inquisition, bespeaks for you an endless round of trouble and greatdisappointment.If you are brought before an inquisition on a charge of wilfulness, you will be unable todefend yourself from malicious slander.InsaneTo dream of being insane, forebodes disastrous results to some newly undertaken work,or ill health may work sad changes in your prospects.To see others insane, denotes disagreeable contact with suffering and appeals from thepoverty-stricken. The utmost care should be taken of the health after this dream.

InscriptionTo dream you see an inscription, foretells you will shortly receive unpleasantcommunications. If you are reading them on tombs, you will be distressed by sickness ofa grave nature. To write one, you will lose a valued friend.InsolventIf you dream that you are insolvent, you will not have to resort to this means to squareyourself with the world, as your energy and pride will enable you to transact business in afair way. But other worries may sorely afflict you.To dream that others are insolvent, you will meet with honest men in your dealings, butby their frankness they may harm you. For a young woman, it means her sweetheart willbe honest and thrifty, but vexatious discords may arise in her affairs.IntemperanceTo dream of being intemperate in the use of your

intellectual forces, you will seek afterfoolish knowledge fail to benefit
yourself, and give pain and displeasure to your friends.If you are
intemperate in love, or other passions, you will reap disease or loss of
fortuneand esteem. For a young woman to thus dream, she will lose a lover
and incur thedispleasure of close friends.IntercedeTo intercede for some
one in your dreams, shows you will secure aid when you desire
itmost.IntermarryTo dream of intermarrying, denotes quarrels and
contentions which will precipitate youinto trouble and loss.InterpreterTo
dream of an interpreter, denotes you will undertake affairs which will
fail in profit.IntestineTo dream of seeing intestines, signifies you are
about to be visited by a grave calamity,which will remove some friend.To
see your own intestines, denotes grave situations are closing around you;
sickness of a

nature to affect you in your daily communications with others threatens
you. Probableloss, with much displeasure, is also denoted.If you think
you lay them upon something, which turns out to be a radiator, and
theybegin to grow hot and make you very uncomfortable, and you ask others
to assist you,and they refuse, it foretells unexpected calamity, which
will probably come in the form ofa desperate illness or a misfortune for
which you will be censured by those formerly yourfriends. You may have
trouble in extricating yourself from an unpromising
predicament.IntoxicationTo dream of intoxication, denotes that you are
cultivating your desires for illicitpleasures.InundationTo dream of
seeing cities or country submerged in dark, seething waters, denotes
greatmisfortune and loss of life through some dreadful calamity.To see
human beings swept away in an inundation, portends bereavements and
despair,making life gloomy and unprofitable.To see a large area inundated
with clear water, denotes profit and ease after seeminglyhopeless
struggles with fortune.See Food.InvalidTo dream of invalids, is a sign of
displeasing companions interfering with your interest.To think you are
one, portends you are threatened with displeasing
circumstances.InvectiveTo dream of using invectives, warns you of
passionate outbursts of anger, which mayestrange you from close
companions.To hear others using them, enemies are closing you in to
apparent wrong and deceits.InventorTo dream of an inventor, foretells you
will soon achieve some unique work which willadd honor to your name. To
dream that you are inventing something, or feel interested insome
invention, denotes you will aspire to fortune and will be successful in
your designs.

InviteTo dream that you invite persons to visit you, denotes that some
unpleasant event is near,and will cause worry and excitement in your
otherwise pleasant surroundings.If you are invited to make a visit, you

will receive sad news.For a woman to dream that she is invited to attend a party, she will have pleasantanticipations, but ill luck will mar them.IronTo dream of iron, is a harsh omen of distress.To feel an iron weight bearing you down, signifies mental perplexities and materiallosses.To strike with iron, denotes selfishness and cruelty to those dependent upon you.To dream that you manufacture iron, denotes that you will use unjust means toaccumulate wealth.To sell iron, you will have doubtful success, and your friends will not be of noblecharacter.To see old, rusty iron, signifies poverty and disappointment.To dream that the price of iron goes down, you will realize that fortune is a very unsafefactor in your life.If iron advances, you will see a gleam of hope in a dark prospectus.To see red-hot iron in your dreams, denotes failure for you by misapplied energy.IroningTo dream of ironing, denotes domestic comforts and orderly business.If a woman dreams that she burns her hands while ironing, it foretells she will haveillness or jealousy to disturb her peace. If she scorches the clothes, she will have a rivalwho will cause her much displeasure and suspicions. If the irons seem too cold, she willlack affection in her home.ItchTo see persons with the itch, and you endeavor to escape contact, you will stand in fearof distressing results when your endeavors will bring pleasant success.

If you dream you have the itch yourself, you will be harshly used, and will defendyourself by incriminating others. For a young woman to have this dream, omens she willfall into dissolute companionship. To dream that you itch, denotes unpleasant avocations.IvoryTo dream of ivory, is favorable to the fortune of the dreamer.To see huge pieces of ivory being carried, denotes financial success and pleasuresunalloyed.IvyTo dream of seeing ivy growing on trees or houses, predicts excellent health and increaseof fortune. Innumerable joys will succeed this dream. To a young woman, it augurs manyprized distinctions. If she sees ivy clinging to the wall in the moonlight, she will haveclandestine meetings with young men.Withered ivy, denotes broken engagements and sadness.JJackdawTo see a jackdaw, denotes ill health and quarrels. To catch one, you will outwit enemies.To kill one, you will come into possession of disputed property.JailTo see others in jail, you will be urged to grant privileges to persons whom you believeto be unworthy.To see negroes in jail, denotes worries and loss through negligence of underlings.For a young woman to dream that her lover is in jail, she will be disappointed in hischaracter, as he will prove a deceiver.See Gaol.

JailerTo see a jailer, denotes that treachery will embarrass your interests and evil women willenthrall you.To see a mob attempting to break open a jail, is a forerunner of evil, and desperatemeasures will be used to extort money and bounties from you.JamTo dream of eating jam, if

pure, denotes pleasant surprises and journeys.To dream of making jam,
foretells to a woman a happy home and appreciative friends.JanitorTo
dream of a janitor, denotes bad management and disobedient children.
Unworthyservants will annoy you.To look for a janitor and fail to find
him, petty annoyances will disturb your otherwiseplacid existence. If you
find him, you will have pleasant associations with strangers, andyour
affairs will have no hindrances.JanuaryTo dream of this month, denotes
you will be afflicted with unloved companions orchildren.JarTo dream of
empty jars, denotes impoverishment and distress.To see them full, you
will be successful.If you buy jars, your success will be precarious and
your burden will be heavy.To see broken jars, distressing sickness or
deep disappointment awaits you.JasperTo dream of seeing jasper, is a
happy omen, bringing success and love.For a young woman to lose a jasper,
is a sign of disagreement with her lover.

JaundiceTo dream that you have the jaundice, denotes prosperity after
temporary embarrassments.To see others with jaundice, you will be worried
with unpleasant companions anddiscouraging prospects.JavelinTo dream of
defending yourself with a javelin, your most private affairs will be
searchedinto to establish claims of dishonesty, and you will prove your
innocence after muchwrangling.If you are pierced by a javelin, enemies
will succeed in giving you trouble.To see others carrying javelins, your
interests are threatened.JawsTo dream of seeing heavy, misshapen jaws,
denotes disagreements, and ill feeling will beshown between friends.If
you dream that you are in the jaws of a wild beast, enemies will work
injury to youraffairs and happiness. This is a vexatious and perplexing
dream.If your own jaws ache with pain, you will be exposed to climatic
changes, and malariamay cause you loss in health and finances.JaybirdTo
dream of a jay-bird, foretells pleasant visits from friends and
interesting gossips.To catch a jay-bird, denotes pleasant, though
unfruitful, tasks.To see a dead jay-bird, denotes domestic unhappiness
and many vicissitudes.JealousyTo dream that you are jealous of your wife,
denotes the influence of enemies andnarrow-minded persons. If jealous of
your sweetheart, you will seek to displace a rival.If a woman dreams that
she is jealous of her husband, she will find many shockingincidents to
vex and make her happiness a travesty.If a young woman is jealous of her
lover, she will find that he is more favorablyimpressed with the charms
of some other woman than herself.

If men and women are jealous over common affairs, they will meet many
unpleasantworries in the discharge of every-day business.JellyTo dream of
eating jelly, many pleasant interruptions will take place.For a woman to
dream of making jelly, signifies she will enjoy pleasant reunions
withfriends.JessamineTo dream of jessamine, denotes you are approximating

some exquisite pleasure, butwhich will be fleeting.JesterTo dream of a jester, foretells you will ignore important things in looking after sillyaffairs.JewTo dream of being in company with a Jew, signifies untiring ambition and anirrepressible longing after wealth and high position, which will be realized to a verysmall extent.To have transactions with a Jew, you will prosper legally in important affairs.For a young woman to dream of a Jew, omens that she will mistake flattery for truth, andfind that she is only a companion for pleasure.For a man to dream of a Jewess, denotes that his desires run parallel with voluptuousnessand easy comfort. He should constitute himself woman's defender.For a Gentile to dream of Jews, signifies worldly cares and profit from dealing withthem.To argue with them, your reputation is endangered from a business standpoint.JewelryTo dream of broken jewelry, denotes keen disappointment in attaining one's highestdesires.If the jewelry be cankered, trusted friends will fail you, and business cares will be onyou.

JewelsTo dream of jewels, denotes much pleasure and riches.To wear them, brings rank and satisfied ambitions.To see others wearing them, distinguished places will be held by you, or by some friend.To dream of jeweled garments, betokens rare good fortune to the dreamer. Inheritance orspeculation will raise him to high positions.If you inherit jewelry, your prosperity will be unusual, but not entirely satisfactory.To dream of giving jewelry away, warns you that some vital estate is threatening you.For a young woman to dream that she receives jewelry, indicates much pleasure and adesirable marriage. To dream that she loses jewels, she will meet people who will flatterand deceive her.To find jewels, denotes rapid and brilliant advancement in affairs of interest. To givejewels away, you will unconsciously work detriment to yourself.To buy them, proves that you will be very successful in momentous affairs, especiallythose pertaining to the heart.Jew's-HarpTo dream of a Jew's-harp, foretells you will experience a slight improvement in youraffairs. To play one, is a sign that you will fall in love with a stranger.JigTo dance a jig, denotes cheerful occupations and light pleasures.To see negroes dancing a jig, foolish worries will offset pleasure.To see your sweetheart dancing a jig, your companion will be possessed with a merry andhopeful disposition.To see ballet girls dancing a jig, you will engage in undignified amusements and followlow desires.JockeyTo dream of a jockey, omens you will appreciate a gift from an unexpected source. For ayoung woman to dream that she associates with a jockey, or has one for a lover, indicatesshe will win a husband out of her station. To see one thrown from a horse, signifies you will be called on for aid by strangers.JollyTo dream that you feel jolly and are enjoying the merriment of companions, you willrealize pleasure from the good behavior of children and have satisfying results inbusiness. If there comes the least rift in the merriment, worry will intermingle with thesuccess of the future.JourneyTo dream that you go on a journey, signifies profit or a disappointment, as the travels arepleasing and successful or as accidents and disagreeable events take active part in yourjourneying.To see your friends start cheerfully on a journey, signifies delightful change and moreharmonious companions than you have heretofore known. If you see them depart lookingsad, it may be many moons before you see them again. Power and loss are implied.To make a long-distance journey in a much shorter time than you expected, denotes youwill accomplish some work in a surprisingly short time, which will be satisfactory in theway of reimbursement.JourneymanTo dream of a journeyman, denotes you are soon to lose money by useless travels. For awoman, this dream brings pleasant trips, though unexpected ones.JoyTo dream that you feel joy over any event, denotes harmony among friends.JubileeTo dream of a jubilee, denotes many pleasureable enterprises in which you will be aparticipant. For a young woman, this is a favorable dream, pointing to matrimony andincrease of temporal blessings.To dream of a religious jubilee, denotes close but comfortable environments.JudgeTo dream of coming before a judge, signifies that disputes will be settled by legalproceedings. Business or divorce cases may assume gigantic proportions. To have thecase decided in your favor, denotes a successful termination to the suit; if decided againstyou, then you are the aggressor and you should seek to right injustice.

Judgment DayTo dream of the judgment day, foretells that you will accomplish some well-plannedwork, if you appear resigned and hopeful of escaping punishment. Otherwise, your workwill prove a failure.For a young woman to appear before the judgment bar and hear the verdict of ``Guilty,''denotes that she will cause much distress among her friends by her selfish andunbecoming conduct. If she sees the dead rising, and all the earth solemnly and fearfullyawaiting the end, there will be much struggling for her, and her friends will refuse heraid. It is also a forerunner of unpleasant gossip, and scandal is threatened. Business mayassume hopeless aspects.JugIf you dream of jugs well filled with transparent liquids, your welfare is being consideredby more than yourself. Many true friends will unite to please and profit you. If the jugsare empty, your conduct will estrange you from friends and station.Broken jugs, indicate sickness and failures in employment.If you drink wine from a jug, you will enjoy robust health and find pleasure in all circles.Optimistic views will possess you.To take an unpleasant drink from a jug, disappointment and disgust will follow pleasantanticipations.JulyTo dream of this month, denotes you will be depressed with gloomy outlooks, but, assuddenly, your spirits will rebound to unimagined pleasure and good fortune.JumpingIf you dream of jumping over any object, you will succeed in every endeavor; but if youjump and fall back, disagreeable affairs will render life almost intolerable.To jump down from a wall, denotes reckless speculations and disappointment in love.Jumping-JackTo dream of a jumping-jack, denotes that idleness and trivial pastimes will occupy yourthoughts to the exclusion of serious and sustaining plans.

JuneTo dream of June, foretells unusual gains in all undertakings.For a woman to think that vegetation is decaying, or that a drouth is devastating the land,she will have sorrow and loss which will be lasting in its effects.JuniperTo dream of seeing a juniper tree, portends happiness and wealth out of sorrow anddepressed conditions. For a young woman, this dreams omens a bright future afterdisappointing love affairs. To the sick, this is an augury of speedy recovery.To eat, or gather, the berries of a juniper tree, foretells trouble and sickness.JuryTo dream that you are on the jury, denotes dissatisfaction with your employments, andyou will seek to materially change your position.If you are cleared from a charge by the jury, your business will be successful and affairswill move your way, but if you should be condemned, enemies will overpower you andharass you beyond endurance.JusticeTo dream that you demand justice from a person, denotes that you are threatened withembarrassments through the false statements of people who are eager for your downfall.If some one demands the same of you, you will find that your conduct and reputation arebeing assailed, and it will be extremely doubtful if you refute the charges satisfactorily.KKaleidoscopeKaleidoscopes working before you in a dream, portend swift changes with little offavorable promise in them.

KangarooTo see a kangaroo in your dreams, you will outwit a wily enemy who seeks to place youin an unfavorable position before the public and the person you are striving to win.If a kangaroo attacks you, your reputation will be in jeopardy. If you kill one, you willsucceed in spite of enemies and obstacles. To see a kangaroo's hide, denotes that you arein a fair way to success.KatydidsTo dream of hearing katydids, is a prognostic of misfortune and unusual dependence onothers. If any sick person ask you what they are, foretells there will be surprising eventsin your present and future.For a woman to see them, signifies she will have a quarrelsome husband or lover.KegTo dream of a keg, denotes you will have a struggle to throw off oppression. Brokenones, indicate separation from family or friends.KettlesTo see kettles in your dream, denotes great and laborious work before you.To see a kettle of boiling water, your struggles will soon end and a change will come toyou.To see a broken kettle, denotes failure after a mighty effort to work out a path to success.For a young woman to dream of handling dark kettles, foretells disappointment in loveand marriage; but a light-colored kettle brings to her absolute freedom from care, and herhusband will be handsome and worthy.To dream of keys, denotes unexpected changes.If the keys are lost, unpleasant adventures will affect you.To find keys, brings domestic peace and brisk turns to business.Broken keys, portends separation either through death or jealousy.For a young woman to dream of losing the key to any personal ornament, denotes shewill have quarrels with her lover, and will suffer much disquiet therefrom. If she dreamsof unlocking a door with a key, she will have a new lover and have over-confidence inhim. If she locks a door with a key, she will be successful in selecting a husband. If she

gives the key away, she will fail to use judgment in conversation and darken her ownreputation.KeyholeTo dream that you spy upon others through a keyhole, you will damage some person bydisclosing confidence. If you catch others peeping through a keyhole, you will have falsefriends delving into your private matters to advance themselves over you.To dream that you cannot find the keyhole, you will unconsciously injure a friend.KidTo dream of a kid, denotes you will not be over-scrupulous in your morals or pleasures.You will be likely to bring grief to some loving heart.KidneysTo dream about your kidneys, foretells you are threatened with a serious illness, or therewill be trouble in marriage relations for you.If they act too freely, you will be a party to some racy intrigue. If they refuse to performtheir work, there will be a sensation, and to your detriment. If you eat kidney-stew, someofficious person will cause you disgust in some secret lover affair.KillingTo dream of killing a defenseless man, prognosticates sorrow and failure in affairs.If you kill one in defense, or kill a ferocious beast, it denotes victory and a rise inposition.KingTo dream of a king, you are struggling with your might, and ambition is your master.To dream that you are crowned king, you will rise above your comrades and co-workers.If you are censured by a king, you will be reproved for a neglected duty.For a young woman to be in the presence of a king, she will marry a man whom she willfear. To receive favors from a king, she will rise to exalted positions and be congeniallywedded.

KissTo dream that you see children kissing, denotes happy reunions in families andsatisfactory work.To dream that you kiss your mother, you will be very successful in your enterprises, andbe honored and beloved by your friends.To kiss a brother or sister, denotes much pleasure and good in your association.To kiss your sweetheart in the dark, denotes dangers and immoral engagements.To kiss her in the light, signifies honorable intentions occupy your mind always inconnection with women.To kiss a strange woman, denotes loose morals and perverted integrity.To dream of kissing illicitly, denotes dangerous past-times. The indulgence of a lowpassion may bring a tragedy into well-thought-of homes.To see your rival kiss your sweetheart, you are in danger of losing her esteem.For married people to kiss each other, denotes that harmony is prized in the home life.To dream of kissing a person on the neck, denotes passionate inclinations and weakmastery of self.If you dream of kissing an enemy, you will make advance towards reconciliation with anangry friend.For a young woman to dream that some person sees her kiss her lover, indicates thatspiteful envy is entertained for her by a false friend. For her to see her lover kiss another,she will be disappointed in her hopes of marriage.KitchenTo dream of a kitchen, denotes you will be forced to meet emergencies which willdepress your spirits. For a woman to dream that her kitchen is clear. and orderly, foretellsshe will become the mistress of interesting fortunes.KiteTo dream of flying a kite, denotes a great show of wealth, or business, but with little truesoundness to it all.To see the kite thrown upon the ground, foretells disappointment and failure.

To dream of making a kite, you will speculate largely on small means and seek to win theone you love by misrepresentations.To see children flying kites, denotes pleasant and light occupation. If the kite ascendsbeyond the vision high hopes and aspirations will resolve themselves intodisappointments and loss.KittenFor a woman to dream of a beautiful fat, white kitten, omens artful deception will bepractised upon her, which will almost ensnare her to destruction, but her good sense andjudgment will prevail in warding off unfortunate complications. If the kittens are soiled,or colored and lean, she will be victimized into glaring indiscretions.To dream of kittens, denotes abominable small troubles and vexations will pursue andwork you loss, unless you kill the kitten, and then you will overcome these worries.To see snakes kill kittens, you have enemies who in seeking to injure you will work harmto themselves.See Cats.KnapsackTo see a knapsack while dreaming, denotes you will find your greatest pleasure awayfrom the associations of friends. For a woman to see an old dilapidated one, meanspoverty and disagreeableness for her.KneeTo dream that your knees are too large, denotes sudden ill luck for you. If they are stiffand pain you, swift and fearful calamity awaits you.For a woman to dream that she has well-formed and smooth knees, predicts she willhave many admirers, but none to woo her in wedlock.If they are soiled, sickness from dissipation is portended. If they are unshapely, unhappychanges in her fortune will displace ardent hopes.To dream of knees is an unfortunate omen.KnifeTo dream of a knife is bad for the dreamer, as it portends separation and quarrels, andlosses in affairs of a business character.

To see rusty knives, means dissatisfaction, and complaints of those in the home, andseparation of lovers.Sharp knives and highly polished, denotes worry. Foes are ever surrounding you.Broken knives, denotes

defeat whatever the pursuit, whether in love or business.To dream that
you are wounded with a knife, foretells domestic troubles, in
whichdisobedient children will figure largely. To the unmarried, it
denotes that disgrace mayfollow.To dream that you stab another with a
knife, denotes baseness of character, and youshould strive to cultivate a
higher sense of right.Knife GrinderTo dream of a knife grinder, foretells
unwarrantable liberties will be taken with yourpossessions. For a woman,
this omens unhappy unions and much drudgery.KnittingFor a woman to dream
of knitting, denotes that she will possess a quiet and peacefulhome,
where a loving companion and dutiful children delight to give
pleasure.For a man to be in a kniting-mill, indicates thrift and a solid
rise in prospects.For a young woman to dream of knitting, is an omen of a
hasty but propitious marriage.For a young woman to dream that she works
in a knitting-mill, denotes that she will havea worthy and loyal lover.
To see the mill in which she works dilapidated, she will meetwith
reverses in fortune and love.KnockerTo dream of using a knocker,
foretells you will be forced to ask aid and counsel ofothers.KnockingTo
hear knocking in your dreams, denotes that tidings of a grave nature will
soon bereceived by you. If you are awakened by the knocking, the news
will affect you the moreseriously.KnotsTo dream of seeing knots, denotes
much worry over the most trifling affairs. If your

sweetheart notices another, you will immediately find cause to censure
him.To tie a knot, signifies an independent nature, and you will refuse
to be nagged byill-disposed lover or friend.KrishnaTo see Krishna in your
dreams, denotes that your greatest joy will be in pursuit of
occultknowledge, and you will school yourself to the taunts of friends,
and cultivate aphilosophical bearing toward life and sorrow.LLabelTo
dream of a label, foretells you will let an enemy see the inside of your
private affairs,and will suffer from the negligence.LaborTo dream that
you watch domestic animals laboring under heavy burdens, denotes thatyou
will be prosperous, but unjust to your servants, or those employed by
you.To see men toiling, signifies profitable work, and robust health. To
labor yourself,denotes favorable outlook for any new enterprise, and
bountiful crops if the dreamer isinterested in farming.LaboratoryTo dream
of being in a laboratory, denotes great energies wasted in unfruitful
enterprisewhen you might succeed in some more practical business.If you
think yourself an alchemist, and try to discover a process to turn other
things intogold, you will entertain far-reaching and interesting
projects, but you will fail to reachthe apex of your ambition. Wealth
will prove a myth, and the woman you love will hold afalse position
towards you.LabyrinthIf you dream of a labyrinth, you will find yourself
entangled in intricate and perplexing

business conditions, and your wife will make the home environment intolerable; childrenand sweethearts will prove ill-tempered and unattractive.If you are in a labyrinth of night or darkness, it foretells passing, but agonizing sicknessand trouble.A labyrinth of green vines and timbers, denotes unexpected happiness from what wasseemingly a cause for loss and despair.In a network, or labyrinth of railroads, assures you of long and tedious journeys.Interesting people will be met, but no financial success will aid you on these journeys.LaceSee to it, if you are a lover, that your sweetheart wears lace, as this dream brings fidelityin love and a rise in position.If a woman dreams of lace, she will be happy in the realization of her most ambitiousdesires, and lovers will bow to her edict. No questioning or imperiousness on their part.If you buy lace, you will conduct an expensive establishment, but wealth will be a solidfriend.If you sell laces, your desires will outrun your resources.For a young girl to dream of making lace, forecasts that she will win a handsome,wealthy husband. If she dreams of garnishing her wedding garments with lace, she willbe favored with lovers who will bow to her charms, but the wedding will be far removedfrom her.LadderTo dream of a ladder being raised for you to ascend to some height, your energetic andnervy qualifications will raise you into prominence in business affairs.To ascend a ladder, means prosperity and unstinted happiness.To fall from one, denotes despondency and unsuccessful transactions to the tradesman,and blasted crops to the farmer.To see a broken ladder, betokens failure in every instance.To descend a ladder, is disappointment in business, and unrequited desires.To escape from captivity, or confinement, by means of a ladder, you will be successful,though many perilous paths may intervene.

To grow dizzy as you ascend a ladder, denotes that you will not wear new honorsserenely. You are likely to become haughty and domineering in your newly acquiredposition.See Hill, Ascend, Fall.LadleTo see a ladle in your dreams, denotes you will be fortunate in the selection of acompanion. Children will prove sources of happiness.If the ladle is broken or uncleanly, you will have a grievous loss.LagoonTo dream of a lagoon, denotes that you will be drawn into a whirlpool of doubt andconfusion through misapplication of your intelligence.LakeFor a young woman to dream that she is alone on a turbulent and muddy lake, foretellsmany vicissitudes are approaching her, and she will regret former extravagances, anddisregard of virtuous teaching.If the water gets into the boat, but by intense struggling she reaches the boat-housesafely, it denotes she will be under wrong persuasion, but will eventually overcome it,and rise to honor and distinction.It may predict the illness of some one near her.If she sees a young couple in the same position as herself, who succeed in rescuingthemselves, she will find that some friend has committed indiscretions, but will succeedin reinstating himself in her favor.To dream of sailing on a clear and smooth lake, with happy and congenial companions,you will have much happiness, and wealth will meet your demands.A muddy lake, surrounded with bleak rocks and bare trees, denotes unhappy terminationsto business and affection.A muddy lake, surrounded by green trees, portends that the moral in your nature willfortify itself against passionate desires, and overcoming the same will direct your energyinto a safe and remunerative channel. If the lake be clear and surrounded by barrenness, aprofitable existence will be marred by immoral and passionate dissipation.To see yourself reflected in a clear lake, denotes coming joys and many ardent friends.

To see foliaged trees reflected in the lake, you will enjoy to a satiety Love's draught ofpassion and happiness.To see slimy and uncanny inhabitants of the lake rise up and menace you, denotes failureand ill health from squandering time, energy and health on illicit pleasures. You willdrain the utmost drop of happiness, and drink deeply of Remorse's bitter concoction.LambTo dream of lambs frolicking in green pastures, betokens chaste friendships and joys.Bounteous and profitable crops to the farmers, and increase of possessions for others.To see a dead lamb, signifies sadness and desolation.Blood showing on the white fleece of a lamb, denotes that innocent ones will suffer frombetrayal through the wrong doing of others.A lost lamb, denotes that wayward people will be under your influence, and you shouldbe careful of your conduct.To see lamb skins, denotes comfort and pleasure usurped from others.To slaughter a lamb for domestic uses, prosperity will be gained through the sacrifice ofpleasure and contentment.To eat lamb chops, denotes illness, and much anxiety over the welfare of children.To see lambs taking nourishment from their mothers, denotes happiness through pleasantand intelligent home companions, and many lovable and beautiful children.To dream that dogs, or wolves devour lambs, innocent people will suffer at the hands ofinsinuating and designing villains.To hear the bleating of lambs, your generosity will be appealed to.To see them in a winter storm, or rain, denotes disappointment in expected enjoymentand betterment of fortune.To own lambs in your dreams, signifies that your environments will be pleasant andprofitable.If you carry lambs in your arms, you will be encumbered with happy cares upon whichyou will lavish a wealth of devotion, and no expense will be regretted in responding toappeals from the objects of your affection.To shear lambs, shows that you will be cold and mercenary. You will be honest, butinhumane.

For a woman to dream that she is peeling the skin from a lamb, and while doing so, shediscovers that it is her child, denotes that she will cause others sorrow which will alsorebound to her grief and loss.See Sheep.LameFor a woman to dream of seeing any one lame, foretells that her pleasures and hopes willbe unfruitful and disappointing.See Cripple.LamentTo dream that you bitterly lament the loss of friends, or property, signifies great strugglesand much distress, from which will spring causes for joy and personal gain.To lament the loss of relatives, denotes sickness or disappointments, which will bring you into closer harmony with companions, and will result in brighter prospects for the future. Lamp To see lamps filled with oil, denotes the demonstration of business activity, from which you will receive gratifying results. Empty lamps, represent depression and despondency To see lighted lamps burning with a clear flame, indicates merited rise in fortune and domestic bliss. If they give out a dull, misty radiance, you will have jealousy and envy, coupled with suspicion, to combat, in which you will be much pleased to find the right person to attack. To drop a lighted lamp, your plans and hopes will abruptly turn into failure. If it explodes, former friends will unite with enemies in damaging your interests. Broken lamps, indicate the death of relatives or friends. To light a lamp, denotes that you will soon make a change in your affairs, which will lead to profit. To carry a lamp, portends that you will be independent and self-sustaining, preferring your own convictions above others. If the light fails, you will meet with unfortunate conclusions, and perhaps the death of friends or relatives.

If you are much affrighted, and throw a bewildering light from your window, enemies will ensnare you with professions of friendship and interest in your achievements. To ignite your apparel from a lamp, you will sustain humiliation from sources from which you expected encouragement and sympathy, and your business will not be fraught with much good. Lamp-Post To see a lamp-post in your dreams, some stranger will prove your staunchiest friend in time of pressing need. To fall against a lamp-post, you will have deception to overcome, or enemies will ensnare you. To see a lamp-post across your path, you will have much adversity in your life. Lance To dream of a lance, denotes formidable enemies and injurious experiments. To be wounded by a lance, error of judgment will cause you annoyance. To break a lance, denotes seeming impossibilities will be overcome and your desires will be fulfilled. Land To dream of land, when it appears fertile, omens good; but if sterile and rocky, failure and dispondency is prognosticated. To see land from the ocean, denotes that vast avenues of prosperity and happiness will disclose themselves to you. Landau To dream that you ride in a landau, with your friend or sweetheart, denotes that incidents of a light, but pleasant character will pass in rapid succession through your life. If the vehicle is overturned, then pleasure will abruptly turn into woe See Fields. Lantern To dream of seeing a lantern going before you in the darkness, signifies unexpected

affluence. If the lantern is suddenly lost to view, then your success will take an unfavorable turn. To carry a lantern in your dreams, denotes that your benevolence will win you many friends. If it goes out, you fail to gain the prominence you wish. If you stumble and break it, you will seek to aid others, and in so doing lose your own station, or be disappointedin some undertaking.To clean a lantern, signifies great possibilities are open to you.To lose a lantern, means business depression, and disquiet in the home.If you buy a lantern, it signifies fortunate deals.For a young woman to dream that she lights her lover's lantern, foretells for her a worthyman, and a comfortable home. If she blows it out, by her own imprudence she will lose achance of getting married.LapTo dream of sitting on some person's lap, denotes pleasant security from vexingengagements. If a young woman dreams that she is holding a person on her lap, she willbe exposed to unfavorable criticism.To see a serpent in her lap, foretells she is threatened with humiliation at the hands ofenemies. If she sees a cat in her lap, she will be endangered by a seductive enemy.Lap DogTo dream of a lap dog, foretells you will be succored by friends in some approachingdilemma If it be thin and ill-looking, there will be distressing occurrences to detract fromyour prospects.Lap RobeTo dream of a lap robe, indicates suspicious engagements will place you under thesurveillance of enemies or friends.To lose one, your actions will be condemned by enemies to injure your affairs.LardTo dream of lard, signifies a rise in fortune will soon gratify you. For a woman to findher hand in melted lard, foretells her disappointment in attempting to rise in socialcircles.

LarkTo see larks flying, denotes high aims and purposes through the attainment of which youwill throw off selfishness and cultivate kindly graces of mind.To hear them singing as they fly, you will be very happy in a new change of abode, andbusiness will flourish.To see them fall to the earth and singing as they fall, despairing gloom will overtake youin pleasure's bewildering delights.A wounded or dead lark, portends sadness or death.To kill a lark, portends injury to innocence through wantonness.If they fly around and light on you, Fortune will turn her promising countenance towardsyou.To catch them in traps, you will win honor and love easily.To see them eating, denotes a plentiful harvest.LatchTo dream of a latch, denotes you will meet urgent appeals for aid, to which you willrespond unkindly. To see a broken latch, foretells disagreements with your dearest friend.Sickness is also foretold in this dream.LatinTo dream of studying this language, denotes victory and distinction in your efforts tosustain your opinion on subjects of grave interest to the public welfare.LaudanumTo dream that you take laudanum, signifies weakness of your own; and that you willhave a tendency to be unduly influenced by others. You should cultivate determination.To prevent others from taking this drug, indicates that you will be the means ofconveying great joy and good to people.To see your lover taking laudanum through disappointment, signifies unhappy affairs andthe loss of a friend.To give it, slight ailments will attack some member of your domestic circle.

LaughingTo dream that you laugh and feel cheerful, means success in your undertakings, andbright companions socially.Laughing immoderately at some weird object, denotes disappointment and lack ofharmony in your surroundings.To hear the happy laughter of children, means joy and health to the dreamer.To laugh at the discomfiture of others, denotes that you will wilfully injure your friendsto gratify your own selfish desires.To hear mocking laughter, denotes illness and disappointing affairs.LaundryTo dream of laundering clothes, denotes struggles, but a final victory in winning fortune.If the clothes are done satisfactorily, then your endeavors will bring complete happiness.If they come out the reverse, your fortune will fail to procure pleasure.To see pretty girls at this work, you will seek pleasure out of your rank.If a laundryman calls at your house, you are in danger of sickness, or of losing somethingvery valuable.To see laundry wagons, portends rivalry and contention.LaurelDreaming of the laurel, brings success and fame. You will acquire new possessions inlove. Enterprises will be laden with gain.For a young woman to wreath laurel about her lover's head, denotes that she will have afaithful man, and one of fame to woo her.Law and LawsuitsTo dream of engaging in a lawsuit, warns you of enemies who are poisoning publicopinion against you. If you know that the suit is dishonest on your part, you will seek todispossess true owners for your own advancement.If a young man is studying law, he will make rapid rise in any chosen profession.For a woman to dream that she engages in a law suit, means she will be calumniated, andfind enemies among friends.

See Judge and Jury.LawnsTo dream of walking upon well-kept lawns, denotes occasions for joy and greatprosperity.To join a merry party upon a lawn, denotes many secular amusements, and businessengagements will be successfully carried on.For a young woman to wait upon a green lawn for the coming of a friend or lover,denotes that her most ardent wishes concerning wealth and marriage will be gratified. Ifthe grass be dead and the lawn marshy, quarrels and separation may be expected.To see serpents crawling in the grass before you, betrayal and cruel insinuations will fillyou with despair.LawyerFor a young woman to dream that she is connected in any way with a lawyer, foretellsthat she will unwittingly commit indiscretions, which will subject her to unfavorable andmortifying criticism.See Attorney.LazyTo dream of feeling lazy, or acting so, denotes you will make a mistake in the formationof enterprises, and will suffer keen disappointment.For a young woman to think her lover is lazy, foretells she will have bad luck in securingadmiration. Her actions will discourage men who mean marriage.LeadTo dream of lead, foretells poor success in any engagement.A lead mine, indicates that your friends will look with suspicion on your money making.Your sweetheart will surprise you with her deceit and ill temper.To dream of lead ore, foretells distress and accidents. Business will assume a gloomycast.To hunt for lead, denotes discontentment, and a constant changing of employment.To melt lead, foretells that by impatience you will bring failure upon yourself and others.

LeakingTo dream of seeing a leak in anything, is usually significant of loss and vexations.LeapingFor a young woman to dream of leaping over an obstruction, denotes that she will gainher desires after much struggling and opposition.See Jumping.LearningTo dream of learning, denotes that you will take great interest in acquiring knowledge,and if you are economical of your time, you will advance far into the literary world.To enter halls, or places of learning, denotes rise from obscurity, and finance will be acongenial adherent.To see learned men, foretells that your companions will be interesting and prominent.For a woman to dream that she is associated in any way with learned people, she will beambitious and excel in her endeavors to rise into prominence.LeatherTo dream of leather, denotes successful business and favorable engagements withwomen. You will go into lucky speculations if you dream that you are dressed in leather.Ornaments of leather, denotes faithfulness in love and to the home.Piles of leather, denotes fortune and happiness.To deal in leather, signifies no change in the disposition of your engagements isnecessary for successful accumulation of wealth.LeavesTo dream of leaves, denotes happiness and wonderful improvement in your business.Withered leaves, indicate false hopes and gloomy forebodings will harass your spirit intoa whirlpool of despondency and loss.If a young woman dreams of withered leaves, she will be left lonely on the road toconjugality. Death is sometimes implied.

If the leaves are green and fresh, she will come into a legacy and marry a wealthy andprepossessing husband.LedgerTo dream of keeping a ledger, you will have perplexities and disappointing conditions tocombat.To dream that you make wrong entries on your ledger, you will have small disputes and aslight loss will befall you.To put a ledger into a safe, you will be able to protect your rights under adversecircumstances.To get your ledger misplaced, your interests will go awry through neglect of duty.To dream that your ledger gets destroyed by fire, you will suffer through the carelessnessof friends.To dream that you have a woman to keep your ledger, you will lose money trying tocombine pleasure with business.For a young woman to dream of ledgers, denotes she will have a solid business man tomake her a proposal of marriage.To dream that your ledger has worthless accounts, denotes bad management and losses;but if the accounts are good, then your business will assume improved conditions.LeechesTo dream of leeches, foretells that enemies will run over your interests.If they are applied to you for medicinal purposes, you will have a serious illness tn yourfamily (if you escape yourself).To see them applied to others, denotes sickness or trouble to friends.If they should bite you, there is danger for you in unexpected places, and you should heedwell this warning.LeewardTo dream of sailing leeward, denotes to the sailor a prosperous and merry voyage. Toothers, a pleasant journey.

LedgerdemainTo dream of practising legerdemain, or seeing others doing so, signifies you will beplaced in a position where your energy and power of planning will be called intostrenuous play to extricate yourself.LegislatureTo dream that you are a member of a legislature, foretells you will be vain of yourpossessions and will treat members of your family unkindly. You will have no realadvancement.LegsIf you dream of admiring well-shaped feminine legs, you will lose your judgment, andact very silly over some fair charmer.To see misshapen legs, denotes unprofitable occupations and ill-tempered comrades.A wounded leg, foretells losses and agonizing attacks of malaria.To dream that you have a wooden leg, denotes that you will bemean yourself in a falseway to your friends.If ulcers are on your legs, it signifies a drain on your income to aid others.To dream that you have three, or more, legs, indicates that more enterprises are plannedin your imagination than will ever benefit you.If you can't use your legs, it portends poverty.To have a leg amputated, you will lose valued friends, and the home influence will renderlife unbearable.For a young woman to admire her own legs, denotes vanity, and she will be repulsed bythe man she admires. If she has hairy legs, she will dominate her husband.If your own legs are clean and well shaped, it denotes a happy future and devoted friends.LemonadeIf you drink lemonade in a dream, you will concur with others in signifying someentertainment as a niggardly device to raise funds for the personal enjoyment of others atyour expense.

LemonsTo dream of seeing lemons on their native trees among rich foliage, denotes jealousytoward some beloved object, but demonstrations will convince you of the absurdity of thecharge.To eat lemons, foretells humiliation and disappointments.Green lemons, denotes sickness and contagion.To see shriveled lemons, denotes divorce, if married, and separation, to lovers.LendingTo dream that you are lending money, foretells difficulties in meeting payments of debtsand unpleasant influence in private.To lend other articles, denotes impoverishment through generosity.To refuse to lend things, you will be awake to your interests and keep the respect offriends.For others to offer to lend you articles, or money, denotes prosperity and closefriendships.LentilIf you dream of lentils, it denotes quarrels and unhealthy surroundings. For a youngwoman, this dream portends dissatisfaction with her lover, but parental advice will causeher to accept the inevitable.LeopardTo dream of a leopard attacking you, denotes that while the future seemingly promisesfair, success holds many difficulties through misplaced confidence.To kill one, intimates victory in your affairs.To see one caged, denotes that enemies will surround but fail to injure you.To see leopards in their native place trying to escape from you, denotes that you will beembarrassed in business or love, but by persistent efforts you will overcome difficulties.To dream of a leopard's skin, denotes that your interests will be endangered by adishonest person who will win your esteem.

LeprosyTo dream that you are infected with this dread disease, foretells sickness, by which youwill lose money and incur the displeasure of others.If you see others afflicted thus, you will meet discouraging prospects and love will turninto indifference.LetterTo dream that you see a registered letter, foretells that some money matters will disruptlong-established relations.For a young woman to dream that she receives such a letter, intimates that she will beoffered a competency, but it will not be on strictly legal, or moral grounds; others mayplay towards her a dishonorable part.To the lover, this bears heavy presentments of disagreeable mating. His sweetheart willcovet other gifts than his own.To dream of an anonymous letter, denotes that you will receive injury from anunsuspected source.To write one, foretells that you will be jealous of a rival, whom you admit to be yoursuperior.To dream of getting letters bearing unpleasant news, denotes difficulties or illness. If thenews is of a joyous character, you will have many things to be thankful for. If the letter isaffectionate, but is written on green, or colored, paper, you will be slighted in love andbusiness. Despondency will envelop you. Blue ink, denotes constancy and affection, alsobright fortune.Red colors in a letter, imply estrangements through suspicion and jealousy, but this maybe overcome by wise maneuvering of the suspected party.If a young woman dreams that she receives a letter from her lover and places it near herheart, she will be worried very much by a good-looking rival. Truthfulness is oftenrewarded with jealousy.If you fail to read the letter, you will lose something either in a business or social way.Letters nearly always bring worry.To have your letter intercepted, rival enemies are working to defame you.To dream of trying to conceal a letter from your sweetheart or wife, intimates that youare interested in unworthy occupations.

To dream of a letter with a black border, signifies distress and the death of some relative.To receive a letter written on black paper with white ink, denotes that gloom anddisappointment will assail you, and friendly interposition will render small relief. If theletter passes between husband and wife, it means separation under sensational charges. Iflovers, look for quarrels and threats of suicide. To business people, it denotesenviousness and covetousness.To dream that you write a letter, denotes that you will be hasty in condemning some oneon suspicion, and regrets will follow.A torn letter, indicates that hopeless mistakes may ruin your reputation.To receive a letter by hand, denotes that you are acting ungenerously towards yourcompanions or sweetheart, and you also are not upright in your dealings.To dream often of receiving a letter from a friend, foretells his arrival, or you will hearfrom him by letter or otherwise.Letter-CarrierIf you dream of a letter-carrier coming with your letters, you will soon receive news ofan unwelcome and an unpleasant character.To hear his whistle, denotes the unexpected arrival of a visitor.If he passes without your mail, disappointment and sadness will befall you.If you give him letters to mail, you will suffer injury through envy or jealousy.To converse with a letter-carrier, you will implicate yourself in some scandalousproceedings.Letter FileTo see a letter file in your dreams, is significant of important news, which will cause youan irksome journey. For a woman, this dream implies distressful news and unfaithfulfriends.LettuceTo see lettuce growing green and thrifty, denotes that you will enjoy some greatly desiredgood, after an unimportant embarrassment.If you eat lettuce, illness will separate you from your lover or companion, or perhaps itmay be petty jealousy.

For a woman to dream of sowing lettuce, portends she will be the cause of her own earlysickness or death.To gather it, denotes your superabundant sensitiveness, and that your jealous dispositionwill cause you unmitigated distress and pain.To buy lettuce, denotes that you will court your own downfall.LiarTo dream of thinking people are liars, foretells you will lose faith in some scheme whichyou had urgently put forward. For some one to call you a liar, means you will havevexations through deceitful persons.For a woman to think her sweetheart a liar, warns her that her unbecoming conduct islikely to lose her a valued friend.LibraryTo dream that you are in a library, denotes that you will grow discontented with yourenvironments and associations and seek companionship in study and the exploration ofancient customs.To find yourself in a library for other purpose than study, foretells that your conduct willdeceive your friends, and where you would have them believe that you had literaryaspirations, you will find illicit assignations.LiceA dream of lice contains much waking worry and distress. It often implies offensiveailments.Lice on stock, foretells famine and loss.To have lice on your body, denotes that you will conduct yourself unpleasantly with youracquaintances.To dream of catching lice, foretells sickness, and that you will cultivate morbidity.LicenseTo dream of a license, is an omen of disputes and loss. Married women will exasperateyour cheerfulness. For a woman to see a marriage license, foretells that she will soonenter unpleasant bonds, which will humiliate her pride.

Life-boatTo dream of being in a life-boat, denotes escape from threatened evil.To see a life-boat sinking, friends will contribute to your distress.To be lost in a life-boat, you will be overcome with trouble, in which your friends willbe included to some extent. If you are saved, you will escape a great calamity.Life-insurance ManTo see life-insurance men in a dream, means that you are soon to meet a stranger whowill contribute to your business interests, and change in your home life is foreshadowed,as interests will be mutual.If they appear distorted or unnatural, the dream is more unfortunate than good.LightIf you dream of light, success will attend you. To dream of weird light, or if the lightgoes out, you will be disagreeably surprised by some undertaking resulting in nothing.To see a dim light, indicates partial success.LighthouseIf you see a lighthouse through a storm, difficulties and grief will assail you, but they willdisperse before prosperity and happiness.To see a lighthouse from a placid sea, denotes calm joys and congenial friends.LightningLightning in your dreams, foreshadows happiness and prosperity of short duration.If the lightning strikes some object near you, and you feel the shock, you will bedamaged by the good fortune of a friend, or you may be worried by gossipers andscandalmongers.To see livid lightning parting black clouds, sorrow and difficulties will follow close on tofortune.If it strikes you, unexpected sorrows will overwhelm you in business or love.To see the lightning above your head, heralds the advent of joy and gain.

To see lightning in the south, fortune will hide herself from you for awhile.If in the southwest, luck will come your way. In the west, your prospects will be brighterthan formally. In the north, obstacles will have to be removed before your prospects willbrighten up. If in the east, you will easily win favors and fortune. Lightning from darkand ominous-looking clouds, is always a forerunner of threats, of loss and ofdisappointments. Business men should stay close to business, and women near theirhusbands or mothers; children and the sick should be looked after closely.Lightning-rodTo see a lightning-rod, denotes that threatened destruction to some cherished work willconfront you. To see one change into a serpent, foretells enemies will succeed in theirschemes against you. If the lightning strikes one, there will be an accident or suddennews to give you sorrow.If you are having one put up, it is a warning to beware how you begin a new enterprise,as you will likely be overtaken by disappointment.To have them taken down, you will change your plans and thereby further your interests.To see many lightning rods, indicates a variety of misfortunes.LilyTo dream of a lily, denotes much chastisement through illness and death. To see liliesgrowing with their rich foliage, denotes early marriage to the young and subsequentseparation through death.To see little children among the flowers, indicates sickness and fragile constitutions tothese little ones.For a young woman to dream of admiring, or gathering, lilies, denotes much sadnesscoupled with joy, as the one she loves will have great physical suffering, if not an earlydissolution. If she sees them withered, sorrow is even nearer than she could havesuspected.To dream that you breathe the fragrance of lilies, denotes that sorrow will purify andenhance your mental qualities.LimeTo dream of lime, foretells that disaster will prostrate you for a time, but you will reviveto greater and richer prosperity than before.

Lime-kilnTo dream of a lime-kiln, foretells the immediate future holds no favor for speculations inlove or business.LimesTo dream of eating limes, foretells continued sickness and adverse straits.LimpTo dream that you limp in your walk, denotes that a small worry will unexpectedlyconfront you, detracting much from your enjoyment.To see others limping, signifies that you will be naturally offended at the conduct of afriend. Small failures attend this dream.See Cripple and Lamed.LinenTo see linen in your dream, augurs prosperity and enjoyment.If a person appears to you dressed in linen garments, you will shortly be the recipient ofjoyful tidings in the nature of an inheritance.If you are apparelled in clean, fine linen, your fortune and fullest enjoyment in life isassured. If it be soiled, sorrow and ill luck will be met with occasionally, mingled withthe good in your life.Linseed OilTo see linseed oil in your dreams, denotes your impetuous extravagance will be checkedby the kindly interference of a friend.LionTo dream of a lion, signifies that a great force is driving you.If you subdue the lion, you will be victorious in any engagement.If it overpowers you, then you will be open to the successful attacks of enemies.To see caged lions, denotes that your success depends upon your ability to cope withopposition.

To see a man controlling a lion in its cage, or out denotes success in business and greatmental power. You will be favorably regarded by women.To see young lions, denotes new enterprises, which will bring success if properlyattended.For a young woman to dream of young lions, denotes new and fascinating lovers.For a woman to dream that she sees Daniel in the lions' den, signifies that by herintellectual qualifications and personal magnetism she will win fortune and lovers to herhighest desire.To hear the roar of a lion, signifies unexpected advancement and preferment withwomen.To see a lion's head over you, showing his teeth by snarls, you are threatened with defeatin your upward rise to power.To see a lion's skin, denotes a rise to fortune and happiness.To ride one, denotes courage and persistency in surmounting difficulties.To dream you are defending your children from a lion with a pen-knife, foretellsenemies will threaten to overpower you, and will well nigh succeed if you allow anyartfulness to persuade you for a moment from duty and business obligations.LipsTo dream of thick, unsightly lips, signifies disagreeable encounters, hasty decision, andill temper in the marriage relation.Full, sweet, cherry lips, indicates harmony and affluence. To a lover, it augursreciprocation in love, and fidelity.Thin

lips, signifies mastery of the most intricate subjects.Sore, or swollen
lips, denotes privations and unhealthful desires.LiquorTo dream of buying
liquor, denotes selfish usurpation of property upon which you haveno
legal claim If you sell it, you will be criticised for niggardly
benevolence.To drink some, you will come into doubtful possession of
wealth, but your generositywill draw around you convivial friends, and
women will seek to entrance and hold you.To see liquor in barrels,
denotes prosperity, but unfavorable tendency toward makinghome pleasant.

If in bottles, fortune will appear in a very tangible form.For a woman to
dream of handling, or drinking liquor, foretells for her a happyBohemian
kind of existence. She will be good natured but shallow minded. To
treatothers, she will be generous to rivals, and the indifference of
lovers or husband will notseriously offset her pleasures or
contentment.LiverTo dream of a disordered liver, denotes a querulous
person will be your mate, andfault-finding will occupy her time, and
disquiet will fill your hours.To dream of eating liver, indicates that
some deceitful person has installed himself in theaffection of your
sweetheart.LizardTo dream of lizards, foretells attacks upon you by
enemies.If you kill a lizard, you will regain your lost reputation or
fortune; but if it should escape,you will meet vexations and crosses in
love and business.For a woman to dream that a lizard crawls up her skirt,
or scratches her, she will havemuch misfortune and sorrow. Her husband
will be a victim to invalidism and she will beleft a widow, and little
sustenance will be eked out by her own labors.LoadTo dream that you carry
a load, signifies a long existence filled with labors of love
andcharity.To fall under a load, denotes your inability to attain
comforts that are necessary to thoselooking to you for subsistence.To see
others thus engaged, denotes trials for them in which you will be
interested.LoadstoneTo dream of a loadstone, denotes you will make
favorable opportunities for your ownadvancement in a material way. For a
young woman to think a loadstone is attracting her,is an omen of happy
changes in her family.LoavesTo dream of loaves of bread, denotes
frugality. If they be of cake, the dreamer has causeto rejoice over his
good fortune, as love and wealth will wait obsequiously upon you.

Broken loaves, bring discontent and bickerings between those who love.To
see loaves multiply phenomenally, prognosticates great success. Lovers
will be happyin their chosen ones.LobsterTo dream of seeing lobsters,
denotes great favors, and riches will endow you.If you eat them, you will
sustain contamination by associating too freely withpleasure-seeking
people.If the lobsters are made into a salad, success will not change
your generous nature, butyou will enjoy to the fullest your ideas of
pleasure.To order a lobster, you will hold prominent positions and

command many subordinates.LockTo dream of a lock, denotes bewilderment. If the lock works at your command, or efforts,you will discover that some person is working you injury. If you are in love, you will findmeans to aid you in overcoming a rival; you will also make a prosperous journey.If the lock resists your efforts, you will be derided and scorned in love and perilousvoyages will bring to you no benefit.To put a lock upon your fiance'e's neck and arm, foretells that you are distrustful of herfidelity, but future episodes will disabuse your mind of doubt.LocketIf a young woman dreams that her lover places a locket around her neck, she will be therecipient of many beautiful offerings, and will soon be wedded, and lovely children willcrown her life. If she should lose a locket, death will throw sadness into her life.If a lover dreams that his sweetheart returns his locket, he will confront disappointingissues. The woman he loves will worry him and conduct herself in a displeasing waytoward him.If a woman dreams that she breaks a locket, she will have a changeable and unstablehusband, who will dislike constancy in any form, be it business or affection.LockjawTo dream that you have lockjaw, signifies there is trouble ahead for you, as some personis going to betray your confidence. For a woman to see others with lockjaw, foretells herfriends will unconsciously detract from her happiness by assigning her unpleasant tasks.

If stock have it, you will lose a friend.LocomotiveTo dream of a locomotive running with great speed, denotes a rapid rise in fortune, andforeign travel. If it is disabled, then many vexations will interfere with business affairs,and anticipated journeys will be laid aside through the want of means.To see one completely demolished, signifies great distress and loss of property.To hear one coming, denotes news of a foreign nature. Business will assume changes thatwill mean success to all classes.To hear it whistle, you will be pleased and surprised at the appearance of a friend whohas been absent, or an unexpected offer, which means preferment to you.LocustTo dream of locusts, foretells discrepancies will be found in your business, for which youwill worry and suffer. For a woman, this dream foretells she will bestow her affectionsupon ungenerous people.LodgerFor a woman to dream that she has lodgers, foretells she will be burdened withunpleasant secrets. If one goes away without paying his bills, she will have unexpectedtrouble with men. For one to pay his bill, omens favor and accumulation of money.Looking-glassFor a woman to dream of a looking-glass, denotes that she is soon to be confronted withshocking deceitfulness and discrepancies, which may result in tragic scenes orseparations.See Mirror.LoomTo dream of standing by and seeing a loom operated by a stranger, denotes muchvexation and useless irritation from the talkativeness of those about you. Somedisappointment with happy expectations are coupled with this dream.To see good-looking women attending the loom, denotes unqualified success to those inlove. It predicts congenial pursuits to the married. It denotes you are drawing closertogether in taste.

For a woman to dream of weaving on an oldtime loom, signifies that she will have athrifty husband and beautiful children will fill her life with happy solicitations.To see an idle loom, denotes a sulky and stubborn person, who will cause you muchanxious care.Lord's PrayerTo dream of repeating the Lord's Prayer, foretells that you are threatened with secret foesand will need the alliance and the support of friends to tide you over difficulties.To hear others repeat it, denotes the danger of some friend.LotteryTo dream of a lottery, and that you are taking great interest in the drawing, you willengage in some worthless enterprise, which will cause you to make an unpropitiousjourney. If you hold the lucky number, you will gain in a speculation which will perplexand give you much anxiety.To see others winning in a lottery, denotes convivialities and amusements, bringing manyfriends together.If you lose in a lottery, you will be the victim of designing persons. Gloomy depressionsin your affairs will result.For a young woman to dream of a lottery in any way, denotes that her careless way ofdoing things will bring her disappointment, and a husband who will not be altogetherreliable or constant.To dream of a lottery, denotes you will have unfavorable friendships in business. Yourlove affairs will produce temporary pleasure.LouseTo dream of a louse, foretells that you will have uneasy feelings regarding your health,and an enemy will give you exasperating vexation.See Lice.LoveTo dream of loving any object, denotes satisfaction with your present environments.To dream that the love of others fills you with happy forebodings, successful affairs willgive you contentment and freedom from the anxious cares of life. If you find that yourlove fails, or is not reciprocated, you will become despondent over some conflicting

question arising in your mind as to whether it is best to change your mode of living or tomarry and trust fortune for the future advancement of your state.For a husband or wife to dream that their companion is loving, foretells great happinessaround the hearthstone, and bright children will contribute to the sunshine of the home.To dream of the love of parents, foretells uprightness in character and a continualprogress toward fortune and elevation.The love of animals, indicates contentment with what you possess, though you may notthink so. For a time, fortune will crown you.LovelyDreaming of lovely things, brings favor to all persons connected with you.For a lover to dream that his sweetheart is lovely of person and character, foretells forhim a speedy and favorable marriage.If through the vista of dreams you see your own fair loveliness, fate bids you, with agleaming light, awake to happiness.LozengesTo dream of lozenges, foretells success in small matters. For a woman to eat or throwthem away, foretells her life will be harassed by little spites from the envious.LuckyTo dream of being lucky, is highly favorable to the dreamer. Fulfilment of wishes may beexpected and pleasant duties will devolve upon you.To the despondent, this dream forebodes an uplifting and a renewal of prosperity.LuggageTo dream of luggage, denotes unpleasant cares. You will be encumbered with peoplewho will prove distasteful to you.If you are carrying your own luggage, you will be so full of your own distresses that youwill be blinded to the sorrows of others.To lose your luggage, denotes some unfortunate speculation or family dissensions To theunmarried, it foretells broken engagements.

LumberTo dream of lumber, denotes many difficult tasks and but little remuneration or pleasure.To see piles of lumber burning, indicates profit from an unexpected source.To dream of sawing lumber, denotes unwise transactions and unhappiness.LuteTo dream of playing on one, is auspicious of joyful news from absent friends.Pleasant occupations follow the dreaming of hearing the music of a lute.LuxuryTo dream that you are surrounded by luxury, indicates much wealth, but dissipation andlove of self will reduce your income.For a poor woman to dream that she enjoys much luxury, denotes an early change in hercircumstances.LyingTo dream that you are lying to escape punishment, denotes that you will act dishonorablytowards some innocent person.Lying to protect a friend from undeserved chastisement, denotes that you will have manyunjust criticisms passed upon your conduct, but you will rise above them and enjoyprominence.To hear others lying, denotes that they are seeking to entrap you. Lynx.To dream of seeing a lynx, enemies are undermining your business and disrupting yourhome affairs. For a woman, this dream indicates that she has a wary woman rivaling herin the affections of her lover. If she kills the lynx, she will overcome her rival.LyreTo dream of listening to the music of a lyre, foretells chaste pleasures and congenialcompanionship. Business will run smoothly.For a young woman to dream of playing on one, denotes that she will enjoy theundivided affection of a worthy man.

MMacadamizeTo dream that you see or travel on a macadamized road, is significant of pleasantjourneys, from which you will derive much benefit. For young people, this dreamforetells noble aspirations.MacaroniTo dream of eating macaroni, denotes small losses. To see it in large quantities, denotesthat you will save money by the strictest economy. For a young woman, this dreammeans that a stranger will enter her life.MachineryTo dream of machinery, denotes you will undertake some project which will give greatanxiety, but which will finally result in good for you.To see old machinery, foretells enemies will overcome in your strivings to build up yourfortune. To become entangled in machinery, foretells loss in your business, and muchunhappiness will follow.Loss from bad deals generally follows this dream.Mad DogTo dream of seeing a mad dog, denotes that enemies will make scurrilous attacks uponyou and your friends, but if you succeed in killing the dog, you will overcome adverseopinions and prosper greatly in a financial way.See Dog.MadnessTo dream of being mad, shows trouble ahead for the dreamer. Sickness, by which youwill lose property, is threatened.To see others suffering under this malady, denotes inconstancy of friends and gloomyending of bright expectations.

For a young woman to dream of madness, foretells disappointment in marriage andwealth.MadstoneTo see a madstone applied to a wound from the fangs of some mad animal, denotes thatyou will endeavor, to the limits of your energy, to shield self from the machinations ofenemies, which will soon envelop you with the pall of dishonorable defeat.MagicTo dream of accomplishing any design by magic, indicates pleasant surprises.To see others practising this art, denotes profitable changes to all who have this dream.To dream of seeing a magician, denotes much interesting travel to those concerned in theadvancement of higher education, and profitable returns to the mercenary.Magic here should not be confounded with sorcery or spiritism. If the reader sointerprets, he may expect the opposite to what is here forecast to follow. True magic isthe study of the higher truths of Nature.MagistrateTo dream of a magistrate, foretells that you will be harassed with threats of law suits andlosses in your business.See Judge and Jury.MagnetTo dream of a magnet, denotes that evil influences will draw you from the path of honor.A woman is probably luring you to ruin. To a woman, this dream foretells that protectionand wealth will be showered upon her.Magnifying-glassTo look through a magnifying-glass in your dreams, means failure to accomplish yourwork in a satisfactory manner. For a woman to think she owns one, foretells she willencourage the attention of persons who will ignore her later.MagpieTo dream of a magpie, denotes much dissatisfaction and quarrels. The dreamer shouldguard well his conduct and speech after this dream.

MaliceTo dream of entertaining malice for any person, denotes that you will stand low in theopinion of friends because of a disagreeable temper. Seek to control your passion.If you dream of persons maliciously using you, an enemy in friendly garb is working youharm.MalletTo dream of a mallet, denotes you will meet unkind treatment from friends on account ofyour ill health. Disorder in the home is indicated.MaltTo dream of malt, betokens a pleasant existence and riches that will advance your station.To dream of taking malted drinks, denotes that you will interest yourself in somedangerous affair, but will reap much benefit therefrom.ManTo dream of a man, if handsome, well formed and supple, denotes that you will enjoy lifevastly and come into rich possessions. If he is misshapen and sour-visaged, you willmeet disappointments and many perplexities will involve you.For a woman to dream of a handsome man, she is likely to have distinction offered her. Ifhe is ugly, she will experience trouble through some one whom she considers a friend.MannersTo dream of seeing ugly-mannered persons, denotes failure to carry out undertakingsthrough the disagreeableness of a person connected with the affair.If you meet people with affable manners, you will be pleasantly surprised by affairs ofmoment with you taking a favorable turn.Man-of-warTo dream of a man-of-war, denotes long journeys and separation from country andfriends, dissension in political affairs is portended.If she is crippled, foreign elements will work damage to home interests.If she is sailing upon rough seas, trouble with foreign powers may endanger privateaffairs.

Personal affairs may also go awry.MansionTo dream that you are in a mansion where there is a haunted chamber, denotes suddenmisfortune in the midst of contentment.To dream of being in a mansion, indicates for you wealthy possessions.To see a mansion from distant points, foretells future advancement.ManslaughterFor a woman to dream that she sees, or is in any way connected with, manslaughter,denotes that she will be desperately scared lest her name be coupled with somescandalous sensation.See Murder.MantillaTo dream of seeing a mantilla, denotes an unwise enterprise which will bring you intounfavorable notice.ManufactoryTo dream of a large manufactory, denotes unusual activity in business circles.ManureTo dream of seeing manure, is a favorable omen. Much good will follow the dream.Farmers especially will feel a rise in fortune.ManuscriptTo dream of manuscript in an unfinished state, forebodes disappointment. If finished andclearly written, great hopes will be realized.If you are at work on manuscript, you will have many fears for some cherished hope, butif you keep the blurs out of your work you will succeed in your undertakings. If it isrejected by the publishers, you will be hopeless for a time, but eventually your mostsanguine desires will become a reality.If you lose it, you will be subjected to disappointment.If you see it burn, some work of your own will bring you profit and much elevation.

MapTo dream of a map, or studying one, denotes a change will be contemplated in yourbusiness. Some disappointing things will occur, but much profit also will follow thechange.To dream of looking for one, denotes that a sudden discontent with your surroundingswill inspire you with new energy, and thus you will rise into better conditions. For ayoung woman, this dream denotes that she will rise into higher spheres by sheerambition.MarbleTo dream of a marble quarry, denotes that you life will be a financial success, but thatyour social surroundings will be devoid of affection.To dream of polishing marble, you will come into a pleasing inheritance.To see it broken, you will fall into disfavor among your associates by defying all moralcodes.MarchTo dream of marching to the strains of music, indicates that you are ambitious to becomea soldier or a public official, but you should consider all things well before making finaldecision.For women to dream of seeing men marching, foretells their inclination for men in publicpositions. They should be careful of their reputations, should they be thrown much withmen.To dream of the month of March, portends disappointing returns in business, and somewoman will be suspicious of your honesty.MareTo dream of seeing mares in pastures, denotes success in business and congenialcompanions. If the pasture is barren, it foretells poverty, but warm friends. For a youngwoman, this omens a happy marriage and beautiful children.See Horse.MarigoldTo dream of seeing marigolds, denotes contentment with frugality should be your aim.

MarinerTo dream that you are a mariner, denotes a long journey to distant countries, and muchpleasure will be connected with the trip.If you see your vessel sailing without you, much personal discomfort will be wroughtyou by rivals.MarketTo dream that you are in a market, denotes thrift and much activity in all occupations.To see an empty market, indicates depression and gloom.To see decayed vegetables or meat, denotes losses in business.For a young woman, a market foretells pleasant changes.MarmaladeTo dream of eating marmalade, denotes sickness and much dissatisfaction.For a young woman to dream of making it, denotes unhappy domestic associations.MarmotTo dream of seeing a marmot, denotes that sly enemies are approaching you in the shapeof fair women.For a young woman to dream of a marmot, foretells that temptation will beset her in thefuture.MarriageFor a woman to dream that she marries an old, decrepit man, wrinkled face and grayheaded, denotes she will have a vast amount of trouble and sickness to encounter. If,while the ceremony is in progress, her lover passes, wearing black and looking at her in areproachful way, she will be driven to desperation by the coldness and lack of sympathyof a friend.To dream of seeing a marriage, denotes high enjoyment, if the wedding guests attend inpleasing colors and are happy; if they are dressed in black or other somber hues, therewill be mourning and sorrow in store for the dreamer.If you dream of contracting a marriage, you will have unpleasant news from the absent.

If you are an attendant at a wedding, you will experience much pleasure from thethoughtfulness of loved ones, and business affairs will be unusually promising.To dream of any unfortunate occurrence in connection with a marriage, foretells distress,sickness, or death in your family.For a young woman to dream that she is a bride, and unhappy or indifferent, foretellsdisappointments in love, and probably her own sickness. She should be careful of herconduct, as enemies are near her.See Bride.MarsTo dream of Mars, denotes that your life will be made miserable and hardly worth livingby the cruel treatment of friends. Enemies will endeavor to ruin you.If you feel yourself drawn up toward the planet, you will develop keen judgment andadvance beyond your friends in learning and wealth.MarshTo dream of walking through marshy places, denotes illness resulting from overwork andworry. You will suffer much displeasure from the unwise conduct of a near relative.MartyrTo dream of martyrs, denotes that false friends, domestic unhappiness and losses inaffairs which concern you most.To dream that you are a martyr, signifies the separation from friends, and enemies willslander you.MaskTo dream that you are wearing a mask, denotes temporary trouble, as your conducttowards some dear one will be misinterpreted, and your endeavors to aid that one will bemisunderstood, but you will profit by the temporary estrangements.To see others masking, denotes that you will combat falsehood and envy.To see a mask in your dreams, denotes some person will be unfaithful to you, and youraffairs will suffer also. For a young woman to dream that she wears a mask, foretells shewill endeavor to impose upon some friendly person.If she unmasks, or sees others doing so, she will fail to gain the admiration sought for.She should demean herself modestly after this dream.

MasonTo dream that you see a mason plying his trade, denotes a rise in your circumstances anda more congenial social atmosphere will surround you.If you dream of seeing a band of the order of masons in full regalia, it denotes that youwill have others beside yourself to protect and keep from the evils of life.MasqueradeTo dream of attending a masquerade, denotes that you will indulge in foolish and harmfulpleasures to the neglect of business and domestic duties.For a young woman to dream that she participates in a masquerade, denotes that she willbe deceived.MastTo dream of seeing the masts of ships, denotes long and pleasant voyages, the making ofmany new friends, and the gaining of new possessions.To see the masts of wrecked ships, denotes sudden changes in your circumstances whichwill necessitate giving over anticipated pleasures.If a sailor dreams of a mast, he will soon sail on an eventful trip.MasterTo dream that you have a master, is a sign of incompetency on your part to commandothers, and you will do better work under the leadership of some strong-willed person.If you are a master, and command many people under you, you will excel in judgment inthe fine points of life, and will hold high positions and possess much wealth.MatKeep away from mats in your dreams, as they will usher you into sorrow andperplexities.MatchTo dream of matches, denotes prosperity and change when least expected.To strike a match in the dark, unexpected news and fortune is foreboded.

MattingTo dream of matting, foretells pleasant prospects and cheerful news from the absent. If itis old or torn, you will have vexing things come before you.MattressTo dream of a mattress, denotes that new duties and responsibilities will shortly beassumed.To sleep on a new mattress, signifies contentment with present surroundings.To dream of a mattress factory, denotes that you will be connected in business withthrifty partners and will soon amass wealth.MausoleumTo dream of a mausoleum, indicates the sickness, death, or trouble of some prominentfriend.To find yourself inside a mausoleum, foretells your own illness.MayTo dream of the month of May, denotes prosperous times, and pleasure for the young.To dream that nature appears freakish, denotes sudden sorrow and disappointmentclouding pleasure.May BugsTo dream of May bugs, denotes an ill-tempered companion where a congenial one wasexpected.MeadowTo dream of meadows, predicts happy reunions under bright promises of futureprosperity.MealsTo dream of meals, denotes that you will let trifling matters interfere with momentousaffairs and business engagements.See Eating.

MeaslesTo dream that you have measles, denotes much worry, and anxious care will interferewith your business affairs.To dream that others have this disease, denotes that you will be troubled over thecondition of others.MeatFor a woman to dream of raw meat, denotes that she will meet with muchdiscouragement in accomplishing her aims. If she sees cooked meat, it denotes that otherswill obtain the object for which she will strive.See Beef.MechanicTo dream of a mechanic, denotes change in your dwelling place and a more activebusiness. Advancement in wages usually follows after seeing mechanics at work onmachinery.MedalTo dream of medals, denotes honors gained by application and industry.To lose a medal, denotes misfortune through the unfaithfulness of others.MedicineTo dream of medicine, if pleasant to the taste, a trouble will come to you, but in a shorttime it will work for your good; but if you take disgusting medicine, you will suffer aprotracted illness or some deep sorrow or loss will overcome you.To give medicine to others, denotes that you will work to injure some one who trustedyou.MelancholyTo dream that you feel melancholy over any event, is a sign of disappointment in whatwas thought to be favorable undertakings.To dream that you see others melancholy, denotes unpleasant interruption in affairs. Tolovers, it brings separation.

MelonTo dream of melons, denotes ill health and unfortunate ventures in business.To eat them, signifies that hasty action will cause you anxiety.To see them growing on green vines, denotes that present troubles will result in goodfortune for you.MemorandumTo dream that you make memoranda, denotes that you will engage in an unprofitablebusiness, and much worry will result for you.To see others making a memorandum, signifies that some person will worry you withappeals for aid.To lose your memorandum, you will experience a slight loss in trade.To find a memorandum, you will assume new duties that will cause much pleasure toothers.MemorialTo dream of a memorial, signifies there will be occasion for you to show patientkindness, as trouble and sickness threatens your relatives.MenagerieTo dream of visiting a menagerie, denotes various troubles.MendicantFor a woman to dream of mendicants, she will meet with disagreeable interferences inher plans for betterment and enjoyment.MendingTo dream of mending soiled garments, denotes that you will undertake to right a wrong atan inopportune moment; but if the garment be clean, you will be successful in adding toyour fortune.For a young woman to dream of mending, foretells that she will be a systematic help toher husband.

MercuryTo dream of mercury, is significant of unhappy changes through the constant oppressionof enemies. For a woman to be suffering from mercurial poison, foretells she will bedeserted by and separated from her family.MerryTo dream being merry, or in merry company, denotes that pleasant events will engageyou for a time, and affairs will assume profitable shapes.MeshesTo dream of being entangled in the meshes of a net, or other like constructions, denotesthat enemies will oppress you in time of seeming prosperity. To a young woman, thisdream foretells that her environments will bring her into evil and consequentabandonment. If she succeeds in disengaging herself from the meshes, she will narrowlyescape slander.MessageTo dream of receiving a message, denotes that changes will take place in your affairs.To dream of sending a message, denotes that you will be placed in unpleasant situations.MetamorphoseTo dream of seeing anything metamorphose, denotes that sudden changes will take placein your life, for good or bad, as the metamorphose was pleasant or frightful.MiceTo dream of mice, foretells domestic troubles and the insincerity of friends. Businessaffairs will assume a discouraging tone.To kill mice, denotes that you will conquer your enemies.To let them escape, is significant of doubtful struggles.For a young woman to dream of mice, warns her of secret enemies, and that deception isbeing practised upon her. If she should see a mouse in her clothing, it is a sign of scandalin which she will figure.

MicroscopeTo dream of a microscope, denotes you will experience failure or small returns in yourenterprises.MidwifeTo see a midwife in your dreams, signifies unfortunate sickness with a narrow escapefrom death.For a young woman to dream of such a person, foretells that distress and calumny willattend her.Mile-PostTo dream you see or pass a mile-post, foretells that you will be assailed by doubtful fearsin business or love.

To see one down, portends accidents are threatening to give disorderto your affairs.MilkTo dream of drinking milk, denotes abundant harvest to the farmer and pleasure in thehome; for a traveler, it foretells a fortunate voyage. This is a very propitious dream forwomen.To see milk in large quantities, signifies riches and health.To dream of dealing in milk commercially, denotes great increase in fortune.To give milk away, shows that you will be too benevolent for the good of your ownfortune.To spill milk, denotes that you will experience a slight loss and suffer temporaryunhappiness at the hands of friends.To dream of impure milk, denotes that you will be tormented with petty troubles.To dream of sour milk, denotes that you will be disturbed over the distress of friends.To dream of trying unsuccessfully to drink milk, signifies that you will be in danger oflosing something of value or the friendship of a highly esteemed person.To dream of hot milk, foretells a struggle, but the final winning of riches and desires.To dream of bathing in milk, denotes pleasures and companionships of congenial friends.See Buttermilk.

MilkingTo dream of milking, and it flows in great streams from the udder, while the cow isrestless and threatening, signifies you will see great opportunities withheld from you, butwhich will result in final favor for you.MillTo dream of a mill, indicates thrift and fortunate undertakings.To see a dilapidated mill, denotes sickness and ill fortune.See Cotton Mill, etc.Mill-DamTo dream that you see clear water pouring over a mill-dam, foretells pleasant enterprises,either of a business or social nature. If the water is muddy or impure, you will meet withlosses, and troubles will arise where pleasure was anticipated.If the dam is dry, your business will assume shrunken proportions.MilletTo see a miller in your dreams, signifies your surroundings will grow more hopeful. Fora woman to dream of a miller failing in an attempt to start his mill, foretells she will bedisappointed in her lover's wealth, as she will think him in comfortable circumstances.MineTo dream of being in a mine, denotes failure in affairs.To own a mine, denotes future wealth.See Coal Mine.MineralTo dream of minerals, denotes your present unpromising outlook will grow directlybrighter. To walk over mineral land, signifies distress, from which you will escape and bebettered in your surroundings.Mineral WaterTo dream of drinking mineral water, foretells fortune will favor your efforts, and you will

enjoy your opportunities to satisfy your cravings for certain pleasures.MiningTo see mining in your dreams, denotes that an enemy is seeking your ruin by bringing uppast immoralities in your life. You will be likely to make unpleasant journeys, if youstand near the mine.If you dream of hunting for mines, you will engage in worthless pursuits.MinisterTo dream of seeing a minister, denotes unfortunate changes and unpleasant journeys.To hear a minister exhort, foretells that some designing person will influence you to evil.To dream that you are a minister, denotes that you will usurp another's rights.See Preacher and Priest.MinuetTo dream of seeing the minuet danced, signifies a pleasant existence with congenialcompanions.To dance it yourself, good fortune and domestic joys are foretold.MinxTo dream of a minx, denotes you will have sly enemies to overcome. If you kill one, youwill win your desires. For a young woman to dream that she is partial to minx furs, shewill find protection and love in some person who will be inordinately jealous.MireTo dream of a minx, denotes you will have sly enemies to overcome.If you kill one, you will win your desires. For a young woman to dream that she is partialto minx furs, she will find protection and love in some person who will be inordinatelyjealous.MirrorTo dream of seeing yourself in a mirror, denotes that you will meet many discouragingissues, and sickness will cause you distress and loss in fortune.

To see a broken mirror, foretells the sudden or violent death of some one related to you.To see others in a mirror, denotes that others will act unfairly towards you to promotetheir own interests.To see animals in a mirror, denotes disappointment and loss in fortune.For a young woman to break a mirror, foretells unfortunate friendships and an unhappymarriage. To see her lover in a mirror looking pale and careworn, denotes death or abroken engagement. If he seems happy, a slight estrangement will arise, but it will be ofshort duration.See Glass.MiserTo dream of a miser, foretells you will be unfortunate in finding true happiness owing toselfishness, and love will disappoint you sorely.For a woman to dream that she is befriended by a miser, foretells she will gain love andwealth by her intelligence and tactful conduct.To dream that you are miserly, denotes that you will be obnoxious to others by yourconceited bearingTo dream that any of your friends are misers, foretells that you will be distressed by theimportunities of others.MistTo dream that you are enveloped in a mist, denotes uncertain fortunes and domesticunhappiness. If the mist clears away, your troubles will be of short duration.To see others in a mist, you will profit by the misfortune of others.MistletoeTo dream of mistletoe, foretells happiness and great rejoicing.To the young, it omens many pleasant pastimesIf seen with unpromising signs, disappointment will displace pleasure or fortune.Mocking-BirdTo see or hear a mocking-bird, signifies you will be invited to go on a pleasant visit tofriends, and your affairs will move along smoothly and prosperously. For a woman to see

a wounded or dead one, her disagreement with a friend or lover is signified.ModelsTo dream of a model, foretells your social affairs will deplete your purse, and quarrelsand regrets will follow. For a young woman to dream that she is a model or seeking to beone, foretells she will be entangled in a love affair which will give her trouble throughthe selfishness of a friend.MolassesTo dream of molasses, is a sign that some one is going to extend you pleasant hospitality,and, through its acceptance, you will meet agreeable and fortunate surprises. To eat it,foretells that you will be discouraged and disappointed in love. To have it smeared onyour clothing, denotes you will have disagreeable offers of marriage, and probably lossesin business.MolesTo dream of moles, indicates secret enemies.To dream of catching a mole, you will overcome any opposition and rise to prominence.To see moles, or such blemishes, on the person, indicates illness and quarrels.MoneyTo dream of finding money, denotes small worries, but much happiness. Changes willfollow.To pay out money, denotes misfortune.To receive gold, great prosperity and unalloyed pleasures.To lose money, you will experience unhappy hours in the home and affairs will appeargloomy.To count your money and find a deficit, you will be worried in making payments.To dream that you steal money, denotes that you are in danger and should guard youractions.To save money, augurs wealth and comfort.To dream that you swallow money, portends that you are likely to become mercenary.

To look upon a quantity of money, denotes that prosperity and happiness are within yourreach.To dream you find a roll of currency, and a young woman claims it, foretells you willlose in some enterprise by the interference of some female friend. The dreamer will findthat he is spending his money unwisely and is living beyond his means. It is a dream ofcaution.Beware lest the innocent fancies of your brain make a place for your money beforepayday.MonkTo dream of seeing a monk, foretells dissensions in the family and unpleasantjourneyings. To a young woman, this dream signifies that gossip and deceit will be usedagainst her.To dream that you are a monk, denotes personal loss and illness.MonkeyTo dream of a monkey, denotes that deceitful people will flatter you to advance their owninterests.To see a dead monkey, signifies that your worst enemies will soon be removed.If a young woman dreams of a monkey, she should insist on an early marriage, as herlover will suspect unfaithfulness.For a woman to dream of feeding a monkey, denotes that she will be betrayed by aflatterer.MonsterTo dream of being pursued by a monster, denotes that sorrow and misfortune holdprominent places in your immediate future.To slay a monster, denotes that you will successfully cope with enemies and rise toeminent positions.MoonTo dream of seeing the moon with the aspect of the heavens remaining normal,prognosticates success in love and business affairs.A weird and uncanny moon, denotes unpropitious lovemaking, domestic infelicities anddisappointing enterprises of a business character.

The moon in eclipse, denotes that contagion will ravage your community.To see the new moon, denotes an increase in wealth and congenial partners in marriage.For a young woman to dream that she appeals to the moon to know her fate, denotes thatshe will soon be rewarded with marriage to the one of her choice. If she sees two moons,she will lose her lover by being mercenary. If she sees the moon grow dim, she will letthe supreme happiness of her life slip for want of womanly tact.To see a blood red moon, indicates war and strife, and she will see her lover march awayin defence of his country.MorgueTo dream that you visit a morgue searching for some one, denotes that you will beshocked by news of the death of a relative or friend.To see many corpses there, much sorrow and trouble will come under your notice.MorningTo see the morning dawn clear in your dreams, prognosticates a near approach of fortuneand pleasure.A cloudy morning, portends weighty affairs will overwhelm you.MoroccoTo see morocco in your dreams, foretells that you will receive substantial aid fromunexpected sources. Your love will be rewarded by faithfulness.MortgageTo dream that you give a mortgage on your property, denotes that you are threatenedwith financial upheavals, which will throw you into embarrassing positions.To take, or hold one, against others, is ominous of adequate wealth to liquidate yourobligations.To find yourself reading or examining mortgages, denotes great possibilities before youof love or gain.To lose a mortgage, if it cannot be found again, implies loss and worry.

MoroseIf you find yourself morose in dreams, you will awake to find the world, as far as you areconcerned, going fearfully wrong.To see others morose, portends unpleasant occupations and unpleasant companions.MortificationTo dream that you feel mortified over any deed committed by yourself, is a sign that youwill be placed in an unenviable position before those to whom you most wish to appearhonorable and just. Financial conditions will fall low.To see mortified flesh, denotes disastrous enterprises and disappointment in love.MosesTo dream that you see Moses, means personal gain and a connubial alliance which willbe a source of sweet congratulation to yourself.MosquitoTo see mosquitoes in your dreams, you will strive in vain to remain impregnable to thesly attacks of secret enemies. Your patience and fortune will both suffer from thesedesigning persons.If you kill mosquitoes, you will eventually overcome obstacles and enjoy fortune anddomestic bliss.MossTo dream of moss, denotes that you will fill dependent positions, unless the moss growsin rich soil, when you will be favored with honors.MothTo see a moth in a dream, small worries will lash you into hurried contracts, which willprove unsatisfactory. Quarrels of a domestic nature are prognosticated.MotherTo see your mother in dreams as she appears in the home, signifies pleasing results fromany enterprise.To hold her in conversation, you will soon have good news from interests you are anxious over.For a woman to dream of mother, signifies pleasant duties and connubial bliss.To see one's mother emaciated or dead, foretells sadness caused by death or dishonor.To hear your mother call you, denotes that you are derelict in your duties, and that youare pursuing the wrong course in business.To hear her cry as if in pain, omens her illness, or some affliction is menacing you.Mother-in-LawTo dream of your mother-in-law, denotes there will be pleasant reconciliations for youafter some serious disagreement. For a woman to dispute with her mother-in-law, shewill find that quarrelsome and unfeeling people will give her annoyance.MountainFor a young woman to dream of crossing a mountain in company with her cousin anddead brother, who was smiling, denotes she will have a distinctive change in her life forthe better, but there are warnings against allurements and deceitfulness of friends. If shebecomes exhausted and refuses to go further, she will be slightly disappointed in notgaining quite so exalted a position as was hoped for by her.If you ascend a mountain in your dreams, and the way is pleasant and verdant, you willrise swiftly to wealth and prominence. If the mountain is rugged, and you fail to reach thetop, you may expect reverses in your life, and should strive to overcome all weakness inyour nature. To awaken when you are at a dangerous point in ascending, denotes that youwill find affairs taking a flattering turn when they appear gloomy.MourningTo dream that you wear mourning, omens ill luck and unhappiness.If others wear it, there will be disturbing influences among your friends causing youunexpected dissatisfaction and loss. To lovers, this dream foretells misunderstanding andprobable separation.MouseFor a woman to dream of a mouse, denotes that she will have an enemy who will annoyher by artfulness and treachery.

Mouse-TrapTo see a mouse-trap in dreams, signifies your need to be careful of character, as waryersons have designs upon you.To see it full of mice, you will likely fall into the hands of enemies.To set a trap, you will artfully devise means to overcome your opponents.See Mice.MudTo dream that you walk in mud, denotes that you will have cause to lose confidence infriendships, and there will be losses and disturbances in family circles.To see others walking in mud, ugly rumors will reach you of some friend or employee.To the farmer, this dream is significant of short crops and unsatisfactory gains fromstock.To see mud on your clothing, your reputation is being assailed. To scrape it off, signifiesthat you will escape the calumny of enemies.MuffTo dream of wearing a muff, denotes that you will be well provided for against thevicissitudes of fortune.For a lover to see his sweetheart wearing a muff, denotes that a worthier man will usurphis place in her affections.MulattoIf a mulatto appears to you in a dream, beware of making new friendships or falling intoassociations with strange women, as you are threatened with loss of money and of highmoral standing.See Negro.MulberriesTo see mulberries in your dreams, denotes that sickness will prevent you from obtainingyour desires, and you will be called upon often to relieve suffering.To eat them, signifies bitter disappointments.

MuleIf you dream that your are riding on a mule, it denotes that you are engaging in pursuitswhich will cause you the greatest anxiety, but if you reach your destination withoutinterruption, you will be recompensed with substantial results.For a young woman to dream of a white mule, shows she will marry a wealthy foreigner,or one who, while wealthy, will not be congenial in tastes. If she dreams of mulesrunning loose, she will have beaux and admirers, but no offers of marriage.To be kicked by a mule, foretells disappointment in love and marriage.To see one dead, portends broken engagements and social decline.MurderTo see murder committed in your dreams, foretells much sorrow arising from themisdeeds of others. Affair will assume dulness. Violent deaths will come under yournotice.If you commit murder, it signifies that you are engaging in some dishonorable adventure,which will leave a stigma upon your name.To dream that you are murdered, foretells that enemies are secretly working to overthrowyou.See Killing and kindred words.MuscleTo dream of seeing your muscle well developed, you will have strange encounters withenemies, but you will succeed in surmounting their evil works, and gain fortune.If they are shrunken, your inability to succeed in your affairs is portended. For a woman,this dream is prophetic of toil and hardships.MuseumTo dream of a museum, denotes you will pass through many and varied scenes in strivingfor what appears your rightful position. You will acquire useful knowledge, which willstand you in better light than if you had pursued the usual course to learning. If themuseum is distasteful, you will have many causes for vexation.MusicTo dream of hearing harmonious music, omens pleasure and prosperity.

Discordant music foretells troubles with unruly children, and unhappiness in thehousehold.Musical InstrumentsTo see musical instruments, denotes anticipated pleasures.If they are broken, the pleasure will be marred by uncongenial companionship. For ayoung woman, this dream foretells for her the power to make her life what she will.MushroomTo see mushrooms in your dreams, denotes unhealthy desires, and unwise haste inamassing wealth, as it may vanish in law suits and vain pleasures.To eat them, signifies humiliation and disgraceful love.For a young woman to dream of them, foretells her defiance of propriety in her pursuit offoolish pleasures.MuskTo dream of musk, foretells unexpected occasions of joy, and lovers will agree and ceaseto be unfaithful.MusselsTo dream of water mussels, denotes small fortune, but contentment and domesticenjoyment.MustacheTo dream that you have a mustache, denotes that your egotism and effrontery will causeyou a poor inheritance in worldly goods, and you will betray women to their sorrow.If a woman dreams of admiring a mustache, her virtue is in danger, and she should bemindful of her conduct.If a man dreams that he has his mustache shaved, he will try to turn from evilcompanions and pleasures, and seek to reinstate himself in former positions of honor.MustardTo see mustard growing, and green, foretells success and joy to the farmer, and to theseafaring it prognosticates wealth.

To eat mustard seed and feel the burning in your mouth, denotes that you will repentbitterly some hasty action, which has caused you to suffer.To dream of eating green mustard cooked, indicates the lavish waste of fortune, andmental strain.For a young woman to eat newly grown mustard, foretells that she will sacrifice wealthfor personal desires.MuteTo converse with a mute in your dreams, foretells that unusual crosses in your life will fityou for higher positions, which will be tendered you.To dream that you are a mute, portends calamities and unjust persecution.MyrrhTo see myrtle in foliage and bloom in your dream, denotes that your desires will begratified, and pleasures will possess you.For a young woman to dream of wearing a sprig of myrtle, foretells to her an earlymarriage with a well-to do and intelligent man.To see it withered, denotes that she will miss happiness through careless conduct.MyrtleTo see myrtle in foliage and bloom in your dream, denotes that your desires will begratified, and pleasures will possess you. For a young woman to dream of wearing a sprigof myrtle, foretells to her an early marriage with a well-to do and intelligent man. To seeit withered, denotes that she will miss happiness through careless conduct.MysteryTo find yourself bewildered by some mysterious event, denotes that strangers will harassyou with their troubles and claim your aid. It warns you also of neglected duties, forwhich you feel much aversion. Business will wind you into unpleasant complications.To find yourself studying the mysteries of creation, denotes that a change will take placein your life, throwing you into a higher atmosphere of research and learning, and thusadvancing you nearer the attainment of true pleasure and fortune.

What's In A Dream - N to S

NNailsTo see nails in your dreams, indicates much toil and small recompense.To deal in nails, shows that you will engage in honorable work, even if it be lowly.To see rusty or broken nails, indicates sickness and failure in business.NakedTo dream that you are naked, foretells scandal and unwise engagements.To see others naked, foretells that you will be tempted by designing persons to leave thepath of duty. Sickness will be no small factor against your success.To dream that you suddenly discover your nudity, and are trying to conceal it, denotesthat you have sought illicit pleasure contrary to your noblest instincts and are desirous ofabandoning those desires.For a young woman to dream that she admires her nudity, foretells that she will win, butnot hold honest men's regard. She will win fortune by her charms. If she thinks herselffill-formed, her reputation will be sullied by scandal. If she dreams of swimming in clearwater naked, she will enjoy illicit loves, but nature will revenge herself by sickness, orloss of charms. If she sees naked men swimming in clear water, she will have manyadmirers. If the water is muddy, a jealous admirer will cause ill-natured gossip about her.NapkinTo dream of a napkin, foretells convivial entertainments in which you will figureprominently. For a woman to dream of soiled napkins, foretells that humiliating affairs

will thrust themselves upon her.NavyTo dream of the navy, denotes victorious struggles with unsightly obstacles, and thepromise of voyages and tours of recreation. If in your dream you seem frightened ordisconcerted, you will have strange obstacles to overcome before you reach fortune. Adilapidated navy is an indication of unfortunate friendships in business or love.See Gunboat.NearsightedTo dream that you are nearsighted, signifies embarrassing failure and unexpected visitsfrom unwelcome persons. For a young woman, this dream foretells unexpected rivalry.To dream that your sweetheart is nearsighted, denotes that she will disappoint you.NeckTo dream that you see your own neck, foretells that vexatious family relations willinterfere with your business.To admire the neck of another, signifies your worldly mindedness will cause brokendomestic ties.For a woman to dream that her neck is thick, foretells that she will become querulous andsomething of a shrew if she fails to control her temper.NecklaceFor a woman to dream of receiving a necklace, omens for her a loving husband and abeautiful home.To lose a necklace, she will early feel the heavy hand of bereavement.NecromancerTo dream of a necromancer and his arts, denotes that you are threatened with strangeacquaintances who will influence you for evil.See Hypnotist.

NeedTo dream that you are in need, denotes that you will speculate unwisely and distressingnews of absent friends will oppress you.To see others in need, foretells that unfortunate affairs will affect yourself with others.NeedleTo use a needle in your dream, is a warning of approaching affliction, in which you willsuffer keenly the loss of sympathy, which is rightfully yours.To dream of threading a needle, denotes that you will be burdened with the care of othersthan your own household.To look for a needle, foretells useless worries.To find a needle, foretells that you will have friends who will appreciate you.To break one, signifies loneliness and poverty.NegroTo dream of seeing a negro standing on your green lawn, is a sign that while yourimmediate future seems filled with prosperity and sweetest joys, there will creep into itunavoidable discord, which will veil all brightness in gloom for a season.To dream of seeing a burly negro, denotes formidable rivals in affection and business.To see a mulatto, constant worries and friction with hirelings is foretold.To dream of a difficulty with a negro, signifies your inability to overcome disagreeablesurroundings. It also denotes disappointments and ill fortune.For a young woman to dream of a negro, she will be constrained to work for her ownsupport, or be disappointed in her lover.To dream of negro children, denotes many little anxieties and crosses.For a young woman to dream of being held by a negro, portends for her manydisagreeable duties. She is likely to meet with and give displeasure. She will quarrel withher dearest friends.Sickness sometimes follows dreams of old negroes.To see one nude, abject despair, and failure to cope with treachery may follow. Enemieswill work you signal harm, and bad news from the absent may be expected.

To meet with a trusty negro in a place where he ought not to be, foretells you will bedeceived by some person in whom you placed great confidence. You are likely to bemuch exasperated over the conduct of a servant or some person under your orders.Delays and vexations may follow.To think that you are preaching to negroes is a warning to protect your interest, as falsefriends are dealing surreptitiously with you. To hear a negro preaching denotes you willbe greatly worried over material matters and servants are giving cause for uneasiness.See Mulatto.NeighborTo see your neighbors in your dreams, denotes many profitable hours will be lost inuseless strife and gossip. If they appear sad, or angry, it foretells dissensions and quarrels.NephewTo dream of your nephew, denotes you are soon to come into a pleasing competency, ifhe is handsome and well looking; otherwise, there will be disappointment and discomfortfor you.NestTo dream of seeing birds' nests, denotes that you will be interested in an enterprise whichwill be prosperous. For a young woman, this dream foretells change of abode.To see an empty nest, indicates sorrow through the absence of a friend.Hens' nests, foretells that you will be interested in domesticities, and children will becheerful and obedient.To dream of a nest filled with broken or bad eggs, portends disappointments and failure.See Birds' Nest.NetsTo dream of ensnaring anything with a net, denotes that you will be unscrupulous in yourdealings and deportment with others.To dream of an old or torn net, denotes that your property has mortgages, or attachments,which will cause you trouble.

Nettles If in your dreams you walk among nettles without being stung, you will be prosperous.To be stung by them, you will be discontented with yourself and make others unhappy.For a young woman to dream of passing through nettles, foretells that she will be offeredmarriage by different men, and her decision will fill her with anxious foreboding.To dream of nettles, is portentous of stringent circumstances and disobedience fromchildren or servants.News To hear good news in a dream, denotes that you will be fortunate in affairs, and haveharmonious companions; but if the news be bad, contrary conditions will exist.Newspaper To dream of newspapers, denotes that frauds will be detected in your dealings, and yourreputation will likewise be affected.To print a newspaper, you will have opportunities of making foreign journeys andfriends.Trying, but failing to read a newspaper, denotes that you will fail in some uncertainenterprise.Newspaper Reporter If in your dreams you unwillingly see them, you will be annoyed with small talk, andperhaps quarrels of a low character.If you are a newspaper reporter in your dreams, there will be a varied course of traveloffered you, though you may experience unpleasant situations, yet there will be somehonor and gain attached.New Year To dream of the new year, signifies prosperity and connubial anticipations. If youcontemplate the new year in weariness, engagement will be entered into inauspiciously.Niece For a woman to dream of her niece, foretells she will have unexpected trials and muchuseless worry in the near future.

Night If you are surrounded by night in your dreams, you may expect unusual oppression andhardships in business. If the night seems to be vanishing, conditions which hithertoseemed unfavorable will now grow bright, and affairs will assume prosperous phases.See Darkness.Nightmare To dream of being attacked with this hideous sensation, denotes wrangling and failure inbusiness. For a young woman, this is a dream prophetic of disappointment and unmeritedslights. It may also warn the dreamer to be careful of her health, and food.Nightingale To dream that you are listening to the harmonious notes of the nightingale, foretells apleasing existence, and prosperous and healthy surroundings. This is a most favorabledream to lovers, and parents.To see nightingales silent, foretells slight misunderstandings among friends.Ninepins To dream that you play ninepins, denotes that you are foolishly wasting your energy andopportunities. You should be careful in the selection of companions. All phases of thisdream are bad.Nobility To dream of associating with the nobility, denotes that your aspirations are not of theright nature, as you prefer show and pleasures to the higher development of the mind.For a young woman to dream of the nobility, foretells that she will choose a lover for hisoutward appearance, instead of wisely accepting the man of merit for her protector.Noise If you hear a strange noise in your dream, unfavorable news is presaged. If the noiseawakes you, there will be a sudden change in your affairs.Noodles To dream of noodles, denotes an abnormal appetite and desires. There is little good inthis dream.

NoseTo see your own nose, indicates force of character, and consciousness of your ability toaccomplish whatever enterprise you may choose to undertake.If your nose looks smaller than natural, there will be failure in your affairs. Hair growingon your nose, indicates extraordinary undertakings, and that they will be carried throughby sheer force of character, or will.A bleeding nose, is prophetic of disaster, whatever the calling of the dreamer may be.NotaryTo dream of a notary, is a prediction of unsatisfied desires, and probable lawsuits. For awoman to associate with a notary, foretells she will rashly risk her reputation, ingratification of foolish pleasure.NovemberTo dream of November, augers a season of indifferent success in all affairs.NumbnessTo dream that you feel a numbness creeping over you, in your dreams, is a sign of illness,and disquieting conditionsNumbersTo dream of numbers, denotes that unsettled conditions in business will cause youuneasiness and dissatisfaction.See Figures.NunsFor a religiously inclined man to dream of nuns, foretells that material joys will interferewith his spirituality. He should be wise in the control of self.For a woman to dream of nuns, foretells her widowhood, or her separation from herlover. If she dreams that she is a nun, it portends her discontentment with presentenvironments.To see a dead nun, signifies despair over the unfaithfulness of loved ones, andimpoverished fortune.

For one to dream that she discards the robes of her order, foretells that longing forworldly pleasures will unfit her for her chosen duties.NuptialFor a woman to dream of her nuptials, she will soon enter upon new engagements, whichwill afford her distinction, pleasure, and harmony.See Marriage.NurseTo dream that a nurse is retained in your home, foretells distressing illness, or unluckyvisiting among friends.To see a nurse leaving your house, omens good health in the family.For a young woman to dream that she is a nurse, denotes that she will gain the esteem ofpeople, through her self-sacrifice. If she parts from a patient, she will yield to thepersuasion of deceit.NursingFor a woman to dream of nursing her baby, denotes pleasant employment.For a young woman to dream of nursing a baby, foretells that she will occupy positionsof honor and trust.For a man to dream of seeing his wife nurse their baby, denotes harmony in his pursuits.NutsTo dream of gathering nuts, augurs successful enterprises, and much favor in love.To eat them, prosperity will aid you in grasping any desired pleasure.For a woman to dream of nuts, foretells that her fortune will be on blissful heights.NutmegsTo dream of nutmegs, is a sign of prosperity, and pleasant journeyings.NymphTo see nymphs bathing in clear water, denotes that passionate desires will find an ecstaticrealization. Convivial entertainments will enchant you.

To see them out of their sphere, denotes disappointment with the world.For a young woman to see them bathing, denotes that she will have great favor andpleasure, but they will not rest strictly within the moral code. To dream that sheimpersonates a nymph, is a sign that she is using her attractions for selfish purposes, andthus the undoing of men.OOakTo dream of seeing a forest of oaks, signifies great prosperity in all conditions of life.To see an oak full of acorns, denotes increase and promotion.If blasted oak, it denotes sudden and shocking surprises.For sweethearts to dream of oaks, denotes that they will soon begin life together underfavorable circumstances.OarTo dream of handling oars, portends disappointments for you, inasmuch as you willsacrifice your own pleasure for the comfort of others.To lose an oar, denotes vain efforts to carry out designs satisfactorily.A broken oar represents interruption in some anticipated pleasure.OathWhenever you take an oath in your dreams, prepare for dissension and altercations onwaking.OatmealTo dream of eating oatmeal, signifies the enjoyment of worthily earned fortune.For a young woman to dream of preparing it for the table, denotes that she will soonpreside over the destiny of others.

OatsTo dream that oats hold the vision, portends a variety of good things. The farmer willespecially advance in fortune and domestic harmony.To see decayed oats, foretells that sorrow will displace bright hopes.ObedienceTo dream that you render obedience to another, foretells for you a common place, apleasant but uneventful period of life.If others are obedient to you, it shows that you will command fortune and high esteem.ObeliskAn obelisk looming up stately and cold in your dreams is the forerunner of melancholytidings.For lovers to stand at the base of an obelisk, denotes fatal disagreements.ObituaryTo dream of writing an obituary, denotes that unpleasant and discordant duties willdevolve upon you.If you read one, news of a distracting nature will soon reach you.ObligationTo dream of obligating yourself in any incident, denotes that you will be fretted andworried by the thoughtless complaints of others.If others obligate themselves to you, it portends that you will win the regard ofacquaintances and friends.ObservatoryTo dream of viewing the heavens and beautiful landscapes from an observatory, denotesyour swift elevation to prominent positions and places of trust. For a young woman thisdream signals the realization of the highest earthly joys. If the heavens are clouded, yourhighest aims will miss materialization.

OccultistTo dream that you listen to the teachings of an occultist, denotes that you will strive toelevate others to a higher plane of justice and forbearance. If you accept his views, youwill find honest delight by keeping your mind and person above material frivolities andpleasures.OceanTo dream of the ocean when it is calm is propitious. The sailor will have a pleasant andprofitable voyage. The business man will enjoy a season of remuneration, and the youngman will revel in his sweetheart's charms.To be far out on the ocean, and hear the waves lash the ship, forebodes disaster inbusiness life, and quarrels and stormy periods in the household.To be on shore and see the waves of the ocean foaming against each other, foretells yournarrow escape from injury and the designs of enemies.To dream of seeing the ocean so shallow as to allow wading, or a view of the bottom,signifies prosperity and pleasure with a commingling of sorrow and hardships.To sail on the ocean when it is calm, is always propitious.OctoberTo imagine you are in October is ominous of gratifying success in your undertakings.You will also make new acquaintances which will ripen into lasting friendships.OculistTo dream of consulting an oculist, denotes that you will be dissatisfied with yourprogress in life, and will use artificial means of advancement.Odd-FellowTo dream of this order, signifies that you will have sincere friends, and misfortune willtouch you but lightly.To join this order, foretells that you will win distinction and conjugal bliss.OdorTo dream of inhaling sweet odors, is a sign of a beautiful woman ministering to yourdaily life, and successful financiering.

To smell disgusting odors, foretells unpleasant disagreements and unreliable servants.OffenseTo dream of being offended, denotes that errors will be detected in your conduct, whichwill cause you inward rage while attempting to justify yourself.To give offense, predicts for you many struggles before reaching your aims.For a young woman to give, or take offense, signifies that she will regret hastyconclusions, and disobedience to parents or guardian.OfferingTo bring or make an offering, foretells that you will be cringing and hypocritical unlessyou cultivate higher views of duty.OfficeFor a person to dream that he holds office, denotes that his aspirations will sometimesmake him undertake dangerous paths, but his boldness will be rewarded with success. Ifhe fails by any means to secure a desired office he will suffer keen disappointment in hisaffairs.To dream that you are turned out of office, signifies loss of valuables.OffspringTo dream of your own offspring, denotes cheerfulness and the merry voices of neighborsand children.To see the offspring of domestic animals, denotes increase in prosperity.OilTo dream of anointing with oil, foretells events in which you will be the particularmoving power.Quantities of oil, prognosticates excesses in pleasurable enterprises.For a man to dream that he deals in oil, denotes unsuccessful love making, as he willexpect unusual concessions.For a woman to dream that she is anointed with oil, shows that she will be open toindiscreet advances.

OilclothTo dream of oilcloth is a warning that you will meet coldness and treachery.To deal in it, denotes uncertain speculations.OintmentTo dream of ointment, denotes that you will form friendships which will prove beneficialand pleasing to you.For a young woman to dream that she makes ointment, denotes that she will be able tocommand her own affairs whether they be of a private or public character.Old Man, or WomanTo dream of seeing an old man, or woman, denotes that unhappy cares will oppress you,if they appear otherwise than serene.See Faces, Men and Women.OlivesGathering olives with a merry band of friends, foretells favorable results in business, anddelightful surprises.If you take them from bottles, it foretells convivialityTo break a bottle of olives, indicates disappointments on the eve of pleasure.To eat them, signifies contentment and faithful friends.OmeletTo see omelet being served in your dream, warns you of flattery and deceit, which isabout to be used against you.To eat it, shows that you will be imposed upon by some one seemingly worthy of yourconfidence.OmnibusTo dream that you are being drawn through the streets in an omnibus, foretellsmisunderstandings with friends, and unwise promises will be made by youSee Carriage.

One-EyedTo see one-eyed creatures in your dreams, is portentous of an over-whelming intimationof secret intriguing against your fortune and happiness.OnionsSeeing quantities of onions in your dreams, represents the amount of spite and envy thatyou will meet, by being successful.If you eat them, you will overcome all opposition.If you see them growing, there will be just enough of rivalry in your affairs, to makethings interesting.Cooked onions, denote placidity and small gains in business.To dream that you are cutting onions and feel the escaping juice in your eyes, denotesthat you will be defeated by your rivals.OperaTo dream of attending an opera, denotes that you will be entertained by congenialfriends, and find that your immediate affairs will be favorable.OpiumTo dream of opium, signifies strangers will obstruct your chances of improving yourfortune, by sly and seductive means.OpulenceFor a young woman to dream that she lives in fairy like opulence, denotes that she will bedeceived, and will live for a time in luxurious ease and splendor, to find later that she ismated with shame and poverty. When young women dream that they are enjoying solidand real wealth and comforts, they will always wake to find some real pleasure, but whenabnormal or fairy-like dreams of luxury and joy seem to encompass them, their wakingmoments will be filled with disappointments; as the dreams are warnings, superinducedby their practicality being supplanted by their excitable imagination and lazy desires,which should be overcome

with energy, and the replacing of practicality on her base. Noyoung woman
should fill her mind with idle day dreams, but energetically strive to
carryforward noble ideals and thoughts, and promising and helpful dreams
will come to herwhile she restores physical energies in sleep.See Wealth.

OrangesSeeing a number of orange trees in a healthy condition, bearing
ripe fruit, is a sign ofhealth and prosperous surroundings.To eat oranges
is signally bad. Sickness of friends or relatives will be a source of
worryto you. Dissatisfaction will pervade the atmosphere in business
circles. If they are fineand well-flavored, there will be a slight
abatement of ill luck. A young woman is likelyto lose her lover, if she
dreams of eating oranges. If she dreams of seeing a fine onepitched up
high, she will be discreet in choosing a husband from many lovers.To slip
on an orange peel, foretells the death of a relative.To buy oranges at
your wife's solicitation, and she eats them, denotes that
unpleasantcomplications will resolve themselves into profit.Orang-UtangTo
dream of an orang-utang, denotes that some person is falsely using your
influence tofurther selfish schemes. For a young woman, it portends an
unfaithful lover.OratorBeing under the spell of an orator's eloquence,
denotes that you will heed the voice offlattery to your own detriment, as
you will be persuaded into offering aid to unworthypeople.If a young
woman falls in love with an orator, it is proof that in her loves she
will beaffected by outward show.OrchardDreaming of passing through
leaving and blossoming orchards with your sweetheart,omens a delightful
consummation of a long courtship. If the orchard is filled withripening
fruit, it denotes recompense for faithful service to those under masters,
and fullfruition of designs for the leaders of enterprises. Happy homes,
with loyal husbands andobedient children, for wives.If you are in an
orchard and see hogs eating the fallen fruit, it is a sign that you will
loseproperty in trying to claim what are not really your own
belongings.To gather the ripe fruit, is a happy omen of plenty to all
classes.Orchards infested with blight, denotes a miserable existence,
amid joy and wealth.To be caught in brambles, while passing through an
orchard, warns you of a jealous rival,or, if married, a private but large
row with your partner.

If you dream of seeing a barren orchard, opportunities to rise to higher
stations in life willbe ignored.If you see one robbed of its verdure by
seeming winter, it denotes that you have beencareless of the future in
the enjoyment of the present.To see a storm-swept orchard, brings an
unwelcome guest, or duties.OrchestraBelonging to an orchestra and
playing, foretells pleasant entertainments, and yoursweetheart will be
faithful and cultivated.To hear the music of an orchestra, denotes that
the knowledge of humanity will at alltimes prove you to be a much-liked

person, and favors will fall unstintedly upon you.OrganTo hear the pealing forth of an organ in grand anthems, signifies lasting friendships andwell-grounded fortune.To see an organ in a church, denotes despairing separation of families, and death,perhaps, for some of them.If you dream of rendering harmonious music on an organ, you will be fortunate in theway to worldly comfort, and much social distinction will be given you.To hear doleful singing and organ accompaniment, denotes you are nearing a wearisometask, and probable loss of friends or position.OrganistTo see an organist in your dreams, denotes a friend will cause you much inconveniencefrom hasty action. For a young woman to dream that she is an organist, foretells she willbe so exacting in her love that she will be threatened with desertion.OrnamentIf you wear ornaments in dreams, you will have a flattering honor conferred upon you.If you receive them, you will be fortunate in undertakings.Giving them away, denotes recklessness and lavish extravagance.Losing an ornament, brings the loss either of a lover, or a good situation.

OrphanCondoling with orphans in a dream, means that the unhappy cares of others will touchyour sympathies and cause you to sacrifice much personal enjoyment.If the orphans be related to you, new duties will come into your life, causingestrangement from friends ant from some person held above mere friendly liking.OstrichTo dream of an ostrich, denotes that you will secretly amass wealth, but at the same timemaintain degrading intrigues with women.To catch one, your resources will enable you to enjoy travel and extensive knowledge.OtterTo see otters diving and sporting in limpid streams is certain to bring the dreamer wakinghappiness and good fortune. You will find ideal enjoyment in an early marriage, if youare single; wives may expect unusual tenderness from their spouses after this dream.OttomanDreams in which you find yourself luxuriously reposing upon an ottoman, discussing theintricacies of love with your sweetheart, foretells that envious rivals will seek to defameyou in the eyes of your affianced, and a hasty marriage will be advised.See Couch.OuijaTo dream of working on an ouija board, foretells the miscarriage of plans and unluckypartnerships.To fail to work, one is ominous of complications, caused by substituting pleasure forbusiness.If it writes fluently, you may expect fortunate results from some well-planned enterprise.If a negro steals it, you will meet with trials and vexations past endurance. To recover it,foretells that grievances will meet a favorable adjustment.OvenFor a woman to dream that her baking oven is red hot, denotes that she will be loved byher own family and friends, for her sweet and unselfish nature. If she is baking,

temporary disappointments await her. If the oven is broken, she will undergo manyvexations from children and servants.OvercoatTo dream of an overcoat, denotes you will suffer from contrariness, exhibited by others.To borrow one, foretells you will be unfortunate through mistakes made by strangers. Ifyou see or are wearing a handsome new overcoat, you will be exceedingly fortunate inrealizing your wishes.Over-AllsFor a woman to dream that she sees a man wearing over-alls, she will be deceived as tothe real character of her lover. If a wife, she will be deceived in her husband's frequentabsence, and the real cause will create suspicions of his fidelity.OwlTo hear the solemn, unearthly sound of the muffled voice of the owl, warns dreamers thatdeath creeps closely in the wake of health and joy. Precaution should be taken that life isnot ruthlessly exposed to his unyielding grasp. Bad tidings of the absent will surelyfollow this dream.To see a dead owl, denotes a narrow escape from desperate illness or death.To see an owl, foretells that you will be secretly maligned and be in danger fromenemies.OxTo see a well-fed ox, signifies that you will become a leading person in your community,and receive much adulation from women.To see fat oxen in green pastures, signifies fortune, and your rise to positions beyondyour expectations. If they are lean, your fortune will dwindle, and your friends will fallaway from you.If you see oxen well-matched and yoked, it betokens a happy and wealthy marriage, orthat you are already joined to your true mate.To see a dead ox, is a sign of bereavement.If they are drinking from a clear pond, or stream, you will possess some long-desiredestate, perhaps it will be in the form of a lovely and devoted woman. If a woman she willwin the embraces of her lover.See Cattle.

OystersIf you dream that you eat oysters, it denotes that you will lose all sense of propriety andmorality in your pursuit of low pleasures, and the indulgence of an insatiate thirst forgaining.To deal in oysters, denotes that you will not be over-modest in your mode of winning asweetheart, or a fortune.To see them, denotes easy circumstances, and many children are promised you.Oyster ShellsTo see oyster shells in your dreams, denotes that you will be frustrated in your attempt tosecure the fortune of another.PPacifyTo endeavor to pacify suffering ones, denotes that you will be loved for your sweetnessof disposition. To a young woman, this dream is one of promise of a devoted husband orfriends.Pacifying the anger of others, denotes that you will labor for the advancement of others.If a lover dreams of soothing the jealous suspicions of his sweetheart, he will find that hislove will be unfortunately placed.PacketTo dream of seeing a packet coming in, foretells that some pleasant recreation is in storefor you.To see one going out, you will experience slight losses and disappointments.PageTo see a page, denotes that you will contract a hasty union with one unsuited to you. Youwill fail to control your romantic impulses.

If a young woman dreams she acts as a page, it denotes that she is likely to participate insome foolish escapade.PagodaTo see a pagoda in your dreams, denotes that you will soon go on a long desired journey.If a young woman finds herself in a pagoda with her sweetheart, many unforeseen eventswill transpire before her union is legalized. An empty one, warns her of separation fromher lover.PailTo dream of full pails of milk, is a sign of fair prospects and pleasant associations.An empty pail is a sign of famine, or bad crops.For a young woman to be carrying a pail, denotes household employment.PainTo dream that you are in pain, will make sure of your own unhappiness. This dreamforetells useless regrets over some trivial transaction.To see others in pain, warns you that you are making mistakes in your life.Paint and PaintingTo see newly painted houses in dreams, foretells that you will succeed with some devisedplan.To have paint on your clothing, you will be made unhappy by the thoughtless criticismsof others.To dream that you use the brush yourself, denotes that you will be well pleased with yourpresent occupation.To dream of seeing beautiful paintings, denotes that friends will assume false positionstowards you, and you will find that pleasure is illusive.For a young woman to dream of painting a picture, she will be deceived in her lover, ashe will transfer his love to another.PalaceWandering through a palace and noting its grandeur, signifies that your prospects are

growing brighter and you will assume new dignity.To see and hear fine ladies and men dancing and conversing, denotes that you willengage in profitable and pleasing associations.For a young woman of moderate means to dream that she is a participant in theentertainment, and of equal social standing with others, is a sign of her advancementthrough marriage, or the generosity of relatives.This is often a very deceitful and misleading dream to the young woman of humblecircumstances; as it is generally induced in such cases by the unhealthy day dreams ofher idle, empty brain. She should strive after this dream, to live by honest work, andrestrain deceitful ambition by observing the fireside counsels of mother, and friends.See Opulence.PalisadeTo dream of the palisades, denotes that you will alter well-formed plans to pleasestrangers, and by so doing, you will impair your own interests.PallTo dream that you see a pall, denotes that you will have sorrow and misfortune.If you raise the pall from a corpse, you will doubtless soon mourn the death of one whomyou love.Pall-bearerTo dream of a pall-bearer, indicates some enemy will provoke your ill feeling, byconstant attacks on your integrity. If you see a pall-bearer, you will antagonize worthyinstitutions, and make yourself obnoxious to friends.PalletTo dream of a pallet, denotes that you will suffer temporary uneasiness over your loveaffairs. For a young woman, it is a sign of a jealous rival.PalmistryFor a young woman to dream of palmistry, foretells she will be the object of suspicion.If she has her palms read, she will have many friends of the opposite sex, but her own sexwill condemn her. If she reads others' hands, she will gain distinction by her intelligentbearing. If a minister's hand, she will need friends, even in her elevation.

Palm Tree Palm trees seen in your dreams, are messages of hopeful situations and happiness of a high order. For a young woman to pass down an avenue of palms, omens a cheerful home and a faithful husband. If the palms are withered, some unexpected sorrowful event will disturb her serenity. **Palsy**To dream that you are afflicted with palsy, denotes that you are making unstable contracts. To see your friend so afflicted, there will be uncertainty as to his faithfulness and sickness, too, may enter your home. For lovers to dream that their sweethearts have palsy, signifies that dissatisfaction over some question will mar their happiness. **Pancake**To dream of eating pancakes, denotes that you will have excellent success in all enterprises undertaken at this time. To cook them, denotes that you will be economical and thrifty in your home. **Pane of Glass**To dream that you handle a pane of glass, denotes that you are dealing in uncertainties. If you break it, your failure will be accentuated. To talk to a person through a pane of glass, denotes that there are obstacles in your immediate future, and they will cause you no slight inconvenience. **Panorama**To dream of a panorama, denotes that you will change your occupation or residence. You should curb your inclinations for change of scene and friends. **Panther**To see a panther and experience fright, denotes that contracts in love or business may be canceled unexpectedly, owing to adverse influences working against your honor. But killing, or over-powering it, you will experience joy and be successful in your undertakings. Your surroundings will take on fair prospects.

If one menaces you by its presence, you will have disappointments in business. Other people will likely recede from their promises to you. If you hear the voice of a panther, and experience terror or fright, you will have unfavorable news, coming in the way of reducing profit or gain, and you may have social discord; no fright forebodes less evil. A panther, like the cat, seen in a dream, portends evil to the dreamer, unless he kills it. **Pantomime**To dream of seeing pantomimes, denotes that your friends will deceive you. If you participate in them, you will have cause of offense. Affairs will not prove satisfactory. **Paper or Parchment**If you have occasion in your dreams to refer to, or handle, any paper or parchment, you will be threatened with losses. They are likely to be in the nature of a lawsuit. For a young woman, it means that she will be angry with her lover and that she fears the opinion of acquaintances. Beware, if you are married, of disagreements in the precincts of the home. **Parables**To dream of parables, denotes that you will be undecided as to the best course to pursue in dissenting to some business complication. To the lover, or young woman, this is a prophecy of misunderstandings and disloyalty. **Paradise**To dream that you are in Paradise, means loyal friends, who are willing to aid you. Thisdream holds out bright hopes to sailors or those about to make a long voyage. Tomothers, this means fair and obedient children. If you are sick and unfortunate, you willhave a speedy recovery and your fortune will ripen. To lovers, it is the promise of wealthand faithfulness.To dream that you start to Paradise and find yourself bewildered and lost, you willundertake enterprises which look exceedingly feasible and full of fortunate returns, butwhich will prove disappointing and vexatious.ParalysisParalysis is a bad dream, denoting financial reverses and disappointment in literaryattainment. To lovers, it portends a cessation of affections.

ParasolTo dream of a parasol, denotes, for married people, illicit enjoyments.If a young woman has this dream, she will engage in many flirtations, some of which willcause her interesting disturbances, lest her lover find out her inclinations.See Umbrella.ParcelTo dream of a parcel being delivered to you, denotes that you will be pleasantly surprisedby the return of some absent one, or be cared for in a worldly way.If you carry a parcel, you will have some unpleasant task to perform.To let a parcel fall on the way as you go to deliver it, you will see some deal fail to gothrough.PardonTo dream that you are endeavoring to gain pardon for an offense which you nevercommitted, denotes that you will be troubled, and seemingly with cause, over youraffairs, but it will finally appear that it was for your advancement. If offense wascommitted, you will realize embarrassment in affairs.To receive pardon, you will prosper after a series of misfortunes.See kindred words.ParentsTo see your parents looking cheerful while dreaming, denotes harmony and pleasantassociates.If they appear to you after they are dead, it is a warning of approaching trouble, and youshould be particular of your dealings.To see them while they are living, and they seem to be in your home and happy, denotespleasant changes for you. To a young woman, this usually brings marriage andprosperity. If pale and attired in black, grave disappointments will harass you.To dream of seeing your parents looking robust and contented, denotes you are underfortunate environments; your business and love interests will flourish. If they appearindisposed or sad, you will find life's favors passing you by without recognition.See Father and Mother.

ParkTo dream of walking through a well-kept park, denotes enjoyable leisure. If you walkwith your lover, you will be comfortably and happily married. Ill-kept parks, devoid ofgreen grasses and foliage, is ominous of unexpected reverses.ParrotParrots chattering in your dreams, signifies frivolous employments and idle gossipamong your friends.To see them in repose, denotes a peaceful intermission of family broils.For a young woman to dream that she owns a parrot, denotes that her lover will believeher to be quarrelsome.To teach a parrot, you will have trouble in your private affairs.A dead parrot, foretells the loss of social friends.ParsleyTo dream of parsley, denotes hard-earned success, usually the surroundings of thedreamer are healthful and lively.To eat parsley, is a sign of good health, but the care of a large family will be yourportion.ParsnipsTo see or eat parsnips, is a favorable omen of successful business or trade, but love willtake on unfavorable and gloomy aspects.PartingTo dream of parting with friends and companions, denotes that many little vexations willcome into your daily life.If you part with enemies, it is a sign of success in love and business.PartnerTo dream of seeing your business partner with a basket of crockery on his back, and,letting it fall, gets it mixed with other crockery, denotes your business will sustain a lossthrough the indiscriminate dealings of your partner. If you reprimand him for it, you will,to some extent, recover the loss.

PartnershipTo dream of forming a partnership with a man, denotes uncertain and fluctuating moneyaffairs. If your partner be a woman, you will engage in some enterprise which you willendeavor to keep hidden from friends.To dissolve an unpleasant partnership, denotes that things will arrange themselvesagreeable to your desires; but if the partnership was pleasant, there will be disquietingnews and disagreeable turns in your affairs.PartridgePartridges seen in your dreams, denotes that conditions will be good in your immediatefuture for the accumulation of property.To ensnare them, signifies that you will be fortunate in expectations.To kill them, foretells that you will be successful, but much of your wealth will be givento others.To eat them, signifies the enjoyment of deserved honors.To see them flying, denotes that a promising future is before you.PartyTo dream of an unknown party of men assaulting you for your money or valuables,denotes that you will have enemies banded together against you. If you escape uninjured,you will overcome any opposition, either in business or love.To dream of attending a party of any kind for pleasure, you will find that life has muchgood, unless the party is an inharmonious one.PassengerTo dream that you see passengers coming in with their luggage, denotes improvement inyour surroundings. If they are leaving you will lose an opportunity of gaining somedesired property. If you are one of the passengers leaving home, you will be dissatisfiedwith your present living and will seek to change it.Passing BellTo hear a passing bell, unexpected intelligence of the sorrow or illness of the absent.To ring one yourself, denotes ill health and reverses.

PasswordTo dream of a password, foretells you will have influential aid in some slight troublesoon to attack you. For a woman to dream that she has given away the password,signifies she will endanger her own standing through seeking frivolous or illicit desires.PasteboardTo dream of pasteboard, denotes that unfaithful friends will deceive you concerningimportant matters. To cut pasteboard, you will throw aside difficulties in your struggle toreach eminent positions.PastryTo dream of pastry, denotes that you will be deceived by some artful person.To eat it, implies heartfelt friendships.If a young woman dreams that she is cooking it, she will fail to deceive others as to herreal intentions.See Pies.PatchTo dream that you have patches upon your clothing, denotes that you will show no falsepride in the discharge of obligations.To see others wearing patches, denotes want and misery are near.If a young woman discovers a patch on her new dress, it indicates that she will findtrouble facing her when she imagines her happiest moments are approaching near. If shetries to hide the patches, she will endeavor to keep some ugly trait in her character fromher lover. If she is patching, she will assume duties for which she has no liking.For a woman to do family patching, denotes close and loving bonds in the family, but ascarcity of means is portended.PatentTo dream of securing a patent, denotes that you will be careful and painstaking with anytask you set about to accomplish. If you fail in securing your patent, you will sufferfailure for the reason that you are engaging in enterprises for which you have no ability.If you buy one, you will have occasion to make a tiresome and fruitless journey.

To see one, you will suffer unpleasantness from illness.Patent MedicineTo dream that you resort to patent medicine in your search for health, denotes that youwill use desperate measures in advancing your fortune, but you will succeed, to thedisappointment of the envious.To see or manufacture patent medicines, you will rise from obscurity to positions aboveyour highest imaginings.PathTo dream that you are walking in a narrow and rough path, stumbling over rocks andother obstructions, denotes that you will have a rough encounter with adversity, andfeverish excitement will weigh heavily upon you.To dream that you are trying to find your path, foretells that you will fail to accomplishsome work that you have striven to push to desired ends.To walk through a pathway bordered with green grass and flowers, denotes your freedomfrom oppressing loves.PaunchTo see a large paunch, denotes wealth and the total absence of refinement.To see a shriveled paunch, foretells illness and reverses.PauperTo dream that you are a pauper, implies unpleasant happenings for you.To see paupers, denotes that there will be a call upon your generosity.See Beggars and kindred words.Pawn-ShopIf in your dreams you enter a pawn-shop, you will find disappointments and losses inyour waking moments.To pawn articles, you will have unpleasant scenes with your wife or sweetheart, andperhaps disappointments in business.For a woman to go to a pawn-shop, denotes that she is guilty of indiscretions, and she is

likely to regret the loss of a friend.To redeem an article, denotes that
you will regain lost positions.To dream that you see a pawn-shop, denotes
you are negligent of your trust and are indanger of sacrificing your
honorable name in some salacious affair.PeachesDreaming of seeing or
eating peaches, implies the sickness of children, disappointingreturns in
business, and failure to make anticipated visits of pleasure; but if you
see themon trees with foliage, you will secure some desired position or
thing after much strivingand risking of health and money.To see dried
peaches, denotes that enemies will steal from you.For a young woman to
dream of gathering luscious peaches from well-filled trees, shewill, by
her personal charms and qualifications, win a husband rich in worldly
goods andwise in travel. If the peaches prove to be green and knotty, she
will meet with unkindnessfrom relatives and ill health will steal away
her attractions.See Orchard.PeacockFor persons dreaming of peacocks,
there lies below the brilliant and flashing ebb andflow of the stream of
pleasure and riches, the slums of sorrow and failure, which threatento
mix with its clearness at the least disturbing influence.For a woman to
dream that she owns peacocks, denotes that she will be deceived in
herestimate of man's honor.To hear their harsh voices while looking upon
their proudly spread plumage, denotes thatsome beautiful and
well-appearing person will work you discomfort and uneasiness
ofmind.PearlsTo dream of pearls, is a forerunner of good business and
trade and affairs of socialnature.If a young woman dreams that her lover
sends her gifts of pearls, she will indeed be mostfortunate, as there
will be occasions of festivity and pleasure for her, besides a loving
andfaithful affianced devoid of the jealous inclinations so ruinous to
the peace of lovers. Ifshe loses or breaks her pearls, she will suffer
indescribable sadness and sorrow throughbereavement or misunderstandings.
To find herself admiring them, she will covet andstrive for love or
possessions with a pureness of purpose.

PearsTo dream of eating pears, denotes poor success and debilitating
health.To admire the golden fruit upon graceful trees, denotes that
fortune will wear a morepromising aspect than formerly.To dream of
gathering them, denotes pleasant surprises will follow quickly
upondisappointment.To preserve them, denotes that you will take reverses
philosophically.Baking them, denotes insipid love and
friendships.PeasDreaming of eating peas, augurs robust health and the
accumulation of wealth. Muchactivity is indicated for farmers and their
women folks.To see them growing, denotes fortunate enterprises.To plant
them, denotes that your hopes are well grounded and they will be
realized.To gather them, signifies that your plans will culminate in good
and you will enjoy thefruits of your labors.To dream of canned peas,
denotes that your brightest hopes will be enthralled inuncertainties for
a short season, but they will finally be released by fortune.To see dried
peas, denotes that you are overtaxing your health.To eat dried peas,
foretells that you will, after much success, suffer a slight decrease

inpleasure or wealth.PebblesFor a young woman to dream of a pebble-strewn walk, she will be vexed with manyrivals and find that there are others with charms that attract besides her own. She whodreams of pebbles is selfish and should cultivate leniency towards others' faults.PecansTo dream of eating this appetizing nut, you will see one of your dearest plans come tofull fruition, and seeming failure prove a prosperous source of gain.To see them growing among leaves, signifies a long, peaceful existence. Failure in loveor business will follow in proportion as the pecan is decayed.

If they are difficult to crack and the fruit is small, you will succeed after much troubleand expense, but returns will be meagre.PelicanTo dream of a pelican, denotes a mingling of disappointments with successes.To catch one, you will be able to overcome disappointing influences.To kill one, denotes that you will cruelly set aside the rights of others.To see them flying, you are threatened with changes, which will impress you with ideasof uncertainty as to good.PenTo dream of a pen, foretells you are unfortunately being led into serious complications byyour love of adventure. If the pen refuses to write, you will be charged with a seriousbreach of morality.PenaltiesTo dream that you have penalties imposed upon you, foretells that you will have dutiesthat will rile you and find you rebellious.To pay a penalty, denotes sickness and financial loss. To escape the payment, you will bevictor in some contest.PencilTo dream of pencils, denotes favorable occupations. For a young woman to write withone, foretells she will be fortunate in marriage, if she does not rub out words; in that case,she will be disappointed in her lover.PennyTo dream of pennies, denotes unsatisfactory pursuits. Business will suffer, and lovers andfriends will complain of the smallness of affection.To lose them, signifies small deference and failures.To find them, denotes that prospects will advance to your improvement.To count pennies, foretells that you will be business-like and economical.

PensionTo dream of drawing a pension, foretells that you will be aided in your labors by friends.To fail in your application for a pension, denotes that you will lose in an undertaking andsuffer the loss of friendships.PeopleSee Crowd.PepperTo dream of pepper burning your tongue, foretells that you will suffer from youracquaintances through your love of gossip.To see red pepper growing, foretells for you a thrifty and an independent partner in themarriage state.To see piles of red pepper pods, signifies that you will aggressively maintain your rights.To grind black pepper, denotes that you will be victimized by the wiles of ingenious menor women. To see it in stands on the table, omens sharp reproaches or quarrels.For a young woman to put it on her food, foretells that she will be deceived by herfriends.PeppermintTo dream of peppermint, denotes pleasant entertainments and interesting affairs.To see it growing, denotes that you will participate in some pleasure in which there willbe a dash of romance.To enjoy drinks in which there is an effusion of peppermint, denotes that you will enjoyassignations with some attractive and fascinating person. To a young woman, this dreamwarns her against seductive pleasures.PerfumeTo dream of inhaling perfume, is an augury of happy incidents.For you to perfume your garments and person, denotes that you will seek and obtainadulation.Being oppressed by it to intoxication, denotes that excesses in joy will impair your

mental qualities.To spill perfume, denotes that you will lose something which affords you pleasure.To break a bottle of perfume, foretells that your most cherished wishes and desires willend disastrously, even while they promise a happy culmination.To dream that you are distilling perfume, denotes that your employments andassociations will be of the pleasantest character.For a young woman to dream of perfuming her bath, foretells ecstatic happenings. If shereceives it as a gift from a man, she will experience fascinating, but dangerous pleasures.PerspirationTo dream that you are in a perspiration, foretells that you will come out of somedifficulty, which has caused much gossip, with new honors.PestTo dream of being worried over a pest of any nature, foretells that disturbing elementswill prevail in your immediate future.To see others thus worried, denotes that you will be annoyed by some displeasingdevelopment.PetticoatTo dream of seeing new petticoats, denotes that pride in your belongings will make youan object of raillery among your acquaintances.To see them soiled or torn, portends that your reputation will be in great danger.If a young woman dream that she wears silken, or clean, petticoats, it denotes that shewill have a doting, but manly husband. If she suddenly perceives that she has left off herpetticoat in dressing, it portends much ill luck and disappointment. To see her petticoatfalling from its place while she is at some gathering, or while walking, she will havetrouble in retaining her lover, and other disappointments may follow.PewterTo dream of pewter, foretells straitened circumstances.See Dishes.

PhantomTo dream that a phantom pursues you, foretells strange and disquieting experiences.To see a phantom fleeing from you, foretells that trouble will assume smallerproportions.See Ghost.PheasantDreaming of pheasants, omens good fellowship among your friends.To eat one, signifies that the jealousy of your wife will cause you to forego friendlyintercourse with your friends.To shoot them, denotes that you will fail to sacrifice one selfish pleasure for the comfortof friends.PhosphorusTo dream of seeing phosphorus, is indicative of evanescent joys.For a young woman, it foretells a brilliant but brief success with admirers.PhotographyIf you see photographs in your dreams, it is a sign of approaching deception.If you receive the photograph of your lover, you are warned that he is not giving you hisundivided loyalty, while he tries to so impress you.For married people to dream of the possession of other persons' photographs, foretellsunwelcome disclosures of one's conduct.To dream that you are having your own photograph made, foretells that you willunwarily cause yourself and others' trouble.PhysicianFor a young woman to dream of a physician, denotes that she is sacrificing her beauty inengaging in frivolous pastimes. If she is sick and thus dreams, she will have sickness orworry, but will soon overcome them, unless the physician appears very anxious, and thenher trials may increase, ending in loss and sorrow.

PianoTo dream of seeing a piano, denotes some joyful occasion.To hear sweet and voluptuous harmony from a piano, signals success and health. Ifdiscordant music is being played, you will have many exasperating matters to consider.Sad and plaintive music, foretells sorrowful tidings.To find your piano broken and out of tune, portends dissatisfaction with your ownaccomplishments and disappointment in the failure of your friends or children to winhonors.To see an old-fashioned piano, denotes that you have, in trying moments, neglected theadvices and opportunities of the past, and are warned not to do so again.For a young woman to dream that she is executing difficult, but entrancing music, shewill succeed in winning an indifferent friend to be a most devoted and loyal lover.PickaxeTo dream of a pickaxe, denotes a relentless enemy is working to overthrow you socially.A broken one, implies disaster to all your interests.PicklesTo dream of pickles, denotes that you will follow worthless pursuits if you fail to callenergy and judgment to your aid.For a young woman to dream of eating pickles, foretells an unambitious career. To dreamof pickles, denotes vexation in love, but final triumph.For a young woman to dream that she is eating them, or is hungry for them, foretells shewill find many rivals, and will be overcome unless she is careful of her private affairs.Impure pickles, indicate disappointing engagements and love quarrels.PickpocketTo dream of a pickpocket, foretells some enemy will succeed in harassing and causingyou loss. For a young woman to have her pocket picked, denotes she will be the object ofsome person's envy and spite, and may lose the regard of a friend through these evilmachinations, unless she keeps her own counsel. If she picks others' pockets, she willincur the displeasure of a companion by her coarse behavior.PicnicTo dream of attending a picnic, foreshadows success and real enjoyment.

Dreams of picnics, bring undivided happiness to the young.Storms, or any interfering elements at a picnic, implies the temporary displacement ofassured profit and pleasure in love or business.See kindred words.PicturesPictures appearing before you in dreams, prognosticate deception and the ill will ofcontemporaries.To make a picture, denotes that you will engage in some unremunerative enterprise.To destroy pictures, means that you will be pardoned for using strenuous means toestablish your rights.To buy them, foretells worthless speculation.To dream of seeing your likeness in a living tree, appearing and disappearing, denotesthat you will be prosperous and seemingly contented, but there will be disappointmentsin reaching out for companionship and reciprocal understanding of ideas and plans.To dream of being surrounded with the best efforts of the old and modern masters,denotes that you will have insatiable longings and desires for higher attainments,compared to which present success will seem poverty-stricken and miserable.See Painting and Photographs.PierTo stand upon a pier in your dream, denotes that you will be brave in your battle forrecognition in prosperity's realm, and that you will be admitted to the highest posts ofhonor.If you strive to reach a pier and fail, you will lose the distinction you most coveted.PiesTo dream of eating pies, you will do well to watch your enemies, as they are planning toinjure you.For a young woman to dream of making pies, denotes that she will flirt with men forpastime. She should accept this warning.See Pastry.

PigTo dream of a fat, healthy pig, denotes reasonable success in affairs. If they arewallowing in mire, you will have hurtful associates, and your engagements will besubject to reproach. This dream will bring to a young woman a jealous and greedycompanion though the chances are that he will be wealthy.See Hog.PigeonTo dream of seeing pigeons and hearing them cooing above their cotes, denotes domesticpeace and pleasure-giving children. For a young woman, this dream indicates an earlyand comfortable union.To see them being used in a shooting match, and, if you participate, it denotes thatcruelty in your nature will show in your dealings, and you are warned of low anddebasing pleasures.To see them flying, denotes freedom from misunderstanding, you will meet agreeableand fortuPilgrimTo dream of pilgrims, denotes that you will go on an extended journey, leaving home andits dearest objects in the mistaken idea that it must be thus for their good.To dream that you are a pilgrim, portends struggles with poverty and unsympatheticcompanions.For a young woman to dream that a pilgrim approaches her, she will fall an easy dupe todeceit. If he leaves her, she will awaken to her weakness of character and strive tostrengthen independent thought.PillTo dream that you take pills, denotes that you will have responsibilities to look after, butthey will bring you no little comfort and enjoyment.To give them to others, signifies that you will be criticised for your disagreeableness.PillowTo dream of a pillow, denotes luxury and comfort.For a young woman to dream that she makes a pillow, she will have encouraging prospects of a pleasant future.PimpleTo dream of your flesh being full of pimples, denotes worry over trifles.To see others with pimples on them, signifies that you will be troubled with illness andcomplaints from others.For a woman to dream that her beauty is marred by pimples, her conduct in home orsocial circles will be criticised by friends and acquaintances. You may have smallannoyances to follow this dream.PincersTo dream of feeling pincers on your flesh, denotes that you will be burdened withexasperating cares. Any dream of pincers, signifies unfortunate incidents.PineappleTo dream of pineapples, is exceedingly propitious. Success will follow in the near future,if you gather pineapples or eat them.To dream that you prick your fingers while preparing a pineapple for the table, you willexperience considerable vexation over matters which will finally bring pleasure andsuccess.Pine TreeTo see a pine tree in a dream, foretells unvarying success in any undertaking. Dead pine,for a woman, represents bereavement and cares.PinsTo dream of pins, augurs differences and quarrels ill families.To a young woman, they warn her of unladylike conduct towards her lover. To dream ofswallowing a pin, denotes that accidents will force you into perilous conditions.To lose one, implies a petty loss or disagreement.To see a bent or rusty pin, signifies that you will lose esteem because of your carelessways.To stick one into your flesh, denotes that some person will irritate you.

PipePipes seen in dreams, are representatives of peace and comfort after many struggles.Sewer, gas, and such like pipes, denotes unusual thought and prosperity in yourcommunity.Old and broken pipe, signifies ill health and stagnation of business.To dream that you smoke a pipe, denotes that you will enjoy the visit of an old friend,and peaceful settlements of differences will also take place.PirateTo dream of pirates, denotes that you will be exposed to the evil designs of false friends.To dream that you are a pirate, denotes that you will fall beneath the society of friendsand former equals.For a young woman to dream that her lover is a pirate, is a sign of his unworthiness anddeceitfulness. If she is captured by pirates, she will be induced to leave her home underfalse pretenses.PistolSeeing a pistol in your dream, denotes bad fortune, generally.If you own one, you will cultivate a low, designing character.If you hear the report of one, you will be made aware of some scheme to ruin yourinterests.To dream of shooting off your pistol, signifies that you will bear some innocent personenvy, and you will go far to revenge the imagined wrong.PitIf you are looking into a deep pit in your dream, you will run silly risks in businessventures and will draw uneasiness about your wooing.To fall into a pit denotes calamity and deep sorrow. To wake as you begin to feel yourselffalling into the pit, brings you out of distress in fairly good shape.To dream that you are descending into one, signifies that you will knowingly risk healthand fortune for greater success.

PitcherTo dream of a pitcher, denotes that you will be of a generous and congenial disposition.Success will attend your efforts.A broken pitcher, denotes loss of friends.PitchforkPitchforks in dreams, denotes struggles for betterment of fortune and great laboring,either physically or mentally.To dream that you are attacked by some person using a pitchfork, implies that you willhave personal enemies who would not scruple to harm you.PlagueTo dream of a plague raging, denotes disappointing returns in business, and your wife orlover will lead you a wretched existence.If you are afflicted with the plague, you will keep your business out of embarrassmentwith the greatest maneuvering. If you are trying to escape it, some trouble, which looksimpenetrable, is pursuing you.PlainFor a young woman to dream of crossing a plain, denotes that she will be fortunatelysituated, if the grasses are green and luxuriant; if they are arid, or the grass is dead, shewill have much discomfort and loneliness.See Prairie.PlaneTo dream that you use a plane, denotes that your liberality and successful efforts will behighly commended.To see carpenters using their planes, denotes that you will progress smoothly in yourundertakings.To dream of seeing planes, denotes congeniality and even success.A love of the real, and not the false, is portended by this dream.

PlanetTo dream of a planet, foretells an uncomfortable journey and depressing work.PlankFor a young woman to dream that she is walking across muddy water on a rotten plank,denotes that she will feel keenly the indifference shown her by one she loves, or othertroubles may arise; or her defence of honor may be in danger of collapse.Walking a good, sound plank, is a good omen, but a person will have to be unusuallycareful in conduct after such a dream.PlasterTo dream of seeing walls plainly plastered, denotes that success will come, but it will notbe stable.To have plaster fall upon you, denotes unmitigated disasters and disclosure.To see plasterers at work, denotes that you will have a sufficient competency to liveabove penury.PlateFor a woman to dream of plates, denotes that she will practise economy and win a worthyhusband. If already married, she will retain her husband's love and respect by the wiseordering of his household.See Dishes.PlayFor a young woman to dream that she attends a play, foretells that she will be courted bya genial friend, and will marry to further her prospects and pleasure seeking. If there istrouble in getting to and from the play, or discordant and hideous scenes, she will beconfronted with many displeasing surprises.See Theater.PleasureTo dream of pleasure, denotes gain and personal enjoyment.See Joy.

PlowTo dream of a plow, signifies unusual success, and affairs will reach a pleasingculmination.To see persons plowing, denotes activity and advancement in knowledge and fortune.For a young woman to see her lover plowing, indicates that she will have a noble andwealthy husband. Her joys will be deep and lasting.To plow yourself, denotes rapid increase in property and joys.PlumsPlums, if they are green, unless seen on trees, are signs of personal and relativediscomfort.To see them ripe, denotes joyous occasions, which, however, will be of short duration.To eat them, denotes that you will engage in flirtations and other evanescent pleasures.To gather them, you will obtain your desires, but they will not prove so solid as you hadimagined.If you find yourself gathering them up from the ground, and find rotten ones among thegood, you will be forced to admit that your expectations are unrealized, and that there isno life filled with pleasure alone.PocketTo dream of your pocket, is a sign of evil demonstrations against you.PocketbookTo find a pocketbook filled with bills and money in your dreams, you will be quite lucky,gaining in nearly every instance your desire. If empty, you will be disappointed in somebig hope.If you lose your pocketbook, you will unfortunately disagree with your best friend, andthereby lose much comfort and real gain.PoinardTo dream of some one stabbing you with a poinard, denotes that secret enemies willcause you uneasiness of mind.

If you attack any person with one of these weapons, you will unfortunately suspect yourfriends of unfaithfulness.Dreaming of poinards, omens evil.See Dagger.PoisonTo fed that you are poisoned in a dream, denotes that some painful influence willimmediately reach you.If you seek to use poison on others, you will be guilty of base thoughts, or the world willgo wrong for you.For a young woman to dream that she endeavors to rid herself of a rival in this way, shewill be likely to have a deal of trouble in securing a lover.To throw the poison away, denotes that by sheer force you will overcome unsatisfactoryconditions.To handle poison, or see others with it, signifies that unpleasantness will surround you.To dream that your relatives or children are poisoned, you will receive injury fromunsuspected sources.If an enemy or rival is poisoned, you will overcome obstacles.To recover from the effects of poison, indicates that you will succeed after worry.To take strychnine or other poisonous medicine under the advice of a physician, denotesthat you will undertake some affair fraught with danger.PokerTo dream of seeing a red hot poker, or fighting with one, signifies that you will meettrouble with combative energy.To play at poker, warns you against evil company; and young women, especially, willlose their moral distinctiveness if they find themselves engaged in this game.Polar BearPolar bears in dreams, are prognostic of deceit, as misfortune will approach you in aseeming fair aspect. Your bitterest enemies will wear the garb of friendship. Rivals willtry to supersede you.

To see the skin of one, denotes that you will successfully overcome any opposition.See Bear.Pole-catTo dream of a pole-cat, signifies salacious scandals.To inhale the odor of a pole-cat on your clothes, or otherwise smell one, you will findthat your conduct will be considered rude, and your affairs will prove unsatisfactory.To kill one, denotes that you will overcome formidable obstacles.PoliceIf the police are trying to arrest you for some crime of which you are innocent, it foretellsthat you will successfully outstrip rivalry.If the arrest is just, you will have a season of unfortunate incidents.To see police on parole, indicates alarming fluctuations in affairs.PolishingTo dream of polishing any article, high attainments will place you in enviable positions.PoliticianTo dream of a politician, denotes displeasing companionships, and incidences where youwill lose time and means.If you engage in political wrangling, it portends that misunderstandings and ill feelingwill be shown you by friends.For a young woman to dream of taking interest in politics, warns her against designingduplicity,PolkaTo dream of dancing the polka, denotes pleasant occupations.See Dancing.

PomegranatePomegranates, when dreamed of, denotes that you will wisely use your talents for theenrichment of the mind rather than seeking those pleasures which destroy morality andhealth.If your sweetheart gives you one, you will be lured by artful wiles to the verge ofdistraction by woman's charms, but inner forces will hold you safe from thralldom.To eat one, signifies that you will yield yourself a captive to the personal charms ofanother.PondTo see a pond in your dream, denotes that events will bring no emotion, and fortune willretain a placid outlook.If the pond is muddy, you will have domestic quarrels.See Water, Puddle and kindred words.PonyTo see ponies in your dreams, signifies moderate speculations will be rewarded withsuccess.PoorTo dream that you, or any of your friends, appear to be poor, is significant of worry andlosses.See Pauper.Poor-HouseTo see a poor-house in your dream, denotes you have unfaithful friends, who will carefor you only as they can use your money and belongings.PopeAny dream in which you see the Pope, without speaking to him, warns you of servitude.You will bow to the will of some master, even to that of women.To speak to the Pope, denotes that certain high honors are in store for you. To see thePope looking sad or displeased, warns you against vice or sorrow of some kind.

PoplarsTo dream of seeing poplars, is an omen of good, if they are in leaf or bloom.For a young woman to stand by her lover beneath the blossoms and leaves of a tulippoplar, she will realize her most extravagant hopes.Her lover will be handsome and polished. Wealth and friends will be hers. If they areleafless and withered, she will meet with disappointments.PoppiesPoppies seen in dreams, represents a season of seductive pleasures and flatteringbusiness, but they all occupy unstable foundations.If you inhale the odor of one, you will be the victim of artful persuasions and flattery.(The mesmeric influence of the poppy inducts one into strange atmospheres, leavingmateriality behind while the subjective self explores these realms as in natural sleep; yetthese dreams do not bear truthful warnings to the material man. Being, in a manner,enforced.)PorcelainTo dream of porcelain, signifies you will have favorable opportunities of progressing inyour affairs. To see it broken or soiled, denotes mistakes will be made which will causegrave offense.PorchTo dream of a porch, denotes that you will engage a new undertakings, and the futurewill be full of uncertainties.If a young woman dreams that she is with her lover on a porch, implies her doubts ofsome one's intentions. To dream that you build a porch, you will assume new duties.PorcupineTo see a porcupine in your dreams, denotes that you will disapprove any new enterpriseand repel new friendships with coldness.For a young woman to dream of a porcupine, portends that she will fear her lover.To see a dead one, signifies your abolishment of ill feelings and possessions.

PorkIf you eat pork in your dreams, you will encounter real trouble, but if you only see pork,you will come out of a conflict victoriously.See Bacon.PorpoiseTo see a porpoise in your dreams, denotes enemies are thrusting your interest aside,through your own inability to keep people interested in you.PorterSeeing a porter in a dream, denotes decided bad luck and eventful happenings.To imagine yourself a porter, denotes humble circumstances.To hire one, you will be able to enjoy whatever success comes to you.To discharge one, signifies that disagreeable charges will be preferred against you.PortfolioTo dream of a portfolio, denotes that your employment will not be to your liking, andyou will seek a change in your location.PortraitTo dream of gazing upon the portrait of some beautiful person, denotes that, while youenjoy pleasure, you can but feel the disquieting and treacherousness of such joys. Yourgeneral affairs will suffer loss after dreaming of portraits.See Pictures, Photographs, and Paintings.PostageTo dream of postage stamps, denotes system and remuneration in business.If you try to use cancelled stamps, you will fall into disrepute.To receive stamps, signifies a rapid rise to distinction.To see torn stamps, denotes that there are obstacles in your way.

PostmanTo dream of a postman, denotes that hasty news will more frequently be of a distressingnature than otherwise.See Letter Carrier.Post-OfficeTo dream of a post-office, is a sign of unpleasant tidings. and ill luck generally.PotTo dream of a pot, foretells that unimportant events will work you vexation. For a youngwoman to see a boiling pot, omens busy employment of pleasant and social duties. Tosee a broken or rusty one, implies that keen disappointment will be experienced by you.PotatoesDreaming of potatoes, brings incidents often of good.To dream of digging them, denotes success.To dream of eating them, you will enjoy substantial gain.To cook them, congenial employment.Planting them, brings realization of desires.To see them rotting, denotes vanished pleasure and a darkening future.PotterTo dream of a potter, denotes constant employment, with satisfactory results. For a youngwoman to see a potter, foretells she will enjoy pleasant engagements.Potter's FieldTo see a potter's field in your dreams, denotes you will have poverty and misery todistress you. For a young woman to walk through a potter's field with her lover, she willgive up the one she loves in the hope of mercenary gain.PoultryTo see dressed poultry in a dream, foretells extravagant habits will reduce your security

in money matters. For a young woman to dream that she is chasing live poultry, foretellsshe will devote valuable time to frivolous pleasure.PowderTo see powder in your dreams, denotes unscrupulous people are dealing with you. Youmay detect them through watchfulness.PrairieTo dream of a prairie, denotes that you will enjoy ease, and even luxury and unobstructedprogress.An undulating prairie, covered with growing grasses and flowers, signifies joyoushappenings.A barren prairie, represents loss and sadness through the absence of friends.To be lost on one, is a sign of sadness and ill luck.PrayerTo dream of saying prayers, or seeing others doing so, foretells you will be threatenedwith failure, which will take strenuous efforts to avert.PreacherTo dream of a preacher, denotes that your ways are not above reproach, and your affairswill not move evenly.To dream that you are a preacher, foretells for you losses in business, and distastefulamusements will jar upon you.To hear preaching, implies that you will undergo misfortune.To argue with a preacher, you will lose in some contest.To see one walk away from you, denotes that your affairs will move with new energy. Ifhe looks sorrowful, reproaches will fall heavily upon you.To see a long-haired preacher, denotes that you are shortly to have disputes withoverbearing and egotistical people.PrecipiceTo dream of standing over a yawning precipice, portends the threatenings of misfortunes and calamities.To fall over a precipice, denotes that you will be engulfed in disaster.See Abyss and Pit.PregnancyFor a woman to dream that she is pregnant, denotes she will be unhappy with herhusband, and her children will be unattractive.For a virgin, this dream omens scandal and adversity. If a woman is really pregnant andhas this dream, it prognosticates a safe delivery and swift recovery of strength.PresentTo receive presents in your dreams, denotes that you will be unusually fortunate.See Gifts.PriestA priest is an augury of ill, if seen in dreams.If he is in the pulpit, it denotes sickness and trouble for the dreamer.If a woman dreams that she is in love with a priest, it warns her of deceptions and anunscrupulous lover. If the priest makes love to her, she will be reproached for her love ofgaiety and practical joking.To confess to a priest, denotes that you will be subjected to humiliation and sorrow.These dreams imply that you have done, or will do, something which will bringdiscomfort to yourself or relatives. The priest or preacher is your spiritual adviser, andany dream of his professional presence is a warning against your own imperfections.Seen in social circles, unless they rise before you as spectres, the same rules will apply asto other friends.See Preacher.PrimroseTo dream of this little flower starring the grass at your feet, is an omen of joys laden withcomfort and peace.

PrinterTo see a printer in your dreams, is a warning of poverty, if you neglect to practiceeconomy and cultivate energy. For a woman to dream that her lover or associate is aprinter, foretells she will fail to please her parents in the selection of a close friend.Printing OfficeTo be in a printing office in dreams, denotes that slander and contumely will threatenyou.To run a printing office is indicative of hard luck.For a young woman to dream that her sweetheart is connected with a printing office,denotes that she will have a lover who is unable to lavish money or time upon her, andshe will not be sensible enough to see why he is so stingy.PrisonTo dream of a prison, is the forerunner of misfortune in every instance, if it encirclesyour friends, or yourself.To see any one dismissed from prison, denotes that you will finally overcome misfortune.See Jail.PrivacyTo dream that your privacy suffers intrusion, foretells you will have overbearing peopleto worry you. For a woman, this dream warns her to look carefully after private affairs. Ifshe intrudes on the privacy of her husband or lover, she will disabuse some one'sconfidence, if not careful of her conversation.Prize FightTo see a prize fight in your dreams, denotes your affairs will give you trouble incontrolling them.Prize FighterFor a young woman to see a prize fighter, foretells she will have pleasure in fast society,and will give her friends much concern about her reputation.

ProcessionTo dream of a procession, denotes that alarming fears will possess you relative to thefulfilment of expectations. If it be a funeral procession, sorrow is fast approaching, andwill throw a shadow around pleasures.To see or participate in a torch-light procession, denotes that you will engage in gaietieswhich will detract from your real merit.ProfanityTo dream of profanity, denotes that you will cultivate those traits which render youcoarse and unfeeling toward your fellow man.To dream that others use profanity, is a sign that you will be injured in some way, andprobably insulted also.ProfitsTo dream of profits, brings success in your immediate future.PromenadeTo dream of promenading, foretells that you will engage in energetic and profitablepursuits.To see others promenading, signifies that you will have rivals in your pursuits.PropertyTo dream that you own vast property, denotes that you will be successful in affairs, andgain friendships.See Wealth.ProstituteTo dream that you are in the company of a prostitute, denotes that you will incur therighteous scorn of friends for some ill-mannered conduct.For a young woman to dream of a prostitute, foretells that she will deceive her lover as toher purity or candor. This dream to a married woman brings suspicion of her husband andconsequent quarrels.See Harlot.

PublicanTo dream of a publican, denotes that you will have your sympathies aroused by some onein a desperate condition, and you will diminish your own gain for his advancement. To ayoung woman, this dream brings a worthy lover; but because of his homeliness she willtrample on his feelings unnecessarily.PublisherTo dream of a publisher, foretells long journeys and aspirations to the literary craft.If a woman dreams that her husband is a publisher, she will be jealous of more than onewoman of his acquaintance, and spicy scenes will ensue.For a publisher to reject your manuscript, denotes that you will suffer disappointment atthe miscarriage of cherished designs. If he accepts it, you will rejoice in the full fruitionof your hopes. If he loses it, you will suffer evil at the hands of strangers.PuddingsTo dream of puddings, denotes small returns from large investments, if you only see it.To eat it, is proof that your affairs will be disappointing.For a young woman to cook, or otherwise prepare a pudding, denotes that her lover willbe sensual and worldly minded, and if she marries him, she will see her love and fortunevanish.PuddleTo find yourself stepping into puddles of clear water in a dream, denotes a vexation, butsome redeeming good in the future. If the water be muddy, unpleasantness will go a fewrounds with you.To wet your feet by stepping into puddles, foretells that your pleasure will work youharm afterwards.PulpitTo dream of a pulpit, denotes sorrow and vexation.To dream that you are in a pulpit, foretells sickness, and unsatisfactory results in businessor trades of any character.

PulseTo dream of your pulse, is warning to look after your affairs and health with close care,as both are taking on debilitating conditions.To dream of feeling the pulse of another, signifies that you are committing depredationsin Pleasure's domain.PumpTo see a pump in a dream, denotes that energy and faithfulness to business will producedesired riches, good health also is usually betokened by this dream.To see a broken pump, signifies that the means of advancing in life will be absorbed byfamily cares. To the married and the unmarried, it intimates blasted energies.If you work a pump, your life will be filled with pleasure and profitable undertakings.PunchTo dream of drinking the concoction called punch, denotes that you will prefer selfishpleasures to honorable distinction and morality.To dream that you are punching any person with a club or fist, denotes quarrels andrecriminations.PupTo dream of pups, denotes that you will entertain the innocent and hapless, and therebyenjoy pleasure. The dream also shows that friendships will grow stronger, and fortunewill increase if the pups are healthful and well formed, and vice versa if they are lean andfilthy.See Dogsand Hound Pups.PurchasesTo dream of purchases usually augurs profit and advancement with pleasure.PurseTo dream of your purse being filled with diamonds and new bills, denotes for youassociations where ``Good Cheer'' is the watchword, and harmony and tender loves willmake earth a beautiful place.See Pocketbook.

PuttyTo dream of working in putty, denotes that hazardous chances will be taken with fortune.If you put in a window-pane with putty, you will seek fortune with poor results.PyramidTo dream of pyramids, denotes that many changes will come to you.If you scale them, you will journey along before you find the gratification of desires. Forthe young woman, it prognosticates a husband who is in no sense congenial.To dream that you are studying the mystery of the ancient pyramids, denotes that youwill develop a love for the mysteries of nature, and you will become learned andpolished.QQuack DoctorTo see a quack doctor in your dreams denotes you will be alarmed over some illness andits improper treatment.Quack MedicineTo dream you take quack medicine shows that you are growing morbid under sometrouble and should overcome it by industrious application to duty. To read theadvertisement of it foretells unhappy companions will wrong and distress you.QuadrilleTo dream of dancing a quadrille foretells that some pleasant engagement will occupyyour time.See Dancing.

QuagmireTo dream of being in a quagmire implies your inability to meet obligations. To see othersthus situated denotes that the failures of others will be felt by you. Illness is sometimesindicated by this dream.QuailTo see quails in your dream is a very favorable omen, if they are alive; if dead, you willundergo serious ill luck.To shoot quail foretells that ill feelings will be shown by you to your best friends.To eat them signifies extravagance in your personal living.QuakerTo dream of a Quaker denotes that you will have faithful friends and fair business. If youare one, you will deport yourself honorably toward an enemy.For a young woman to attend a Quaker meeting portends that she will by her modestmanners win a faithful husband who will provide well for her household.QuarantineTo dream of being in quarantine denotes that you will be placed in a disagreeableposition by the malicious intriguing of enemies.QuarrelQuarrels in dreams portend unhappiness and fierce altercations. To a young woman, it isthe signal of fatal unpleasantries, and to a married woman, it brings separation orcontinuous disagreements.To hear others quarreling denotes unsatisfactory business and disappointing trade.QuarryTo dream of being in a quarry and seeing the workmen busy denotes that you willadvance by hard labor.An idle quarry signifies failure, disappointment, and often death.

QuartetteTo dream of a quartette--and you are playing or singing-- denotes favorable affairs,jolly companions, and good times.To see or hear a quartette foretells that you will aspire to something beyond you.QuayTo dream of a quay denotes that you will contemplate making a long tour in the nearfuture.To see vessels while standing on the quay denotes the fruition of wishes and designs.QueenTo dream of a queen foretells successful ventures. If she looks old or haggard, there willbe disappointments connected with your pleasures.See Empress.QuestionTo question the merits of a thing in your dreams denotes that you will suspect someonewhom you love of unfaithfulness, and you will fear for your speculations.To ask a question foretells that you will earnestly strive for truth and be successful.If you are questioned, you will be unfairly dealt with.QuicksandTo find yourself in quicksand while dreaming, you will meet with loss and deceit.If you are unable to overcome it, you will be involved in overwhelming misfortunes.For a young woman to be rescued by her lover from quicksand, she will possess a worthyand faithful husband, who will still remain her lover.QuillsTo dream of quills denotes to the literary inclined a season of success.To dream of them as ornaments signifies a rushing trade and some remuneration.

For a young woman to be putting a quill on her hat denotes that she will attempt manyconquests, and her success will depend upon her charms.QuiltsTo dream of quilts foretells pleasant and comfortable circumstances. For a young woman,this dream foretells that her practical and wise business-like ways will advance her intothe favorable esteem of

a man who will seek her for a wife.If the quilts are clean but have holes
in them, she will win a husband who appreciates herworth, but he will not
be the one most desired by her for a companion. If the quilts aresoiled,
she will bear evidence of carelessness in her dress and manners and thus
fail tosecure a very upright husband.QuinineTo dream of quinine denotes
you will soon be possessed of great happiness, though yourprospects for
much wealth may be meager. To take some foretells improvement in
healthand energy. You will also make new friends, who will lend you
commercial aid.QuinsyTo dream of being afflicted with this disease
denotes discouraging employments.To see others with it, sickness will
cause you much anxiety.QuoitsTo play at quoits in dreams foretells low
engagements and loss of good employment. Tolose portends of distressing
conditions.RRabbitTo dream of rabbits foretells favorable turns in
conditions, and you will be more pleasedwith your gains than formerly.To
see white rabbits denotes faithfulness in love to the married or single.

To see rabbits frolicing about denotes that children will contribute to
your joys.See Hare.RaccoonTo dream of a raccoon denotes you are being
deceived by the friendly appearance ofenemies.RaceTo dream that you are
in a race foretells that others will aspire to the things you areworking
to possess; but if you win in the race, you will overcome your
competitors.RackTo dream of a rack denotes the uncertainty of the outcome
of some engagement, whichgives you much anxious thought.RacketTo dream of
a racket denotes that you will be foiled in some anticipated pleasure.
For ayoung woman, this dream is ominous of disappointment in not being
able to participatein some amusement that has engaged her
attention.RadishTo dream of seeing a bed of radishes growing is an omen
of good luck. Your friends willbe unusually kind, and your business will
prosper.If you eat them, you will suffer slightly through the
thoughtlessness of some one near toyou.To see radishes or to plant them
denotes that your anticipations will be happily realized.RaffleIf you
dream of raffling any article, you will fall a victim to speculation.If
you are at a church raffle, you will soon find that disappointment is
clouding yourfuture. For a young woman, this dream means empty
expectations.RaftTo dream of a raft denotes that you will go into new
locations to engage in enterprises,

which will prove successful.To dream of floating on a raft denotes
uncertain journeys. If you reach your destination,you will surely come
into good fortune.If a raft breaks or any such mishap befalls it, you or
some friend will suffer from anaccident, or sickness will bear
unfortunate results.RageTo be in a rage and scolding and tearing up
things generally, while dreaming, signifiesquarrels and injury to your
friends.To see others in a rage is a sign of unfavorable conditions for

business and unhappinessin social life.For a young woman to see her lover in a rage denotes that there will be some discordantnote in their love, and misunderstandings will naturally occur.RailingTo dream of seeing railings denotes that some person is trying to obstruct your pathwayin love or business.To dream of holding on to a railing foretells that some desperate chance will be taken byyou to obtain some object upon which you have set your heart. It may be of love, or of amore material form.RailroadIf you dream of a railroad, you will find that your business will need close attention, asenemies are trying to usurp you.For a young woman to dream of railroads, she will make a journey to visit friends andwill enjoy some distinction.To see an obstruction on these roads indicates foul play in your affairs.To walk the cross ties of a railroad signifies a time of worry and laborious work.To walk the rails, you may expect to obtain much happiness from your skillfulmanipulation of affairs.To see a road inundated with clear water foretells that pleasure will wipe out misfortunefor a time, but it will rise, phoenix like, again.

RainTo be out in a clear shower of rain denotes that pleasure will be enjoyed with the zest ofyouth, and prosperity will come to you.If the rain descends from murky clouds, you will feel alarmed over the graveness of yourundertakings.To see and hear rain approaching, and you escape being wet, you will succeed in yourplans, and your designs will mature rapidly.To be sitting in the house and see through the window a downpour of rain denotes thatyou will possess fortune, and passionate love will be requited.To hear the patter of rain on the roof denotes a realization of domestic bliss and joy.Fortune will come in a small way.To dream that your house is leaking during a rain, if the water is clear, foretells that illicitpleasure will come to you rather unexpectedly; but if filthy or muddy, you may expectthe reverse and also exposure.To find yourself regretting some duty unperformed while listening to the rain denotesthat you will seek pleasure at the expense of another's sense of propriety and justice.To see it rain on others foretells that you will exclude friends from your confidence.For a young woman to dream of getting her clothes wet and soiled while out in a raindenotes that she will entertain some person indiscreetly and will suffer the suspicions offriends for the unwise yielding to foolish enjoyments.To see it raining on farm stock foretells disappointment in business and unpleasantness insocial circles.Stormy rains are always unfortunate.RainbowTo see a rainbow in a dream is prognostic of unusual happenings. Affairs will assume amore promising countenance, and crops will give promise of a plentiful yield.For lovers to see the rainbow is an omen of much happiness from their union.To see the rainbow hanging low over green trees signifies unconditional success in anyundertaking.

RaisinsTo dream of eating raisins implies that discouragements will darken your hopes whenthey seem about to be realized.RakeTo dream of using a rake portends that some work which you have left to others willnever be accomplished unless you superintend it yourself.To see a broken rake denotes that sickness or some accident will bring failure to yourplans.To see others raking foretells that you will rejoice in the fortunate condition of others.RamTo dream that a ram pursues you foretells that some misfortune threatens you.To see one quietly grazing denotes that you will have powerful friends who will use theirbest efforts for your good.See Sheep and Lamb.RambleTo dream that you are rambling through the country denotes that you will be oppressedwith sadness and the separation from friends, but your worldly surroundings will be allthat one could desire. For a young woman, this dream promises a comfortable home butearly bereavement.RamrodTo dream of a ramrod denotes unfortunate adventures. You will have cause for grief. Fora young woman to see one bent or broken foretells that a dear friend or lover will fail her.RansomTo dream that a ransom is made for you, you will find that you are deceived and workedfor money on all sides. For a young woman, this is prognostic of evil, unless some onepays the ransom and relieves her.RapeTo dream that rape has been committed among your acquaintances denotes that you will

be shocked at the distress of some of your friends.For a young woman to dream that she has been the victim of rape foretells that she willhave troubles, which will wound her pride, and her lover will be estranged.RapidsTo imagine that you are being carried over rapids in a dream denotes that you will sufferappalling loss from the neglect of duty and the courting of seductive pleasures.RaspberryTo see raspberries in a dream foretells you are in danger of entanglements, which willprove interesting before you escape from them.For a woman to eat them means distress over circumstantial evidence in some occurrencecausing gossip.RatTo dream of rats denotes that you will be deceived and injured by your neighbors.Quarrels with your companions is also foreboded.To catch rats means you will scorn the baseness of others and worthily outstrip yourenemies.To kill one denotes your victory in any contest.See Mice.Rat-TrapTo dream of falling into a rat-trap denotes that you will be victimized and robbed ofsome valuable object.To see an empty one foretells the absence of slander or competition.A broken one denotes that you will be rid of unpleasant associations.To set one, you will be made aware of the designs of enemies, but the warning willenable you to outwit them.See Mouse-trap.

Rattan CaneTo dream of a rattan cane foretells that you will depend largely upon the judgment ofothers, and you should cultivate independence in planning and executing your ownaffairs.RattleTo dream of seeing a baby play with its rattle omens peaceful contentment in the home,and enterprises will be honorable and full of gain. To a young woman, it augurs an earlymarriage and tender cares of her own.To give a baby a rattle denotes unfortunate investments.RavenTo dream of a raven denotes reverse in fortune and inharmonious surroundings. For ayoung woman, it is implied that her lover will betray her.See Crow.RazorTo dream of a razor portends disagreements and contentions over troubles.To cut yourself with one denotes that you will be unlucky in some deal which you areabout to make.Fighting with a razor foretells disappointing business, and that some one will keep youharassed almost beyond endurance.A broken or rusty one brings unavoidable distress.ReadingTo be engaged in reading in your dreams denotes that you will excel in some work,which appears difficult.To see others reading denotes that your friends will be kind and are well disposed.To give a reading or to discuss reading, you will cultivate your literary ability.Indistinct, or incoherent reading, implies worries and disappointments.

ReapersTo dream of seeing reapers busy at work at their task denotes prosperity andcontentment. If they appear to be going through dried stubble, there will be a lack ofgood crops, and business will consequently fall off.To see idle ones denotes that some discouraging event will come in the midst ofprosperity.To see a broken reaping machine signifies loss of employment or disappointment intrades.ReceptionTo dream of attending a reception denotes that you will have pleasant engagements.Confusion at a reception will work you disquietude.See Entertainment.RefrigeratorTo see a refrigerator in your dreams portends that your selfishness will offend and injuresome one who endeavors to gain an honest livelihood.To put ice in one brings the dreamer into disfavor.RegisterTo dream that some one registers your name at a hotel for you denotes you will undertakesome work which will be finished by others.If you register under an assumed name, you will engage in some guilty enterprise whichwill give you much uneasiness of mind.ReindeerTo dream of a reindeer signifies faithful discharge of duties, and remaining staunch tofriends in their adversity.To drive them foretells that you will have hours of bitter anguish, but friends will attendyou.ReligionIf you dream of discussing religion and feel religiously inclined, you will find much tomar the calmness of your life, and business will turn a disagreeable front to you.

If a young woman imagines that she is over religious, she will disgust her lover with herefforts to act ingenuous innocence and goodness.If she is irreligious and not a transgressor, it foretells that she will have that independentfrankness and kind consideration for others, which wins for women profound respect, andlove from the opposite sex as well as her own; but if she is a transgressor in the eyes ofreligion, she will find that there are moral laws, which, if disregarded, will place heroutside the pale of honest recognition. She should look well after her conduct. If sheweeps over religion, she will be disappointed in the desires of her heart. If she is defiant,but innocent of offence, she will shoulder burdens bravely, and stand firm againstdeceitful admonitions.If you are self-reproached in the midst of a religious excitement, you will find that youwill be almost induced to give up your own personality to please some one whom youhold in reverent esteem.To see religion declining in power denotes that your life will be more in harmony withcreation than formerly. Your prejudices will not be so aggressive.To dream that a minister in a social way tells you that he has given up his work foretellsthat you will be the recipient of unexpected tidings of a favorable nature, but if in aprofessional and warning way, it foretells that you will be overtaken in your deceitfulintriguing, or other disappointments will follow.(These dreams are sometimes fulfilled literally in actual life. When this is so, they mayhave no symbolical meaning. Religion is thrown around men to protect them from vice,so when they propose secretly in their minds to ignore its teachings, they are likely to seea minister or some place of church worship in a dream as a warning against theircontemplated action. If they live pure and correct lives as indicated by the church, theywill see little of the solemnity of the church or preachers.)RentTo dream that you rent a house is a sign that you will enter into new contracts, which willprove profitable.To fail to rent out property denotes that there will be much inactivity in business.To pay rent signifies that your financial interest will be satisfactory.If you can't pay your rent, it is unlucky for you, as you will see a falling off in trade, andsocial pleasures will be of little benefit.ReprieveTo be under sentence in a dream and receive a reprieve foretells that you will overcomesome difficulty which is causing you anxiety.

For a young woman to dream that her lover has been reprieved, denotes that she willsoon hear of some good luck befalling him, which will be of vital interest to her.ReptileIf a reptile attacks you in a dream, there will be trouble of a serious nature ahead for you.If you succeed in killing it, you will finally overcome obstacles.To see a dead reptile come to life, denotes that disputes and disagreements, which werethought to be settled, will be renewed and pushed with bitter animosity.To handle them without harm to yourself foretells that you will be oppressed by the illhumor and bitterness of friends, but you will succeed in restoring pleasant relations.For a young woman to see various kinds of reptiles, she will have many conflictingtroubles. Her lover will develop fancies for others. If she is bitten by any of them, shewill be superseded by a rival.RescueTo dream of being rescued from any danger denotes that you will be threatened withmisfortune, and will escape with a slight loss.To rescue others foretells that you will be esteemed for your good deeds.ResignTo dream that you resign any position signifies that you will unfortunately embark innew enterprises.To hear of others resigning denotes that you will have unpleasant tidings.ResurrectionTo dream that you are resurrected from the dead, you will have some great vexation, butwill eventually gain your desires. To see others resurrected, denotes unfortunate troubleswill be lightened by the thoughtfulness of friendsResuscitateTo dream that you are being resuscitated, denotes that you will have heavy losses, butwill eventually regain more than you lose, and happiness will attend you.To resuscitate another, you will form new friendships, which will give you prominenceand pleasure.

RevelationTo dream of a revelation, if it be of a pleasant nature, you may expect a bright outlook,either in business or love; but if the revelation be gloomy you will have manydiscouraging features to overcome.RevengeTo dream of taking revenge is a sign of a weak and uncharitable nature, which if notproperly governed, will bring you troubles and loss of friends.If others revenge themselves on you, there will be much to fear from enemies.RevivalTo dream you attend a religious revival foretells family disturbances and unprofitableengagements.If you take a part in it, you will incur the displeasure of friends by your contrary ways.See Religion.RevolverFor a young woman to dream that she sees her sweetheart with a revolver denotes thatshe will have a serious disagreement with some friend and probably separation from herlover.See Pistol.RheumatismTo feel rheumatism attacking you in a dream foretells unexpected delay in theaccomplishment of plans.To see others so afflicted brings disappointments.RhinestonesTo dream of rhinestones denotes pleasures and favors of short duration. For a youngwoman to dream that a rhinestone proves to be a diamond foretells she will be surprisedto find that some insignificant act on her part will result in good fortune.

RhinocerosTo dream that you see a rhinoceros foretells you will have a great loss threatening youand that you will have secret troubles. To kill one shows that you will bravely overcomeobstacles.RhubarbTo dream of rhubarb growing denotes that pleasant entertainments will occupy your timefor a while.To cook it foretells spirited arguments in which you will lose a friend.To eat it denotes dissatisfaction with present employment.RibTo dream of seeing ribs, denotes poverty and misery.RibbonSeeing ribbons floating from the costume of any person in your dreams indicates you willhave gay and pleasant companions, and practical cares will not trouble you greatly.For a young woman to dream of decorating herself with ribbons, she will soon have adesirable offer of marriage, but frivolity may cause her to make a mistake. If she seesother girls wearing ribbons, she will encounter rivalry in her endeavors to secure ahusband. If she buys them, she will have a pleasant and easy place in life. If she feelsangry or displeased about them, she will find that some other woman is dividing herhonors and pleasures with her in her social realm.RiceRice is good to see in dreams, as it foretells success and warm friendships. Prosperity toall trades is promised, and the farmer will be blessed with a bounteous harvest.To eat it signifies happiness and domestic comfort.To see it mixed with dirt or otherwise impure denotes sickness and separation fromfriends.For a young woman to dream of cooking it shows she will soon assume new duties,which will make her happier, and she will enjoy wealth.

RichesTo dream that you are possessed of riches denotes that you will rise to high places byyour constant exertion and attention to your affairs.See Wealth.RiddlesTo dream that you are trying to solve riddles denotes you will engage in some enterprisewhich will try your patience and employ your money.The import of riddles is confusion and dissatisfaction.RideTo dream of riding is unlucky for business or pleasure. Sickness often follows this dream.If you ride slowly, you will have unsatisfactory results in your undertakings.Swift riding sometimes means prosperity under hazardous conditions.Riding SchoolTo attend a riding school foretells some friend will act falsely by you, but you will throwoff the vexing influence occasioned by it.RingTo dream of wearing rings denotes new enterprises in which you will be successful.A broken ring foretells quarrels and unhappiness in the married state and separation tolovers.For a young woman to receive a ring denotes that worries over her lover's conduct willcease, as he will devote himself to her pleasures and future interest.To see others with rings denotes increasing prosperity and many new friends.RingwormsTo dream of having ringworms appear on you, you will have a slight illness, and someexasperating difficulty in the near future.To see them on others, beggars and appeals for charity will beset you.

RiotTo dream of riots foretells disappointing affairs.To see a friend killed in a riot, you will have bad luck in all undertakings, and the death,or some serious illness, of some person will cause you distress.RisingTo dream of rising to high positions denotes that study and advancement will bring youdesired wealth.If you find yourself rising high into the air, you will come into unexpected riches andpleasures, but you are warned to be careful of your engagements, or you may incurdispleasing prominence.RivalTo dream you have a rival is a sign that you will be slow in asserting your rights and willlose favor with people of prominence.For a young woman, this dream is a warning to cherish the love she already holds, as shemight unfortunately make a mistake in seeking other bonds.If you find that a rival has outwitted you, it signifies that you will be negligent in yourbusiness, and that you love personal ease to your detriment.If you imagine that you are the successful rival, it is good for your advancement, and youwill find congeniality in your choice of a companion.RiverIf you see a clear, smooth, flowing river in your dream, you will soon succeed to theenjoyment of delightful pleasures, and prosperity will bear flattering promises.If the waters are muddy or tumultuous, there will be disagreeable and jealous contentionsin your life.If you are water-bound by the overflowing of a river, there will be temporaryembarrassments in your business, or you will suffer uneasiness lest some privateescapade will reach public notice and cause your reputation harsh criticisms.If while sailing upon a clear river you see corpses in the bottom, you will find that troubleand gloom will follow swiftly upon present pleasures and fortune.To see empty rivers denotes sickness and unusual ill-luck.

RoadTraveling over a rough, unknown road in a dream signifies new undertakings, which willbring little else than grief and loss of time.If the road is bordered with trees and flowers, there will be some pleasant and unexpectedfortune for you. If friends accompany you, you will be successful in building an idealhome, with happy children and faithful wife, or husband.To lose the road foretells that you will make a mistake in deciding some question of tradeand suffer loss in consequence.RoastTo see or eat roast in a dream is an omen of domestic infelicity and secret treachery.To see a rocket ascending in your dream foretells sudden and unexpected elevation,successful wooing, and faithful keeping of the marriage vows.To see them falling, unhappy unions may be expected.Rocking-ChairRocking-chairs seen in dreams bring friendly intercourse and contentment with anyenvironment.To see a mother, wife, or sweetheart in a rocking chair is ominous of the sweetest joysthat earth affords.To see vacant rocking-chairs forebodes bereavement or estrangement. The dreamer willsurely merit misfortune in some form.RocksTo dream of rocks denotes that you will meet reverses, and that there will be discord andgeneral unhappiness.To climb a steep rock foretells immediate struggles and disappointing surroundings.See Stones.RogueTo see or think yourself a rogue foretells you are about to commit some indiscretionwhich will give your friends uneasiness of mind. You are likely to suffer from a passingmalady.

For a woman to think her husband or lover is a rogue foretells she will be painfullydistressed over neglect shown her by a friend.Rogue's GalleryTo dream that you are in a rogue's gallery, foretells you will be associated with peoplewho will fail to appreciate you. To see your own picture, you will be overawed by atormenting enemy.Roman CandleTo see Roman candles while dreaming is a sign of speedy attainment of covetedpleasures and positions.To imagine that you have a loaded candle and find it empty denotes that you will bedisappointed with the possession of some object which you have long striven to obtain.RoofTo find yourself on a roof in a dream denotes unbounded success. To become frightenedand think you are falling, signifies that, while you may advance, you will have no firmhold on your position.To see a roof falling in, you will be threatened with a sudden calamity.To repair, or build a roof, you will rapidly increase your fortune.To sleep on one proclaims your security against enemies and false companions. Yourhealth will be robust.Roof CornerTo see a person dressed in mourning sitting on a roof corner foretells there will beunexpected and dismal failures in your business.Affairs will appear unfavorable in love.RooksTo dream of rooks denotes that while your friends are true, they will not afford you thepleasure and contentment for which you long, as your thoughts and tastes will outstriptheir humble conception of life.A dead rook denotes sickness or death in your immediate future.

RoosterTo dream of a rooster foretells that you will be very successful and rise to prominence,but you will allow yourself to become conceited over your fortunate rise.To see roosters fighting foretells altercations and rivals.See Chickens.RootsTo dream of seeing roots of plants or trees denotes misfortune, as both business andhealth will go into decline.To use them as medicine warns you of approaching illness or sorrow.RopesRopes in dreams signify perplexities and complications in affairs, and uncertain lovemaking.If you climb one, you will overcome enemies who are working to injure you.To descend a rope brings disappointment to your most sanguine moments.If you are tied with them, you are likely to yield to love contrary to your judgment.To break them signifies your ability to overcome enmity and competition.To tie ropes or horses denotes that you will have power to control others as you maywish.To walk a rope signifies that you will engage in some hazardous speculation, but willsurprisingly succeed. To see others walking a rope, you will benefit by the fortunateventures of others.To jump a rope foretells that you will startle your associates with a thrilling escapadebordering upon the sensational.To jump rope with children shows that you are selfish and overbearing; failing to see thatchildren owe very little duty to inhuman parents. To catch a rope with the foot, denotesthat under cheerful conditions you will be benevolent and tender in your administrations.To dream that you let a rope down from an upper window to people below, thinking theproprietors would be adverse to receiving them into the hotel, denotes that you willengage in some affair which will not look exactly proper to your friends, but the samewill afford you pleasure and interest. For a young woman, this dream is indicative of pleasures which do not bear the stamp of propriety.RosebushTo see a rosebush in foliage but no blossoms denotes prosperous circumstances areenclosing you. To see a dead rosebush, foretells misfortune and sickness for you orrelatives.RosemaryRosemary, if seen in dreams, denotes that sadness and indifference will causeunhappiness in homes where there is every appearance of prosperity.RosesTo dream of seeing roses blooming and fragrant denotes that some joyful occasion isnearing, and you will possess the faithful love of your sweetheart.For a young woman to dream of gathering roses shows she will soon have an offer ofmarriage, which will be much to her liking.Withered roses signify the absence of loved ones.White roses, if seen without sunshine or dew, denote serious if not fatal illness.To inhale their fragrance brings unalloyed pleasure.For a young woman to dream of banks of roses, and that she is gathering and tying theminto bouquets, signifies that she will be made very happy by the offering of some personwhom she regards very highly.RosetteTo wear or see rosettes on others while in dreams is significant of frivolous waste oftime; though you will experience the thrills of pleasure, they will bring disappointments.RougeTo dream of using rouge denotes that you will practice deceit to obtain your wishes.To see others with it on their faces warns you that you are being artfully used to furtherthe designs of some deceitful persons.If you see it on your hands, or clothing, you will be detected in some scheme.If it comes off of your face, you will be humiliated before some rival, and lose your lover

by assuming unnatural manners.RoundaboutTo dream of seeing a roundabout denotes that you will struggle unsuccessfully toadvance in fortune or love.RowboatTo dream that you are in a rowboat with others denotes that you will derive muchpleasure from the companionship of gay and worldly persons. If the boat is capsized, youwill suffer financial losses by engaging in seductive enterprises.If you find yourself defeated in a rowing race, you will lose favors to your rivals withyour sweetheart. If you are the victor, you will easily obtain supremacy with women.Your affairs will move agreeably.RubberTo dream of being clothed in rubber garments, is a sign that you will have honorsconferred upon you because of your steady and unchanging stand of purity and morality.If the garments are ragged or torn, you should be cautious in your conduct, as scandal isready to attack your reputation.To dream of using "rubber" as a slang term, foretells that you will be easy to please inyour choice of pleasure and companions.If you find that your limbs will stretch like rubber, it is a sign that illness is threateningyou, and you are likely to use deceit in your wooing and business.To dream of rubber goods, denotes that your affairs will be conducted on a secret basis,and your friends will fail to understand your conduct in many instances.RubbishTo dream of rubbish, denotes that you will badly manage your affairs.RubyTo dream of a ruby, foretells you will be lucky in speculations of business or love. For awoman to lose one, is a sign of approaching indifference of her lover.RudderTo dream of a rudder, you will soon make a pleasant journey to foreign lands, and newfriendships will be formed.

A broken rudder, augurs disappointment and sickness.RuinsTo dream of
ruins, signifies broken engagements to lovers, distressing conditions
inbusiness, destruction to crops, and failing health. To dream of ancient
ruins, foretells thatyou will travel extensively, but there will be a
note of sadness mixed with the pleasure inthe realization of a
long-cherished hope. You will feel the absence of some friend.RumTo dream
of drinking rum, foretells that you will have wealth, but will lack
moralrefinement, as you will lean to gross pleasures.See other
intoxicating drinks.RunningTo dream of running in company with others, is
a sign that you will participate in somefestivity, and you will find that
your affairs are growing towards fortune. If you stumbleor fall, you will
lose property and reputation.Running alone, indicates that you will
outstrip your friends in the race for wealth, andyou will occupy a higher
place in social life.If you run from danger, you will be threatened with
losses, and you will despair ofadjusting matters agreeably. To see others
thus running, you will be oppressed by thethreatened downfall of
friends.To see stock running, warns you to be careful in making new
trades or undertaking newtasks.RuptureTo dream that you are ruptured,
denotes you will have physical disorders or disagreeablecontentions. If
it be others you see in this condition, you will be in danger
ofirreconcilable quarrels.RustTo dream of rust on articles, old pieces of
tin, or iron, is significant of depression of yoursurroundings. Sickness,
decline in fortune and false friends are filling your sphere.

RyeTo see rye, is a dream of good, as prosperity envelopes your future in
brightest promises.To see coffee made of rye, denotes that your pleasures
will be tempered with soundjudgment, and your affairs will be managed
without disagreeable friction.To see stock entering rye fields, denotes
that you will be prosperous.Rye BreadTo see or eat rye bread in your
dreams, foretells you will have a cheerful andwell-appointed
home.SSaddleTo dream of saddles, foretells news of a pleasant nature,
also unannounced visitors. Youare also, probably, to take a trip which
will prove advantageous.SafeTo dream of seeing a safe, denotes security
from discouraging affairs of business andlove.To be trying to unlock a
safe, you will be worried over the failure of your plans notreaching
quick maturity.To find a safe empty, denotes trouble.SaffronSaffron seen
in a dream warns you that you are entertaining false hopes, as bitter
enemiesare interfering secretly with your plans for the future.To drink a
tea made from saffron, foretells that you will have quarrels and
alienations inyour family.

SageTo dream of sage, foretells thrift and economy will be practised by your servants orfamily. For a woman to think she has too much in her viands, omens she will regretuseless extravagance in love as well as fortune.SailingTo dream of sailing on calm waters, foretells easy access to blissful joys, and immunityfrom poverty and whatever brings misery.To sail on a small vessel, denotes that your desires will not excel your power ofpossessing them.See Ocean and Sea.SailorTo dream of sailors, portends long and exciting journeys.For a young woman to dream of sailors, is ominous of a separation from her loverthrough a frivolous flirtation. If she dreams that she is a sailor, she will indulge in someunmaidenly escapade, and be in danger of losing a faithful lover.SaladTo dream of eating salad, foretells sickness and disagreeable people around you.For a young woman to dream of making it, is a sign that her lover will be changeable andquarrelsome.SalmonDreaming of salmon, denotes that much good luck and pleasant duties will employ yourtime.For a young woman to eat it, foretells that she will marry a cheerful man, with means tokeep her comfortable.SaltSalt is an omen of discordant surroundings when seen in dreams. You will usually findafter dreaming of salt that everything goes awry, and quarrels and dissatisfaction showthemselves in the family circle.To salt meat, portends that debts and mortgages will harass you.

For a young woman to eat salt, she will be deserted by her lover for a more beautiful andattractive girl, thus causing her deep chagrin.SaltpeterTo dream of saltpeter, denotes change in your living will add loss to some unconquerablegrief.SalveTo dream of salve, denotes you will prosper under adverse circumstances and convertenemies into friends.SamplesTo dream of receiving merchandise samples, denotes improvement in your business. Fora traveling man to lose his samples, implies he will find himself embarrassed in businessaffairs, or in trouble through love engagements. For a woman to dream that she isexamining samples sent her, denotes she will have chances to vary her amusements.SandTo dream of sand, is indicative of famine and losses.SanskritTo dream of Sanskrit, denotes that you will estrange yourself from friends in order toinvestigate hidden subjects, taking up those occupying the minds of cultured andprogressive thinkers.SapphireTo dream of sapphire, is ominous of fortunate gain, and to woman, a wise selection in alover.SardinesTo eat sardines in a dream, foretells that distressing events will come unexpectedly uponyou.For a young woman to dream of putting them on the table, denotes that she will beworried with the attentions of a person who is distasteful to her.

SardonyxTo dream of sardonyx, signifies gloomy surroundings will be cleared away by yourenergetic overthrow of poverty. For a woman, this dream denotes an increase in herpossessions, unless she loses or throws them away, then it might imply a disregard ofopportunities to improve her condition.SashTo dream of wearing a sash, foretells that you will seek to retain the affections of aflirtatious person.For a young woman to buy one, she will be faithful to her lover, and win esteem by herfrank, womanly ways.SatanTo dream of Satan, foretells that you will have some dangerous adventures, and you willbe forced to use strategy to keep up honorable appearances.To dream that you kill him, foretells that you will desert wicked or immoral companionsto live upon a higher plane.If he comes to you under the guise of literature, it should be heeded as a warning againstpromiscuous friendships, and especially flatterers.If he comes in the shape of wealth or power, you will fail to use your influence forharmony, or the elevation of others.If he takes the form of music, you are likely to go down before his wiles.If in the form of a fair woman, you will probably crush every kindly feeling you mayhave for the caresses of this moral monstrosity.To feel that you are trying to shield yourself from satan, denotes that you will endeavorto throw off the bondage of selfish pleasure, and seek to give others their best deserts.See Devil.SausageTo dream of making sausage, denotes that you will be successful in many undertakings.To eat them, you will have a humble, but pleasant home.

SawTo dream that you use a hand-saw, indicates an energetic and busy time, and cheerfulhome life.To see big saws in machinery, foretells that you will superintend a big enterprise, and thesame will yield fair returns. For a woman, this dream denotes that she will be esteemed,and her counsels will be heeded.To dream of rusty or broken saws, denotes failure and accidents.To lose a saw, you will engage in affairs which will culminate in disaster.To hear the buzz of a saw, indicates thrift and prosperity.To find a rusty saw, denotes that you will probably restore your fortune.To carry a saw on your back, foretells that you will carry large, but profitable,responsibilities.SawdustTo dream of sawdust, signifies that grievous mistakes will cause you distress andquarreling in your home.ScabbardTo dream of a scabbard, denotes some misunderstanding will be amicably settled. If youwonder where your scabbard can be, you will have overpowering difficulties to meet.ScaffoldTo dream of a scaffold, denotes that you will undergo keen disappointment in failing tosecure the object of your affection.To ascend one, you will be misunderstood and censured by your friends for some action,which you never committed.To decend one, you will be guilty of wrong doing, and you will suffer the penalty.To fall from one, you will be unexpectedly surprised while engaged in deceiving andworking injury to others.ScaldheadTo see any one with a scaldhead in your dreams, there will be uneasiness felt over the sickness or absence of some one near to you.If you dream that your own head is thus afflicted, you are in danger of personal illness oraccidents.ScaldingTo dream of being scalded, portends that distressing incidents will blot out pleasurableanticipations.ScalesTo dream of weighing on scales, portends that justice will temper your conduct, and youwill see your prosperity widening.For a young woman to weigh her lover, the indications are that she will find him of solidworth, and faithfulness will balance her love.ScandalTo dream that you are an object of scandal, denotes that you are not particular to selectgood and true companions, but rather enjoy having fast men and women contribute toyour pleasure. Trade and business of any character will suffer dulness after this dream.For a young woman to dream that she discussed a scandal, foretells that she will conferfavors, which should be sacred, to some one who will deceive her into believing that he ishonorably inclined. Marriage rarely follows swiftly after dreaming of scandal.ScarcityTo dream of scarcity, foretells sorrow in the household and failing affairs.Scarlet FeverTo dream of scarlet fever, foretells you are in danger of sickness, or in the power of anenemy. To dream a relative dies suddenly with it, foretells you will be overcome byvillainous treachery.SceptreTo imagine in your dreams that you wield a sceptre, foretells that you will be chosen byfriends to positions of trust, and you will not disappoint their estimate of your ability.To dream that others wield the sceptre over you, denotes that you will seek employmentunder the supervision of others, rather than exert your energies to act for yourself.

SchoolTo dream of attending school, indicates distinction in literary work. If you think you areyoung and at school as in your youth, you will find that sorrow and reverses will makeyou sincerely long for the simple trusts and pleasures of days of yore.To dream of teaching a school, foretells that you will strive for literary attainments, butthe bare necessities of life must first be forthcoming.To visit the schoolhouse of your childhood days, portends that discontent anddiscouraging incidents overshadows the present.School TeacherTo dream of a school teacher, denotes you are likely to enjoy learning and amusements ina quiet way. If you are one, you are likely to reach desired success in literary and otherworks.ScissorsTo dream of scissors is an unlucky omen; wives will be jealous and distrustful of theirhusbands, and sweethearts will quarrel and nag each other into crimination andrecrimination. Dulness will overcast business horizons.To dream that you have your scissors sharpened, denotes that you will work to do thatwhich will be repulsive to your feelings.To break them, there will be quarrels, and probable separations for you.To lose them, you will seek to escape from unpleasant tasks.ScorpionTo dream of a scorpion, foretells that false friends will improve opportunities toundermine your prosperity. If you fail to kill it, you will suffer loss from an enemy'sattack.Scrap-bookTo dream of a scrap-book, denotes disagreeable acquaintances will shortly be made.ScratchTo scratch others in your dream, denotes that you will be ill-tempered and fault-findingin your dealings with others.

If you are scratched, you will be injured by the enmity of some deceitful person.Scratch HeadTo dream that you scratch your head, denotes strangers will annoy you by their flatteringattentions, which you will feel are only shown to win favors from you.Screech-OwlTo dream that you hear the shrill startling notes of the screech-owl, denotes that you willbe shocked with news of the desperate illness, or death of some dear friend.ScrewTo dream of seeing screws, denotes that tedious tasks must be performed, andpeevishness in companions must be combated. It also denotes that you must beeconomical and painstaking.SculptorTo dream of a sculptor, foretells you will change from your present position to one lesslucrative, but more distinguished.For a woman to dream that her husband or lover is a sculptor, foretells she will enjoyfavors from men of high position.ScumTo dream of scum, signifies disappointment will be experienced by you over socialdefeats.ScytheTo dream of a scythe, foretells accidents or sickness will prevent you from attending toyour affairs, or making journeys. An old or broken scythe, implies separation fromfriends, or failure in some business enterprise.SeaTo dream of hearing the lonely sighing of the sea, foretells that you will be fated to spenda weary and unfruitful life devoid of love and comradeship.Dreams of the sea, prognosticate unfulfilled anticipations, while pleasures of a materialform are enjoyed, there is an inward craving for pleasure that flesh cannot requite.

For a young woman to dream that she glides swiftly over the sea with her lover, therewill come to her sweet fruition of maidenly hopes, and joy will stand guard at the door ofthe consummation of changeless vows.See Ocean.Sea FoamFor a woman to dream of sea foam, foretells that indiscriminate and demoralizingpleasures will distract her from the paths of rectitude. If she wears a bridal veil of seafoam, she will engulf herself in material pleasure to the exclusion of true refinement andinnate modesty. She will be likely to cause sorrow to some of those dear to her, throughtheir inability to gratify her ambition.SealTo dream that you see seals, denotes that you are striving for a place above your power tomaintain.Dreams of seals usually show that the dreamer has high aspirations and discontent willharass him into struggles to advance his position.SeamstressTo see a seamstress in a dream, portends you will be deterred from making pleasant visitsby unexpected luck.SeaportTo dream of visiting a seaport, denotes that you will have opportunities of traveling andacquiring knowledge, but there will be some who will object to your anticipated tours.SeatTo think, in a dream, that some one has taken your seat, denotes you will be tormented bypeople calling on you for aid. To give a woman your seat, implies your yielding to somefair one's artfulness.Secret OrderTo dream of any secret order, denotes a sensitive and excited organism, and the ownershould cultivate practical and unselfish ideas and they may soon have opportunities forhonest pleasures, and desired literary distinctions.There is a vision of selfish and designing friendships for one who joins a secret order.

Young women should heed the counsel of their guardians, lest they fall into discreditablehabits after this dream.If a young woman meets the head of the order, she should oppose with energy and moralrectitude against allurements that are set brilliantly and prominently before those of hersex. For her to think her mother has joined the order, and she is using her best efforts tohave her mother repudiate her vows, denotes that she will be full of love for her parents,yet will wring their hearts with anguish by thoughtless disobedience.To see or hear that the leader is dead, foretells severe strains, and trials will eventuallyend in comparative good.SeducerFor a young woman to dream of being seduced, foretells that she will be easilyinfluenced by showy persons.For a man to dream that he has seduced a girl, is a warning for him to be on his guard, asthere are those who will falsely accuse him. If his sweetheart appears shocked or angryunder these proposals, he will find that the woman he loves is above reproach. If sheconsents, he is being used for her pecuniary pleasures.SeedTo dream of seed, foretells increasing prosperity, though present indications appearunfavorable.SentryTo dream of a sentry, denotes that you will have kind protectors, and your life will besmoothly conducted.SerenadeTo hear a serenade in your dream, you will have pleasant news from absent friends, andyour anticipations will not fail you.If you are one of the serenaders, there are many delightful things in your future.SerpentsTo dream of serpents, is indicative of cultivated morbidity and depressed surroundings.There is usually a disappointment after this dream.See Snakes and Reptile.

ServantTo dream of a servant, is a sign that you will be fortunate, despite gloomy appearances.Anger is likely to precipitate you into useless worries and quarrels.To discharge one, foretells regrets and losses.To quarrel with one in your dream, indicates that you will, upon waking, have real causefor censuring some one who is derelict in duty.To be robbed by one, shows that you have some one near you, who does not respect thelaws of ownership.SewingTo dream of sewing on new garments, foretells that domestic peace will crown yourwishes.ShakersTo dream of seeing members of the sect called Shakers in a dream, denotes that you willchange in your business, and feel coldness growing towards your sweetheart.If you imagine you belong to them, you will unexpectedly renounce all former ties, andseek new pleasures in distant localities.Shaking HandsFor a young woman to dream that she shakes hands with some prominent ruler, foretellsshe will be surrounded with pleasures and distinction from strangers. If she avails herselfof the opportunity, she will stand in high favor with friends. If she finds she must reachup to shake hands, she will find rivalry and opposition. If she has on gloves, she willovercome these obstacles.To shake hands with those beneath you, denotes you will be loved and honored for yourkindness and benevolence. If you think you or they have soiled hands, you will findenemies among seeming friends.For a young woman to dream of shaking hands with a decrepit old man, foretells she willfind trouble where amusement was sought.ShakspeareTo dream of Shakspeare, denotes that unhappiness and dispondency will work muchanxiety to momentous affairs, and love will be stripped of passion's fever.

To read Shakspeare's works, denotes that you will unalterably attach yourself to literaryaccomplishments.ShampooTo dream of seeing shampooing going on, denotes that you will engage in undignifiedaffairs to please othersTo have your own head shampooed, you will soon make a secret trip, in which you willhave much enjoyment, if you succeed in keeping the real purport from your family orfriends.ShantyTo dream of a shanty, denotes that you will leave home in the quest of health. This alsowarns you of decreasing prosperity.SharkTo dream of sharks, denotes formidable enemies.To see a shark pursuing and attacking you, denotes that unavoidable reverses will sinkyou into dispondent foreboding.To see them sporting in clear water, foretells that while you are basking in the sunshineof women and prosperity, jealousy is secretly, but surely, working you disquiet, andunhappy fortune.To see a dead one, denotes reconciliation and renewed prosperity.ShaveTo merely contemplate getting a shave, in your dream, denotes you will plan for thesuccessful development of enterprises, but will fail to generate energy sufficient tosucceed.ShavingTo dream that you are being shaved, portends that you will let imposters defraud you.To shave yourself, foretells that you will govern your own business and dictate to yourhousehold, notwithstanding that the presence of a shrew may cause you quarrels.If your face appears smooth, you will enjoy quiet, and your conduct will hot bequestioned by your companions. If old and rough, there will be many squalls or, thematrimonial sea.

If your razor is dull and pulls your face, you will give your friends cause to criticize yourprivate life.If your beard seems gray, you will be absolutely devoid of any sense of justice to thosehaving claims upon you.For a woman to see men shaving, foretells that her nature will become sullied byindulgence in gross pleasures.If she dreams of being shaved, she will assume so much masculinity that men will turnfrom her in disgust.ShawlTo dream of a shawl, denotes that some one will offer you flattery and favor.To lose your shawl, foretells sorrow and discomfort. A young woman is in danger ofbeing jilted by a good-looking man, after this dream.ShearsTo see shears in your dream, denotes that you will become miserly and disagreeable inyour dealings.To see them broken, you will lose friends and standing by your eccentric demeanor.SheavesTo dream of sheaves, denotes joyful occasions. Prosperity holds before you a panoramaof delightful events, and fields of enterprise and fortunate gain.SheepTo dream of shearing them, denotes a season of profitable enterprises will shower downupon you.To see flocks of sheep, there will be much rejoicing among farmers, and other trades willprosper.To see them looking scraggy and sick, you will be thrown into despair by the miscarriageof some plan, which promised rich returns.To eat the flesh of sheep, denotes that ill-natured persons will outrage your feelings.See Lamb and Ram.

Sheet IronTo see sheet iron in your dream, denotes you are unfortunately listening to theadmonition of others. To walk on it, signifies distasteful engagements.ShellsTo walk among and gather shells in your dream, denotes extravagance. Pleasure willleave you naught but exasperating regrets and memories.See Mussels and Oysters.ShelterTo dream that you are building a shelter, signifies that you will escape the evil designs ofenemies.If you are seeking shelter, you will be guilty of cheating, and will try to justify yourself.ShelvesTo see empty shelves in dreams, indicates losses and consequent gloom.Full shelves, augurs happy contentment through the fulfillment of hope and exertions.See Store.ShepherdTo see shepherds in your dreams watching their flocks, portends bounteous crops andpleasant relations for the farmer, also much enjoyment and profit for others.To see them in idleness, foretells sickness and bereavement.SheriffTo dream of seeing a sheriff, denotes that you will suffer great uneasiness over theuncertain changes which loom up before you.To imagine that you are elected sheriff or feel interested in the office, denotes that youwill participate in some affair which will afford you neither profit nor honor.To escape arrest, you will be able to further engage in illicit affairs.See Bailiff and Police.

ShipTo dream of ships, foretells honor and unexpected elevation to ranks above your mode oflife.To hear of a shipwreck is ominous of a disastrous turn in affairs. Your female friends willbetray you.To lose your life in one, denotes that you will have an exceeding close call on your life orhonor.To see a ship on her way through a tempestuous storm, foretells that you will beunfortunate in business transactions, and you will be perplexed to find means of hidingsome intrigue from the public, as your partner in the affair will threaten you withbetrayal.To see others shipwrecked, you will seek in vain to shelter some friend from disgrace andinsolvency.ShirtTo dream of putting on your shirt, is a sign that you will estrange yourself from yoursweetheart by your faithless conduct.To lose your shirt, augurs disgrace in business or love.A torn shirt, represents misfortune and miserable surroundings.A soiled shirt, denotes that contagious diseases will confront you.Shirt-StudsTo dream of shirt-studs, foretells you will struggle to humor your pride, and will usuallybe successful. If they are diamonds, and the center one is larger than the others, you willenjoy wealth, or have an easy time, surrounded by congenial friends.ShoemakerTo see a shoemaker in your dream, warns you that indications are unfavorable to youradvancement. For a woman to dream that her husband or lover is a shoemaker, foretellscompetency will be hers; her wishes will be gratified.ShoesTo dream of seeing your shoes ragged and soiled, denotes that you will make enemies byyour unfeeling criticisms.

enemies are seducing the confidence of your friends.For a woman to use it in her dreams, foretells complications which will involve herseparation from a favored friend.

SoapTo dream of soap, foretells that friendships will reveal interesting entertainment. Farmerswill have success in their varied affairs.For a young woman to be making soap, omens a substantial and satisfactory competencywill be hers.SocialistTo see a socialist in your dreams, your unenvied position among friends andacquaintances is predicted. Your affairs will be neglected for other imaginary duties.Soda FountainTo dream of being at a soda fountain, denotes pleasure and profit after many exasperatingexperiences.To treat others to this and other delectable iced drinks; you will be rewarded in yourefforts, though the outlook appears full of contradictions. Inharmonious environments,and desired results will be forthcoming.SonTo dream of your son, if you have one, as being handsome and dutiful, foretells that hewill afford you proud satisfaction, and will aspire to high honors. If he is maimed, orsuffering from illness or accident, there is trouble ahead for you.For a mother to dream that her son has fallen to the bottom of a well, and she hears cries,it is a sign of deep grief, losses and sickness. If she rescues him, threatened danger willpass away unexpectedly.SootIf you see soot in your dreams, it means that you will meet with ill success in youraffairs. Lovers will be quarrelsome and hard to please.SoldTo dream that you have sold anything, denotes that unfavorable business will worry you.SoldiersTo see soldiers marching in your dreams, foretells for you a period of flagrant excesses,but at the same time you will be promoted to elevations above rivals.

SpectaclesTo dream of spectacles, foretells that strangers will cause changes in your affairs. Fraudswill be practised on your credulity.To dream that you see broken spectacles, denotes estrangement caused by fondness forillegal pleasures.SpiceTo dream of spice, foretells you will probably damage your own reputation in search ofpleasure. For a young woman to dream of eating spice, is an omen of deceitfulappearances winning her confidence.SpiderTo dream of a spider, denotes that you will be careful and energetic in your labors, andfortune will be amassed to pleasing proportions.To see one building its web, foretells that you will be happy and secure in your ownhome.To kill one, signifies quarrels with your wife or sweetheart.If one bites you, you will be the victim of unfaithfulness and will suffer from enemies inyour business.If you dream that you see many spiders hanging in their webs around you, foretells mostfavorable conditions, fortune, good health and friends.To dream of a large spider confronting you, signifies that your elevation to fortune willbe swift, unless you are in dangerous contact.To dream that you see a very large spider and a small one coming towards you, denotesthat you will be prosperous, and that you will feel for a time that you are immenselysuccessful; but if the large one bites you, enemies will steal away your good fortune. Ifthe little one bites you, you will be harassed with little spites and jealousies. To imaginethat you are running from a large spider, denotes you will lose fortune in slightingopportunities. If you kill the spider you will eventually come into fair estate. If itafterwards returns to life and pursues you, you will be oppressed by sickness andwavering fortunes.For a young woman to dream she sees gold spiders crawling around her, foretells that herfortune and prospect for happiness will improve, and new friends will surround her.

Spider WebTo see spider webs, denotes pleasant associations and fortunate ventures.SpinningTo dream that you are spinning, means that you will engage in some enterprise, whichwill be all you could wish.Spirit or SpecterTo see spirits in a dream, denotes that some unexpected trouble will confront you. If theyare white-robed, the health of your nearest friend is threatened, or some businessspeculation will be disapproving. If they are robed in black, you will meet with treacheryand unfaithfulness.If a spirit speaks, there is some evil near you, which you might avert if you would listento the counsels of judgment.To dream that you hear spirits knocking on doors or walls, denotes that trouble will ariseunexpectedly.To see them moving draperies, or moving behind them, is a warning to hold control overyour feelings, as you are likely to commit indiscretions. Quarrels are also threatened.To see the spirit of your friend floating in your room, foretells disappointment andinsecurity.To hear music supposedly coming from spirits, denotes unfavorable changes and sadnessin the household.SpittingTo dream of spitting, denotes unhappy terminations of seemingly auspiciousundertakings. For some one to spit on you, foretells disagreements and alienation ofaffections.SpleenTo dream of spleen, denotes that you will have a misunderstanding with some party whowill injure you.SplendorTo dream that you live in splendor, denotes that you will succeed to elevations, and willreside in a different state to the one you now occupy.

To see others thus living, signifies pleasure derived from the interest that friends take inyour welfare.SplinterTo dream of splinters sticking into your flesh, denotes that you will have many vexationsfrom members of your family or from jealous rivals.If while you are visiting you stick a splinter in your foot, you will soon make, or receive,a visit which will prove extremely unpleasant. Your affairs will go slightly wrongthrough your continued neglect.SpongesSponges seen in a dream, denote that deception is being practised upon you.To use one in erasing, you will be the victim of folly.SpoolsTo dream of spools of thread, indicates some long and arduous tasks, but which whencompleted will meet your most sanguine expectations. If they are empty, there will bedisappointments for you.SpoonsTo see, or use, spoons in a dream, denotes favorable signs of advancement. Domesticaffairs will afford contentment.To think a spoon is lost, denotes that you will be suspicious of wrong doing.To steal one, is a sign that you will deserve censure for your contemptible meanness inyour home.To dream of broken or soiled spoons, signifies loss and trouble.SpringTo dream that spring is advancing, is a sign of fortunate undertakings and cheerfulcompanions.To see spring appearing unnaturally, is a foreboding of disquiet and losses.

SpurTo dream of wearing spurs, denotes that you will engage in some unpleasant controversy.To see others with them on, foretells that enmity is working you trouble.SpyTo dream that spies are harassing you, denotes dangerous quarrels and uneasiness.To dream that you are a spy, denotes that you will make unfortunate ventures.Spy GlassTo dream that you are looking through a spy-glass, denotes that changes will soon occurto your disadvantage.To see a broken or imperfect one, foretells unhappy dissensions and loss of friends.SquallTo dream of squalls, foretells disappointing business and unhappiness.SquintingTo dream that you see some person with squinting eyes, denotes that you will be annoyedwith unpleasant people.For a man to dream that his sweetheart, or some good-looking girl, squints her eyes athim, foretells that he is threatened with loss by seeking the favors of women. For a youngwoman to have this dream about men, she will be in danger of losing her fair reputation.SquirrelTo dream of seeing squirrels, denotes that pleasant friends will soon visit you. You willsee advancement in your business also.To kill a squirrel, denotes that you will be unfriendly and disliked.To pet one, signifies family joy.To see a dog chasing one, foretells disagreements and unpleasantness among friends.

StableTo dream of a stable, is a sign of fortune and advantageous surroundings.To see a stable burning denotes successful changes, or it may be seen in actual life.StagTo see stags in your dream, foretells that you will have honest and true friends, and willenjoy delightful entertainments.Stage DriverTo dream of a stage driver, signifies you will go on a strange journey in quest of fortuneand happiness.StainTo see stain on your hands, or clothing, while dreaming, foretells that trouble over smallmatters will assail you.To see a stain on the garments of others, or on their flesh, foretells that some person willbetray you.StairsTo dream of passing up a stairs, foretells good fortune and much happiness.If you fall down stairs, you will be the object of hatred and envy.To walk down, you will be unlucky in your affairs, and your lovemaking will beunfavorable.To see broad, handsome stairs, foretells approaching riches and honors.To see others going down stairs, denotes that unpleasant conditions will take the place ofpleasure.To sit on stair steps, denotes a gradual rise in fortune and delight.StallTo dream of a stall, denotes impossible results from some enterprise will be expected byyou.

StallionTo dream of a stallion, foretells prosperous conditions are approaching you, in which youwill hold a position which will confer honor upon you.To dream you ride a fine stallion, denotes you will rise to position and affluence in aphenomenal way; however, your success will warp your morality and sense of justice. Tosee one with the rabies, foretells that wealthy surroundings will cause you to assumearrogance, which will be distasteful to your friends, and your pleasures will be deceitful.StammerTo dream that you stammer in your conversation, denotes that worry and illness willthreaten your enjoyment. To hear others stammer, foretells that unfriendly persons willdelight in annoying you and giving you needless worry.Standard BearerTo dream that you are a standard-bearer, denotes that your occupation will be pleasant,but varied.To see others acting as standard-bearers, foretells that you will be jealous and envious ofsome friend.StarsTo dream of looking upon clear, shining stars, foretells good health and prosperity. Ifthey are dull or red, there is trouble and misfortune ahead.To see a shooting or falling star, denotes sadness and grief.To see stars appearing and vanishing mysteriously, there will be some strange changesand happenings in your near future.If you dream that a star falls on you, there will be a bereavement in your family.To see them rolling around on the earth, is a sign of formidable danger and trying times.StarvingTo dream of being in a starving condition, portends unfruitful labors and a dearth offriends.To see others in this condition, omens misery and dissatisfaction with presentcompanions and employment.

StatuesTo see statues in dreams, signifies estrangement from a loved one. Lack of energy willcause you disappointment in realizing wishes.StealingTo dream of stealing, or of seeing others commit this act, foretells bad luck and loss ofcharacter.To be accused of stealing, denotes that you will be misunderstood in some affair, andsuffer therefrom, but you will eventually find that this will bring you favor.To accuse others, denotes that you will treat some person with hasty inconsideration.SteepleTo see a steeple rising from a church, is a harbinger of sickness and reverses.A broken one, points to death in your circle, or friends.To climb a steeple, foretells that you will have serious difficulties, but will surmountthem.To fall from one, denotes losses in trade and ill health.StepsTo dream that you ascend steps, denotes that fair prospects will relieve former anxiety.To decend them, you may look for misfortune.To fall down them, you are threatened with unexpected failure in your affairs.See Stairs.Step SisterTo dream of a step-sister, denotes you will have unavoidable care and annoyance uponyou.StethoscopeTo dream of a stethoscope, foretells calamity to your hopes and enterprises. There will betroubles and recriminations in love.

SticksTo dream of sticks, is an unlucky omen.StillbornTo dream of a stillborn infant, denotes that some distressing incident will come beforeyour notice.StiltsTo dream of walking on stilts, denotes that your fortune is in an insecure condition.To fall from them, or feel them break beneath you, you will be precipitated intoembarrassments by trusting your affairs to the care of others.StingTo feel that any insect stings you in a dream, is a foreboding of evil and unhappiness.For a young woman to dream that she is stung, is ominous of sorrow and remorse fromover-confidence in men.StockingsTo dream of stockings, denotes that you will derive pleasure from dissolutecompanionship.For a young woman to see her stockings ragged, or worn, foretells that she will be guiltyof unwise, if not immoral conduct. To dream that she puts on fancy stockings, she will befond of the attention of men, and she should be careful to whom she shows preference. Ifwhite ones appear to be on her feet, she is threatened with woeful disappointment orillness.See Knitting.StoneTo see stones in your dreams, foretells numberless perplexities and failures.To walk among rocks, or stones, omens that an uneven and rough pathway will be yoursfor at least a while.To make deals in ore-bearing rock lands, you will be successful in business after manylines have been tried. If you fail to profit by the deal, you will have disappointments. Ifanxiety is greatly felt in closing the trade, you will succeed in buying or selling

something that will prove profitable to you.Small stones or pebbles, implies that little worries and vexations will irritate you.If you throw a stone, you will have cause to admonish a person.If you design to throw a pebble or stone at some belligerent person, it denotes that someevil feared by you will pass because of your untiring attention to right principles.See Rock.Stone MasonTo see stone masons at work while dreaming, foretells disappointment.To dream that you are a stone mason, portends that your labors will be unfruitful, andyour companions will be dull and uncongenial.Storage BatteryYou are likely to suffer from a passing malady.StoreTo dream of a store filled with merchandise, foretells prosperity and advancement.An empty one, denotes failure of efforts and quarrels.To dream that your store is burning, is a sign of renewed activity in business andpleasure.If you find yourself in a department store, it foretells that much pleasure will be derivedfrom various sources of profit.To sell goods in one, your advancement will be accelerated by your energy and theefforts of friends.To dream that you sell a pair of soiled, gray cotton gloves to a woman, foretells that youropinion of women will place you in hazardous positions. If a woman has this dream, herpreference for some one of the male sex will not be appreciated very much by him.StormTo see and hear a storm approaching, foretells continued sickness, unfavorable business,and separation from friends, which will cause added distress. If the storm passes, youraffliction will not be so heavy.

See Hurricane and Rain.StrawIf you dream of straw, your life is threatened with emptiness and failure.To see straw piles burning, is a signal of prosperous times.To feed straw to stock, foretells that you will make poor provisions for those dependingupon you.StrawberriesTo dream of strawberries, is favorable to advancement and pleasure. You will obtainsome long wished-for object.To eat them, denotes requited love.To deal in them, denotes abundant harvest and happiness.StreetTo dream that you are walking in a street, foretells ill luck and worries. You will almostdespair of reaching the goal you have set up in your aspirations.To be in a familiar street in a distant city, and it appears dark, you will make a journeysoon, which will not afford the profit or pleasure contemplated. If the street is brilliantlylighted, you will engage in pleasure, which will quickly pass, leaving no comfort.To pass down a street and feel alarmed lest a thug attack you, denotes that you areventuring upon dangerous ground in advancing your pleasure or business.Street PosterTo dream that you are a street-poster, denotes that you will undertake some unpleasantand unprofitable work.To see street-posters at work, foretells disagreeable news.StrugglingTo dream of struggling, foretells that you will encounter serious difficulties, but if yougain the victory in your struggle, you will also surmount present obstacles.

StumbleIf you stumble in a dream while walking or running, you will meet with disfavor, andobstructions will bar your path to success, but you will eventually surmount them, if youdo not fall.StumpsTo dream of a stump, foretells you are to have reverses and will depart from your usualmode of living. To see fields of stumps, signifies you will be unable to defend yourselffrom the encroachments of adversity. To dig or pull them up, is a sign that you willextricate yourself from the environment of poverty by throwing off sentiment and prideand meeting the realities of life with a determination to overcome whatever oppositionyou may meet.SuckleTo see the young taking suckle, denotes contentment and favorable conditions forsuccess is unfolding to you.See Nursing.SuffocatingTo dream that you are suffocating, denotes that you will experience deep sorrow andmortification at the conduct of some one you love. You should be careful of your healthafter this dream.See Smoke.SugarTo dream of sugar, denotes that you will be hard to please in your domestic life, and willentertain jealousy while seeing no cause for aught but satisfaction and secure joys. Theremay be worries, and your strength and temper taxed after this dream.To eat sugar in your dreams, you will have unpleasant matters to contend with for awhile, but they will result better than expected.To price sugar, denotes that you are menaced by enemies.To deal in sugar and see large quantities of it being delivered to you, you will barelyescape a serious loss.To see a cask of sugar burst and the sugar spilling out, foretells a slight loss.

To hear a negro singing while unloading sugar, some seemingly insignificant affair willbring you great benefit, either in business or social states.Sugar TongsTo dream of sugar-tongs, foretells that disagreeable tidings of wrong-doings will bereceived by you.SuicideTo commit suicide in a dream, foretells that misfortune will hang heavily over you.To see or hear others committing this deed, foretells that the failure of others will affectyour interests.For a young woman to dream that her lover commits suicide, her disappointment by thefaithlessness of her lover is accentuated.SulphurTo dream of sulphur, warns you to use much discretion in your dealings, as you arethreatened with foul play.To see sulphur burning, is ominous of great care attendant upon your wealth.To eat sulphur, indicates good health and consequent pleasure.SunTo dream of seeing a clear, shining sunrise, foretells joyous events and prosperity, whichgive delightful promises.To see the sun at noontide, denotes the maturity of ambitions and signals unboundedsatisfaction.To see the sunset, is prognostic of joys and wealth passing their zenith, and warns you tocare for your interests with renewed vigilance.A sun shining through clouds, denotes that troubles and difficulties are losing hold onyou, and prosperity is nearing you.If the sun appears weird, or in an eclipse, there will be stormy and dangerous times, butthese will eventually pass, leaving your business and domestic affairs in better forms thanbefore.

SunshadeTo dream of seeing young girls carrying sunshades, foretells prosperity and exquisitedelights.A broken one, foretells sickness and death to the young.SurgeonTo dream of a surgeon, denotes you are threatened by enemies who are close to you inbusiness. For a young woman, this dream promises a serious illness from which she willexperience great inconvenience.Surgical InstrumentsTo see surgical instruments in a dream, foretells dissatisfaction will be felt by you at theindiscreet manner a friend manifests toward you.SwallowTo dream of swallows, is a sign of peace and domestic harmony.To see a wounded or dead one, signifies unavoidable sadness.SwampTo walk through swampy places in dreams, foretells that you will be the object ofadverse circumstances. Your inheritance will be uncertain, and you will undergo keendisappointments in your love matters.To go through a swamp where you see clear water and green growths, you will take holdon prosperity and singular pleasures, the obtaining of which will be attended with dangerand intriguing.See Marsh.SwanTo dream of seeing white swans floating upon placid waters, foretells prosperousoutlooks and delightful experiences.To see a black swan, denotes illicit pleasure, if near clear water.A dead swan, foretells satiety and discontentment.To see them flying, pleasant anticipations will be realized soon.

SwearingTo dream of swearing, denotes some unpleasant obstructions in business. A lover willhave cause to suspect the faithfulness of his affianced after this dream.To dream that you are swearing before your family, denotes that disagreements will soonbe brought about by your unloyal conduct.SweepingTo dream of sweeping, denotes that you will gain favor in the eyes of your husband, andchildren will find pleasure in the home.If you think the floors need sweeping, and you from some cause neglect them, there willbe distresses and bitter disappointments awaiting you in the approaching days.To servants, sweeping is a sign of disagreements and suspicion of the intentions ofothers.SweetheartTo dream that your sweetheart is affable and of pleasing physique, foretells that you willwoo a woman who will prove a joy to your pride and will bring you a good inheritance.If she appears otherwise, you will be discontented with your choice before the marriagevows are consummated. To dream of her as being sick or in distress, denotes that sadnesswill be intermixed with joy.If you dream that your sweetheart is a corpse, you will have a long period of doubt andunfavorable fortune.See Lover, Hugging, and Kissing.Sweet OilSweet oil in dreams, implies considerate treatment will be withheld from you in someunfortunate occurrence.Sweet TasteTo dream of any kind of a sweet taste in your mouth, denotes you will be praised for yourpleasing conversation and calm demeanor in a time of commotion and distress.To dream that you are trying to get rid of a sweet taste, foretells that you will oppress andderide your friends, and will incur their displeasure.

SwellingTo dream that you see yourself swollen, denotes that you will amass fortune, but youregotism will interfere with your enjoyment.To see others swollen, foretells that advancement will meet with envious obstructions.SwimmingTo dream of swimming, is an augury of success if you find no discomfort in the act. Ifyou feel yourself going down, much dissatisfaction will present itself to you.For a young woman to dream that she is swimming with a girl friend who is an artist inswimming, foretells that she will be loved for her charming disposition, and her littlelove affairs will be condoned by her friends.To swim under water, foretells struggles and anxieties.See Diving and Bathing.Swiss CheeseTo dream of Swiss cheese, foretells that you will come into possession of substantialproperty, and healthful amusements will be enjoyed.SwitchTo dream of a switch, foretells changes and misfortune.A broken switch, foretells disgrace and trouble.To dream of a railroad switch, denotes that travel will cause you much loss andinconvenience.To dream of a switch, signifies you will meet discouragements in momentous affairs.SwordTo dream that you wear a sword, indicates that you will fill some public position withhonor.To have your sword taken from you, denotes your vanquishment in rivalry.To see others bearing swords, foretells that altercations will be attended with danger.A broken sword, foretells despair.

SybilTo dream of a sybil, foretells that you will enjoy assignations and other demoralizingpleasures.SymphonyTo dream of symphonies, heralds delightful occupations.See Music.SynagogueTo dream of a synagogue, foretells that you have enemies powerfully barricading yourentrance into fortune's realms. If you climb to the top on the outside, you will overcomeoppositions and be successful.If you read the Hebrew inscription on a synagogue, you will meet disaster, but willeventually rebuild your fortunes with renewed splendor.See Church.SyringeTo dream of a syringe, denotes that false alarm of the gravity of a relative's condition willreach you. To see a broken one, foretells you are approaching a period of ill health orworry over slight mistakes in business.

What's In A Dream - T to Z

TTableTo dream of setting a table preparatory to a meal, foretells happy unions and prosperouscircumstances.To see empty tables, signifies poverty or disagreements.To clear away the table, denotes that pleasure will soon assume the form of trouble andindifference.To eat from a table without a cloth, foretells that you will be possessed of an independentdisposition, and the prosperity or conduct of others will give you no concern.To see a table walking or moving in some mysterious way, foretells that dissatisfactionwill soon enter your life, and you will seek relief in change.To dream of a soiled cloth on a table, denotes disobedience from servants or children,and quarreling will invariably follow pleasure.To see a broken table, is ominous of decaying fortune.To see one standing or sitting on a table, foretells that to obtain their desires they will beguilty of indiscretions.To see or hear table-rapping or writing, denotes that you will undergo change of feelingstowards your friends, and your fortune will be threatened. A loss from the depreciation ofrelatives or friends is indicated.

TacksTo dream of tacks, means to you many vacations and quarrels.For a woman to drive one, foretells she will master unpleasant rivalry.If she mashes her finger while driving it, she will be distressed over unpleasant tasksTadpoleTo dream of tadpoles, foretells uncertain speculation will bring cause for uneasiness inbusiness. For a young woman to see them in clear water, foretells she will form a relationwith a wealthy but immoral man.TailTo dream of seeing only the tail of a beast, unusual annoyance is indicated wherepleasures seemed assured.To cut off the tail of an animal, denotes that you will suffer misfortune by your owncarelessness.To dream that you have the tail of a beast grown on you, denotes that your evil ways willcause you untold distress, and strange events will cause you perplexity.TailorTo dream of a tailor, denotes that worries will arise on account of some journey to bemade.To have a misunderstanding with one, shows that you will be disappointed in theoutcome of some scheme.For one to take your measure, denotes that you will have quarrels and disagreements.TalismanTo dream that you wear a talisman, implies you will have pleasant companions and enjoyfavors from the rich. For a young woman to dream her lover gives her one, denotes shewill obtain her wishes concerning marriage.TalkingTo dream of talking, denotes that you will soon hear of the sickness of relatives, andthere will be worries in your affairs.

To hear others talking loudly, foretells that you will be accused of interfering in theaffairs of others. To think they are talking about you, denotes that you are menaced withillness and disfavor.TallowTo dream of tallow, forebodes that your possessions of love and wealth will quicklyvanish.TambourineTo dream of a tambourine, signifies you will have enjoyment in some unusual eventwhich will soon take place.TankTo dream of a tank, foretells you will be prosperous and satisfied beyond yourexpectations. To see a leaking tank, denotes loss in your affairs.TanneryTo dream of a tannery, denotes contagion and other illness. Loss in trade is portended.To dream that you are a tanner, denotes that you will have to engage in work which is notto your taste, but there will be others dependent upon you.To buy leather from a tannery, foretells that you will be successful in your undertakings,but will not make many friends.TapeTo dream of tape, denotes your work will be wearisome and unprofitable. For a womanto buy it, foretells she will find misfortune laying oppression upon her.TapestryTo dream of seeing rich tapestry, foretells that luxurious living will be to your liking, andif the tapestries are not worn or ragged, you will be able to gratify your inclinations.If a young woman dreams that her rooms are hung with tapestry, she will soon wed someone who is rich and above her in standing.TapewormTo dream you see a tapeworm, or have one, denotes disagreeable prospects for health or

for pleasure.TarIf you see tar in dreams, it warns you against pitfalls and designs of treacherous enemies.To have tar on your hands or clothing, denotes sickness and grief.TarantulaTo see a tarantula in your dream, signifies enemies are about to overwhelm you with loss.To kill one, denotes you will be successful after much ill-luck.TargetTo dream of a target, foretells you will have some affair demanding your attention fromother more pleasant ones. For a young woman to think she is a target, denotes herreputation is in danger through the envy of friendly associates.TasselsTo see tassels in a dream, denotes you will reach the height of your desires and ambition.For a young woman to lose them, denotes she will undergo some unpleasant experience.TattooTo see your body appearing tattooed, foretells that some difficulty will cause you tomake a long and tedious absence from your home.To see tattooes on others, foretells that strange loves will make you an object of jealousy.To dream you are a tattooist, is a sign that you will estrange yourself from friendsbecause of your fancy for some strange experience.TaxesTo dream that you pay your taxes, foretells you will succeed in destroying evil influencesrising around you. If others pay them, you will be forced to ask aid of friends. If you areunable to pay them, you will be unfortunate in experiments you are making.TeaTo dream that you are brewing tea, foretells that you will be guilty of indiscreet actions,and will feel deeply remorseful.

To see your friends drinking tea, and you with them, denotes that social pleasures willpall on you, and you will seek to change your feelings by serving others in their sorrows.To see dregs in your tea, warns you of trouble in love, and affairs of a social nature.To spill tea, is a sign of domestic confusion and grief.To find your tea chest empty, unfolds much disagreeable gossip and news.To dream that you are thirsty for tea, denotes that you will be surprised with uninvitedguests.TeacupsTo dream of teacups, foretells that affairs of enjoyment will be attended by you. For awoman to break or see them broken, omens her pleasure and good fortune will be marredby a sudden trouble. To drink wine from one, foretells fortune and pleasure will becombined in the near future.TeakettleTo dream you see a teakettle, implies sudden news which will be likely to distress you.For a woman to pour sparkling, cold water from a teakettle, she will have unexpectedfavor shown her.TearsTo dream that you are in tears, denotes that some affliction will soon envelope you.To see others shedding tears, foretells that your sorrows will affect the happiness ofothers.TeasingTo find yourself teasing any person while dreaming, denotes that you will be loved andsought after because of your cheerful and amiable manners. Your business will beeventually successful.To dream of being teased, denotes that you will win the love of merry and well-to-dopersons.For a young woman to dream of being teased, foretells that she will form a hastyattachment, but will not be successful in consummating an early marriage.

TeethAn ordinary dream of teeth augurs an unpleasant contact with sickness, or disquietingpeople.If you dream that your teeth are loose, there will be failures and gloomy tidings.If the doctor pulls your tooth, you will have desperate illness, if not fatal; it will belingering.To have them filled, you will recover lost valuables after much uneasiness.To clean or wash your teeth, foretells that some great struggle will be demanded of youin order to preserve your fortune.To dream that you are having a set of teeth made, denotes that severe crosses will fallupon you, and you will strive to throw them aside.If you lose your teeth, you will have burdens which will crush your pride and demolishyour affairs.To dream that you have your teeth knocked out, denotes sudden misfortune. Either yourbusiness will suffer, or deaths or accidents will come close to you.To examine your teeth, warns you to be careful of your affairs, as enemies are lurkingnear you.If they appear decayed and snaggled, your business or health will suffer from intensestrains.To dream of spitting out teeth, portends personal sickness, or sickness in your immediatefamily.Imperfect teeth is one of the worst dreams. It is full of mishaps for the dreamer. A loss ofestates, failure of persons to carry out their plans and desires, bad health, depressedconditions of the nervous system for even healthy persons.For one tooth to fall out, foretells disagreeable news; if two, it denotes unhappy statesthat the dreamer will be plunged into from no carelessness on his part. If three fall out,sickness and accidents of a very serious nature will follow.Seeing all the teeth drop out, death and famine usually will prevail. If the teeth aredecayed and you pull them out, the same, only yourself, is prominent in the case.To dream of tartar or any deposit falling off of the teeth and leaving them sound andwhite, is a sign of temporary indisposition, which will pass, leaving you wiser in regardto conduct, and you will find enjoyment in the discharge of duty.

To admire your teeth for their whiteness and beauty, foretells that pleasant occupationsand much happiness will be experienced through the fulfilment of wishes.To dream that you pull one of your teeth and lose it, and feeling within your mouth withyour tongue for the cavity, and failing to find any, and have a doctor for the same, but tono effect, leaving the whole affair enveloped in mystery, denotes that you are about toenter into some engagement which does not exactly please you, and which you decide toignore, but will later take it up and secretly prosecute it to your own disquietingsatisfaction and under the suspicion of friends.To dream that a dentist cleans your teeth perfectly, and the next morning you find themrusty, foretells you will believe your interest secure concerning some person or position,but you will find that they have succumbed to the blandishments of an artful man orwoman.TelegramTo dream that you receive a telegram, denotes that you will soon receive tidings of anunpleasant character. Some friend is likely to misrepresent matters which are of muchconcern to you.To send a telegram is a sign that you will be estranged from some one holding a placenear you, or business will disappoint you.If you are the operator sending these messages, you will be affected by them onlythrough the interest of others.To see or be in a telegraph office, foretells unfortunate engagements.TelephoneTo dream of a telephone, foretells you will meet strangers who will harass and bewilderyou in your affairs. For a woman to dream of talking over one, denotes she will havemuch jealous rivalry, but will overcome all evil influences. If she cannot hear well inconversing over one, she is threatened with evil gossip, and the loss of a lover.TelescopeTo dream of a telescope, portends unfavorable seasons for love and domestic affairs, andbusiness will be changeable and uncertain.To look at planets and stars through one, portends for you journeys which will afford youmuch pleasure, but later cause you much financial loss.To see a broken telescope, or one not in use, signifies that matters will go out of theordinary with you, and trouble may be expected.

TempestTo dream of tempests, denotes that you will have a siege of calamitous trouble, andfriends will treat you with indifference.See Storms.TemptationTo dream that you are surrounded by temptations, denotes that you will be involved insome trouble with an envious person who is trying to displace you in the confidence offriends. If you resist them, you will be successful in some affair in which you have muchopposition.TenantFor a landlord to see his tenant in a dream, denotes he will have business trouble andvexation. To imagine you are a tenant, foretells you will suffer loss in experiments of abusiness character. If a tenant pays you money, you will be successful in someengagements.TenpinsIf you dream at playing at tenpins, you will doubtless soon engage in some affair whichwill bring discredit upon your name, and you will lose your money and true friendship.To see others engaged in this dream, foretells that you will find pleasure in frivolouspeople and likely lose employment.For a young woman to play a successful game of tenpins, is an omen of light pleasures,but sorrow will attend her later.TentTo dream of being in a tent, foretells a change in your affairs.To see a number of tents, denotes journeys with unpleasant companions.If the tents are torn or otherwise dilapidated, there will be trouble for you.TerrorTo dream that you feel terror at any object or happening, denotes that disappointmentsand loss will envelope you.To see others in terror, means that unhappiness of friends will seriously affect you.

TextTo dream of hearing a minister reading his text, denotes that quarrels will lead toseparation with some friend.To dream that you are in a dispute about a text, foretells unfortunate adventures for you.If you try to recall a text, you will meet with unexpected difficulties.If you are repeating and pondering over one, you will have great obstacles to overcome ifyou gain your desires.ThatchTo dream that you thatch a roof with any quickly, perishable material, denotes thatsorrow and discomfort will surround you.If you find that a roof which you have thatched with straw is leaking, there will bethreatenings of danger, but by your rightly directed energy they may be averted.ThawTo dream of seeing ice thawing, foretells that some affair which has caused you muchworry will soon give you profit and pleasure.To see the ground thawing after a long freeze, foretells prosperous circumstances.TheaterTo dream of being at a theater, denotes that you will have much pleasure in the companyof new friends. Your affairs will be satisfactory after this dream. If you are one of theplayers, your pleasures will be of short duration.If you attend a vaudeville theater, you are in danger of losing property through sillypleasures. If it is a grand opera, you will succeed in you wishes and aspirations.If you applaud and laugh at a theater, you will sacrifice duty to the gratification of fancy.To dream of trying to escape from one during a fire or other excitement, foretells that youwill engage in some enterprise, which will be hazardous.ThermometerTo dream of looking at a thermometer, denotes unsatisfactory business, anddisagreements in the home.

To see a broken one, foreshadows illness. If the mercury seems to be falling, your affairswill assume a distressing shape. If it is rising, you will be able to throw off badconditions in your business.ThiefTo dream of being a thief and that you are pursued by officers, is a sign that you willmeet reverses in business, and your social relations will be unpleasant.If you pursue or capture a thief, you will overcome your enemies.See Stealing.ThighTo dream of seeing your thigh smooth and white, denotes unusual good luck andpleasure.To see wounded thighs, foretells illness and treachery.For a young woman to admire her thigh, signifies willingness to engage in adventures,and she should heed this as a warning to be careful of her conduct.ThimbleIf you use a thimble in your dreams, you will have many others to please besidesyourself. If a woman, you will have your own position to make.To lose one, foretells poverty and trouble. To see an old or broken one, denotes that youare about to act unwisely in some momentous affair.To receive or buy a new thimble, portends new associations in which you will findcontentment.To dream that you use an open end thimble, but find that it is closed, denotes that youwill have trouble, but friends will aid you in escaping its disastrous consequences.ThirstTo dream of being thirsty, shows that you are aspiring to things beyond your presentreach; but if your thirst is quenched with pleasing drinks, you will obtain your wishes.To see others thirsty and drinking to slake it, you will enjoy many favors at the hands ofwealthy people.

ThornsTo dream of thorns, is an omen of dissatisfaction, and evil will surround every effort toadvancement.If the thorns are hidden beneath green foliage, you prosperity will be interfered with bysecret enemies.ThreadTo dream of thread, denotes that your fortune lies beyond intricate paths.To see broken threads, you will suffer loss through the faithlessness of friends.See Spools.ThreshingTo dream of threshing grain, denotes great advancement in business and happinessamong families. But if there is an abundance of straw and little grain, unsuccessfulenterprises will be undertaken.To break down or have an accident while threshing, you will have some great sorrow inthe midst of prosperity.ThroatTo dream of seeing a well-developed and graceful throat, portends a rise in position.If you feel that your throat is sore, you will be deceived in your estimation of a friend,and will have anxiety over the discovery.ThroneIf you dream of sitting on a throne, you will rapidly rise to favor and fortune.To descend from one, there is much disappointment for you.To see others on a throne, you will succeed to wealth through the favor of others.ThumbTo dream of seeing a thumb, foretells that you will be the favorite of artful persons anduncertain fortune.

If you are suffering from a sore thumb, you will lose in business, and your companionswill prove disagreeable. To dream that you have no thumb, implies destitution andloneliness. If it seems unnaturally small, you will enjoy pleasure for a time. If abnormallylarge, your success will be rapid and brilliant.A soiled thumb indicates gratification of loose desires. If the thumb has a very long nail,you are liable to fall into evil through seeking strange pleasures.ThunderTo dream of hearing thunder, foretells you will soon be threatened with reverses in yourbusiness.To be in a thunder shower, denotes trouble and grief are close to you.To hear the terrific peals of thunder, which make the earth quake, portends great loss anddisappointment.TickleTo dream of being tickled, denotes insistent worries and illness.If you tickle others, you will throw away much enjoyment through weakness and folly.TicksTo dream you see ticks crawling on your flesh, is a sign of impoverished circumstancesand ill health. Hasty journeys to sick beds may be made.To mash a tick on you, denotes that you will be annoyed by treacherous enemies.To see in your dreams large ticks on stock, enemies are endeavoring to get possession ofyour property by foul means.TigerTo dream of a tiger advancing towards you, you will be tormented and persecuted byenemies. If it attacks you, failure will bury you in gloom. If you succeed in warding itoff, or killing it, you will be extremely successful in all your undertakings.To see one running away from you, is a sign that you will overcome opposition, and riseto high positions.To see them in cages, foretells that you will foil your adversaries.To see rugs of tiger skins, denotes that you are in the way to enjoy luxurious ease andpleasure.

TillTo dream of seeing money and valuables in a till, foretells coming success. Your loveaffairs will be exceedingly favorable. An empty one, denotes disappointed expectations.TimberTo see timber in your dreams, is an augury of prosperous times and peacefulsurroundings.If the timber appears dead, there are great disappointments for you.See Forest.TipsyTo dream that you are tipsy, denotes that you will cultivate a jovial disposition, and thecares of life will make no serious inroads into your conscience.To see others tipsy, shows that you are careless as to the demeanor of your associates.ToadTo dream of toads, signifies unfortunate adventures. If a woman, your good name isthreatened with scandal.To kill a toad, foretells that your judgment will be harshly criticised.To put your hands on them, you will be instrumental in causing the downfall of a friend.TobaccoTo dream of tobacco, denotes success in business affairs, but poor returns in love.To use it, warns you against enemies and extravagance.To see it growing, foretells successful enterprises. To see it dry in the leaf, ensures goodcrops to farmers, and consequent gain to tradesmen.To smoke tobacco, denotes amiable friendships.TocsinTo dream of hearing a tocsin sounded, augurs a strife from which you will comevictorious. For a woman, this is a warning of separation from her husband or lover.

ToddyTo dream of taking a toddy, foretells interesting events will soon change your plan ofliving.TomatoesTo dream of eating tomatoes, signals the approach of good health. To see them growing,denotes domestic enjoyment and happiness.For a young woman to see ripe ones, foretells her happiness in the married state.TombTo dream of seeing tombs, denotes sadness and disappointments in business.Dilapidated tombs omens death or desperate illness.To dream of seeing your own tomb, portends your individual sickness ordisappointments.To read the inscription on tombs, foretells unpleasant duties.TongueTo dream of seeing your own tongue, denotes that you will be looked upon with disfavorby your acquaintances.To see the tongue of another, foretells that scandal will villify you.To dream that your tongue is affected in any way, denotes that your carelessness intalking will get you into trouble.ToothlessTo dream that you are toothless, denotes your inability to advance your interests, and illhealth will cast gloom over your prospects.To see others toothless, foretells that enemies are trying in vain to calumniate you.Tooth-PicksTo dream of tooth-picks, foretells that small anxieties, and spites will harass youunnecessarily if you give them your attention.If you use one, you will be a party to a friend's injury.

TopazTo see topaz in a dream, signifies Fortune will be liberal in her favors, and you will havevery pleasing companions. For a woman to lose topaz ornaments, foretells she will beinjured by jealous friends who court her position. To receive one from another beside arelative, foretells an interesting love affair will occupy her attention.TopsTo dream of a top, denotes that you will be involved in frivolous difficulties.To see one spinning, foretells that you will waste your means in childish pleasures.To see a top, foretells indiscriminate friendships will involve you in difficulty.TorchTo dream of seeing torches, foretells pleasant amusement and favorable business.To carry a torch, denotes success in love making or intricate affairs. For one to go out,denotes failure and distress.See Lantern and Lamp.TornadoIf you dream that you are in a tornado, you will be filled with disappointment andperplexity over the miscarriage of studied plans for swift attainment of fortune.See Hurricane.TorrentTo dream that you are looking upon a rushing torrent, denotes that you will have unusualtrouble and anxiety.TortureTo dream of being tortured, denotes that you will undergo disappointment and griefthrough the machination of false friends.If you are torturing others, you will fail to carry out well-laid plans for increasing yourfortune.If you are trying to alleviate the torture of others, you will succeed after a struggle inbusiness and love.

TouristTo dream that you are a tourist, denotes that you will engage in some pleasurable affairwhich will take you away from your usual residence.To see tourists, indicates brisk but unsettled business and anxiety in love.TowerTo dream of seeing a tower, denotes that you will aspire to high elevations. If you climbone, you will succeed in your wishes, but if the tower crumbles as you descend, you willbe disappointed in your hopes.See Ladder.ToysTo see toys in dreams, foretells family joys, if whole and new, but if broken, death willrend your heart with sorrow.To see children at play with toys, marriage of a happy nature is indicated.To give away toys in your dreams, foretells you will be ignored in a social way by youracquaintances.TradeTo dream of trading, denotes fair success in your enterprise. If you fail, trouble andannoyances will overtake you.TragedyTo dream of a tragedy, foretells misunderstandings and grievious disappointments.To dream that you are implicated in a tragedy, portends that a calamity will plunge youinto sorrow and peril.TrainTo see a train of cars moving in your dreams, you will soon have cause to make ajourney.To be on a train and it appears to move smoothly along, though there is no track, denotesthat you will be much worried over some affair which will eventually prove a source ofprofit to you.

To see freight trains in your dreams, is an omen of changes which will tend to yourelevation.To find yourself, in a dream, on top of a sleeping car, denotes you will make a journeywith an unpleasant companion, with whom you will spend money and time that could beused in a more profitable and congenial way, and whom you will seek to avoid.TraitorTo see a traitor in your dream, foretells you will have enemies working to despoil you. Ifsome one calls you one, or if you imagine yourself one, there will be unfavorableprospects of pleasure for you.TransfigurationTo dream of the transfiguration, foretells that your faith in man's own nearness to Godwill raise you above trifling opinions, and elevate you to a worthy position, in whichcapacity you will be able to promote the well being of the ignorant and persecuted.To see yourself transfigured, you will stand high in the esteem of honest and prominentmen.TrapTo dream of setting a trap, denotes that you will use intrigue to carry out your designs.If you are caught in a trap, you will be outwitted by your opponents.If you catch game in a trap, you will flourish in whatever vocation you may choose.To see an empty trap, there will be misfortune in the immediate future.An old or broken trap, denotes failure in business, and sickness in your family mayfollow.TravelingTo dream of traveling, signifies profit and pleasure combined. To dream of travelingthrough rough unknown places, portends dangerous enemies, and perhaps sickness.Over bare or rocky steeps,signifies apparent gain, but loss and disappointment willswiftly follow. If the hills or mountains are fertile and green, you will be eminentlyprosperous and happy.To dream you travel alone in a car, denotes you may possibly make an eventful journey,and affairs will be worrying. To travel in a crowded car, foretells fortunate adventures,and new and entertaining companions.

See Journey.TrayTo see trays in your dream, denotes your wealth will be foolishly wasted, and surprises ofunpleasant nature will shock you. If the trays seem to be filled with valuables, surpriseswill come in the shape of good fortune.TreasuresTo dream that you find treasures, denotes that you will be greatly aided in your pursuit offortune by some unexpected generosity.If you lose treasures, bad luck in business and the inconstancy of friends is foretold.TreesTo dream of trees in new foliage, foretells a happy consummation of hopes and desires.Dead trees signal sorrow and loss.To climb a tree is a sign of swift elevation and preferment.To cut one down, or pull it up by the roots, denotes that you will waste your energies andwealth foolishly.To see green tress newly felled, portends unhappiness coming unexpectedly upon scenesof enjoyment, or prosperity.See Forest.TrenchesTo see trenches in dreams, warns you of distant treachery. You will sustain loss if notcareful in undertaking new enterprises, or associating with strangers.To see filled trenches, denotes many anxieties are gathering around you.See Ditch.TriangleTo dream of a triangle, foretells separation from friends, and love affairs will terminate indisagreements.

TripeTo see tripe in a dream, means sickness and danger.To eat tripe, denotes that you will be disappointed in some serious matter.TripletsTo dream of seeing triplets, foretells success in affairs where failure was feared.For a man to dream that his wife has them, signifies a pleasant termination to some affairwhich has been long in dispute.To hear newly-born triplets crying, signifies disagreements which will be hastilyreconciled to your pleasure.For a young woman to dream that she has triplets, denotes that she will suffer loss anddisappointment in love, but will succeed to wealth.TrophyTo see trophies in a dream, signifies some pleasure or fortune will come to you throughthe endeavors of mere acquaintances.For a woman to give away a trophy, implies doubtful pleasures and fortune.TrousersTo dream of trousers, foretells that you will be tempted to dishonorable deeds.If you put them on wrong side out, you will find that a fascination is fastening its holdupon you.TroutTo dream of seeing trout, is significant of growing prosperity. To eat some, denotes thatyou will be happily conditioned.To catch one with a hook, foretells assured pleasure and competence. If it falls back intothe water, you will have a short season of happiness.To catch them with a seine, is a sign of unparalleled prosperity.To see them in muddy water shows that your success in love will bring you to grief anddisappointments.

TrowelTo dream of a trowel, denotes you will experience reaction in unfavorable business, andwill vanquish poverty. To see one rusty or broken, unavoidable ill luck is fastapproaching you.TrumpetTo dream of a trumpet, denotes that something of unusual interest is about to befall you.To blow a trumpet, signifies that you will gain your wishes.TrunkTo dream of trunks, foretells journeys and ill luck. To pack your trunk, denotes that youwill soon go on a pleasant trip.To see the contents of a trunk thrown about in disorder, foretells quarrels, and a hastyjourney from which only dissatisfaction will accrue.Empty trunks foretell disappointment in love and marriage.For a drummer to check his trunk, is an omen of advancement and comfort. If he findsthat his trunk is too small for his wares, he will soon hear of his promotion, and hisdesires will reach gratification.For a young woman to dream that she tries to unlock her trunk and can't, signifies thatshe will make an effort to win some wealthy person, but by a misadventure she will loseher chance. If she fails to lock her trunk, she will be disappointed in making a desiredtrip.TrussTo see a truss in your dream, your ill health and unfortunate business engagements arepredicted.TrustsTo dream of trusts, foretells indifferent success in trade or law.If you imagine you are a member of a trust, you will be successful in designs of aspeculative nature.

TubTo dream of seeing a tub full of water, denotes domestic contentment. An empty tubproclaims unhappiness and waning of fortune.A broken tub, foretells family disagreements and quarrels.TumbleTo dream that you tumble off of any thing, denotes that you are given to carelessness,and should strive to be prompt with your affairs.To see others tumbling, is a sign that you will profit by the negligence of others.TunnelTo dream of going through a tunnel is bad for those in business and in love.To see a train coming towards you while in a tunnel, foretells ill health and change inoccupation.To pass through a tunnel in a car, denotes unsatisfactory business, and much unpleasantand expensive travel.To see a tunnel caving in, portends failure and malignant enemies.To look into one, denotes that you will soon be compelled to face a desperate issue.TurfTo dream of a racing turf, signifies that you will have pleasure and wealth at yourcommand, but your morals will be questioned by your most intimate friends.To see a green turf, indicates that interesting affairs will hold your attention.TurkeyTo dream of seeing turkeys, signifies abundant gain in business, and favorable crops tothe farmer.To see them dressed for the market, denotes improvement in your affairs.To see them sick, or dead, foretells that stringent circumstances will cause your pride tosuffer.To dream you eat turkey, foretells some joyful occasion approaching.

To see them flying, denotes a rapid transit from obscurity to prominence. To shoot themas game, is a sign that you will unscrupulously amass wealth.Turkish BathsTo dream of taking a Turkish bath, foretells that you will seek health far from your homeand friends, but you will have much pleasurable enjoyment.To see others take a Turkish bath, signifies that pleasant companions will occupy yourattention.TurnipsTo see turnips growing, denotes that your prospects will brighten, and that you will bemuch elated over your success.To eat them is a sign of ill health. To pull them up, denotes that you will improve youropportunities and your fortune thereby.To eat turnip greens, is a sign of bitter disappointment. Turnip seed is a sign of futureadvancement.For a young woman to sow turnip seed, foretells that she will inherit good property, andwin a handsome husband.TurpentineTo dream of turpentine, foretells your near future holds unprofitable and discouragingengagements. For a woman to dream that she binds turpentine to the wound of another,shows she will gain friendships and favor through her benevolent acts.TurquoiseTo dream of a turquoise, foretells you are soon to realize some desire which will greatlyplease your relatives. For a woman to have one stolen, foretells she will meet withcrosses in love. If she comes by it dishonestly, she must suffer for yielding to hastysusceptibility in love.TurtleTo dream of seeing turtles, signifies that an unusual incident will cause you enjoyment,and improve your business conditions.To drink turtle soup, denotes that you will find pleasure in compromising intrigue.

TweezersTo see tweezers in a dream, denotes uncomfortable situations will fill you withdiscontent, and your companions will abuse you.TwineTo see twine in your dream, warns you that your business is assuming complicationswhich will be hard to overcome.See Thread.TwinsTo dream of seeing twins, foretells security in business, and faithful and lovingcontentment in the home.If they are sickly, it signifies that you will have disappointment and grief.TypeTo see type in a dream, portends unpleasant transactions with friends. For a woman toclean type, foretells she will make fortunate speculations which will bring love andfortune.TyphoidTo dream that you are affected with this malady, is a warning to beware of enemies, andlook well to your health.If you dream that there is an epidemic of typhoid, there will be depressions in business,and usual good health will undergo disagreeable changes.UUglyTo dream that you are ugly, denotes that you will have a difficulty with your sweetheart,and your prospects will assume a depressed shade.

If a young woman thinks herself ugly, she will conduct herself offensively toward herlover, which will probably cause a break in their pleasant associations.UlcerTo see an ulcer in your dream, signifies loss of friends and removal from loved ones.Affairs will remain unsatisfactory.To dream that you have ulcers, denotes that you will become unpopular with your friendsby giving yourself up to foolish pleasures.UmbrellaTo dream of carrying an umbrella, denotes that trouble and annoyances will beset you.To see others carrying them, foretells that you will be appealed to for aid by charity.To borrow one, you will have a misunderstanding, perhaps, with a warm friend.To lend one, portends injury from false friends. To lose one, denotes trouble with someone who holds your confidence.To see one torn to pieces, or broken, foretells that you will be misrepresented andmaligned.To carry a leaky one, denotes that pain and displeasure will be felt by you towards yoursweetheart or companions.To carry a new umbrella over you in a clear shower, or sunshine, omens exquisitepleasure and prosperity.UncleIf you see your uncle in a dream, you will have news of a sad character soon.To dream you see your uncle prostrated in mind, and repeatedly have this dream, youwill have trouble with your relations which will result in estrangement, at least for a time.To see your uncle dead, denotes that you have formidable enemies.To have a misunderstanding with your uncle, denotes that your family relations will beunpleasant, and illness will be continually present.UndergroundTo dream of being in an underground habitation, you are in danger of losing reputationand fortune.

To dream of riding on an underground railway, foretells that you will engage in somepeculiar speculation which will contribute to your distress and anxiety.See Cars.UndressTo dream that you are undressing, foretells, scandalous gossip will overshadow you.For a woman to dream that she sees the ruler of her country undressed, signifies sadnesswill overtake anticipated pleasures. She will suffer pain through the apprehension of evilto those dear to her.To see others undressed, is an omen of stolen pleasures, which will rebound with grief.UnfortunateTo dream that you are unfortunate, is significant of loss to yourself, and trouble forothers.UniformTo see a uniform in your dream, denotes that you will have influential friends to aid youin obtaining your desires.For a young woman to dream that she wears a uniform, foretells that she will luckilyconfer her favors upon a man who appreciated them, and returns love for passion. If shediscards it, she will be in danger of public scandal by her notorious love for adventure.To see people arrayed in strange uniforms, foretells the disruption of friendly relationswith some other Power by your own government. This may also apply to families orfriends. To see a friend or relative looking sad while dressed in uniform, or as a soldier,predicts ill fortune or continued absence.United States Mail BoxTo see a United States mail box, in a dream, denotes that you are about to enter intotransactions which will be claimed to be illegal.To put a letter in one, denotes you will be held responsible for some irregularity ofanother.UnknownTo dream of meeting unknown persons, foretells change for good, or bad as the person isgood looking, or ugly, or deformed.

To feel that you are unknown, denotes that strange things will cast a shadow of ill luckover you.See Mystery.UrgentTo dream that you are supporting an urgent petition, is a sign that you will engage insome affair which will need fine financiering to carry it through successfully.UrinalTo dream of a urinal, disorder will predominate in your home.UrineTo dream of seeing urine, denotes ill health will make you disagreeable and unpleasantwith your friends.To dream that you are urinating, is an omen of bad luck, and trying seasons to love.UrnTo dream of an urn, foretells you will prosper in some respects, and in others disfavorwill be apparent. To see broken urns, unhappiness will confront you.UsurerTo find yourself a usurer in your dreams, foretells that you will be treated with coldnessby your associates, and your business will decline to your consternation.If others are usurers, you will discard some former friend on account of treachery.UsurperTo dream that you are a usurper, foretells you will have trouble in establishing a goodtitle to property.If others are trying to usurp your rights, there will be a struggle between you and yourcompetitors, but you will eventually win.For a young woman to have this dream, she will be a party to a spicy rivalry, in whichshe will win.

VVaccinateTo dream of being vaccinated, foretells that your susceptibility to female charms will beplayed upon to your sorrow.To dream that others are vaccinated, shows you will fail to find contentment where it issought, and your affairs will suffer decline in consequence.For a young woman to be vaccinated on her leg, foreshadows her undoing throughtreachery.VagrantTo dream that you are a vagrant, portends poverty and misery. To see vagrants is a signof contagion invading your community. To give to a vagrant, denotes that yourgenerosity will be applauded.ValentineTo dream that you are sending valentines, foretells that you will lose opportunities ofenriching yourself.For a young woman to receive one, denotes that she will marry a weak, but ardent loveragainst the counsels of her guardians.ValleyTo find yourself walking through green and pleasant valleys, foretells greatimprovements in business, and lovers will be happy and congenial. If the valley is barren,the reverse is predicted. If marshy, illness or vexations may follow.Vapor BathTo dream of a vapor bath, you will have fretful people for companions, unless you dreamof emerging from one, and then you will find that your cares will be temporary.VarnishingTo dream of varnishing anything, denotes that you will seek to win distinction byfraudulent means.

To see others varnishing, foretells that you are threatened with danger from the endeavorof friends to add to their own possessions.VaseTo dream of a vase, denotes that you will enjoy sweetest pleasure and contentment in thehome life.To drink from a vase, you will soon thrill with the delights of stolen love.To see a broken vase, foretells early sorrow. For a young woman to receive one, signifiesthat she will soon obtain her dearest wish.VatTo see a vat in your dreams, foretells anguish and suffering from the hands of cruelpersons, into which you have unwittingly fallen.VaticanTo dream of the vatican, signifies unexpected favors will fall within your grasp. You willform the acquaintance of distinguished people, if you see royal personages speaking tothe Pope.VaultTo dream of a vault, denotes bereavement and other misfortune. To see a vault forvaluables, signifies your fortune will surprise many, as your circumstances will appear tobe meagre. To see the doors of a vault open, implies loss and treachery of people whomyou trust.VegetablesTo dream of eating vegetables, is an omen of strange luck. You will think for a time thatyou are tremendously successful, but will find to your sorrow that you have been grosslyimposed upon.Withered, or decayed vegetables, bring unmitigated woe and sadness.For a young woman to dream that she is preparing vegetables for dinner, foretells that shewill lose the man she desired through pique, but she will win a well-meaning and faithfulhusband. Her engagements will be somewhat disappointing.

VehicleTo ride in a vehicle while dreaming, foretells threatened loss, or illness.To be thrown from one, foretells hasty and unpleasant news. To see a broken one, signalsfailure in important affairs.To buy one, you will reinstate yourself in your former position. To sell one, denotesunfavorable change in affairs.VeilTo dream that you wear a veil, denotes that you will not be perfectly sincere with yourlover, and you will be forced to use stratagem to retain him.To see others wearing veils, you will be maligned and defamed by apparent friends.An old, or torn veil, warns you that deceit is being thrown around you with sinisterdesign.For a young woman to dream that she loses her veil, denotes that her lover sees throughher deceitful ways and is likely to retaliate with the same.To dream of seeing a bridal veil, foretells that you will make a successful change in theimmediate future, and much happiness in your position.For a young woman to dream that she wears a bridal veil, denotes that she will engage insome affair which will afford her lasting profit and enjoyment. If it gets loose, or anyaccident befalls it, she will be burdened with sadness and pain.To throw a veil aside, indicates separation or disgrace.To see mourning veils in your dreams, signifies distress and trouble, and embarrassmentin business.VeinTo see your veins in a dream, insures you against slander, if they are normal.To see them bleeding, denotes that you will have a great sorrow from which there will beno escape.To see them swollen, you will rise hastily to distinction and places of trust.

VelvetTo dream of velvet, portends very successful enterprises. If you wear it, some distinctionwill be conferred upon you.To see old velvet, means your prosperity will suffer from your extreme pride.If a young woman dreams that she is clothed in velvet garments, it denotes that she willhave honors bestowed upon her, and the choice between several wealthy lovers.VeneerTo dream that you are veneering, denotes that you will systematically deceive yourfriends, your speculations will be of a misleading nature.VentriloquistTo dream of a ventriloquist, denotes that some treasonable affair is going to provedetrimental to your interest.If you think yourself one, you will not conduct yourself honorably towards people whotrust you.For a young woman to dream she is mystified by the voice of a ventriloquist, foretellsthat she will be deceived into illicit adventures.VerandaTo dream of being on a veranda, denotes that you are to be successful in some affairwhich is giving you anxiety.For a young woman to be with her lover on a veranda, denotes her early and happymarriage.To see an old veranda, denotes the decline of hopes, and disappointment in business andlove.VerminVermin crawling in your dreams, signifies sickness and much trouble. If you succeed inridding yourself of them, you will be fairly successful, but otherwise death may come toyou, or your relatives.See Locust.

VertigoTo dream that you have vertigo, foretells you will have loss in domestic happiness, andyour affairs will be under gloomy outlooks.VesselsTo dream of vessels, denotes labor and activity.See Ships and similar words.VexedIf you are vexed in your dreams, you will find many worries scattered through your earlyawakening.If you think some person is vexed with you, it is a sign that you will not shortly reconcilesome slight misunderstanding.VicarTo dream of a vicar, foretells that you will do foolish things while furious with jealousyand envy.For a young woman to dream she marries a vicar, foretells that she will fail to awakereciprocal affection in the man she desires, and will live a spinster, or marry to keep frombeing one.ViceTo dream that you are favoring any vice, signifies you are about to endanger yourreputation, by letting evil persuasions entice you.If you see others indulging in vice, some ill fortune will engulf the interest of somerelative or associate.VictimTo dream that you are the victim of any scheme, foretells that you will be oppressed andover-powered by your enemies. Your family relations will also be strained.To victimize others, denotes that you will amass wealth dishonorably and prefer illicitrelations, to the sorrow of your companions.

VictoryTo dream that you win a victory, foretells that you will successfully resist the attacks ofenemies, and will have the love of women for the asking.VillageTo dream that you are in a village, denotes that you will enjoy good health and findyourself fortunately provided for.To revisit the village home of your youth, denotes that you will have pleasant surprises instore and favorable news from absent friends.If the village looks dilapidated, or the dream indistinct, it foretells that trouble andsadness will soon come to you.VineTo dream of vines, is propitious of success and happiness. Good health is in store forthose who see flowering vines. If they are dead, you will fail in some momentousenterprise.To see poisonous vines, foretells that you will be the victim of a plausible scheme andyou will impair your health.VinegarTo dream of drinking vinegar, denotes that you will be exasperated and worried intoassenting to some engagement which will fill you with evil foreboding.To use vinegar on vegetables, foretells a deepening of already distressing affairs.To dream of vinegar at all times, denotes inharmonious and unfavorable aspects.VineyardTo dream of a vineyard, denotes favorable speculations and auspicious love-making.To visit a vineyard which is not well-kept and filled with bad odors, denotesdisappointment will overshadow your most sanguine anticipations.ViolenceTo dream that any person does you violence, denotes that you will be overcome byenemies.

If you do some other persons violence, you will lose fortune and favor by yourreprehensible way of conducting your affairs.VioletsTo see violets in your dreams, or gather them, brings joyous occasions in which you willfind favor with some superior person.For a young woman to gather them, denotes that she will soon meet her future husband.To see them dry, or withered, denotes that her love will be scorned and thrown aside.ViolinTo see, or hear a violin in dreams, foretells harmony and peace in the family, andfinancial affairs will cause no apprehension.For a young woman to play on one in her dreams, denotes that she will be honored andreceive lavish gifts.If her attempt to play is unsuccessful, she will lose favor, and aspire to things she nevercan possess.A broken one, indicates sad bereavement and separation.ViperTo dream of a viper, foretells that calamities are threatening you. To dream that amany-hued viper, and capable of throwing itself into many pieces, or unjointing itself,attacks you, denotes that your enemies are bent on your ruin and will work unitedly, yetapart, to displace you.VirginTo dream of a virgin, denotes that you will have comparative luck in your speculations.For a married woman to dream that she is a virgin, foretells that she will suffer remorseover her past, and the future will hold no promise of better things.For a young woman to dream that she is no longer a virgin, foretells that she will rungreat risk of losing her reputation by being indiscreet with her male friends.For a man to dream of illicit association with a virgin, denotes that he will fail toaccomplish an enterprise, and much worry will be caused him by the appeals of people.His aspirations will be foiled through unwarranted associations.

VisitIf you visit in your dreams, you will shortly have some pleasant occasion in your life.If your visit is unpleasant, your enjoyment will be marred by the action of maliciouspersons.For a friend to visit you, denotes that news of a favorable nature will soon reach you. Ifthe friend appears sad and travel-worn, there will be a note of displeasure growing out ofthe visit, or other slight disappointments may follow. If she is dressed in black or whiteand looks pale or ghastly, serious illness or accidents are predicted.VisionsTo dream that you have a strange vision, denotes that you will be unfortunate in yourdealings and sickness will unfit you for pleasant duties.If persons appear to you in visions, it foretells uprising and strife of families or state.If your friend is near dissolution and you are warned in a vision, he will appear suddenlybefore you, usually in white garments. Visions of death and trouble have such closeresemblance, that they are sometimes mistaken one for the other.To see visions of any order in your dreams, you may look for unusual developments inyour business, and a different atmosphere and surroundings in private life. Things will bereversed for a while with you. You will have changes in your business and private lifeseemingly bad, but eventually good for all concerned.The Supreme Will is always directed toward the ultimate good of the race.VitriolIf you see vitriol in your dreams, it is a token of some innocent person being censured byyou.To throw it on people, shows you will bear malice towards parties who seek to favor you.For a young woman to have a jealous rival throw it in her face, foretells that she will bethe innocent object of some person's hatred. This dream for a business man, denotesenemies and much persecution.VoiceTo dream of hearing voices, denotes pleasant reconciliations, if they are calm andpleasing; high-pitched and angry voices, signify disappointments and unfavorablesituations.

To hear weeping voices, shows that sudden anger will cause you to inflict injury upon afriend.If you hear the voice of God, you will make a noble effort to rise higher in unselfish andhonorable principles, and will justly hold the admiration of high-minded people.For a mother to hear the voice of her child, is a sign of approaching misery, perplexityand grievous doubts.To hear the voice of distress, or a warning one calling to you, implies your own seriousmisfortune or that of some one close to you. If the voice is recognized, it is oftenominous of accident or illness, which may eliminate death or loss.VolcanoTo see a volcano in your dreams, signifies that you will be in violent disputes, whichthreaten your reputation as a fair dealing and honest citizen.For a young woman, it means that her selfishness and greed will lead her into intricateadventures.VomitTo dream of vomiting, is a sign that you will be afflicted with a malady which willthreaten invalidism, or you will be connected with a racy scandal.To see others vomiting, denotes that you will be made aware of the false pretenses ofpersons who are trying to engage your aid.For a woman to dream that she vomits a chicken, and it hops off, denotes she will bedisappointed in some pleasure by the illness of some relative. Unfavorable business anddiscontent are also predicted.If it is blood you vomit, you will find illness a hurried and unexpected visitor. You willbe cast down with gloomy forebodings, and children and domesticity in general will allyto work you discomfort.VoteIf you dream of casting a vote on any measure, you will be engulfed in a commotionwhich will affect your community.To vote fraudulently, foretells that your dishonesty will overcome your betterinclinations.

VoucherTo dream of vouchers, foretells that patient toil will defeat idle scheming to arrest fortunefrom you.To sign one, denotes that you have the aid and confidence of those around you, despitethe evil workings of enemies.To lose one, signifies that you will have a struggle for your rights with relatives.VowTo dream that you are making or listening to vows, foretells complaint will be madeagainst you of unfaithfulness in business, or some love contract. To take the vows of achurch, denotes you will bear yourself with unswerving integrity through some difficulty.To break or ignore a vow, foretells disastrous consequences will attend your dealings.VoyageTo make a voyage in your dreams, foretells that you will receive some inheritancebesides that which your labors win for you.A disastrous voyage brings incompetence, and false loves.VulturesTo dream of vultures, signifies that some scheming person is bent on injuring you, andwill not succeed unless you see the vulture wounded, or dead.For a woman to dream of a vulture, signifies that she will be overwhelmed with slanderand gossip.WWadingIf you wade in clear water while dreaming, you will partake of evanescent, but exquisitejoys. If the water is muddy, you are in danger of illness, or some sorrowful experiences.

To see children wading in clear water is a happy prognostication, as you will be favoredin your enterprises.For a young woman to dream of wading in clear foaming water, she will soon gain thedesire nearest her heart.See Bathing.WaddingWadding, if seen in a dream, brings consolation to the sorrowing, and indifference tounfriendly criticism.WaferWafer, if seen in a dream, purports an encounter with enemies. To eat one, suggestsimpoverished fortune.For a young woman to bake them, denotes that she will be tormented and distressed byfears of remaining in the unmarried state.WagerTo dream of making a wager, signifies that you will resort to dishonest means to forwardyour schemes.If you lose a wager, you will sustain injury from base connections with those out of yoursocial sphere.To win one, reinstates you in favor with fortune.If you are not able to put up a wager, you will be discouraged and prostrated by theadverseness of circumstances.WagesWages, if received in dreams, brings unlooked for good to persons engaging in newenterprises.To pay out wages, denotes that you will be confounded by dissatisfaction.To have your wages reduced, warns you of unfriendly interest that is being taken againstyou.An increase of wages, suggests unusual profit in any undertaking.

WagonTo dream of a wagon, denotes that you will be unhappily mated, and many troubles willprematurely age you.To drive one down a hill, is ominous of proceedings which will fill you with disquiet,and will cause you loss.To drive one up hill, improves your worldly affairs.To drive a heavily loaded wagon, denotes that duty will hold you in a moral position,despite your efforts to throw her off.To drive into muddy water, is a gruesome prognostication, bringing you into a vortex ofunhappiness and fearful foreboding.To see a covered wagon, foretells that you will be encompassed by mysterious treachery,which will retard your advancement.For a young woman to dream that she drives a wagon near a dangerous embankment,portends that she will be driven into an illicit entanglement, which will fill her withterror, lest she be openly discovered and ostracised. If she drives across a clear stream ofwater, she will enjoy adventure without bringing opprobrium upon herself.A broken wagon represents distress and failure.WagtailTo see a wagtail in a dream, foretells that you will be the victim of unpleasant gossip, andyour affairs will develop unmistakable loss.WaifTo dream of a waif, denotes personal difficulties, and especial ill-luck in business.WailA wail falling upon your ear while in the midst of a dream, brings fearful news of disasterand woe.For a young woman to hear a wail, foretells that she will be deserted and left alone indistress, and perchance disgrace.See Weeping.

Waist and Shirt-WaistTo dream of a round full waist, denotes that you will be favored by an agreeabledispensation of fortune.A small, unnatural waist, foretells displeasing success and recriminating disputes.For a young woman to dream of a nice, ready-made shirt-waist, denotes that she willwin admiration through her ingenuity and pleasing manners.To dream that her shirt-waist is torn, she will be censured for her illicit engagements. Ifshe is trying on a shirt-waist, she will encounter rivalry in love, but if she succeeds inadjusting the waist to her person, she will successfully combat the rivalry and win theobject of her love.WaiterTo dream of a waiter, signifies you will be pleasantly entertained by a friend. To see onecross or disorderly, means offensive people will thrust themselves upon your hospitality.WakeTo dream that you attend a wake, denotes that you will sacrifice some importantengagement to enjoy some ill-favored assignation.For a young woman to see her lover at a wake, foretells that she will listen to theentreaties of passion, and will be persuaded to hazard honor for love.WalkingTo dream of walking through rough brier, entangled paths, denotes that you will be muchdistressed over your business complications, and disagreeable misunderstandings willproduce coldness and indifference.To walk in pleasant places, you will be the possessor of fortune and favor.To walk in the night brings misadventure, and unavailing struggle for contentment.For a young woman to find herself walking rapidly in her dreams, denotes that she willinherit some property, and will possess a much desired object.See Wading.Walking StickTo see a walking stick in a dream, foretells you will enter into contracts without proper

deliberation, and will consequently suffer reverses. If you use one in walking, you will bedependent upon the advice of others. To admire handsome ones, you will entrust yourinterest to others, but they will be faithful.WalletTo see wallets in a dream, foretells burdens of a pleasant nature will await your discretionas to assuming them. An old or soiled one, implies unfavorable results from your labors.WallsTo dream that you find a wall obstructing your progress, you will surely succumb toill-favored influences and lose important victories in your affairs.To jump over it, you will overcome obstacles and win your desires. To force a breach ina wall, you will succeed in the attainment of your wishes by sheer tenacity of purpose.To demolish one, you will overthrow your enemies. To build one, foretells that you willcarefully lay plans and will solidify your fortune to the exclusion of failure, or designingenemies.For a young woman to walk on top of a wall, shows that her future happiness will soonbe made secure. For her to hide behind a wall, denotes that she will form connections thatshe will be ashamed to acknowledge. If she walks beside a base wall. she will soon haverun the gamut of her attractions, and will likely be deserted at a precarious time.WalnutTo dream of walnuts, is an omen significant of prolific joys and favors.To dream that you crack a decayed walnut, denotes that your expectations will end inbitterness and regretable collapse.For a young woman to dream that she has walnut stain on her hands, foretells that shewill see her lover turn his attention to another, and she will entertain only regrets for her past indiscreet conduct.WaltzTo see the waltz danced, foretells that you will have pleasant relations with a cheerfuland adventuresome person.For a young woman to waltz with her lover, denotes that she will be the object of muchadmiration, but none will seek her for a wife. If she sees her lover waltzing with a rival,she will overcome obstacles to her desires with strategy. If she waltzes with a woman,she will be loved for her virtues and winning ways. If she sees persons whirling in thewaltz as if intoxicated, she will be engulfed so deeply in desire and pleasure that it will be

a miracle if she resists the impassioned advances of her lover and male acquaintances.WantTo dream that you are in want, denotes that you have unfortunately ignored the realitiesof life, and chased folly to her stronghold of sorrow and adversity.If you find yourself contented in a state of want, you will bear the misfortune whichthreatens you with heroism, and will see the clouds of misery disperse.To relieve want, signifies that you will be esteemed for your disinterested kindness, butyou will feel no pleasure in well doing.WarTo dream of war, foretells unfortunate conditions in business, and much disorder andstrife in domestic affairs.For a young woman to dream that her lover goes to war, denotes that she will hear ofsomething detrimental to her lover's character.To dream that your country is defeated in war, is a sign that it will suffer revolution of abusiness and political nature. Personal interest will sustain a blow either way.If of victory you dream, there will be brisk activity along business lines, and domesticitywill be harmonious.WardrobeTo dream of your wardrobe, denotes that your fortune will be endangered by yourattempts to appear richer than you are.If you imagine you have a scant wardrobe, you will seek association with strangers.WarehouseTo dream of a warehouse, denotes for you a successful enterprise. To see an empty one,is a sign that you will be cheated and foiled in some plan which you have given muchthought and maneuvering.WarrantTo dream that a warrant is being served on you, denotes that you will engage in someimportant work which will give you great uneasiness as to its standing and profits.To see a warrant served on some one else, there will be danger of your actions bringing

you into fatal quarrels or misunderstandings. You are likely to be justly indignant withthe wantonness of some friend.WartsIf you are troubled with warts on your person, in dreams, you will be unable tosuccessfully parry the thrusts made at your honor.To see them leaving your hands, foretells that you will overcome disagreeableobstructions to fortune.To see them on others, shows that you have bitter enemies near you. If you doctor them,you will struggle with energy to ward off threatened danger to you and yours.WashboardTo see a washboard in your dreams, is indicative of embarrassment. If you see a woman using one, it predicts that you will let women rob you of energy and fortune. A broken one, portends that you will come to grief and disgraceful deeds through fast living. Wash-Bowl To dream of a wash-bowl, signifies that new cares will interest you, and afford much enjoyment to others. To bathe your face and hands in a bowl of clear water, denotes that you will soon consummate passionate wishes which will bind you closely to some one who interested you, but before passion enveloped you. If the bowl is soiled, or broken, you will rue an illicit engagement, which will give others pain, and afford you small pleasure. Washer Woman A washer woman seen in dreams, represents infidelity and a strange adventure. For the business man, or farmer, this dream indicates expanding trade and fine crops. For a woman to dream that she is a washer woman, denotes that she will throw decorum aside in her persistent effort to hold the illegal favor of men. Washing To dream that you are washing yourself, signifies that you pride yourself on the numberless liaisons you maintain.

See Wash Bowl or Bathing. Wasp Wasps, if seen in dreams, denotes that enemies will scourge and spitefully villify you. If one stings you, you will feel the effect of envy and hatred. To kill them, you will be able to throttle your enemies, and fearlessly maintain your rights. Waste To dream of wandering through waste places, foreshadows doubt and failure, where promise of success was bright before you. To dream of wasting your fortune, denotes you will be unpleasantly encumbered with domestic cares. Watch To dream of a watch, denotes you will be prosperous in well-directed speculations. To look at the time of one, your efforts will be defeated by rivalry. To break one, there will be distress and loss menacing you. To drop the crystal of one, foretells carelessness, or unpleasant companionship. For a woman to lose one, signifies domestic disturbances will produce unhappiness. To imagine you steal one, you will have a violent enemy who will attack your reputation. To make a present of one, denotes you will suffer your interest to decline in the pursuance of undignified recreations. Water To dream of clear water, foretells that you will joyfully realize prosperity and pleasure. If the water is muddy, you will be in danger and gloom will occupy Pleasure's seat. If you see it rise up in your house, denotes that you will struggle to resist evil, but unless you see it subside, you will succumb to dangerous influences. If you find yourself baling it out, but with feet growing wet, foreshadows trouble, sickness, and misery will work you a hard task, but you will forestall them by your watchfulness. The same may be applied to muddy water rising in vessels. To fall into muddy water, is a sign that you will make many bitter mistakes, and will suffer poignant grief therefrom.

To drink muddy water, portends sickness, but drinking it clear and refreshing bringsfavorable consummation of fair hopes.To sport with water, denotes a sudden awakening to love and passion.To have it sprayed on your head, denotes that your passionate awakening to love willmeet reciprocal consummation.The following dream and its allegorical occurrence in actual life is related by a youngwoman student of dreams:"Without knowing how, I was (in my dream) on a boat, I waded throughclear blue water to a wharfboat, which I found to be snow white, butrough and splintry. The next evening I had a delightful male caller, buthe remained beyond the time prescribed by mothers and I was severelycensured for it."The blue water and fairy white boat were the disappointing prospects in the symbol.Water-CarrierTo see water-carriers passing in your dreams, denotes that your prospects will befavorable in fortune, and love will prove no laggard in your chase for pleasure.If you think you are a water-carrier, you will rise above your present position.WaterfallTo dream of a waterfall, foretells that you will secure your wildest desire, and fortunewill be exceedingly favorable to your progress.Water LilyTo dream of a water lily, or to see them growing, foretells there will be a closecommingling of prosperity and sorrow or bereavement.WavesTo dream of waves, is a sign that you hold some vital step in contemplation, which willevolve much knowledge if the waves are clear; but you will make a fatal error if you seethem muddy or lashed by a storm.See Ocean and Sea.

Wax TaperTo dream of lighting wax tapers, denotes that some pleasing occurrence will bring youinto association with friends long absent.To blow them out, signals disappointing times, and sickness will forestall expectedopportunities of meeting distinguished friends.WayTo dream you lose your way, warns you to disabuse your mind of lucky speculations, asyour enterprises threaten failure unless you are painstaking in your management ofaffairs.See Road and Path.WealthTo dream that you are possessed of much wealth, foretells that you will energeticallynerve yourself to meet the problems of life with that force which compels success.To see others wealthy, foretells that you will have friends who will come to your rescuein perilous times.For a young woman to dream that she is associated with wealthy people, denotes that shewill have high aspirations and will manage to enlist some one who is able to furtherthem.WeaselTo see a weasel bent on a marauding expedition in your dreams, warns you to beware ofthe friendships of former enemies, as they will devour you at an unseemly time.If you destroy them, you will succeed in foiling deep schemes laid for your defeat.WeatherTo dream of the weather, foretells fluctuating tendencies in fortune. Now you areprogressing immensely, to be suddenly confronted with doubts and rumblings of failure.To think you are reading the reports of a weather bureau, you will change your place ofabode, after much weary deliberation, but you will be benefited by the change.To see a weather witch, denotes disagreeable conditions in your family affairs.To see them conjuring the weather, foretells quarrels in the home and disappointment in business.WeavingTo dream that you are weaving, denotes that you will baffle any attempt to defeat you inthe struggle for the up-building of an honorable fortune.To see others weaving shows that you will be surrounded by healthy and energeticconditions.WebTo dream of webs, foretells deceitful friends will work you loss and displeasure. If theweb is non-elastic, you will remain firm in withstanding the attacks of the enviouspersons who are seeking to obtain favors from you.WeddingTo attend a wedding in your dream, you will speedily find that there is approaching youan occasion which will cause you bitterness and delayed success.For a young woman to dream that her wedding is a secret is decidedly unfavorable tocharacter. It imports her probable downfall.If she contracts a worldly, or approved marriage, signifies she will rise in the estimationof those about her, and anticipated promises and joys will not be withheld.If she thinks in her dream that there are parental objections, she will find that herengagement will create dissatisfaction among her relatives. For her to dream her loverweds another, foretells that she will be distressed with needless fears, as her lover willfaithfully carry out his promises.For a person to dream of being wedded, is a sad augury, as death will only be eluded by amiracle. If the wedding is a gay one and there are no ashen, pale-faced or black-robedministers enjoining solemn vows, the reverses may be expected.For a young woman to dream that she sees some one at her wedding dressed inmourning, denotes she will only have unhappiness in her married life. If at another'swedding, she will be grieved over the unfavorable fortune of some relative or friend. Shemay experience displeasure or illness where she expected happiness and health. Thepleasure trips of others or her own, after this dream, may be greatly disturbed byunpleasant intrusions or surprises.See Marriage and Bride.

Wedding ClothesTo see wedding clothes, signifies you will participate in pleasing works and will meetnew friends. To see them soiled or in disorder, foretells you will lose close relations withsome much-admired person.Wedding RingFor a woman to dream her wedding ring is bright and shining, foretells that she will beshielded from cares and infidelity.If it should be lost or broken, much sadness will come into her life through death anduncongeniality.To see a wedding ring on the hand of a friend, or some other person, denotes that youwill hold your vows lightly and will court illicit pleasure.WedgeTo dream of a wedge, denotes you will have trouble in some business arrangementswhich will be the cause of your separation from relatives.Separation of lovers or friends may also be implied.WedlockTo dream that you are in the bonds of an unwelcome wedlock, denotes you will beunfortunately implicated in a disagreeable affair.For a young woman to dream that she is dissatisfied with wedlock, foretells herinclinations will persuade her into scandalous escapades.For a married woman to dream of her wedding day, warns her to fortify her strength andfeelings against disappointment and grief. She will also be involved in secret quarrels andjealousies. For a woman to imagine she is pleased and securely cared for in wedlock, is apropitious dream.WeedingTo dream that you are weeding, foretells that you will have difficulty in proceeding withsome work which will bring you distinction.To see others weeding, you will be fearful that enemies will upset your plans.

WeepingWeeping in your dreams, foretells ill tidings and disturbances in your family.To see others weeping, signals pleasant reunion after periods of saddened estrangements.This dream for a young woman is ominous of lovers' quarrels, which can only reachreconciliation by self-abnegation.For the tradesman, it foretells temporary discouragement and reverses.WeevilTo dream of weevils, portends loss in trade and falseness in love.WeighingTo dream of weighing, denotes that you are approaching a prosperous period, and if youset yourself determinedly toward success you will victoriously reap the full fruition ofyour labors.To weigh others, you will be able to subordinate them to your interest.For a young woman to weigh with her lover, foretells that he will be ready at all times tocomply with her demands.WellTo dream that you are employed in a well, foretells that you will succumb to adversitythrough your misapplied energies. You will let strange elements direct your course.To fall into a well, signifies that overwhelming despair will possess you. For one to cavein, promises that enemies' schemes will overthrow your own.To see an empty well, denotes you will be robbed of fortune if you allow strangers toshare your confidence.To see one with a pump in it, shows you will have opportunities to advance yourprospects.To dream of an artesian well, foretells that your splendid resources will gain youadmittance into the realms of knowledge and pleasure.To draw water from a well, denotes the fulfilment of ardent desires. If the water isimpure, there will be unpleasantness.

WelcomeTo dream that you receive a warm welcome into any society, foretells that you willbecome distinguished among your acquaintances and will have deference shown you bystrangers. Your fortune will approximate anticipation.To accord others welcome, denotes your congeniality and warm nature will be yourpassport into pleasures, or any other desired place.Welsh RarebitsTo dream of preparing or eating Welsh rarebits, denotes that your affairs will assume acomplicated state, owing to your attention being absorbed by artful women andenjoyment of neutral fancies.WetTo dream that you are wet, denotes that a possible pleasure may involve you in loss anddisease. You are warned to avoid the blandishments of seemingly well-meaning people.For a young woman to dream that she is soaking wet, portends that she will bedisgracefully implicated in some affair with a married man.Wet NurseTo dream that you are a wet nurse, denotes that you will be widowed or have the care ofthe aged, or little children.For a woman to dream that she is a wet nurse, signifies that she will depend on her ownlabors for sustenance.WhaleTo dream of seeing a whale approaching a ship, denotes that you will have a strugglebetween duties, and will be threatened with loss of property.If the whale is demolished, you will happily decide between right and inclination, andwill encounter pleasing successes.If you see a whale overturn a ship, you will be thrown into a whirlpool of disasters.WhaleboneTo see or work with whalebone in your dreams, you still form an alliance which willafford you solid benefit.

WheatTo see large fields of growing wheat in your dreams, denotes that your interest will takeon encouraging prospects.If the wheat is ripe, your fortune will be assured and love will be your joyous companion.To see large clear grains of wheat running through the thresher, foretells that prosperityhas opened her portals to the fullest for you.To see it in sacks or barrels, your determination to reach the apex of success is soon to becrowned with victory and your love matters will be firmly grounded.If your granary is not well covered and you see its contents getting wet, foretells thatwhile you have amassed a fortune, you have not secured your rights and you will seeyour interests diminishing by the hand of enemies.If you rub wheat from the head into your hand and eat it, you will labor hard for successand will obtain and make sure of your rights.To dream that you climb a steep hill covered with wheat and think you are pullingyourself up by the stalks of wheat, denotes you will enjoy great prosperity and thus beable to distinguish yourself in any chosen pursuit.WheelsTo see swiftly rotating wheels in your dreams, foretells that you will be thrifty andenergetic in your business and be successful in pursuits of domestic bliss.To see idle or broken wheels, proclaims death or absence of some one in your household.WhetstoneTo dream of a whetstone, is significant of sharp worries and close attention is needed inyour own affairs, if you avoid difficulties.You are likely to be forced into an uncomfortable journey.WhipTo dream of a whip, signifies unhappy dissensions and unfortunate and formidablefriendships.WhirlpoolTo dream of a whirlpool, denotes that great danger is imminent in your business, and,

unless you are extremely careful, your reputation will be seriously blackened by somedisgraceful intrigue.WhirlwindTo dream that you are in the path of a whirlwind, foretells that you are confronting achange which threatens to overwhelm you with loss and calamity.For a young woman to dream that she is caught in a whirlwind and has trouble to keeper skirts from blowing up and entangling her waist, denotes that she will carry on asecret flirtation and will be horrified to find that scandal has gotten possession of hername and she will run a close risk of disgrace and ostracism.WhiskyTo dream of whisky in bottles, denotes that you will be careful of your interests,protecting them with energy and watchfulness, thereby adding to their proportion.To drink it alone, foretells that you will sacrifice your friends to your selfishness.To destroy whisky, you will lose your friends by your ungenerous conduct.Whisky is not fraught with much good. Disappointment in some form will likely appear.To see or drink it, is to strive and reach a desired object after many disappointments. Ifyou only see it, you will never obtain the result hoped and worked for.WhisperingTo dream of whispering, denotes that you will be disturbed by the evil gossiping ofpeople near you.To hear a whisper coming to you as advice or warning, foretells that you stand in need ofaid and counsel.WhistleTo hear a whistle in your dream, denotes that you will be shocked by some sadintelligence, which will change your plans laid for innocent pleasure.To dream that you are whistling, foretells a merry occasion in which you expect to figurelargely. This dream for a young woman indicates indiscreet conduct and failure to obtainwishes is foretold.

White LeadTo dream of white lead, denotes relatives or children are in danger because of yourcarelessness. Prosperity will be chary of favor.White MothTo dream of a white moth, foretells unavoidable sickness, though you will be tempted toaccuse yourself or some other with wrong-doing, which you think causes the complaint.For a woman to see one flying around in the room at night, forebodes unrequited wishesand disposition which will effect the enjoyment of other people. To see a moth flying andfinally settling upon something, or disappearing totally, foreshadows death of friends orrelatives.WhitewashTo dream that you are whitewashing, foretells that you will seek to reinstate yourselfwith friends by ridding yourself of offensive habits and companions.For a young woman, this dream is significant of well-laid plans to deceive others andgain back her lover who has been estranged by her insinuating bearing toward him.WidowTo dream that you are a widow, foretells that you will have many troubles throughmalicious persons.For a man to dream that he marries a widow, denotes he will see some cherishedundertaking crumble down in disappointment.WifeTo dream of your wife, denotes unsettled affairs and discord in the home.To dream that your wife is unusually affable, denotes that you will receive profit fromsome important venture in trade.For a wife to dream her husband whips her, foretells unlucky influences will cause harshcriticism in the home and a general turmoil will ensue.WigTo dream you wear a wig, indicates that you will soon make an unpropitious change.To lose a wig, you will incur the derision and contempt of enemies. To see otherswearing wigs, is a sign of treachery entangling you.

WildTo dream that you are running about wild, foretells that you will sustain a serious fall or accident.To see others doing so, denotes unfavorable prospects will cause you worry and excitement.**Wild Man**To see a wild man in your dream, denotes that enemies will openly oppose you in your enterprises. To think you are one foretells you will be unlucky in following out your designs.**Will**To dream you are making your will, is significant of momentous trials and speculations.For a wife or any one to think a will is against them, portends that they will have disputes and disorderly proceedings to combat in some event soon to transpire.If you fail to prove a will, you are in danger of libelous slander. To lose one is unfortunate for your business.To destroy one, warns you that you are about to be a party to treachery and deceit.**Willow**To dream of willows, foretells that you will soon make a sad journey, but you will be consoled in your grief by faithful friends.**Wind**To dream of the wind blowing softly and sadly upon you, signifies that great fortune will come to you through bereavement.If you hear the wind soughing, denotes that you will wander in estrangement from one whose life is empty without you.To walk briskly against a brisk wind, foretells that you will courageously resist temptation and pursue fortune with a determination not easily put aside. For the wind to blow you along against your wishes, portends failure in business undertakings and disappointments in love. If the wind blows you in the direction you wish to go you will find unexpected and helpful allies, or that you have natural advantages over a rival or competitor.

WindmillTo see a windmill in operation in your dreams, foretells abundant accumulation of fortune and marked contentment To see one broken or idle, signifies adversity coming unawares.**Window**To see windows in your dreams, is an augury of fateful culmination to bright hopes. You will see your fairest wish go down in despair. Fruitless endeavors will be your portion.To see closed windows is a representation of desertion. If they are broken, you will be hounded by miserable suspicions of disloyalty from those you love.To sit in a window, denotes that you will be the victim of folly. To enter a house through a window, denotes that you will be found out while using dishonorable means to consummate a seemingly honorable purpose.To escape by one, indicates that you will fall into a trouble whose toils will hold you unmercifully close.To look through a window when passing and strange objects appear, foretells that you will fail in your chosen avocation and lose the respect for which you risked health and contentment.**Wine**To dream of drinking wine, forebodes joy and consequent friendships.To dream of breaking bottles of wine, foretells that your love and passion will border on excess.To see barrels of wine, prognosticates great luxury. To pour it from one vessel into another, signifies that your enjoyments will be varied and you will journey to many notable places.To dream of dealing in wine denotes that your occupation will be remunerative.For a young woman to dream of drinking wine, indicates she will marry a wealthygentleman, but withal honorable.Wine-CellarTo dream of a wine-cellar, foretells superior amusements or pleasure will come in yourway, to be disposed of at your bidding.

Wine-GlassTo dream of a wine-glass, foretells that a disappointment will affect you seriously, asyou will fail to see anything pleasing until shocked into the realization of trouble.WingsTo dream that you have wings, foretells that you will experience grave fears for thesafety of some one gone on a long journey away from you.To see the wings of fowls or birds, denotes that you will finally overcome adversity andrise to wealthy degrees and honor.WinterTo dream of winter, is a prognostication of ill-health and dreary prospects for thefavorable progress of fortune. After this dream your efforts will not yield satisfactoryresults.WireTo dream of wire, denotes that you will make frequent but short journeys which will beto your disparagement.Old or rusty wire, signifies that you will be possessed of a bad temper, which will givetroubles to your kindred.To see a wire fence in your dreams, foretells that you will be cheated in some trade youhave in view.WisdomTo dream you are possessed of wisdom, signifies your spirit will be brave under tryingcircumstances, and you will be able to overcome these trials and rise to prosperous living.If you think you lack wisdom, it implies you are wasting your native talents.WitchTo dream of witches, denotes that you, with others, will seek adventures which willafford hilarious enjoyment, but it will eventually rebound to your mortification. Businesswill suffer prostration if witches advance upon you, home affairs may be disappointing.WitnessTo dream that you bear witness against others, signifies you will have great oppression

through slight causes. If others bear witness against you, you will be compelled to refusefavors to friends in order to protect your own interest. If you are a witness for a guiltyperson, you will be implicated in a shameful affair.WizardTo dream of a wizard, denotes you are going to have a big family, which will cause youmuch inconvenience as well as displeasure. For young people, this dream implies lossand broken engagements.WolfTo dream of a wolf, shows that you have a thieving person in your employ, who will alsobetray secrets.To kill one, denotes that you will defeat sly enemies who seek to overshadow you withdisgrace. To hear the howl of a wolf, discovers to you a secret alliance to defeat you inhonest competition.WomenTo dream of women, foreshadows intrigue.To argue with one, foretells that you will be outwitted and foiled.To see a dark-haired woman with blue eyes and a pug nose, definitely determines yourwithdrawal from a race in which you stood a showing for victory. If she has brown eyesand a Roman nose, you will be cajoled into a dangerous speculation. If she has auburnhair with this combination, it adds to your perplexity and anxiety. If she is a blonde, youwill find that all your engagements will be pleasant and favorable to your inclinations.Wooden ShoeTo dream of a wooden shoe, is significant of lonely wanderings and pennilesscircumstances. Those in love will suffer from unfaithfulness.WoodsTo dream of woods, brings a natural change in your affairs. If the woods appear green,the change will be lucky. If stripped of verdure, it will prove calamitous.To see woods on fire, denotes that your plans will reach satisfactory maturity. Prosperitywill beam with favor upon you.To dream that you deal in firewood, denotes that you will win fortune by determinedstruggle.

Wood-PileTo dream of a wood-pile, denotes unsatisfactory business and misunderstandings in love.WoolTo dream of wool, is a pleasing sign of prosperous opportunities to expand your interests.To see soiled, or dirty wool, foretells that you will seek employment with those whodetest your principles.WorkTo dream that you are hard at work, denotes that you will win merited success byconcentration of energy.To see others at work, denotes that hopeful conditions will surround you.To look for work, means that you will be benefited by some unaccountable occurrence.Work HouseTo dream that you are in a workhouse denotes that some event will work you harm andloss.See Prison.WorkshopTo see workshops in your dreams, foretells that you will use extraordinary schemes toundermine your enemies.WormsTo dream of worms, denotes that you will be oppressed by the low intriguing ofdisreputable persons.For a young woman to dream they crawl on her, foretells that her aspirations will alwaystend to the material. If she kills or throws them off, she will shake loose from the materiallethargy and seek to live in morality and spirituality.To use them in your dreams as fish bait, foretells that by your ingenuity you will use yourenemies to good advantage.

WoundTo dream that you are wounded, signals distress and an unfavorable turn in business.To see others wounded, denotes that injustice will be accorded you by your friends.To relieve or dress a wound, signifies that you will have occasion to congratulateyourself on your good fortune.WreathTo dream that you see a wreath of fresh flowers, denotes that great opportunities forenriching yourself will soon present themselves before you.A withered wreath bears sickness and wounded love.To see a bridal wreath, foretells a happy ending to uncertain engagements.WrecksTo see a wreck in your dream, foretells that you will be harassed with fears of destitutionor sudden failure in business.See other like words.WritingTo dream that you are writing, foretells that you will make a mistake which will almostprove your undoing.To see writing, denotes that you will be upbraided for your careless conduct and a lawsuitmay cause you embarrassment.To try to read strange writing, signifies that you will escape enemies only by making nonew speculation after this dream.See Letters.Y

YachtTo see a yacht in a dream, denotes happy recreation away from business and troublesomeencumbrances. A stranded one, represents miscarriage of entertaining engagements.YankeeTo dream of a Yankee, foretells that you will remain loyal and true to your promise andduty, but if you are not careful you will be outwitted in some transaction.Yard StickTo dream of a yard stick, foretells much anxiety will possess you, though your affairsassume unusual activity.YarnTo dream of yarn, denotes success in your business and an industrious companion in yourhome.For a young woman to dream that she works with yarn, foretells that she will be proudlyrecognized by a worthy man as his wife.YawningIf you yawn in your dreams, you will search in vain for health and contentment.To see others yawning, foretells that you will see some of your friends in a miserablestate. Sickness will prevent them from their usual labors.YearnTo feel in a dream that you are yearning for the presence of anyone, denotes that you willsoon hear comforting tidings from your absent friends.For a young woman to think her lover is yearning for her, she will have the pleasure ofsoon hearing some one making a long-wished-for proposal. If she lets him know thatshe is yearning for him, she will be left alone and her longings will grow apace.Yellow BirdTo see a yellow bird flitting about in your dreams, foretells that some great event willcast a sickening fear of the future around you. To see it sick or dead, foretells that youwill suffer for another's wild folly.

Yew TreeTo dream of a yew tree, is a forerunner of illness and disappointment. If a young womansits under one, she will have many fears to rend her over her fortune and the faithfulnessof her lover. If she sees her lover standing by one, she may expect to hear of his illness,or misfortune. To admire one, she will estrange herself from her relatives by amesalliance.To visit a yew tree and find it dead and stripped of its foliage, predicts a sad death in yourfamily. Property will not console for this loss.YieldTo dream you yield to another's wishes, denotes that you will throw away by weakindecision a great opportunity to elevate yourself.If others yield to you, exclusive privileges will be accorded you and you will be elevatedabove your associates.To receive poor yield for your labors, you may expect cares and worries.YokeTo dream of seeing a yoke, denotes that you will unwillingly conform to the customs andwishes of others.To yoke oxen in your dreams, signifies that your judgment and counsels will be acceptedsubmissively by those dependent upon you. To fail to yoke them, you will be anxiousover some prodigal friend.YoungTo dream of seeing young people, is a prognostication of reconciliation of familydisagreements and favorable times for planning new enterprises.To dream that you are young again, foretells that you will make mighty efforts to recalllost opportunities, but will nevertheless fail.For a mother to see her son an infant or small child again, foretells that old wounds willbe healed and she will take on her youthful hopes and cheerfulness. If the child seems tobe dying, she will fall into ill fortune and misery will attend her.To see the young in school, foretells that prosperity and usefulness will envelope youwith favors.

Yule LogTo dream of a yule log, foretells that your joyous anticipations will be realized by yourattendance at great festivities.ZZebraTo dream of a zebra, denotes that you will be interested in varying and fleetingenterprises.To see one wild in his native country, foretells that you will pursue a chimerical fancywhich will return you unsatisfactory pleasure upon possession.ZenithTo dream of the zenith, foretells elaborate prosperity, and your choice of suitors will besuccessful.ZephyrTo dream of soft zephyrs, denotes that you will sacrifice fortune to obtain the object ofyour affection and will find reciprocal affection in your wooing.If a young woman dreams that she is saddened by the whisperings of the zephyrs, shewill have a season of disquietude by the compelled absence of her lover.ZincTo work with or to see zinc in your dreams, indicates substantial and energetic progress.Business will assume a brisk tone in its varying departments.To dream of zinc ore promises the approach of eventful success.ZodiacTo dream of the zodiac is a prognostication of unparalleled rise in material worth, butalso indicates alloyed peace and happiness.

11804698R00127

Printed in Germany
by Amazon Distribution
GmbH, Leipzig